BURNT HORIZON

Ian Chapman

Book One in the Northumbrian Western Series

First published by Lakeland Writers in 2015.

www.lakelandwriters.co.uk

ISBN: 978-1-910875-04-9

Visit www.lakelandwriters.co.uk to learn more about other
books available.

NORTHUMBRIAN WESTERNS

These were formed out of a few crazy ideas in a pub in Northern England. Over five years they evolved through numerous drafts and short stories into a series of novels.

Blending empirically based scenarios with Spaghetti Westerns, the books link dystopia, noir-fiction and border history into a unique set of stories.

Burnt Horizon is book one. Book two is *Blighted Land* and the third is *Blasphemous Isle.*

ABOUT THE AUTHOR

Ian Chapman was born and raised in Northumberland, only leaving when he was lured to the Midlands to study Economics at the University of Wolverhampton. He was so impressed with the place he went on to gain a PGCE and MA in International Studies, staying in the Midlands to teach economics and strategy at a number of colleges and universities. When not teaching he wrote stories or rode one of his three motorbikes with the odd Glastonbury Festival thrown in.

Moving north to Lancaster he took an MA in Creative Writing at St Martin's College before completing a PhD at Lancaster University. Around this time he had a play performed and won a (small) poetry competition. He also had several short stories published.

He now lives on the edge of the Lake District, still teaching and writing but the motorbikes have been replaced by three children.

To Debs and the kids.

CHAPTER ONE

On the road

Just after noon we cleared the Border Forest and came onto the moors that rolled off into the distance, a crisped blanket that lay across Northumberland, lit by the unyielding sun. That was when I spotted the car behind us. It was a silver BMW, closing on us fast. This was a real problem. We were on the run from Maxwell and he only ran BMs, old 2020's machines, and here was one on our tail.

I dropped a gear and accelerated hard, a hiccup coming from our Lotus's massive-mileage engine. The steering wheel juddered and shook, the motor missing a beat, coughing as it fought fuel through its grafted-on carburettors.

'What's up, Trent?' said Jamie.

I flicked a thumb backward and he checked his door mirror.

'Ah, man. I knew Kelso was a mistake.'

'Forget Kelso.'

But we both knew that it was because of Kelso that

Maxwell was on our tail. Because we'd taken something of his, now secreted in the Evora's chassis. Something that people were willing to pay a lot for. Kill for.

That was how we'd lost our partner, Lawson.

We passed a derelict Transit van stripped bare by the scavengers, the neo-reivers who were out here. We both glanced over at it then at the road, a stretch of holed and cracked tarmac rushing under the Lotus's nose.

'Can we outrun them?'

'We can try.' I slipped the car from sixth gear to fifth, rammed the accelerator down. The engine revved up towards the redline and howled as the speedo wavered at a ton-twenty. The whole car shook. I fought with the steering and Jamie gripped his grab handle.

But still the BMW grew in the mirror.

Soon two of Maxwell's men were visible, a couple of suits. There was no way we'd outrun them, not with the car the way it was. I lifted my foot off the accelerator and the engine tone dropped. The landscape slowed.

'What now?'

'Pull level, pop a couple of shots, then whip round.'

Jamie nodded at this, racking the bolt on his Browning. He knew the routine, one that we'd done several times. Before they knew what was what I'd have the Lotus around and we'd be off in the opposite direction. With any luck their car would be crippled. Even if it wasn't we'd get some space between us.

Soon enough the men came alongside, one pointing towards the verge. I waved at them all friendly and co-operative. Then Jamie lowered his window. Raised his gun and aimed. As usual he went for a wheel. The suits were open mouthed as he cracked off two shots and their front tyre blew with a thud. It flapped around and set the BM into a yaw. As they snaked and slowed I swung the steering to the right before yanking on the handbrake, pushing in the clutch and bracing myself. With the brake on the rear wheels locked and the car skidded, ready for me to shove into first, put the power back on and disappear up the road. I released the handbrake's button but nothing happened. It had jammed. I pressed and shoved it but it wouldn't budge and the car continued to slide. I smacked the lever, leant my weight on it, but it didn't move.

The Evora spun and the tyres screamed and the body shook. The moorland and road spun round. We were pushed from one side to the other, as the steering fought against me and the back wheels juddered. The BMW appeared in front of us, to the side; the suits with their waxy faces, as the world whirled around. There was a growl from the engine and a sound from Jamie like a low moan, or maybe it was from me. My foot slid off the clutch as I braced for us to slam into the other car, its nose ready to smash through the side of the Lotus and crush us. We slid some more then stopped.

In front was moorland, light and dark browns that went on without end. The Evora's ignition lights glowed and Jamie slumped forward in his seat, one hand on his head and the other on the gun as he muttered to himself. My hand was still on the brake, the other knotted on the steering wheel. There was no sign of the BMW.

I undid my seatbelt, turned the ignition off and sat there. The car smelled of burning rubber and hot metal. 'You all right?' I said. My voice was hollow, distant. The moors spun around in my head.

'Hmm,' said Jamie.

The engine sighed and gurgled as coolant moved around the radiator. I pushed the cigarette lighter in, reached into my jacket and took out a joint made with best Fife home-grown. Then I slid out of the car to lean against the door frame.

The Evora sat on the edge of the road facing back the way we'd come. There was no sign of the BMW, just tyre tracks, thick black lines that twisted and swirled with one set leading to our car. The others went off to the side, towards the moors. I bent and touched them, my fingers on the warm rubber, and I was reminded of some place a long, long time ago. When I looked back at the moorland there was a town in the distance. Stone buildings that ran off along the edge of a valley. Then there was a pop, the only sound in the still air. When I looked again the town had vanished, a mirage in the heat.

Jamie stepped out holding the hot cigarette lighter. I took it and lit the joint, drawing hard. Then he reached back into the car, leaning on his walking stick, taking out his rifle.

He slid his gun over his shoulder and we followed the tracks onto the moor, through the thick grass and dried earth as the tyre marks disappeared into a depression. There was a pool in it, the remnant of a bigger pond. The edge was baked mud and in the middle was a patch of water a few centimetres deep. The upturned five-series was in the pool with the chassis at eye level, revealing the rear axle and the underside of the engine and the semi-trailing arms. The water reflected the sky, cloudless, blue, as if the BMW was airborne.

'Some mess.' Jamie's gun was levelled at the vehicle.

The windows of the car were cracked and smeared

with blood. One of the suit's arms was pressed up against the glass. No one moved inside. The metal ticked as it cooled. There were hisses as the oil and fuel and coolant shifted around. It smelled of burning oil, diesel and fried brakes.

'Maxwell won't like this.'

'You think?' He did like to state the obvious.

'Should we get them out? See if, they're okay?'

'What, like they did for Lawson?' Maxwell was the enemy, so were his men.

'We can't just leave them —?'

'We can. We have to. We've got our deal to make.'

I passed the joint to him and he finished it, throwing the roach into the water. I had a pretty good idea what was going through his head: that he was back in that bus with his parents when he was a kid. On his way to start a new life in the highlands. The bus that got rammed off the road by reivers with a bulldozer. They left him in it for hours, surrounded by injured people; dead bodies. He'd never given me the full story but I'd heard enough to know it had shaken him up.

The BMW ticked and pinged. Whatever we did Maxwell was going to be really pissed off. These cars were classics, irreplaceable pieces of engineering. And he couldn't afford to lose men, two-a-penny that they were.

'Trent, come on, at least check they're, you know…' Jamie gave me that look, the one that meant I had to be decent, better than the other scum on the road. I wanted to say to him, Jamie forget these thugs, it's not like you stuck in that bus. But the last time I did that he had a fit.

I moved forward through the shallow water taking the passenger door. There was blood across the window, the suit's arm askew, no sign of any airbag. When the door opened he hung out, his arms dangling beside his head, like he was doing a Mexican Wave or something. There was blood all over and his face was twisted towards us, eyes open but unfocussed. I'd seen enough dead people to know he was one of them.

The driver's side door was harder to release. Jamie pulled at the edge of the wing where it fouled the hinge and it popped open. The second suit's face was obscured by the airbag, his arms wrapped round it. Even in a car this old it still worked. When I felt his wrist there was a pulse, weak but there. His chest rose and fell, tiny movements.

'Well?' said Jamie. The gun was lowered at his side.

I was tempted to say nothing, shrug and imply he was dead. But Jamie knew me better than that. We'd been partners since '36 and he could read me, tell when I was lying or hiding stuff.

'Well?'

'He's alive, but we can't — '

'Trent…'

I took a deep breath. 'All right.'

So that was that. We set to rescuing the suit.

It took us a good half-hour to ease him loose, having to shift the airbag and seatbelt before we could roll him out, manhandle his big body with his crew-cut head. We slid him across the muddied pond. It was a stupid thing to do, an act that was going to end in tears. But as soon as we'd opened the car, leaving him was no longer an option. Not with Jamie around.

We carried him over to the Evora. Jamie stopped every few steps to rest his bad leg as the body hung between the two of us. He was a heavy built fella, some fat but a lot of muscle, like most of Maxwell's mob.

Getting him onto the tiny back seats of our car wasn't easy. We shifted our bags, squeezing one in the rear hatch with the LPG cylinder, Jamie's gun and our stash of grass. I examined him again once he was in. His breathing was shallow and there was a pulse but it was weak. If he faltered I'd turf him out, dump him on the moors. But the big lunk was still hanging on. I insisted that we tied his hands. Jamie wasn't keen but he went along with it.

I went back to the BMW and checked it over. The boot was hard to open with the car at that angle but it dropped wide enough for me to poke around. There were a couple of sleeping bags, spare clothes and a can of bio-diesel. Maxwell always ran oil-burners so that was no use to us.

Going over the rest of the car I found a rifle with several rounds. There was some cash in the dead man's jacket, a nice wad of Edinburgh notes, so I took it.

Jamie was leaning against the Evora, next to the cracked headlamp and Lotus symbol too filthy to read. I handed him the gun and he checked it over, lining up the sights on a hillock, taking aim and pulling the trigger. It didn't fire so he opened the breech and poked around. Stripping it down he shook his head. 'What now, Trent?'

'We need to get moving.'

'What about him?' he said, jerking his finger towards the injured thug in the back of our car, napping like a big baby. 'He needs medical care.'

I did know a place that had a hospital. Or had once had a hospital. It was half a day's drive from the deal. Somewhere I'd been thinking about a lot recently, what with this being a special trade, not like our normal type.

This was the one we'd do then vanish.

Maybe it was time to go back to Setmarch. My home town, the place I was run out of decades ago. Now was my last chance to settle up, put things to rest. Catch up with one or two people.

So I said, 'Let's go to Setmarch.' All bright and cheery, like it hadn't been on my mind for some time. But just saying the town's name gave me a weird feeling as if going over a dip in the road or having the first sip of whisky of the day. My fingers drummed on the roof of the car.

'Setmarch?' He slid the rounds out of the gun then chucked it into the back of the car.

I looked away. 'There's a hospital. Somewhere we can stay.' The place had probably closed years ago.

'Okay,' he said. 'That's what he needs.'

With that we got back into our car.

After starting up I messed with the handbrake's button. It released straight away. I shoved the Lotus into first, revving the engine, pulling off slow. No point wasting what little fuel we had.

CHAPTER TWO

Stop Off

We drove south, away from the border, putting distance between us and the upturned BMW, taking it steady but not stopping. The moorland stretched off into the distance, parched and lifeless, patched by black where the dried heather had caught light. The road was empty of vehicles in front or behind. Like most of our runs we were alone. Just us, and the suit, in the Lotus.

I'd done so many trips it was hard to keep track. Years I'd been out here, decades. All this time out in the wilds travelling back and forth sometimes with someone, sometimes on my own. For some people being on the road was a choice, a life they wanted. But for me it was just something that happened, something that had landed on me and I'd had to accept. Even the driving didn't get me fired-up anymore — with fuel being rare we had to take it slowly most of the time. Hundred mile trips took half a day, sometimes longer. It was fine but no more than that.

The suit made a sound in the back like he was clearing his throat.

'Think he's okay?' said Jamie

'Do I give a shit?'

Jamie sighed and turned towards him, putting his hand to his neck then moving the bag wedged around him.

'How is he?' I said, trying to sound more concerned.

'He's all right, not that you care.'

The road rolled past and Jamie sat twisted round to watch him. Despite being born into all this chaos he had his soft side. Part of it was what had happened in the bus but there was something else. Maybe it was because he was younger than me. It was hard to say. One thing was sure — he'd lived through all the worst stuff. By the time he was at school collapse was getting going. There was one thing after another. Some week there was a run on a bank. Another, a series of power cuts. Businesses went bust, many of them well known companies, ones we thought too big to fail. All the time fuel prices crept up. The government lurched through a whole load of emergency measures that made life harder. Street lights went off, policing was cut back, services disappeared: hospitals, schools. Bit by bit the old world died. Sometimes it felt like it was going to be all right, that the latest actions would sort things out. Then petrol stations would run dry and there'd be queues at the ones still pumping; gangs of men turning up in vans. They'd jump the line as they waved axes and pointed shotguns.

There was talk of martial law but the military were busy elsewhere at the time, fighting to secure oil supplies in the Middle East. It was only when our forces were pushed out by the Chinese, Russians and Indians that they came home. We lost out to the new powers and that really signalled the end.

It wasn't long before Murgatroy's government fell. The hapless coalition he'd tried to hold together unravelled on January 14, 2034. And that was it. I was couriering then but I remember hearing about it while drinking in the Cross Keys, Biggar, when the Scots were already running their own affairs. As Lawson and me holed up in the bar, away from the sleet lashing against the window, there was a cheer when the news came over the radio.

With the government gone the military got their chance to run things for a while with the British League throwing their weight around as well. But even they couldn't keep control of the whole country. After another five or so years it all really fell apart. That was when it was at its worst. Marauding gangs and shortages of everything.

By the 2040s it'd settled into a weird sort of pattern. Towns looked inward and did whatever they needed to stop things falling further apart, working hand to mouth, while the bigger cities went for committees and elders, making their own rules. But the roads were chaos. Only the people who had to be out there were there.

By then me, Lawson and Jamie had our patch. We had our usual routes where we ferried things back and forward in our car, one of us sitting shotgun, usually Jamie. We made a good team, the three of us. Lawson and me took turns driving and Jamie did the shooting. He was good with a gun, very good, and you could tell by looking at him he was. Lawson was good as well but with other things. Not good enough though it seemed. He'd never felt like one of those who wasn't going to make it.

Which was why we were quitting.

This was the final run. After the deal we'd be able to leave the business. Do whatever we wanted. We'd have enough money to set ourselves up somewhere. Away from northern England, possibly on the continent. Find the places I'd been told about — where people worked together not against each other.

Before that there was the deal to do. The suit to drop off. Then we'd be free. Jamie and me.

A clattering sound came from the back and the car pitched up and down like we'd hit something. But the road was clear of debris and the suit was lying still. More noises came from the rear, this time popping.

'Trent?' said Jamie.

'Just a misfire.' I slowed down and pulled up in at the edge of the road not far from a derelict pub. To the left was the vallum from Hadrian's Wall filled with discarded debris off stripped vehicles: rusted panels, shattered glass and perished trim, the kind of stuff that couldn't be reused. The junk lay in the shade as the sun dipped down over the moors to the west.

The car stalled, coolant gurgling in the engine bay,

'It needs to cool down,' I said. There was a track to the right, going off into a patch of sickly trees. Before Jamie had time to argue I started the car up and headed for it keeping the revs up as the engine misfired. 'Short stop off then we can carry on.'

'Just a short one.' He gave me an eyeballing but said no more.

We bounced along the rough road past pine trees, many bare of needles but enough to hide us from the road. The track widened out to a churned area of dried grass. Rotted tyres lay off to one side and the remains of a fire in the middle. I stopped the Lotus and stepped out. Our passenger lay like a big baby in the back of the car. A big, stupid, dangerous baby.

A crow rattled around in one of the trees, cawing and flapping off. Jamie joined me, resting against the car. The smell of the pine trees mixed with petrol fumes.

'Light's fading.' He turned the collar up on his donkey jacket. 'You need to sort the car.' With that he leant in and saw to the suit, puffing up his pillow no doubt. I'd just as soon smother him and dump his body in the trees.

I opened the engine's cover and pulled off the plug leads. They were thick with grease and dust so I scraped off some of the dirt using a twig. Once cleaned I pushed them back on hard to ensure good contact. It wasn't going to do much but gave the impression I was busy, keeping Jamie happy while I had time to think. Then I went into the boot to grab some tools, tapping the jerry-can and LPG cylinders so they each gave out a sound, one higher pitched than the other. This was wrecking the engine, all the mixes of fuels we ran it on. One day propane, another ethanol. I closed the boot. Long shadows lay across us from the trees, one patch of ground still lit orange by the setting sun. If I could keep us here for the evening there was more chance the suit wouldn't make it. If he died in the night that would mean we could dump him and not have to lug him around, one of the enemy clogging up our car. But that would that mean a visit to Setmarch was off the list.

Jamie came round and stood next to me, taking his weight on his walking stick. 'Listen,' he said, 'the guy in the back, he's not good. He needs care but it's getting late.' He pointed up to the sky, a deepening blue. 'We're losing light. Might not be a good idea being on the road.'

I nodded, all concerned, as I put away the tools and

shut the hatch on the engine.

We found a spot well away from the road and made a fire with the branches that were lying around. Jamie insisted on dragging our unwanted guest to lie with us. His body was heavier than ever and smelled of sweat, maybe piss. At least out here he wouldn't relieve himself on the car seats. We leant him against a log then heated a tin of beans. Jamie strummed on his guitar, his gun on the ground beside him. He played a vintage pop song then stopped.

His face flickered in the fire light. 'Any idea what's up with the car?'

'Probably the plugs.'

We started to eat and he picked on at his food, saying nothing more. After we'd finished the beans he checked on Maxwell's man then tidied up, making small talk about the glow from the fire, how there was light in the sky even though it was late on. We avoided talking about the serious stuff like the car's problems, our journey to Setmarch. The deal we were going to do.

We bedded down on opposite sides of the fire, Jamie near our guest. As the logs crackled I lay back under the now dark sky. Aside from popping of the burning wood it was silent.

For some time I gazed up at the stars in the still air.

Then a growl came from some way off, the low throb of an engine. The sound rose and fell as a vehicle short shifted through gears, slowing to stop on the road nearby.

CHAPTER THREE

Drive In

I kicked earth onto the fire then went over to the Lotus. Light caught the trees, a spotlight that played across the branches swinging round to show fragments of the woods around us, skeletal in the darkness.

Jamie joined me as I leant against the car, his gun in his hand. 'What the hell is it?'

'Big,' I said.

The engine of the vehicle rattled a rough tick-over as voices shouted over the sound. I slid around the car and moved into the trees. Twigs snapped under my boots as I pushed through the closely packed trunks, my arms raised to deflect branches away from my face. Light flicked across the boughs above me to show branches as sharp shadows, twisted and pointed. There was a gap off to the right that gave a route towards the road, lit for seconds by the spotlight.

I stumbled my way through and the engine revved up, then there was a clunk when it slid into gear and moved onto the track towards the Lotus. The light dipped down and the voices came again.

There was a chance they'd spotted the Lotus's tyre marks fresh on the ground.

Coming to the edge of the trees I slid behind a trunk, peered round. There was the vehicle at the side of the road, some big old lorry, the kind not often seen anymore. Two men stood on the ground while another hung off the cab and shone the light. All wore overalls and as one moved through the spot-lamp's beam the letters AHI showed on his back. He had a shotgun in his hand. Another passed through the light and he had the same letters on his overalls.

My fingers drummed on the tree. This didn't look good. Either they were part of a gang or some big organisation. No one wore letters on their back anymore.

The two on the track kicked the gravel and the third man shifted the lamp around stopping it just above me. I stayed still as the light blazed in the branches. The men shouted something and one of them laughed. If they'd spotted me the best option was to duck back, take them towards Jamie and hope he'd be ready with his gun; that they weren't crack shots with theirs.

The light dipped onto me, straight on. This was it. As soon as they moved I'd run.

Then it flicked up and a crow flew out of the tree. The shotgun fired, then again and the lamp swung around.

There was nothing for a moment, just the idle of the engine. Then the men all got into the cab and the light went off. With a clank and gruff drone the lorry reversed off the track. It turned and growled down the road. The sound faded as I went towards the car using my lighter to see the way. Back at the Lotus Jamie had his rifle set up on the roof.

'That you, Trent?' he said.

'Yeah, it's me.'

He slid his gun down and we sat by the dead fire. 'What was that about?'

'Some fellas shooting at birds.'

'Seriously?'

'So it seems.'

'Think they'll come back?'

'Don't think so.'

'Jesus, Trent. I've not seen anything like that.'

Then he went on and on about it, how weird it was and so on, me agreeing and not adding much. Not letting on how unsettled it made me.

Eventually I went round to my bedding and he took the hint. He fumbled around in the dark as I slid into my sleeping bag. In a short time I heard him snoring but I lay awake, waiting for more sounds on the road.

There was no sign of the lorry but I didn't sleep. I thought about the town we were headed to. This place I hadn't seen for twenty-odd years, filled with people I'd known. Somewhere I'd promised never to return to. A place I'd called home.

Memories floated up and I forced them back down. Maybe visiting would purge them. Cleanse me of Setmarch.

At first light I packed up, the only sound being the crows in the trees. Jamie slept on. I was tempted to take a branch to Maxwell's man, smack him over his thick head. But I let him be. When Jamie awoke he checked over his patient before we ate some ham we'd picked up in Jedburgh. Then we loaded the car. Jamie asked me about the lorry and what it was about but I didn't say much. I was too tired to come up with theories.

With everything loaded we drove off. The sun lit the moors browns and golds as we joined the road.

The car sounded better to begin with but soon deteriorated. By the time we crested the rise into Setmarch's valley it was like a bag of spanners.

Down below us was the town — this town I'd not been to for so long. Decades.

Some of it was familiar: the rows of terraced houses and estates of semi-detacheds. Roofs that spread out before us.

A new addition was the factory. A great dark lump. It was near the centre of town and spewed out smoke, creamy grey clouds that rolled up the valley. Partway up the opposite hillside was the winding-gear of a pit, another new feature. Coal spoils spread out around it and blackened the ground.

As we drove down the hill, the gradient matched the feeling I had, like I'd jumped off a riverbank and was about to land in the water. Cold filthy water. Rattles came from the car's engine, the steering wheel vibrating in my hand as we juddered past a sign, rusted, scratched and stained, it said, *Welcome to Setmarch, home of Armstrong Heavy Industries*. Buildings appeared along the road, coated with soot.

Jamie had his hand on his gun. 'So is this it?'

We passed blackened shops and houses. 'Yeah. This is it.' I sounded nearly as unimpressed as him. The sun disappeared behind the factory's smoke and ash dropped on the car.

As we came to a junction the Lotus stalled. I cranked it

over and it started, backfiring. A car drove past then a donkey pulling a cart followed by a lorry. The lorry was like the one I'd seen the night before. I didn't share this with Jamie. He stared at it, frowning.

The Evora lurched forward to join the road, past the men all wearing filthy overalls with AHI on the back. Just like the fellas I'd seen.

We parked by a baker's shop with windows of mismatched panes. The Lotus's engine ran-on then misfired to a stop. Dark buildings enclosed us beneath that hazy sun.

Jamie loosened his donkey jacket, gazed at the shops and men in overalls. 'What now, Trent?'

A woman walked towards us, dark haired, slim, her head down.

For a second I thought it was her.

At last I let myself think her name, Laura. Laura who I'd not seen since I left all those years ago. This woman pushed a pram, a rickety thing with a red-faced brat in it. Then she looked up, sucking on a roll-up, cheeks hollowed. The nose was too broad, eyes small. Nothing like Laura.

'Trent?'

'Yeah?'

'What now?'

The woman passed by. Her shapeless backside shuffled off into the distance. I turned back towards the suit. He was breathing but there was no other movement. 'There once was a hospital at the far end of town,' I said. 'If it's still open, we drop him off then get the car sorted out.'

Jamie slid his window down. 'You know this place?'

'A little.'

People passed by with expressionless faces. Dead eyes. Along the road music came from a pub, uneven piano playing that faded in and out in the warm air.

'I don't want to be staying here long, Trent.'

I thrust my thumb backwards. 'It was your plan to bring him.'

He pursed his lips but said nothing else.

The Evora took three attempts to start then stalled as we reversed onto the road. It misfired all the way to the hospital, past buildings with AHI stamped all over them. The original shops had gone – Wright's Department Store, Smith's newsagents, Taylor's Bicycles. All replaced by AHI groceries, butchers and clothing. There was still a petrol station, now AHI of course. Two cars queued up at it. Wrecks but working cars. Billboards shouted: AHI IMITATION TOBACCO, JUST LIKE THE REAL THING; AHI, WE CAN REBUILD THE OLD WORLD. Telling people what to do or not do.

The hospital was still open but it was now called AHI Hospital, not Setmarch General. Another part of the Armstrong Empire. It was the same building, an old 1990s place but tiles were missing from the roof, guttering hanging off, windows cracked. The main door was repaired with hardboard.

We untied Maxwell's man but it took a good ten minutes to get some help with him. Even then they just dragged him out of the car to dump him on a rickety stretcher. He was hauled into the building and abandoned in the waiting room.

Me and Jamie sat there, the suit prone beside us, alongside the grey-faced wrinklies and men in overalls with their hacking coughs; women who held sickly children squirming on their laps.

Ceiling tiles were cracked or missing, wiring hanging down through the gaps. It didn't look like the hospital I remembered, the one we'd gone to with sprains and breakages. Where Harry had stayed after his first bike accident. Rory with his virus. The place we'd visited Mum in those last days.

I leant over to Jamie. 'We could just leave him. They'll sort him out.'

'No way, Trent.'

'He'll be fine.'

'No!'

When some of the patients looked round I kept quiet. Jamie had his arms crossed and that annoyed expression he sometimes wore so we waited with the sick of Setmarch.

After half an hour a doctor came over. His white coat was grubby, splatted with something dark; his eyes bloodshot and chin thick with stubble. 'Follow me,' he said. Then he was off.

We pushed the trolley along a dim passageway, its brick walls roughly painted, cries and moans merging with the clip-clop of the doctor's segged shoes. He led us into a long ward. Beds were crammed in with little room to squeeze between them. Sallow faced men lay there — some asleep, others staring at the ceiling. It smelled of damp and bleach. The doctor indicated an empty bed with grey sheets, ruffled and holed. 'Are you on the plan?' he said. 'AHI healthcare plan?'

'We can pay cash,' said Jamie.

The doctor held the suit's wrist, marked by the rope that had tied him. 'What's up with him?'

'Car accident.'

'You have money?'

'Can't you just check him over?' I said. 'A quick examination?'

Maxwell's man lay there, eyes rolled up, open enough to show the whites, chest barely moving as he breathed. He wasn't going to make it.

'Afraid not,' said the doctor.

I put my hand on my pocket but couldn't face bringing the money out. It took Jamie to reach in and take out some notes, about a third of the Scottish tenners lifted from the dead man. He handed several of them over and hung onto the rest.

The doctor examined them. 'No A-pounds? AHI pounds?'

'This is all we have,' I said. 'If it won't do…'

'It'll do.' He waved to a nurse, a heavy-built woman in discoloured uniform. While he counted the money she lifted the man onto the bed, sliding his jacket off.

As Jamie and me turned to go the doctor tapped me on the arm. 'What's his name?'

I looked at Maxwell's man. 'Bob,' I said. 'Bob Shaftoe.'

The doctor frowned but wrote it down on chart at the foot of the bed. He started to examine him and we left.

Jamie stopped in the hospital's doorway, where several men in overalls smoked and spat. 'What now?'

'We pick up provisions, sort the car and go.'

'Is this town okay? I don't want another Motherwell.'

'It'll all be fine. I promise,' I said. 'This is a good town.'

Normally it was me who led but this time I let him go ahead. I couldn't bear to have his eyes on me after I'd lied to him.

CHAPTER FOUR

Fix Up

It was Sunday and a lot of places were shut. Seemed Setmarch respected the Sabbath. Since there was nowhere to buy food I talked to Jamie about staying a night. I pointed out that we had to sort the car and stock up; that there was a week before the deal and we'd still have time to go to the coast, something we'd talked about ages ago, something to look forward to. 'We'll have time for all that and you can check up on your precious suit before we leave,' I said.

This sealed it for him, and he agreed to stay one night. This suited me. Time for a catch up then gone.

We spent ages driving round town until we found a guest house that was open, some converted terraced house on Front Street called *Valley View*. It smelled of cat piss and stale smoke but it was cheap. We parked the Evora round the back, locking it and jamming the transmission. This was our extra security measure — a bolt down through the floor into a tapped hole in the gear-change linkage. Once screwed into place it locked the car in sixth gear. For good measure we had a chain on the steering wheel as well. Jamie was still fidgety about leaving the car with the payload in it but I told him it was fine. Mrs Newry, the woman who ran the place, said she'd keep an eye on it, for what that was worth.

We stashed our bags in the room and Jamie sprawled out on the bed. I lay on mine and for a while neither of us moved. All our time on the road meant we appreciated a real bed.

'Hey Trent,' he said. 'Haven't you got a car to fix?'

'In a minute.'

'We need that sorted...'

'All right, all right.'

He was really whining on. I slid off the bed and made my way down to the yard. Church bells rang across town announcing evening service as I opened the engine cover. The smell of petrol fumes floated out and I prodded the still-warm cam-covers tarnished with age. Black stains collared the distributor I'd had grafted on by that mechanic in Stranraer, a decent fit but never oil-tight. Another fella had fitted the carbs lifted off an old Ford. They'd kept the car going after the fuel injection system packed in. This was a precious vehicle. A car that had been entrusted to me by Harry, my brother. My dead brother.

Before setting to work I brought out the tools and spare spark plugs, old and worn themselves but still serviceable. I had a pile of spares for the car: piston rings, valves, cam chains and a gasket set, enough to keep it going for decades, but fitting those kind of things was beyond me. If it was more than spark plugs or fuelling we were stuck. I popped off the plug caps and unscrewed the first plug.

The pattern of the bells changed. Not many places still had church bells. Not ones that worked.

I slipped the plug out. It was coated with carbon, a charred lump. I slid a replacement in and tightened it.

One by one I took the plugs out. Each was covered in soot. I replaced them and set the soiled ones on an old crate where they lay like artefacts.

For a second the bells stopped then started again. Maybe it was Rory's church. Preacher Rory. My brother. The other brother.

He'd stayed here and had always banged on about starting his own church when I was a kid. Maybe he'd done it.

The plugs were changed. That was all I could do for now. I stashed the old ones and put the tools away. Locked the car up and left it in the yard.

Jamie was in a decent mood when I went up to the room. He cleaned his gun while his three precious objects were set out on the bed: his guitar, old phone and the shopping magazine. It was easy to tell when he was stressed as he'd turn on the phone, coaxing to life its weak battery that we endlessly had to recharge in the Lotus, pressing the bright squares that marked its screen, opening images stored in its memory or starting programs that were no longer linked to anything.

But today it just lay there, inactive. 'Everything okay?' he said.

'Fine.'

'The car's done?'

'Yes, all sorted,' I said, much more strongly than I believed.

'Great.' He started shifting all his stuff around,

arranging it on the bed. 'Should we leave? Get out of this town?'

'We've booked the room.'

'So what?'

I looked out of the window, at the smoke that hung over the houses. There was somewhere I needed to visit before we left. 'Not yet. We'll head out first thing tomorrow. See the suit then go to the coast.' I picked the two things that would pull his strings.

'You reckon?'

'Yeah, let's have a drink, unwind. We've got this place for the night.'

Although Jamie reached for his phone, it was only to slide it into its pouch and stash it in his bag.

'Don't take your gun,' I said. 'Might stir up trouble.' Lots of bars had no-gun rules.

He grunted and packed it away.

I rolled a spliff of our precious home-grown grass, one of the perks of being couriers across the border. This had become a nice little industry. There was a steady output of weed from greenhouses in Fife with its long summer nights and benign gangs.

I slid the joint into my pocket and we went out. Jamie checked that the door was locked several times.

We headed into town where smoggy clouds hung overhead, backlit by the evening sun. We passed the abandoned Belmont Hotel and the library that was now a warehouse with an Armstrong sign on it; the derelict town park, now a tip, pilled high with rotting rubbish.

Beside it was a church. This was the church I'd been dragged to as a kid, where we'd gone along for Christmas and Easter services. The building was intact with a solid front door and some glass in the windows but the stonework was loose, stained with soot. It had been so much of our childhood, something that had mattered to my mother. After her funeral we never went again.

I slowed as we passed it. There was singing from inside from the evening service.

Beside the front door was Rory's name. My brother was now the vicar. There was a picture of him as well, a rough sketch on a sign, all hair and crazed eyes, like he'd always been. A board was up that said *Church of Reform, Abstinence and Piousness,* replacing the original name.

He'd be in there now leading the service.

'Trent?' said Jamie. I'd stopped moving.

I pointed into the centre of town. 'Bound to be some bars this way.'

He nodded, walked on and started to talk about his plans, once we'd done the deal. He'd not even noticed how well I knew my way around. Beyond the church I steered us into Back Lane. This was where I really wanted to go. There were shouts and cheers coming from a pub as we shuffled up the soot-stained cobbles. A filthy sign hung from one hinge beside a glass-panelled door that had *The Feathers* etched into it.

'It looks like a decent pub,' I said, almost off the cuff, even though a smile was fighting to form on my lips. The Feathers was somewhere I'd not been to for over two decades. A place rammed full of memories. It was more run down than the last time I'd seen it, that weekend when everything had really unravelled, but it was still here. Maybe she was still here too. There was a cheer from inside and smoky air rolled out as I tugged the door open.

Part of me thought it was a bad idea; digging up the

past sometimes was, that's why it had worked so well with Jamie and me. When it came to history we didn't tend to ask or tell. I knew a little about him and he knew bits about me but no more than we needed.

But there were logical reasons why we'd come to town. We'd done the right thing with Maxwell's man and it was a good idea to fix the Evora and pick up provisions. While we were here there was no harm seeing the old place. Old friends. This all made sense.

The inside of the pub hadn't changed much. The floor was bare floorboard and the walls off-white. There was a bar on the left. There were a dozen small tables but on this evening all apart from one were pushed up against the far wall. A crowd of men clustered in the middle of the room.

There were two people at the centre of the huddle. One was a fella in his late twenties, short haired in a black tracksuit, an immaculate tracksuit. His shoulders were slumped, face screwed up; angry. He held five playing cards. His opponent was a woman in her forties, dark haired, in checked shirt and jeans.

It was her, Laura. Slim as ever, her hair shorter but other than that the same. There was a drumming sound in my head and my fingers seemed to have a mind of their own, like someone else's hands were stuck on the end of my arms.

She showed her cards and the crowd cheered. The fella shook his head and stared at the floor. People held money in the air, laughed and shouted, moving across the room to the bar. The fella lurched off after them and she stayed at the table.

Maybe I smiled or made some sound but whatever it

was it caused Jamie to turn towards me. Before he got to say something clever I strolled over to Laura and stood behind her, him following after me. 'Nice hand,' I said, all calm, like we always met up like this and there was no history between us.

She stopped counting her money and turned. Her eyes were as deep and dark as they'd been. Deeper and darker. 'Christ,' she said. For a second there was a hint of a smile, then it was gone.

'Hello Laura.'

People shifted tables back across the room, scraping them across the floor. She stayed in her seat and set her money out in front of her.

I didn't move. 'You win much?'

'I can't believe you've just turned up like this.'

'Well, here I am.' It was hard to believe myself. She examined the money but Jamie was watching me, really giving me an eyeballing.

When she stood up we were face to face. 'You've some nerve,' she said. 'After what you did.' She smelled great, like warm biscuits fresh out the oven. Without a word she stepped back and swung her hand, slapping me hard across the face. The sound rattled through my head. Everyone stared, the tables no longer moving.

'I guess I deserved that,' I said. My voice was small, hollow.

'You did indeed.'

The tables scraped across the floor again. She was still mad at me, which wasn't surprising, but now I was back I could tell her what happened. Why I'd left the way I had.

To give me something to do with my hands I picked up her cards, shuffling them. 'Looks like you've kept your game up.'

'I heard you were dead.'

With a laugh I eased the cards into a pocket on the front of her blouse, slipping the pack over her breast, that warm flesh, pushing my luck, taking a gamble. She always liked men who gambled. 'You not going to buy us a drink?'

'Are you serious?' She stared at me with those dark eyes. 'Oh, my god, you are serious!' She frowned and played with her money, sliding it into her jeans then running her fingers through her hair, playing with it, just like she used to do. Then she crossed her arms, leaning to one side, staying like that for some time as people in the pub moved around, the fella she'd beaten drinking a small beer over at the bar, shoulders hunched.

Then she poked me on the chest. 'What the hell, huh? Whisky isn't it?'

'Yeah.'

'What about your friend here?' She looked Jamie up and down. 'You a whisky drinker?'

'No. I'll have a beer,' he said.

She pulled out a banknote and wrapped it around her finger then swung round and strolled over to the bar. I watched her go, how her jeans clung to her legs and backside, tight but not too much, showing off her body.

Jamie tapped me. 'Hey, what was all that about?'

'An old friend.'

'Friend or flame?'

Laura chatted to the barman, flicked her hair to the side. She'd hardly aged, still looking like a woman in her twenties.

'So, Trent, where does she fit in all this, eh?'

I took out the joint and examined it, just to check the skins, make sure they were joined up properly. Jamie was starting to pester, something we'd agreed not to do. Rather than give some lame excuse I lit the joint and smoked.

Laura came over with a whisky, a bottle of beer and a small glass for herself. She raised her drink and smiled, a proper big smile that nearly hit her eyes. 'Here's to you being less of an arse-hole than last time.'

'Cheers,' I said. She and Jamie stared at me like something in a museum. 'This is great whisky,' I said, drinking.

Leaning towards me she sniffed the smoke I blew out. 'Real grass?' Without asking she took the spliff off me, drew it out of my lips with those slim fingers, slid it into her own mouth, smoking it, eyes closed.

Then there were raised voices over at the bar. Someone pushed through people. It was the fella Laura had beaten in the game. He marched over and stood before us, his arm extended to show his tattoos — the Nissan logo, AHI and a code: VQ35DE. More importantly he had a piece on him, some old semi-automatic, worn but polished, sitting in a special pocket stitched into the front of his tracksuit bottoms. I'd not spotted that before.

He pointed at Laura, shifting round. 'Hey, bitch, I want a rematch.'

Everyone in the pub watched him, and us

'You're drunk. Go home and sleep it off,' she said.

He waggled his finger stepping from one foot to the other. His nostrils flared and he pulled back his lips to show grey teeth. 'You're a fucking cheat.' He was one of the town boys but he was full of booze and ready for trouble. Normally I would have laid him out on the spot, nothing nasty but enough to make a point, floor him before he pulled his gun. But I knew not to do that in front of everyone. Not in a small town where I didn't know what the score was. Not any more.

Laura smoked the spliff and smiled. 'I cheated? Really?' She gave a good show but he wasn't backing off.

'You took my money.'

She laughed, putting her glass down and stepping back. 'You lost it, okay?'

'I know a fucking cheat.' He straightened up and leant his head back, touching the grip of his pistol. 'I want my money.'

'You lost it, Sikey. That's how the game goes...'

Jamie put his beer down, standing in front of him. 'Just back off.'

Sikey looked Jamie up and down, like he'd not noticed him before.

Then his gun was out but it was in Jamie's hand, whipped out of Sikey's pants and now thrust in his face.

'That's my semi,' said Sikey.

'That's right.' Jamie slid his free hand across the gun, touching on the chamber indicator. 'And it's loaded and ready.'

'My fucking gun.'

They were eye to eye, the pistol in Sikey's face. No one moved in the pub as Jamie's finger caressed the trigger. Laura raised the joint up but couldn't get it into her mouth. If Jamie fired that was our time in town blown along with Sikey's brains.

For an age we all stood there ready for the shot to ring out, Sikey to fall backwards, blood spraying out. His body slumping onto the floor. Jamie kept his hand on the gun, finger on the trigger. He and Sikey stared it out.

Then someone cleared his throat at the far side.

With a grunt Sikey moved backwards, his strides wide, exaggerated. He glanced round the room, at the people. Pointing at Jamie he said, 'Clever move. Bet you think you're smart, eh?' He swaggered over to the door, pulled it open and lurched out.

Once the door had slammed shut Jamie lowered the pistol.

'That was close,' I said.

Jamie inspected the gun, popped out the magazine, racking the slide and taking out the round. 'Think so?'

Laura smoked, drawing really hard on the joint. Her free hand was in her hair again, curling one lock round a finger, round and round. She moved over towards me, picking up her drink, downing it and putting the glass back on the table.

'Thanks,' she said.

'No problem,' said Jamie.

There was a moment where none of us spoke, as other drinkers milled around, talking, watching us, especially Jamie with the gun. We stood there in a pub that I hadn't been to for decades. Next to her as she looked me up and down, her face flushed, hard to read.

Jamie put the round back in the magazine, clicked it into the pistol.

She pointed over to the door. 'Fancy catching some air?'

Outside it was warm despite being dusk. Sikey was halfway up the road, pulling up his tracksuit bottoms as he lurched off, a pool of piss left steaming in front of the pub. Laura stubbed the joint out with a flourish of her wrist before she leant against the wall. We were so close I could have leant over, put my arm around her.

'That was something,' she said.

'What should we do with the Glock?' said Jamie, holding the gun up.

'The what?'

'His gun.'

She shut her eyes and raised her hand to her forehead. 'We'll have to give it back. Return it.'

Jamie thrust it towards her and she took it, holding the grip between her fingers so it was upside down as if contaminated. Then she slid it down onto her hip and laughed, too loud and for too long.

There was a rumble from the sky, from the clouds above the smoke and she looked up. 'Sounds like there's a storm coming.'

Jamie glanced up. 'Sounds like it's here.'

Raindrops plopped down on us, filthy beads of water. Then more came. She swung the gun under her armpit, pointing it backwards. 'Time to go, I think.' She tapped me on the arm, a little touch but something, as she disappeared back into the pub.

I wanted to follow her but we'd stirred the place up enough. There was a chance Sikey'd be back with some friends, all tooled up.

Jamie pulled his donkey jacket around his shoulders. 'Come on, we're going to get wet.'

I shrugged. 'Yeah.'

We walked away from the pub and across town as the rain fell.

Along the road Sikey was in a doorway, watching, staring. He pointed at us then disappeared into the shadows.

CHAPTER FIVE

Memories

Back in our room Jamie lay on his bed messing with his phone, the light colouring his face. Muted sounds came from it, music and voices. Recordings by forgotten owners; sounds from the past. He'd pulled the curtains so the phone was the only source of light. He did that until the batteries faded.

'So the car'll be ready to go?' He was invisible in the dark.

'Just need to warm it up and check the mixture.'

He grunted, the bed creaking as he shuffled around, stashed his phone. Within a couple of minutes his breathing had slowed. Aside from the rain rattling on the window were few noises in the building: dripping water, Jamie snoring.

I hadn't lied to him. With the fouled plugs replaced that was the car fixed and there was nothing stopping us leaving town. Maybe the carbs needed a tweak to stop further carbonising but that was it. Then we were back on the road. Away from Setmarch.

The rain slackened and sounds from the factory drifted across the town, this place I'd tried to forget. Clanks came from the distant machinery as I pushed memories of my earlier life out of my head.

Seeing Laura had been good but things had changed. All those years on the road had left their mark on me. Here she was in this town, running her own business, settled, at home. Maybe coming here had been a mistake but we'd be gone soon. Forever.

Still, we'd had good times me and her. Much better than anything since.

I twisted and turned in the bed refusing to relive what we'd done together. I fought images of the past, thrashed around and couldn't settle.

I must have fallen asleep just before sunrise. When I woke up Jamie was looking at me.

'Well?' he said.

'Well what?'

'Are you going to check the car over? Warm it up and do whatever to the mixture?' He stared at me until I pulled on my clothes and left the room.

I went down to the Evora, morning sun lighting the yard. The air was the freshest it had been since coming to town but already there was a whiff of sulphur and soot. I undid the transmission lock and started the car, holding it at two-thousand revs on full choke. It ran well without misfire and after a minute I let it tick-over, going round the back and working the throttle by hand. The mixture seemed fine so I wasn't going to mess with it.

Jamie appeared and stood over me.

'All done?'

'Nearly,' I said.

'This isn't going to be another Kelso is it Trent?'

'This is nothing like Kelso.'

'You know what I mean.'

'We got out of that one—'

'Lawson didn't.' Jamie came closer, too close. 'And what about him in the hospital?'

'The suit? What about him?'

'Should we go and see him? Before we go?'

'No. Not a chance.'

'You promised.'

'I've changed my mind.'

'Trent…'

'All right. Maybe. If there's time.'

'There's time.'

With that he left, leaving me with my hands in the engine bay. At least he wasn't hanging around, badgering me. This really was nothing like Kelso but it wasn't surprising it was still on his mind. It had been a real disaster. The worst thing that had happened to us in all our years on the road.

We'd not meant to stay at Maxwell's place, that great country house on the edge of Kelso, the heart of his empire. But after trading some ammo he'd strung us along, saying that there was a cash-flow problem, that he couldn't pay us straight away.

Even though it was a really fancy place it wasn't great hanging out with all his thugs, being stuck there waiting for payment that might never come. Maxwell had this reputation for swinging one way then another, sometimes coughing up the cash and other times failing to deliver; playing dirty, wiping out the competition and dumping their bodies in the River Tweed.

But while we were waiting around Lawson heard something from one of the suits, a conversation when they'd been drinking, about a special payload that they'd just acquired.

Lawson told me about this as we sat out one evening by the ha-ha, looking across the drought-mottled lawns that led down to the river.

'I'm not sure what it is,' he said. 'But they think it's worth a bomb.'

'No idea at all?'

'It's not physically big, from what they said. I reckon it's in the main safe, in that room up on the first floor of the West Pavilion.'

'They told you all this?'

Lawson laughed. 'I did a little sniffing around as well. Heard a gadgie quote Maxwell, saying they'd be able to step up operations with it. Move into new territory and wipe out competitors.'

'Could just be talk.'

Lawson narrowed his eyes that way he always did, giving me a cock-eyed grin. 'We should take it. If it is that special we could sell it on.'

'Yeah? If we could get away with it.'

'Think big, Trent. Think big.'

So we decided to go for it, giving Jamie the edited version of the story seeing as he got so jumpy. He still didn't seem sure but we convinced him it would set up the three of us for good. Then he was in.

We waited until Thursday when most of the men were off on a trade. The house was never left empty but at least it was quiet. As a few of them cleaned Maxwell's BMs me and Lawson went up to the West Pavilion. He was to break the safe while I kept watch.

He went into the room and I stood on the landing beneath one of Maxwell's oil paintings of the estate. Normally this kind of stuff took no time, but he was ages. I expected one of the suits to turn up. Someone I'd have to stall or deal with.

Lawson appeared with his bag, wearing a smile but soaked with sweat.

'Tough job?' I said. He grunted, giving the bag to me then he was off, taking the long route out while I went straight down. We split up to avoid suspicion.

Before I got halfway this fella appeared, a typical suit, all clean cut; nasty. The way he went for me it was obvious that he knew what we'd done. Must have been an alarm on the safe or somewhere. Without a word he grabbed for the bag and I swung it hard, right in his midriff, folding him up before I uppercut him on the chin. As he fell forward he latched onto the handle, tightening his fist.

'Leave it,' I said. When he didn't I stamped on his hand. He cried out but clung on. So I kicked him in the face, a spray of blood coming out, shooting out across the sleeve of his jacket and the bag. He still wouldn't release so I kicked again, this time in the ribs, really hard, making him curl his hands around himself, letting go. He lay still on the floor, his eyes closed, breathing roughly.

Then I was off.

There was no sign of Lawson in the passageway, no one around, just the click-clack of my feet on the bare floorboards, the bag up against my chest. Lawson's job had been to open the safe, no more than that. If he'd listened to me he'd be back at the car with Jamie, ready to go.

Fast footsteps approached from up ahead so I ducked into one of the doorways into a posh-carpeted room with antique vases, old paintings and fancy tables, the finery Maxwell had inherited when he booted the real owner out. The room smelled musty, stale. How long had this taken — half an hour? More? I'd told Jamie to go after twenty minutes, counting down on the Evora's clock, our only timepiece. Lawson never usually took more than seconds on a safe.

Well, he had this time. Still, being Jamie, there was a chance he'd waited.

The footsteps passed and I ventured out. When I turned the corner I saw Lawson. He was laid out on his back, no blood or anything but his head was twisted to the far right, like he was looking over his shoulder. A position no living man would lie in.

I wanted to stop, shift his head and arrange him better, at least leave him with some dignity, for old times' sake. All the things we'd done together. But there was no point, no time. Instead I buried all those thoughts and carried on to the end of the passageway. I took a deep breath, grabbed the handle of the door and stepped outside.

Four men were on the drive by the lawn. They milled around two BMWs, Maxwell's estate stretching off behind them into the distance. I turned the bag so the bloodied side was against me.

One of them shouted a greeting and I waved, carrying on along the driveway to the Evora that was still there, facing the gateway and escape. Even as I approached I expected it to pull off.

Then there was a shout. The door to the building burst open and another suit ran out holding a pistol. Behind him was the one I'd kicked around. As they came after me, the men at the cars looked across, starting towards me.

I ran and shouted to Jamie, telling him start up, get ready to go. As I did, the barrel of his rifle appeared out of the passenger window. It hung there for a few seconds then there was a loud crack. The cry behind me said he'd caught one of the men.

I chucked the bag in the back and leapt into the driver's seat. Jamie was twisted round on the passenger side with his gun still aimed at my pursuers. There was another shot but he swore, sliding the rifle back in. The car's engine was running so I shoved it into gear, flooring the accelerator and we shot off.

'Where's Lawson?' he said.

'He didn't make it.'

He said nothing to that, as we charged down the drive and onto the main road.

Later, when we stopped off on the edge of the Border Forest he asked what had happened and I said a little, told him the basics. After we'd eaten he went off on his own, probably to think it all through. Him and Lawson had spent quite a bit of time together. I'd known Lawson even longer. It was hard to believe he was gone.

While Jamie was away I investigated the payload. I took it out, opening it up. It didn't look like much, a metal cylinder, with odd writing on it saying *HMS Gehenna*, loads of documents inside, technical stuff. Plans of a ship and sea charts. It hardly seemed worth all the fuss. Lawson's death.

But there were sections that mentioned it was Top Secret with Ministry of Defence stamps. They were the things that worried me. And that Maxwell had seen it as important, a game changer or whatever he'd called it. All it all, it had given me a really bad feeling.

CHAPTER SIX

Ready to go

By mid-morning the Lotus was ready for a test drive. I drove round the block, getting it up into third, a slight hunting from the engine but nothing serious. It drove all right at low speed. I would have opened it up but there were loads of people about, crossing the road, hanging around. A lot of them kids, a few in school uniform, women with toddlers, all just hanging around. Between them mingled men in AHI overalls. As I accelerated up Front Street lads pointed, the engine hiccupping and cracking out a loud backfire as it picked up speed. Apart from that it was fine so I drove back and parked in the yard.

Jamie was waiting with the bags packed when I went to fetch him. I helped him down the stairs and loaded the car then we slid in ready to go. Crowds blocked our way but sounding the horn cleared the pavement. As we tried to pull onto the road several men in overalls came over, blocking the way.

I opened the window. 'What's going on?'

'You can't go, not now.'

I tried to drive round them but more men appeared, repeating the line about me not being able to go. Edging the car forward caused them to pound on the car's roof and bonnet. Then one of them whipped out a shotgun and levelled it at us. Jamie grabbed for his rifle and I put my hand onto his arm. After a few seconds he lowered it.

The shotgun stayed on us so I raised a hand in submission and backed the Lotus off the pavement, the men following us all the way to the passageway. Once they'd turned away I drove forward again, trying to burst through onto the road. The Lotus's snout make it onto the tarmac but the men were back, this time really pissed off. Two of them grabbed at the doors trying to pull Jamie and me out. Jamie had his locked and I hung onto the grab handle of mine, preventing it opening. Another fella kicked at the wing while the fourth tried to rip open the bonnet. The one with the gun stood in front of us shaking his head, the barrels pointed at me. I slid the car into reverse, still hanging onto the door with my other hand as we backed away from the road. The men stayed put while we reversed into the back yard.

'Jesus Christ, Trent. What now?'

'I don't know.'

'Let's go again. Blast our way out.' Jamie raised his gun and opened his window. The men were still on the pavement watching.

I grabbed Jamie's arm. 'We can't fight all of them.'

After a second he lowered the Browning. 'Some place this.'

'Looks like we'll have to wait.'

He said nothing more and we sat in the car.

'Should we see what's up?' I said.

I got out of the car and a few seconds later he followed.

We went out into the crowds towards the left, away from the men. Jamie pulled his rifle tight against his back, his other hand on his walking stick. The pavements were rammed with people of all ages who nudged and elbowed one another, the smell of sweat mixing with whiffs of stale beer and fake tobacco smoke. We stood there for some time, waiting. When Jamie asked some woman what was going on she laughed then turned away. Others refused to answer us.

Voices were raised nearby and the crowd shifted, a man swearing as he stepped aside. Then Laura appeared, shoving her way along the packed pavement, carrying a basket with bottles in it, dressed in an old jumper and dark trousers. She stopped and faced us, messing with her hair even though it was pulled up. 'Trent?' she said. 'I thought you were off?'

I moved over towards her, jostled by the people around us so that my arm was pushed up against her. Jamie was to my side.

'We are,' he said. 'Once these lot clear off.'

She gave a little nod, maybe frowned. Between the smoke and sweat I could smell her, some perfume. There was a cheer from the crowd and people moved forward, pushing to get nearer the road.

'I can't believe I've got caught up in all this,' she said.

I stretched up but couldn't see what the crowd were looking at. 'What's going on?'

'All the ghouls are out. Get out the way if you can. I have to get back…' She shoved past us, glancing at the road. 'Hey, if you're around later, come round for dinner.'

'Yeah,' I said. 'We'll see.'

'Hope Street. Number seventeen.' With a wave she was gone, as the crowd muttered and shifted.

There were shouts as a lorry approached from the centre of town. The vehicle crept nearer, a distorted announcement being played through a PA system.

'What *is* this?' Jamie had his hand on his gun.

The lorry stopped a little way off and a voice came over the noise of the engine and crowd. 'This is what happens!' it announced. 'This is the punishment for those who break the rules!' There were cracks, sounds of a man crying out then a woman's scream. Then there was applause and the voice said something, drowned out by all the noise.

The lorry started towards us and there was another cheer. It was a flatbed vehicle with frames on the back, wooden structures. Strapped to them were two people, a man and a woman. Both were bent forward and tied in place. The man was bare-backed, naked to the waist, the woman similar. Each wore bloody marks across their skin. Standing next to them were two of AHI's thugs in threadbare tracksuits, grins across their flushed faces as they brandished whips. Beside them was a man in a polo-shirt and pressed trousers, mid-sixties, fat. His thinning hair was spiked up with gel, his cold eyes scanning the crowd. He held onto the frame built onto the vehicle. There was applause as he approached.

'Who's this?' said Jamie to a woman next to him.

She laughed, pointing at him. 'He doesn't recognise Armstrong!' There was laughter around us but it died down when the lorry came close.

Armstrong stood, proud of his role, as his flogged victims lay before him, the track-suited men laughing. For a second his eyes met mine. There was a look on his face, annoyance or something. Then the lorry was off down Leeson Hill.

Even though the spectacle had passed no one seemed keen to move.

Jamie messed with his rifle, always a bad sign. 'What a place.'

'Yeah.' I didn't know what Armstrong's look had meant but I didn't like it.

Jamie slid his gun off and looked along the barrel before leaning on it as a second walking stick. 'Should we go to the hospital? Check on that guy?'

'Do we have to? '

'You said we would. Anyway, look at the crowds, we're not going anywhere.'

People milled around and the men in overalls still blocked the side roads. Seeing Armstrong and his lorry had unsettled me so I didn't argue further. 'Fine,' I said. So we set off for the hospital on foot.

As we went across town the crowds thinned and Jamie started to chatter, going on about the town and how it reminded him of places he'd been to. We passed the off licence where lads with armfuls of empty bottles queued to get refunds; the billboards telling people not to go to work drunk; not to damage Armstrong Industries' property. Across the road three cars queued for the petrol station, the sign said *AHI Fuel available today*. The cars smoked and backfired, two men arguing from their windows as they both aimed for the single petrol pump.

'And we're still going to the coast before the deal?'

'Yeah,' I said. 'Of course.'

We carried on in silence but the way he walked I could

tell he was happier. Or less pissed off, at least.

The hospital was busy when we arrived, several dilapidated ambulances parked outside as stretchers were carried in. A man in a white coat checked the wallet of a patient as we approached. With a shake of his head he directed the stretcher off to a side door, away from the main entrance.

In the waiting area a woman argued with a doctor, waving her hands at him as he tapped a clipboard. Patients sat around, grey faced, some coughing, waiting to have their healthcare credentials checked before receiving treatment, or being thrown out.

The place was so badly run there was a fair chance Maxwell's man hadn't made it.

The argumentative woman was dragged away by two security men in filthy overalls. She shouted and kicked as she went, her voice echoing through the building. We carried on along the dim passageways to the ward we'd been to before. The beds were as closely packed as last time but a couple were empty. One of the vacant ones was the suit's. I guessed he'd died and they'd taken him off to the mortuary or whatever pit they put the bodies in. In some ways, it was a shame, after all that effort, but it was for the best really, ugly thug that he was.

'He's not here. He's not made it,' I said

'Wait a minute.'

'Let's go, Jamie.'

A nurse came over, a skinny woman with yellowed teeth. Her uniform was threadbare at the front with torn sleeves. 'It's not visiting hours yet.' She pointed at Jamie's rifle. 'You shouldn't have that in here.'

'We've lost our friend.' Jamie pointed to the empty bed.

'He was here.'

'You'll have to come back. Not now.'

Jamie reached into his jacket and pulled out a bundle of cash, the remainder of his money from the suit. 'We're paying his fee. Where is he?'

I was ready to commiserate with Jamie, pat him on the back and say we'd done our best when the nurse pointed to the far end of the ward, where a curtain was pulled round a bed.

'He's been moved,' she said. She stared at the money, as he counted some off. 'There's a discretionary charge for out of hours.' She grabbed several of the notes and shoved them into her skirt pocket, glancing around.

'How is he?' I asked. With any luck he was in a coma.

'Stable. Not up to walking, though.' There was coughing from the opposite end of the ward followed by the sound of retching. 'Don't be all day.' Then she went off, slipping the money out, counting it.

So he was still alive. That was a disappointment. All I had to hope for was brain damage and some serious injuries.

But when we pulled the curtain aside Maxwell's man stared at us. There didn't seem to be a mark on him. He'd been changed into scruffy blue pyjamas and stubble grew on his heavy jaw. The name label on the bed frame now read M. Nixon. His cold grey eyes were on us, hard. 'I thought you'd come back,' he said.

Jamie sat down. 'How are you?'

Nixon laughed. 'What the fuck do you care?'

'We brought you here,' I said.

'Where's Johnson?'

'Who?'

'The co-driver. My partner.'

'He didn't make it,' said Jamie.

'You bastards.'

'We rescued you and brought you here—'

'You drove us off the road. Then you finished off Johnson.'

'Come on, Jamie,' I said, 'let's go.' If we'd not been in a hospital with other people around I'd have finished Nixon off, stuck a pillow over his mean-looking face and choked the life out of him, despite what Jamie thought. 'We're not needed here.'

Nixon bared his teeth. 'Once I'm out I'll get you. Both of you. If I could walk properly I'd have you now.'

'Fuck you,' I said before coaxing Jamie out and away from him. With a last glance at Nixon we left the ward.

We walked out of the hospital past an empty ambulance as the driver changed a tyre.

'Jesus, Trent, he wasn't very appreciative.'

'I said we should have left him.'

'We saved his life.'

Joining the road we made straight for the guesthouse. 'Look, soon we're off and we'll never see him or this place again.'

'Thank god,' said Jamie. 'Thank god.'

CHAPTER SEVEN

Bikers

The roads were quiet enough for us to just to drive out of town, past the few kids being herded back to school and the workers returning to the factory. With the choke on and light throttle the Lotus ran fine, quite well even, picking up speed as we passed the old paper factory and ruined industrial estate, crossing the river by the East Bridge, aiming for the by-pass.

We came to the junction for the old road to Laybridge, a route I'd used as a racetrack in the past. Ahead was the by-pass, the main dual carriageway to the city.

'On our own now,' I said.

Jamie said nothing, possibly thinking about what happened with Nixon. Maybe he felt bad about picking him up and thought it was his fault. Actually it was his fault and he was right to feel bad about it, but I wasn't about to say so. Not yet, anyway.

As we joined the main road I opened the Lotus up. The only traffic was some big thing, way off, probably one of Armstrong's lorries. Aiming towards the city I revved the engine up to three thousand but it misfired and lost power so I backed off. Jamie glanced over and I smiled at him, as if it was okay and I'd expected this, which it wasn't and I hadn't.

Cruising at just below thirty suited the car, also making it easier to steer around the debris and potholes. This was slower than we normally went, not fast enough to stick it in top even. Still, with no other traffic we'd be fine to make it to the city.

'Can't we go faster?' said Jamie.

'Don't want to thrash it after doing work on the engine.'

'I thought you only changed the plugs?'

'Don't want them to get glazed.'

'I see.' He had one hand on his stick and the other on his rifle, his phone charging at his feet. He stared ahead, out at the empty road and fields, still damp from the previous day's downpour, steaming from the heat. The browned vegetation seeming to have gained nothing from the rain, bushes, trees and hedges all leafless and crisped.

The vehicle behind us crept up in the mirror. I'd expected it to turn off for Setmarch but it still lumbered on. It was a flat fronted thing, painted dull colours, probably taking freight of some sort. Though unusual it wasn't that surprising. It was probably on its way to the city.

We passed a cart of misshapen vegetables, pulled by a horse with a peeling coat and knotted mane.

On the downhill section to the Laybridge roundabout the thing behind us surged forward, coming up close. It was an old bus, a double-decker painted greens and browns, the upper windows patched with board. As it grew behind us I dropped the Evora a gear and gave it more throttle. For a second it pulled and picked up speed before coughing and losing power.

The bus slipped into the outside lane and overtook us. Its flank was marked with graffiti and dents. Apart from the driver there seemed to be only women and children on board. They were filthy and tattooed, dressed in biker jackets and they stared out at us, blank expressions, neither friendly nor antagonistic.

'Christ, Trent,' said Jamie. 'Can't we outrun this?'

Rather than argue or try to push the Lotus I braked hard, planning to pull it in behind the double decker. But as we dropped back the identity of the bus's owners became clear. Behind it was a massive trailer, the width and length of the bus, set low with a drop-down ramp. On it were motorbikes facing backwards, each with a rider, mostly male. The bikes had smashed fairings and fuel tanks patched with sheet metal, their chains loose on worn sprockets.

I'd never seen them before but I knew who they were. What they were. Each area had its own troublemaker, neo-reivers, and these seemed to be the ones round Setmarch. Some bike gang that had appeared in the last few decades. The bikers stared at us, looks of hate. Starter motors whinnied and several of the bikers jumped on kick-starts.

'Shit, Trent.' Jamie had his gun up and he racked the bolt and shifted forward to get out of the window. To take aim.

'We can't take them all on,' I said. This was bad, really bad and he was making it worse. 'Lower the gun, Jamie.'

'A couple of shots, that's all. Take a tyre out on the bus.'

'That won't work.'

These reivers were like wasps. You either killed them all or left them alone. Even if only one of them survived he'd be after us forever.

Jamie still had his gun lined up so I pushed the Lotus, giving it as much accelerator as it could bear, coming level with the front of the bus, ahead of the bikers. We kept this position for several minutes, Jamie now spun round so he could aim back at the bus. As we approached the roundabout the bus braked but I kept the speed up, flying onto it and letting the Lotus's suspension balance out, maintaining the power as the tyres cried out. Jamie hung on, shouting something, lowering his gun at last. When the rear end threatened to kick out I backed off a little, taking us right the way round then onto the back road. Easing the Lotus up through the gears I went towards Laybridge veering to the left for the old quarry track. The speed of the turning sent the car sideways down the road, bouncing on a mud-filled pothole before we stopped by some dead bushes, facing the main road. I reversed further into the undergrowth.

Soon the bikers appeared on the road and roared past.

'You should have put your gun down,' I said

'What the hell for?'

'It didn't help.'

'I could have taken a tyre out. Scared them.'

'People like that don't scare.'

We sat in silence as the bike engines disappeared off into the distance, Jamie messing with his gun. Though I was pissed off with him there was no point saying any more.

A minute later we set off in the opposite direction.

'What now?' said Jamie.

'Get the car fixed. So we can outrun people like that.'

'Where are we going to do that?'

'Setmarch would seem the best place.'

'Would it? Would it really?'

He said nothing more as I drove us back onto the by-pass and towards Setmarch. But he gripped his gun and pursed his lips which told me enough.

So we went back to the town, mist rolling in from the east, joining the smoke to form a warm creamy smog. We parked at the back of the guesthouse again, Jamie staying in the car while I went in to talk to Mrs Newry. She was fine about us staying and even knew of a decent garage nearby.

When I returned to the car Jamie had his phone out, pressing icons and flicking through pictures. He let me take the bags while he entertained himself.

Once everything had been taken up he followed me to the room. Then he lay on the bed, still messing with his phone.

I left him like that as I drove along Front Street in the fog, a sultry blanket, following the directions I'd been given.

Dan's place was far away, up a cobbled lane. It was tin roofed with big old wooden doors, thick with paint, that stood propped open. I parked and went in. There was a man and a younger lad at the far end of the garage setting out tools.

'Are you Dan?' I said to the older one. He wore greasy overalls, his hair similarly oiled, slicked back, stubble on his heavy jowls.

'Who's asking?' he said.

I pulled out our roll of cash. 'I need some work doing

on my car.'

He perked up at this and came forward, watching me count the money.

'Okay. But have to be local currency,' he said. 'Setmarch pounds.'

'Fine.' I slid the notes away and drove the Lotus in, him and the lad at the side, their eyes on the Evora, this ancient sports machine. It rolled across the cracked concrete up to the far end, the engine misfiring all the way. It filled the garage with the smell of part-burnt fuel.

When I turned the ignition off there were a series of rattles before it died. Then I felt around with the bolt down into the floor, screwing it into place, locking the car in gear. If Dan ran the engine he'd have to push the clutch in. I tightened the bolt with a short spanner before folding back the carpet and tucking it under the centre consul.

I slid out and faced Dan. 'Is it safe here?'

'Lock it at night,' he said. 'I live next door. Be fine.'

I popped the engine cover, joining him as he raised it up.

'Not seen one of these for a while,' he said. 'Toyota engine?'

'Yeah. It's running rough. Not sure what's wrong.'

He mopped the sweat off his forehead, as the tin roof ticked, still warm from the morning sun. Leaning around the engine he shut one eye, prodding bits. 'Carb conversion. Some electrics gone.'

Then he eased me aside, descending on the engine, the lad slipping the plug caps off while Dan grabbed a dial and attachment, what looked like a compression gauge. Taking a plug out, they screwed the gauge into its place and the lad slid into the car. He tried to put it into neutral but gave up, pushing the clutch in and cranking the engine over.

The Lotus's engine whirred on its starter, unable to fire up with the plug leads off.

Dan sucked his teeth, shook his head. When the engine stopped he unscrewed another plug, grabbing his oil can and squirting a little in before connecting the tester. Again the lad turned the engine over, Dan frowning, muttering to himself. They repeated this for three more. Dan reacted the same each time.

'Well?' I said.

'Valves bust.'

'You sure?'

'Must be with those readings.' He slid the plug he was holding back in as the lad flopped out of the car. They both came and faced me, expectant.

'Can you fix it?' I said.

'Not without the parts.'

Going into the back of the car I pulled out my old rucksack. It held the spare gasket set, piston rings and other parts. I drew the box of valves out. They stared at it, the wrappings bearing Toyota RX 350 and 24, faded printing on peeling labels.

'Fuck,' said the lad.

Dan reached out as if to touch them, then retracted his hand. 'New spares, still in the packet?'

'Be careful with them,' I said, clenching the box tightly.

Dan and the lad gazed at the parts, transfixed.

'You will look after them?' My hands were really gripping the valves. Was this a mistake, trusting them with the parts? Two fellas I'd never seen before. But without them we'd never get away.

Dan nodded. 'Aye, be fine here. Fine.'

'You'll lock the place up?'

'Aye, like I said.'

'How long to fit them?'

'Couple of days. Maybe three.' Dan took the replacement components, slipping them from me, putting them on a cleared section of the bench. Then they both leant over the engine, undoing bolts and removing parts. They lifted the filter up to show the blackened orifices of the carburettor. I stepped backwards, shouldering my rucksack, drumming my fingers on the Evora's flank, feeling the scratches and dents on its dark green paintwork, its history. The payload was in this car, behind the panels and deep inside the chassis. With one last touch of the bodywork I wandered out of the garage.

Outside there was a graveyard of donor vehicles: a Passat with no front end, a Peugeot, gutted and de-glassed and a Citroen Picasso devoid of doors or wheels. They seemed to float above the ground in the mist. Clanks and whistles came from the garage as Dan and the lad worked on the Lotus, the car that held our valuable cargo. But it was something really unusual, something that even if he found it, Dan wouldn't understand. There was a slight risk leaving the car with them but I'd jammed the gear linkage and they'd lock up. They weren't bright enough to go picking around the car, looking for stuff that shouldn't be there.

With one last glance at the car I left.

At the end of the lane Jamie was waiting. He leant on his stick and his gun was over his shoulder. There was no greeting or smile when he saw me.

'You all right?' I said.

He said nothing but joined me as I crossed the road. The sun fought through the muggy smog.

'Looks like the valves are shot,' I said.

'Is that serious?'

'Looks like they can sort it.'

'How long?'

'Not long. But we need to sort out money.' I stopped outside the old Barclays Bank, now run by Armstrong, of course. 'Don't worry, this is all going to work out.'

'So you say.' He followed me in, looking all huffy. There were only a few people in the bank: a couple of old women at the counter and some thick-set fella behind them. The counter itself only had one serving point that was glassed, the rest being boarded up with wood. At our side a row of cashpoints stood screen-less and gutted and the mortgage office was piled with busted furniture. The information desk had been replaced by scruffy chairs where two lads in tracksuits sat, one holding a shotgun. They gave Jamie and me a good looking over. One of the older women was arguing with the cashier who shook her head, closed her eyes. This carried on for some time on until one of the track-suited lads went over and shoved the old women out, both crying. The thick set man dumped a bag full of coins. These were weighed out as he watched and we waited.

When it was our turn I rolled out the Scottish notes we'd picked up. 'What's the charge?' I said.

'Twenty per cent,' said the cashier.

'That's ridiculous.'

She shrugged and sat back, arms crossed. The security lads started to move around.

'Come on, Trent,' said Jamie. 'Easy come and all that.'

'Hardly easy,' I said. The cashier counted out our notes, all with Armstrong pictured on them but younger and thinner than he now was.

When we came out of the bank the mist had thickened. There was no traffic apart from one vehicle. A big dark shadow that emerged out of the mist.

Accompanied by a gruff engine sound, the bikers' bus appeared.

CHAPTER EIGHT

Dinner

The bus rattled past, parking at the side of the road, a great lump in the fog lit by flickering interior lights. As it positioned itself we stopped beside the butchers, staying close to the building, muffled whines coming from starter-motors and the hollow thud-thud of bump starting. Motors caught and the bikers rode their machines off the trailer, shifting in the smog to discordant engine sounds.

'Shit, Trent, what should we do?'

No one seemed to take much notice of them as they raced up the Front Street and they paid no heed to us standing on the pavement. After giving the townsfolk a show they pulled in further up the road, headlamps on and engines ticking over, handlebarred silhouettes lining up.

'Let's head back to the guesthouse,' I said, shoving our money deep into my jacket.

Jamie followed but he had his hand on his gun as we passed by the bikes. They'd parked their machines in a circle, leaving space for a big tourer in the centre. It dwarfed the others, the gills in its fairing catching the headlamp beams. Its rider was spot-lit as he leant against its tank running his fingers through the plaits in his hair, watching as some women brought bottles from the bus, passing them around. Beside him was a shaven headed man, tattooed, with chains encircling his body.

'So, we're prisoners. Trapped here,' said Jamie

'We could have a few beers, go on a pub crawl round town…'

He jerked his thumb back at the bikers. 'Not while they're here. Let's just grab something. Go back to the room.'

So we carried on, stopping at a shop for pies and at the off-licence for booze. Men appeared out of the fog, their overalls as yet unmarked by the coal dust they'd later wear, making their way to factory for the afternoon shift. Some muttered to one another but most were silent, heads down

Ahead there were raised voices and a dog barked, a deep grunt. Figures jumped around on the pavement. Getting closer we saw it was Sikey. He was with two other thugs, track-suited town-lads full of lunchtime beer. They had this older fella up against the rusted railings of the derelict park. He was grey-haired, stooped, dressed in AHI overalls. The lads laughed and passed a rucksack between one another. As the man grasped for it they shoved him, spat on him, one brandishing a cosh. Sikey stood back, hands in the pockets of his tracksuit. There was no sign of his pistol. The dog with him was a big Rottweiler that growled and slavered. Other men on their way to work crossed the road, keeping out of their way, leaving Sikey to it.

One of the lads opened the bag and tipped the contents

out. A bottle thudded onto the ground and hissed foamy beer. A paper-wrapped bundle joined it on the pavement and the other lad kicked it, knocking the sandwiches out. As the man grasped for them the lads stamped on his fingers, roaring with laughter. Then Sikey loosened his hold on the dog so it leapt forward and munched up the food before licking the beer, growling so the man recoiled back. With him pinned against the railings the dog barked and snapped at him. One of the lads glanced over at us, towards Jamie who'd now taken his rifle out of the bag. He had the thing aimed at Sikey's head.

The lad tapped Sikey's arm so he turned towards us as well, his eyes flicking between Jamie and me, back onto the gun. We stood like that for a minute as the mist wafted round us.

Then Sikey spat on the road. Jerking his head he said something to the lads and they went off, shouting, striding out, one of them dragging the dog.

Jamie lowered his gun.

'What the hell are you up to?' I said.

'Just helping out.'

As they disappeared up the road the man knelt down, examining what was left of his lunch. The sandwiches were chewed and scattered across the ground. Rather than give Jamie a lecture on the dangers of helping I went to the man. Jamie shouldered his gun before joining us. Stooping down I grabbed up the bottle of beer. It was split and the rest of the beer glugged out.

'We've got beer,' said Jamie.

'Yeah,' I said. 'We have got beer.'

I opened my bag and gave the man a bottle and pie from what we'd just bought. He took them and slid them away, muttering his thanks before saying he had to go and join the two-till-ten shift. He patted each of us on the arm and did up his rucksack and was off, flicking spit off his overalls.

I gave Jamie a hard stare, just so he knew what a nuisance he was.

'You know how I am with bullies,' he said.

'I know. But that was one of your beers we gave away. And your pie.'

'I'll survive.'

Jamie's rifle was swung down at his side as we headed back via the disused park and ruined play area, past a group of lads playing football on an abandoned car park. They belted the ball into the mist and ran after it.

Once we were in our room we sipped the beer and shared the remaining pie, Jamie messing with his phone while I stared out of the window into the fog, listening to the sounds of the distant bikes as they fired up, drove up and down Front Street and stopped again. At least our car was in a garage not parked in the open.

As the batteries faded Jamie put down his phone and picked up his guitar, strumming, playing something from back in the twenties. A pop song from when such things still existed. While he worked his way through several others I watched the patterns on the ceiling: reflections and light from the bikes' headlamps.

After a while he put the guitar down and leafed through his catalogue, looking at page after page of electrical appliances, toys, things long gone, then he came to one page that showed pans. 'Are we going to Laura's?' he said.

I'd forgotten about Laura and her invitation for dinner. Outside the window there were shouts and the sound of something smashing.

'So, are we going?'

Hearing her name stirred up something and I said. 'Yeah,' without even thinking about it.

So we tidied ourselves up, took turns in the bathroom down the hall with its sink and lukewarm running water. Quite a treat. Jamie put his best shoes on and brushed down his donkey jacket.

Then we went off across town. We had no idea what time it was, since neither of us had a watch, but it must have been early evening and it seemed as good a time as any to go. On the way a biker appearing out of Back Lane, his hair matted with something and vomit down the front of his leathers. He shoved us out of the way and stumbled into the Grey Bull, others following, also drunk, none taking any notice of us.

Before carrying on we checked on the garage. The lane was silent, faint light coming from Dan's place next door. Behind us the bikers shouted and sang, an engine firing up and dying.

'Looks all right,' I said.

Jamie pivoted on his stick. He didn't say anything but after a minute walked off.

We continued across town, the bikers thinning out as we went. I knew where Hope Street was, off Faith Avenue, always a reasonable part of town. Now it felt really up-market, the terraced houses having spotless windows, front doors that gleamed, a rainbow of colours that appeared out of the mist. We stopped at number seventeen, with its glossed woodwork and brass letterbox, the pavement swept and shit-free. Opposite was a fenced garden of trees and shrubs.

Jamie leant on his stick and kicked the doorstep with his winkle-picker. 'Hey, are you sure this is the right place?'

'It's where she said.' I knocked.

The door opened and Laura stood there. She was in a dark dress and had her hair tied up but in a fancy style, not like when she was working. The dress clung to her body, pulling in at her waist. 'Hello fellas, pleased you made it.' She smiled, stepping back and the smell of cooked meat and vegetables came out. A whiff of herbs, some garlic.

She led us along a passageway with white walls and polished floorboards, to the back of the house, into a dining room joined to the kitchen. A table was set for three with a jug of cider in the middle, as if she'd never doubted we'd come.

'We've decided to stay around for a few days.' I said.

'While our car's fixed,' said Jamie.

'Great. Sit where you fancy.' She went off into to the kitchen, the dress shifting on her as she walked.

We were immobile, standing in the alien environment. The room was cream with a blacked stove and a window out onto the darkening yard. There were pictures on the wall, landscapes and abstracts. In the kitchen there was a fridge and proper cooker, devices I'd not seen for years. A ceiling lamp lit the room, its light bulb showing in the lampshade. We gazed up at it.

Jamie was the first to move, sitting at one end of the table. I sat at the other, pouring us all a drink. Laura came over with a pan and ladled food onto Jamie's plate, loads of it, rich and full of meat, potatoes that held their shape. Resting her elbow on my shoulder she served me, leaning forward so I could see into her dress. 'So how long are you around?'

'What meat is this?' said Jamie, now staring at the food rather the lamp.

'Mutton. Good cuts.' Once her own food was out, she put the pan back and joined us. 'Well, it's good you're here.' She picked up her fork and started to eat.

Neither of us moved, the food too good to touch, peas that were green. Carrots bright orange.

Laura stopping eating. 'You not hungry?'

At this we grabbed our cutlery, Jamie slicing into a potato as I shoved a chunk of meat onto my fork, putting it into my mouth, taking in the rich gravy and succulent mutton. It tasted of herbs and had a sweetness, some saltiness, sharp yet tender.

She bit into slice of carrot and licked gravy off the edge of her fork. 'How long are you around?'

Jamie scooped up meat. 'Not long.'

'Couple of days,' I said.

I piled loads on my fork, cramming it in, overloading on the flavours.

The three of us ate and drank in her smart house, this civilised setting. Whatever I'd expected her place to be like, this wasn't it. Meeting her in The Feathers had been like the old days, which seemed all right, but being here made it all different, like grown-ups. How grown-ups used to live before The Collapse. All those years on the road and I'd never thought of having my own place. A house. That kind of thing didn't seem like an option. It was me and the car, later on with Lawson and Jamie. Everything I owned fitting into a bag.

But with the deal, there was a chance to change all that. Settle down, buy a house even. Live forever in one spot.

'You okay?' said Laura.

'Yeah,' I said. My fork was halfway to my mouth with piece of cabbage on it.

'Is the food all right?'

'Yeah.' I slid it into my mouth, chewed it. 'It's great.'

She smiled then told us how nice it was to have guests for dinner, that most of the people she knew had settled down, got kids, didn't go out much. Though I was listening I didn't have much to add. No one I knew had settled down.

After the meal we went through into the sitting room, where we had something that tasted almost like tea. Or how I remembered it. When I got out our grass to roll up a spliff she shook her head.

'Not in the house,' she said.

Jamie gazed around. 'It's a nice house.'

The room had an old-fashioned fireplace, blacked iron with tiles round it. There was a wooden mantelpiece and polished floorboards. White walls and patterned curtains, only a little worn. 'Yeah, nice,' I said. 'Very civilised. Must cost you something.'

'The rent's not bad,' she said. 'Worth it. It's a nice part of town. I can park out the back without worrying.'

'You have a car?'

'My reward. Years of hard work.'

That was something. Our car was our business. Our home. Having one for pleasure, that was another thing. And here we were in her sitting room with books lined up on shelves, more pictures on the wall. All lit by a table lamp, another decadence.

When we'd first met she'd rented a flat above The Feathers. That had seemed impressive at the time, though the shelves had held bottles of gin and whisky, not books. There were ashtrays dotted around the room, often overflowing.

It had been a party place. We'd had plenty of good times there. Drinks and people round for a smoke.

Celebrations.

Like the one for her twenty-first, back in the twenties. 2023 it would have been. Eighth of June. I could still remember when her birthday was.

She thought I'd forgotten, dropping loads of hints and me playing stupid. Eventually she came out and said she wanted to do something so I said, 'Let's go for a beer,' moaning that birthdays weren't worth celebrating. We went to the White Hart, giving Harry and everyone time to set out her flat.

It was a warm summer evening and we sat in the Hart's yard as a rock band played an acoustic set, like all bands did due to the power cuts. Laura drank her gin, showing me the shoes her mother had bought her.

I said I only wanted one drink, that I fancied going back to the flat. On the way she took a huff, standing on the edge of the market place and refusing to walk any further. She wore a new dress that she'd bought for the occasion, a light green one, short and tight fitting. Even as she pointed at me and told me what a shit I was, I couldn't help thinking that she looked great. I apologised for spoiling her birthday and coaxed her back, letting her open the door.

There was a cheer as she went in and they all sang happy birthday. Then she turned to me, crying. 'You bastard,' she said, putting her arms around me. That was when I gave her the necklace. It had cost me a bomb. I'd bought a decent one, all the way from Africa made from a string of amethysts. She went quiet when she put it on.

We drank all night and into the early hours, dancing to music played by Harry's friend. As the sun began to rise we left a couple of the lads singing while we snuck off to the bedroom.

There we gripped each other as if we daren't let go. We'd made love in the faint light of dawn.

Now here I was in her fancy front room, decades later.

Jamie sipped his tea. 'That Sikey is some guy. Thinks he owns the place.'

She laughed. 'He does. At any rate, his boss does. Armstrong just keeps buying everything up.'

'At least he leaves you alone,' I said.

'For now.'

I drank my tea and watched her hold her cup, how she held the handle, her thin fingers splayed out.

Jamie eased himself up. 'I need to pay a visit.' He limped out.

Laura opened a dented tin. It had picture of chocolates on it. There were homemade biscuits inside. 'Want one?' she said.

'It's kind of weird being here.'

'I bet.' She passed a biscuit over to me, her hand resting on mine as she placed it. Her skin was warm, soft. Then she reached down and took one for herself, biting it and dabbing the crumbs on her lips.

'You still sore about the old days?' I said. 'About me leaving?'

She ran her fingers through her hair. 'I think so, yes.'

'I didn't plan it that way.' Outside a cart rattled past. I took a bite of the biscuit and chewed. It was oaty, dry but tasted good. I needed to say something about what had happened, without it sounding like a feeble excuse. Instead I made small talk. 'How are your parents?'

'Died in the late thirties. Within a year of each other.'

'Sorry.'

She shrugged. I couldn't even get the small talk right.

Jamie came back in, staring at the tin of biscuits. 'Hey, don't hog the snacks,' he said.

Laura passed the tin to him as he sat down but she looked at me.

Jamie picked out a biscuit. 'Well, being stuck in this town is a pain, but this almost makes up for it.'

'From you, that's a compliment for sure,' I said, smiling at Laura and she smiled back but her fingers were in her hair, twirling a lock round and round.

CHAPTER NINE

Raided

We didn't stay much after that, Jamie all fidgety. The goodbye was awkward, ending with the three of us shaking hands.

As Jamie and me crossed town we met more of the bikers, four of them wrestling on Hill Terrace while another threw-up beside the pie shop. A window was smashed at the Grey Bull and several bust chairs lay on the pavement. We passed the lane to Dan's garage and there was no sign of any of them. Going into the guesthouse we heard singing coming from the bikers' bus.

Jamie flicked through his catalogue but soon fell asleep. I lay awake, the candle out but light coming in from outside as the bikers fired up their machines, riding up and down Front Street. They did that for what felt like hours, taking turns, engines idling in between. After that there was music, old rap stuff.

Even if it had been quiet I'd have struggled to sleep, the evening at Laura's rolling around my head. Her in that neat house with all that stuff. Settled and content. Happy.

Eventually a heavy engine sounded, raised voices, probably AHI people, and the music stopped. No more bikes revved up and there were just few shouts. Things being dropped.

By sunrise it was silent. At that point I fell asleep, reliving the evening at Laura's, mixing it with the past.

I woke up to scraping and hammering noises. Outside, men swept the pavement and rinsed shop fronts. I stared out of the window at them for a few minutes then got ready.

Jamie only woke when I opened the door to leave. 'Where you going?'

'See how Dan's doing with the car.'

He grunted and slid out of bed and I shut the door on him as he shuffled around the room.

The bikers' bus was just starting when I got outside. There was a cloud of smoke as it revved up then thudded into gear. It growled past with an AHI lorry following it. Several bikers clung to their bikes but most were inside, slumped against the windows.

The men clearing up placed bottles and broken furniture into a cart hitched to a donkey. The door to the AHI off-licence had been smashed and another team worked on cleaning inside.

The debris thinned as I carried on up Front Street but at the bottom of the lane to Dan's there were oily rags and bolts strewn on the ground. Emptied containers discarded on the road. They led in a trail up towards the garage.

The garage where our car was with its valuable cargo.

I carried on up the road to the garage, walking faster and faster. Dan was standing in the open doorway, parts all around him. Tools dropped and scattered. The lad was at the back screwing a pin-board back onto the wall.

The Lotus was still there, parked in the same spot. They hadn't taken it.

'They came in the early hours,' said Dan. 'Bust the door open.'

Shoving past him I circled the car, stopping near the rear, stooping down and feeling underneath. The bodywork was intact, the chassis untouched. They hadn't found our load.

'I chased them out. Came down with my old jack-handle, waved it around, shouted.'

'Yeah?' That was hard to imagine but at least our car was fine. The engine compartment was pushed shut and I lifted it, seeing the exposed pistons and cylinder blocks. The hoses and wires hanging free. On the bench were the cylinder heads, stained and carbonised. Maybe Dan would need to replace some tools to finish the job.

Jamie came in and joined me. 'What's happening?'

Dan was fidgeting around. 'See, they took some spanners but it was the parts that will really cause a problem…'

'Bikers paid a visit,' I said to Jamie. 'Car is intact, though.' I tapped the dismantled parts, the combustion chambers and valves, chipped and misshapen, more like fungi than engine components.

Dan stood alongside me. 'See this is the tricky bit.' He prodded a valve in its seat. 'That was what they took. Your new valves.'

'Valves?' I said. The bikers had taken our spares.

'Fuck,' said Jamie.

The lad came and joined Dan and they faced us.

For a second I said nothing, didn't move. The valves

had gone, those parts I'd put some much effort into finding, trading for them in York years ago, as part of my strategy to keep the Evora on the road forever. I'd kept them safe, away from scum like Maxwell. Now they were gone. Stolen from Dan's.

I moved up to Dan, got really close. 'Have you any idea how much effort it took to get them?'

He stared at me, eyes wide. 'I dunno—' The lad backed away from us.

'Why didn't you stop them? Why the fuck didn't you stop them?' I grabbed hold of him, twisted his overalls in my hands, the coarse material. Him smelling of sweat. Fear. He hadn't stopped them and now the car couldn't be fixed. I had half a mind to crack him over the head.

Jamie had his hand on my arm. 'Trent.' He dragged me.

Letting go of Dan I went out into the lane led by Jamie. The smoke above the town cleared, giving a glimpse of blue sky, then it was back to the usual grey.

For some minutes I stood there, Jamie alongside me. I should never have given the valves to Dan. Never trusted him.

'Jesus Christ, Trent, what now? How are we going to make the deal?' Jamie was next to me, all expectant as if I'd come up with some instant solution. Just like that.

'I don't fucking know.'

There was clattering from the garage as Dan and the lad tidied up. They really weren't bothered. Maybe it was worth going in, kicking them around, roughing them up. They'd been entrusted with the car and fucked up. They'd let the bikers take the valves.

Going back to the doorway I gave Dan a good

eyeballing, letting him know how I felt. Him and the lad stopped what they were doing, glancing at each other. Knocking them around wasn't a solution but it was a way to get my feelings out of me. That car was an heirloom and family treasure. I'd spend years looking after it and now it was so much scrap.

'Trent?' Jamie was at my side. 'We need to think about what we're doing.'

'Do we?' I was thinking about what I was going to do to Dan and the lad. How I was going to make them appreciate what a calamity this was.

'Trent, we need a plan.'

I turned away from the garage, taking a deep breath, my fingers drumming on my leg like crazy. The valves were gone. That was that. Kicking the mechanics around wouldn't fix it, tempting as it was.

We had two options now: get another car or patch this one up. Neither was appealing.

'They've really dropped us in it.' I flicked my thumb back at Dan and the lad.

'Don't blame them, Trent. This is your fault. Yours.' Now it was Jamie's turn to get wound up. 'You brought us here. You left the car. It's your fucking fault.'

'Come on Jamie —'

'Jesus Christ, Trent, this is turning into a real mess. A complete fuck up.' He punctuated his words with prods on my chest, jabs that became sharper as he continued, going on about how important the deal was and that we should never have come to the town. While he rattled on it got me thinking. Maybe there was a solution. Though I was tempted to patch up the Lotus and go as it was, the chance of being outrun was too high. Getting another car wasn't an option, seeing as the load was stashed in the chassis, and the Evora was such a great car in other ways. With the repairs done it would last us years.

So that was it. We had to fix the Evora; get the valves back.

Eventually Jamie ran out of steam and rested his hand on his walking stick.

'Finished?' I said.

He shrugged. 'You need to sort this out. Make sure we can do the deal…'

'I will.'

'Fine.'

Then he turned and walked off, before I had time to discuss a plan, how I was going to get the car back on the road and escape the place.

'Where you going?'

'Back to the room, Trent, back to the room. This is your fault. You sort it.'

I could have argued, made my case but I let him go.

Dan stopped tidying and came to apologise.

'Tell me about the bikers,' I said. I was calm now. Ready to sort this out. If the bikers were like the other reivers they'd never go more than a day's journey from their base. This was their march and they'd have a camp nearby.

'They took the valves. Like I said.'

'I know that. Where do they go? Where do they stash their stuff?'

He stared at me. 'The bikers?'

'Yes, the fucking bikers. Where's their base?'

After a moment's thought he gabbled on about a camp they had, a place at the far side of the woods. 'Ripton,' he said. 'Past Ripton Mill. Where the activity centre used to be. Far side of the woods, over the river.'

I knew the place, well out of town but reachable with some help. I told him to tidy up and promised to get the valves back.

Then I set off to organise the other details, the sun now fighting through the smoky air, not a breath of breeze to be felt.

First I had to contact Sandhu, the guy we were making the deal with.

Asking around in a nearby hardware shop I found out where the couriers did the drop offs and pick-ups. They met up behind the derelict council offices, in what had been the main car park.

When I went there I found a couple of fellas hanging around, one with a package the other empty handed. There were no cars. I went across to the far side, well away from them so they didn't get too edgy. I took my jacket off and sat on a busted wall, the sun now bearing down on the cracked and holed tarmac.

The two men shuffled around at the other side of the car park. It was a good sign them being here. Cars were obviously expected.

Once I rearranged with Sandhu we'd be fine. There was just the complication of picking up the valves. Getting them back. I'd sort out the details later but I'd done worse. We'd need a lift up to the bikers' camp. A pick up afterwards. Escaping Kelso had been trickier. Still, Lawson hadn't made that.

Piano playing drifted in from across the road in the warm air, accompanied by singing, a male voice, old sounding. The song was a pop song, one from when I was a kid. About being lucky or something.

An old Peugeot 308 drove in. The man with the package went over and I followed him, hanging around but trying not to unsettle them. Once the load was handed over, payment made I sidled up, keeping away from his car as we chatted through his window. Turned out he was heading north later, which was no use to me.

The Peugeot left and the fella walked off leaving me and the other man. We kept our distance but there was no sign anything was going to kick off. A few minutes later a Vauxhall Insignia rolled in. The man went to the car and identified himself. Then he was handed a small container. He opened it and sniffed it before handing over cash. I kept out of the way while that went on, only going over once he'd walked off.

The Vauxhall driver was fidgety when I approached, but softened when he saw my roll of money. Seemed he was off to the city, which was perfect. Scribbling down an address and note to Sandhu I gave him a little cash. In the message I suggested the deal be delayed a week, giving us time to grab the valves. Fix our car. I stressed to Sandhu that we would be there. The driver looked reliable and I told him there'd be more money if I got a reply. We'd already sorted out our password me and Sandhu. As long as a message came back with *Gold Jag* in it, I knew we were sweet.

The next part of the plan was working out how to get to the camp. We needed transport and driver. A decent car and someone we could trust. Someone like Laura and her car.

So I went to The Feathers.

It was stinking hot when I went in, the windows all

open. Laura sat on a bar stool, a glass in front of her and her jacket off, using a homemade fan to flap air through the top of her thin dress, onto her body.

Seeing me she straightened up, smiling before ordering me a whisky. 'Still here?'

'Seems so.'

The barman brought my drink, clearing the glasses from in front of us as Laura gave him some instructions, about reordering beer and cider. Apart from two men at the far side there was only us in.

A bead of sweat ran down her forehead and she wafted air from the fan into her dress. 'It's so hot in here.' The material stuck to her shoulders and the nape of her neck was red, flushed. Then she took an ice cube out of her drink, something that was never normally seen in the summer, chunks of ice. She ran it across her forehead, down the side of her face and onto her neck, holding it there. The ice melted sending a ribbon of water down her skin, into her cleavage. 'I'm so hot.'

'Yeah.' She was that all right.

'So what's happening with your car? All going okay?'

This was my cue. 'Not quite.'

'Oh?'

'Yeah. Problem with the parts. I might need a little help.'

'Anything I can do?' She smiled and moved closer.

'Maybe.'

'Must be hard keeping it on the road. Out there.' She waved around the room with her hand.

'Yeah.'

She leant towards me, her warm arm on mine. 'What's it like? Moving around all the time; different towns;

different deals? Different women?' At the last point she raised an eyebrow.

'Rough. Dangerous. Sometimes boring.'

'Must be some interesting bits.'

I took a swig of the whisky, cooled by the chunk of ice. What a luxury that was. Being on the road wasn't great but it was real, not like this town. Laura bent in towards me, ready for a story. I had some real horror ones but she didn't need to hear those

'Here's one,' I said. 'From a couple of summers ago.' Then I went on to tell her about Dumfries. The time we'd met that big-mouth in the Hole in the Wall.

He'd shouted off for ages, telling everyone in the bar how he was going to sort us out and take all our gear, just because we'd not laughed at his joke.

He waited for us in the street, just in front of the Mid-Steeple, a semi-automatic in his hand, waving it at us. Without warning he started shooting, bullets flying all over the place, into windows, catching some old drunk walking by. Jamie just knelt down, took out his Browning, aimed and hit him in the leg. Enough to have him collapse down but not do long-term damage. I walked over and took the fella's piece then we were off. The locals tended to him and the wounded drunk as we left.

We traded that gun in the end, paying for a night of drinking in Galashiels. Selling someone's gun was an extreme thing to do, but he was a real arse-hole and deserved it. And it paid for a good night out, though Jamie had a little too much to drink. I'd had to carry him to the hotel where he puked all over the place. He'd been a right state.

She laughed at this, slapping me on the arm like it was

really funny. I had plenty more stories but they weren't so enjoyable. About the hours sitting in the car, Jamie with his gun to hand, me scanning the road for neo-reivers or gangs. The abandoned villages with mass graves. Piles of human bones. Places where strangers got strung up and left as a warning.

Yes, I had plenty of stories.

We finished our drinks and she ordered some more, giving further instructions to the barman and checking order sheets. We talked about the town, how much it had changed, with AHI now running just about everything. How crazy the world had become since the wars. What things were like when we were kids with cars everywhere, computers, television, all that stuff. Things Jamie asked about but didn't really understand.

Then I went for the big one. 'About me going—'

'Don't, Trent.'

'I didn't mean to leave like that.'

'Trent, please.' She put a finger on my lip, a soft warm finger. 'Fancy grabbing some food?' she said.

'Yeah.' There was no harm in spending the rest of the day with her, catching up. We went back so many years, longer than almost anyone else I knew.

Looking at her now it was hard to believe that was over two decades ago.

It all had started here, at that Christmas party in The Feathers, the one for drivers like me and Harry who'd been employed by Borthwick's haulage firm, before the business had closed in The Collapse, like most things in the town. Long before Armstrong appeared and reshaped Setmarch in his own style.

I'd gone along to the party with Harry, standing at the

bar because we hadn't known many people. Laura was working that night. She was in tight fitting jumper and jeans. Nothing fancy but it looked great on her. Her hair was up and she had flushed cheeks from all the work, adding to the glow around her. When she took a smoking break I went out as well. In those days when there were laws on such things. I stood near her in that freezing yard.

'You got a light,' she said.

I lit her cigarette with my Zippo, watching as she closed her eyes to inhale. We stood and smoked as the sound of voices came from the pub. There was no music or laughter, just low mutterings.

'Quite a party,' I said.

'You think?'

I laughed. 'No. Not really.'

'Well, let's spice it up.'

Then she led me back in, putting the jukebox on full volume, playing old songs. She took my hand and led me to the far side of the room where there were no tables. She strutted around to Eminem with me in tow. Everyone else just watched as we made fools of ourselves. She was so full of energy.

Harry tapped me on the shoulder to say he was going, giving me a wink, so Laura and me danced on, drank until the bar was shutting and I helped her tidy up, both of us talking all the time.

Then we went upstairs, drank some more, listened to music.

And I spent the night there.

The next day we didn't go out of the flat. Outside kids skated on the icy pavements, the sky blue and clear, as we lay entwined in her bedroom.

That's how it had all started.

Here we were together again, years later, but now just friends. No more than that.

'Lunch at mine?' She grabbed her jacket, heading over to the side exit, the one that led into the alley and I joined her, opening the door for her. She stepped out and I hung onto it, running an ice cube from my glass across my forehead, closing my eyes and letting the whisky-infused water run down my skin.

Then she cried out. I sprung out to find Sikey there, his tattooed arm shoved down the front of her dress and his hand over her mouth. A double-barrelled shotgun swung at me from the side, its stock hitting me in the gut, a solid blow that folded me up. On its second swing the gun swished past my head. I found myself facing an unshaven lad in a tracksuit, his belly hanging out of the bust zip of the jacket.

He raised the shotgun up, laughing. 'Gotcha.'

CHAPTER TEN

Sikey

Before the fella had time to cock the gun I kicked him in the groin and he let out a sigh, his grip slipping as he went to hold himself.

Sikey still had his hand pushed into Laura's bra as she twisted and squirmed. He shook his head. 'You know, you shouldn't have messed with me Glock.'

'Yeah?' I elbowed the wheezing lad in the tracksuit before he had time to pull himself together, taking his shotgun off him. 'Let go of her.'

'You shouldn't mess with someone's gun.'

'Really?' I aimed the shotgun at Sikey. 'Five seconds to let her go.' As the lad in the tracksuit shuffled around I cracked him over the head with my free hand, not too hard but enough to keep him out of the way.

Sikey grinned and pulled his hand out of Laura's dress, going for his pistol. 'Fuck you,' he said. Then he cried out and let go of her, blood running from the hand that had been over her mouth, teeth marks showing 'Bitch!'

She pushed him away, kicking him in the shin. 'You

piece of shit.'

Before he grabbed his pistol I was beside him, ramming the shotgun into his chest. 'Hands up.'

'You serious?'

I jabbed him with the shotgun and he raised his arms, blood running down his tattoos. Although he looked over at his accomplice he kept his hands up.

I gave the shotgun to Laura then grabbed Sikey's semi, taking out the magazine, racking the gun like Jamie had so the round dropped out into my hand. I shoved it and the magazine into my pocket, returning the empty pistol to him. The lad in the tracksuit was now standing sideways against the wall, rubbing his crotch so I manoeuvred him into a half nelson, leading him out of the alley. Laura prodded Sikey and he came along with us.

At the pavement I let go of the lad and pushed him forward while Laura shoved Sikey so that he was beside him. The four of us stood there in the hazy heat, as people skirted us when they saw the gun in Laura's hand.

'Second time we've disarmed you,' I said, taking the shotgun from Laura, dangling it limply.

Sikey spat on my foot. Neither he nor the lad moved or gave an impression of coming at us so I led Laura off, hanging the shotgun over my arm. As we passed a low wall I shoved the loose round into the magazine and threw it all over the wall.

'You all right?' I said.

'I'm okay, thanks.' She pulled closer to me, running her hands through her hair. 'But I think it's best you escort me home.' That did seem sensible so I walked along with her. Behind us Sikey and his side-kick were at the wall where I'd thrown the magazine so I hurried Laura along, my

hand on her waist. Sloppy as they were they would soon
have the rounds in Sikey's gun.

Laura leant against me, her body warm and soft,
contrasting with the shotgun's hard edges.

'I need a favour,' I said. 'A lift in your car.'

'Okay.'

'To the bikers camp, if you know where it is.'

She straightened up at this. 'Oh, I know where it is all
right.' Though still walking she slowed, her body tense
beside me. 'That's not a great place to go, Trent.'

'It's not by choice.'

'They don't just let people stroll in.'

'I'm sure.'

She picked up the pace again, saying nothing, taking
deep breaths.

'If you can drop us nearby, that will do,' I said. 'They
have something I need.'

'I bet they do.'

'If it's too much trouble…'

'Well, it is trouble. Anything with the bikers is.'

For a while we walked on in silence but she seemed to
loosen up. Being so close to her was odd, pleasant.

'When do you need to go?' she said.

'Soon as possible. Tomorrow, if we can.'

'They don't welcome guests…' She sighed. 'You'd have
to go early. First light. After the patrol and before the
bikers are on the road.'

'So you'll help us?'

'I shouldn't. I really shouldn't…. Only on two
conditions.'

'Go on.'

'I pick you up in town at six am and we meet the next

day at the same time. No waiting around.'

'That it?'

'And I'll drop you this side of the woods. Well away from them. I don't want to lose my car. You'll have to cut through, cross the river. Make your own way.'

'We can do that.'

'Okay.' She went on to describe her car and where she'd pick us up, going on to talk about some event that was on in town, not anything I needed to know about. Her body was pushed up against me, warm, soft. Pleasant as this was there was no time for relaxing. Sikey and his thugs were slack, lazy from years in a small town. But they were still nasty pieces of work and would want to get us back. I gripped the shotgun tightly.

At her house Laura stopped at the doorstep. 'Ready for something to eat?' She played with her key, staying close by me.

Although the offer of food and an afternoon at hers sounded great, there was stuff to sort out and going in would complicate things, probably lead to something else that there wasn't time for. Not with the Sikey and his people and the bikers' camp to think about.

'I need to organise a few things, for tomorrow.'

'Just a quick bite –'

'Thanks, but no.'

She nodded and slid her key into the lock. 'Right, see you tomorrow.' Then she leant over and pulled me by my shirt, kissing me hard on the lips, wrapping her arms around me and holding me there for a few seconds, her body pressed against me, her mouth tasting of gin and something sweet.

When we separated she smiled. 'See you tomorrow,

then.'

'Yeah.'

Then she went in, leaving me on the doorstep. A moment later I walked off, back across town towards the guesthouse. The shotgun was still in my hand and I swung it as I went.

As I came to the end of Belmont Street a figure watched me from an alleyway. He wore a grey suit with something wrapped around his head.

It was Nixon. He was out and about in town. Cocking the gun I sprinted across the road towards him, into the alley, the weapon raised, ready to finish him off this time. I pulled the trigger, the barrels pointed in his direction. Nothing happened. Pulling the second trigger the gun fired, the sound thundering off the walls. The air was filled with smoke. I rushed forward, wafting it away, looking for his body. There was no sign of him.

The lane at the end of the passageway was also empty.

After a few minutes hanging around I headed back, the gun gripped tight, watching for him. But he never reappeared. There were just workers who made their way to work, the air above them thick with smoke, the smell of sulphur, part burnt coal. No one looked at the gun, me, made eye-contact. They shuffled by in their AHI overalls, past AHI shops selling AHI products. Anyone who stepped out of line ended up on Armstrong's lorry, or whatever other punishments he had, while thugs like Nixon ran free.

Some town.

CHAPTER ELEVEN

Woods

When I got back Jamie was lying on the bed, his phone at his side. After telling him about the valves and how we could get them, I showed him the shotgun, leaving out details about the time I'd spent with Laura. Seeing Nixon. He said nothing about the car but looked the gun over, declaring it junk and chucking it under the bed.

Then he messed with his phone the battery struggling to light it.

When he picked up his magazine I said, 'We need to get sorted.'

'Right,' he said, casting his things aside and getting up.

For the rest of the day we prepared for our trip to the bikers' camp. Jamie didn't say much as he organised what he wanted to take, now and then giving me a glance. I went out and bought a map and food in town. Back at the room we sorted everything on the bed and loaded it into our rucksacks. He insisted on having the map, snatching it up and shoving it into his bag, alongside his gun and ammo, a blanket and spare clothes.

We had an early night and he was already up when I awoke, dressed and staring out of the window at the predawn glow.

'I'm sorry about this,' I said.

'Look, Trent, I'm going on this wild-goose chase, but don't expect me to be all chatty.'

So we walked out in silence, stopping at the side of the road where Laura had said.

He slid a bottle of whisky out of his rucksack, taking a swig and laying the bag on the pavement. He eased himself down and sat on it, turning up the collar on his donkey jacket. As the sun rose up behind us it lit a billboard opposite, giving a pink hue to the wording that said: AHI HEALTHCARE. PAY NOW OR SUFFER LATER.

A lorry growled past, overtaking a donkey laden up with sacks. Even this early there was traffic, and people. Workers filed along the pavement, all grey overalls, expressionless, the smell of coal and sweat on them.

'Is our car going to be okay?' Jamie said.

'Yeah…'

'How long till the deal?'

'Nearly two weeks from now. Plenty of time.' I didn't bother mentioning that this was just a request to Sandhu. That I didn't know if he'd go along with it. A red Ford Mondeo came down the road, a late model but old, like all cars. Its paintwork gleamed in the early light, its bumpers and panels intact, the only modifications being hasps and staples added to the doors, for padlocks to secure them. This was Laura's car, even tidier than she'd described. The Mondeo slowed and pulled over as Jamie struggled up.

Laura joined us, friendly, excited even. 'Great morning, fellas, don't you think?'

'Is it?' Jamie said.

We stashed our bags in the boot and I slid in next to her, Jamie leaning against the door frame. The interior smelled like cars used to smell, of clean carpets and fresh plastic.

'You coming?' I said.

'Aye, I'm coming, give me a minute.' He joined us saying nothing as Laura revved up and we left Setmarch.

Once out of town, clear of the plant's smoke, the sun burnt down on us. We passed by fields of dried earth where diseased pigs picked at scraps; sickly sheep on the higher ground. Soon we were onto moorland, dotted with saplings and up ahead a thick forest rolled off into the distance, the trees well foliated, unlike the soot-specked ones in Setmarch. The road twisted and undulated as Laura pushed the Mondeo. She set the car up well for the corners, feeding the power in on the apex between smooth gear changes.

'Listen, Laura, can't you take us all the way?' said Jamie.

'I don't want them to take my car. They're not worried about doing things like that.'

'Well, you could pull in and we could walk the last part.'

'I don't want to get into problems. This car is really useful.'

I turned to face him. 'It'll be fine.'

'So you keep saying, Trent,' he said. 'So you keep saying.'

'Tell him it'll be fine, Laura.'

Laura glanced at him. 'Trent thinks it'll be fine, Jamie.'

The road turned to the right and curved over a bridge. There was a wrecked car by the side of the river, its rusted shell blackened where it had been burnt, a charred skeleton of steel.

'Bikers did that,' said Laura. 'I don't want that happening to this motor.'

Black tyre tracks marked the road, circles and zigzags where the bikers had performed stunts. Laura swung the car off to the left, towards the woods, down a track. The Mondeo bounced and pitched and the steering wheel twitched in her hands. As we entered the trees she eased the brakes on and the wheels locked, the ABS light flashing on the dash.

'You fellas ready to go?' she said.

We were enclosed by branches heavy with leaves and trunks that receded off into the gloom. 'Yeah,' I said. Maybe I'd got too settled in Setmarch, not thought through how difficult this was going to be.

Laura switched the engine off and pointed. 'Straight on until you meet the river. Then cross and aim for the high ground. It's to the west after that. You can't miss it.'

The sky was clear blue above the forest. I knew where we were headed but it was going to be tough cutting through this way. I stepped out and opened the rear hatch. Wind hissed in the trees and there was a gurgle from a stream nearby.

Laura came round and joined me. 'You be careful out there.'

I lifted out the bags. 'I will.'

'Watch yourself with those crazy bikers.'

'Yeah.'

Jamie shuffled round and joined us, all hunched up,

eyes moving fast as he lifted his rucksack up,

'All set?' I said.

He shrugged. Maybe getting away from town would pick him up.

Laura closed the rear hatch. 'Well, see you in tomorrow.' She put her arm around me, hugged me, holding on tight. She was warm and smelled of soap. She kissed me on the cheek but I turned my head so we kissed on the lips, nothing major but something to remember, a memory for when I was out in the wilds. We pulled apart but she stayed close, her body leant against me. Her eyes were dark, soft, impossible to read.

Jamie nudged up against me. 'Should we get going?'

'Yeah.' I moved away from Laura and the sun shone down across the trees, lighting her with yellow light that gave her a glow, brightened her face and put life in her eyes.

Shouldering my bag I joined Jamie.

'Bye, Laura,' he said.

'Bye.' She smiled at me and got into the car, starting it and swinging round before pulling off with a spray of gravel. It accelerated along the road, disappearing into the distance. Then there was just us and the trees.

I adjusted my rucksack and left the track, going into the shade of the woods with Jamie struggling after me on the rough ground. A few minutes on we were surrounded by the forest, great larch trees grown leggy, some dead and fallen. The ground was a carpet of leaves; thin needles that smelled of decay. Slowing down I let Jamie catch up.

'Which way?' he said.

I pointed my hand ahead. 'Are you all right?'

'Me? I'm fine.' Then he led off, working his stick hard

as he crossed the rough ground.

We walked on for several hours, in patchy light falling through the branches, as we pushed through dry ferns and decaying leaves. The ground undulated over dried up stream beds and around the roots of ancient oaks and beech, some dead, rotted.

When we came to a slope Jamie stopped, leaning against his stick, sweat running down his forehead. 'Is this really the best way?'

Some bird called from way off, a rough squawk that rolled out through the trees, fading as it flew off.

'Only way, it seems,' I said.

'It's taking ages.'

'We're going the shortest way.'

'This is killing me. I'm thirsty.'

There was a rumble from a river up ahead and a murmur of wind in the branches. The trees above us were sycamores, tall, sparsely leafed, while clumps of heather covered the ground around us.

'Can we have a drink?'

'Yeah,' I said, taking my bag off. There was a low moan followed by a scrambling sound, probably a squirrel. I opened the bag, taking out a bottle and passing it to him.

He drank then leant forward, wiping his forehead. 'We should be at the coast today.'

'I know.'

'Doing the deal in a couple of days.' He passed the bottle back to me and I dabbed some on my forehead and neck. Even shaded by the trees it was warm. With my jacket off I laid back on the heather.

'We'll be crossing the river soon.' Branches rattled as something moved in them but there was no sign of anything above.

'This place creeps me out.' He reached for the bottle and drank some more. 'Can we eat now?'

'I guess.' The sun was high above the trees. It was midmorning, seeming later after our early start. Feeling around in my rucksack I found the bread and cheese wrapped in paper. It was jammed in next to our stash of grass, something I wasn't leaving in the guest house. Pulling the cheese out I unwrapped it. It was hard, rubbery and smelled of dope. I tore a piece off, then bread, giving some to him and taking a little for myself. We sat and ate.

'Listen, Trent.'

I gazed up into the trees. Compared to the Border Forest this place seemed tame, almost safe.' Yeah?'

'Can you tell me one of the stories? About years ago?'

'Now?' This was one of his things. Getting me to recount memories — telling him how it used to be. He'd not done it in the town but here it was again. Him and Laura were keen to squeeze tales out of me.

'Come on. What else are we going to do?'

'All right,' I said. This time I picked the holiday to India. The one when I was about ten. He said nothing as I recounted how busy the airport was. The time flying. Staying in a hotel. Going into the jungle by jeep. The exotic markets and food and drink. All the people on the beaches.

At the end of the story he thanked me.

'No problem,' I said, lying back. The leaves moved above us, rippling in the breeze. This place was so much quieter than the town.

'It's good to have time to chat. Just the two of us.

Without Laura—'

'Yeah, but she has helped us. She gave us a lift. We'd have been stuck without her.'

'Pity she's part of the town. Mixed up in it all.'

'Mixed up in what?'

'Well, I just meant that, maybe, only maybe she's—'

'Maybe what?' I sat up.

'Forget it.'

He stared down the hillside and ate his food. Laura had done nothing but help and had no love of Armstrong and his thugs. He'd have known that if he'd seen Sikcy outside the pub. There was no point explaining it to him. Once he had some idea in his head that was it.

I tore off more bread and chewed on it. A breeze blew through the trees, hissing through the branches, wafting the smell of rotting leaves around us. I stood up, shaking crumbs off myself and pulling my jacket on. After putting the remaining food away I grabbed the water bottle off him, closing my bag and shouldering it.

'Come on. We've got some way to go.'

He struggled up. 'Listen, Trent, I didn't mean to sound —'

'It's fine.' I started off down the hill. 'It's all fine.'

I kept ahead of him so I didn't have to hear his moaning.

We walked down to the riverbank, where the vegetation gave way to stones worn smooth. The water rushed past, dropping down over the rocks, gurgling and rumbling, taking small branches with it. The river was clear, free of sediment so that the stones in the riverbed were visible in the shallows.

Jamie came and stood alongside me, staring down into

the water, his chin jerked out. 'I didn't mean to be critical,' he said.

This probably wasn't easy for him, struggling over the rough ground. And Setmarch hadn't been that great, all that hanging around. This wasn't how things usually went. In the past we'd stopped at a town, had a few drinks and were gone in the morning.

'It's all right,' I said.

The river rushed past.

'Christ, it's full,' he said.

'Must have been a storm up the valley.'

'You think we need to go further up?'

The river moved quickly, smooth apart from the eddies between the rocks.

'Here will be fine.' I took my rucksack off then my jacket, boots and socks, stashing them in my bag and rolling up my pants.

He didn't move.

As I waded out, the water rushed over my legs, drawing all the heat from them. The loose pebbles shifted under my feet as I carried on and the force of the current made me lean against the flow. With my rucksack over my head I continued across the slippery stones.

Jamie stood on the shore.

I waved to him. 'It's fine.'

One eyelet at a time he undid the laces on his winkle-pickers before sliding his socks off, stashing them in the shoes which he held as he wobbled into the water. In his other hand was his rucksack with his stick attached and the Browning poking out of the top. 'Ah, man, this is freezing, Trent.'

'Yeah.' My feet lay like albino flatfish amongst the rocks

of the riverbed. They'd lost all feeling as if I'd had someone else's feet stitched on. I inched across the river with him following.

When we got half way I stopped. I was wet up to my waist and my rucksack shifted around, unbalancing me. There was a roar as the river dropped down between two boulders, worn smooth by the flow. 'Jamie, careful, it's deeper here.'

He leant forward with his bag hanging off to one side. 'Trent?'

'Yeah?'

'You know I can't swim.'

I laughed.

'I'm serious. I never learnt.'

'I can't either.'

I'd learned as a kid but hadn't tried for decades. There weren't a lot of swimming pools around these days, especially on the road. I stepped out into the deeper water and sank in to my chest, the icy water filling my clothes, making me gasp.

The current whipped at me, shoving me downstream and I lost my footing, flapped in the water. There was a stick wedged between two rocks not far away and I reached out for it. My hand slipped on the slimy wood so I grabbed again, failing to grasp it, swallowing some water. The current pushed me under, my rucksack a dead weight on my back, tugging me down. I clawed at it, knowing this could be it, that Jamie wouldn't save me. Within a minute I'd be out of air, sucking in water, drowning. Dead.

Then one foot settled on firm ground and I pushed off, surfacing in calmer water that was waist-deep. I drew a great breath, lovely fresh air, throwing my bag onto an exposed rock and grabbed a sapling growing at the waters' edge. Holding on I inhaled great lungfuls of air, shaking the water out of my eyes and ears. Jamie was watching. 'Listen, Jamie, I don't think this is a good idea.'

He gave me some look I couldn't figure out before rearranging his rucksack and shoes, closing his eyes. Then he stepped out and sank under, disappearing into the water.

CHAPTER TWELVE

Lost

His hands flailed around but I couldn't reach them. The end of his rifle and stick were the only other things visible.

'Jamie?' I shouted. 'Jamie?' I dived into the freezing torrent and grabbed for him, finding his arm but losing it as the water swirled and roared, dragging us off. I felt something, his shirt or jacket, and grasped it, pushing against the rocks as we were forced against them, as sky, treetops and dark water swirled around us. Curling into a ball I held onto him as we smashed into the riverbed and rolled along, enclosed in the water until we were shoved against a great boulder. I grasped hold of it, dragging him out, raising his head up. 'Jamie?'

His eyes were shut.

I hauled his limp body into the shallows, through the freezing water and lay him on dry rocks. He breathed but didn't open his eyes. 'Jamie?'

Then he stared up at me. 'Jesus, Trent.'

I helped him onto the shore and lay him out before collected dry wood, piling up kindling and thicker branches. With him wrapped in his jacket I made a fire, warming water and giving it to him in a tin mug. Having a fire so close to the bikers' camp wasn't the best thing to do but it burned hot and didn't give off much smoke. Anyway, he needed to dry out. While he drank I walked up and down the riverbank, looking into the pools and shallows, searching for his rucksack. There was no sign of it. We had my bag with all the dope in it but we'd lost the map, and his gun. We shouldn't have brought it, really. There was no way we were going to outgun the bikers in their own camp. But now we'd lost it.

When I got back to the fire Jamie held the mug close, pulling his jacket around him.

'Any sign of my bag?' he said.

'No. No sign. Look, we're going to have to get going soon.'

'Can't we keep looking for it? Anyway, I'm freezing.'

This part of the woods was tall pines, cutting out the sun, making it cooler than where we'd been before. But it was still warm enough, especially by the fire. I fished through my bag, sorting out dry clothes for him. There was a shirt, pants and a pair of socks, all my spares. 'Here you go.'

As I repacked my rucksack he tugged the socks onto his feet. 'Ah, Trent, this is so stupid.'

'The river was fuller than I expected.'

'And I've lost my fucking stick and gun.' He stood and pulled the pants on. They were too big and hung off the end of his legs. He flapped them around. 'We shouldn't have come here.'

'You're just saying that because you're cold.'

'I'm saying it because it's true, isn't it.'

We were here and we had the valves to get. Things hadn't worked out too well but it was still doable. But I wasn't going to argue with Jamie when he was wet and pissed off. I stacked the fire up and we sat by it for some time. There was no way we'd sneak into the camp in daylight so there was no rush.

With another couple of mugs of hot water in him he got some colour back in his skin.

Sliding my rucksack on I kicked soil on the fire. 'Are you ready?'

'You know we'll never fix that car. You're more bothered about it than you are about us. Something has happened to you, Trent. That town has screwed with your head.'

I pushed the embers of the fire around, coating them in dirt so they wouldn't smoke. 'Come on.'

I led him off up between tall sycamores, sparsely leafed, through the ferns and leaf-litter. At top of the rise there were pines, thickly packed. It was dark amongst them, the ground covered in dead branches that crunched under our feet. As well as losing the gun we'd lost the map. It was all memory and guesswork now.

He leant against a stump. 'Well, Trent, which way?'

There were all these trees around us and somewhere behind was the river. We needed to head to the west. The sun was visible through the foliage, straight ahead. 'This way.' I veered off to my right, guessing it was early afternoon and this would take us west. I wasn't really sure. But I needed to lead Jamie, keep his spirits up.

We left the pines, going back into the sycamores. The sun shone through and dappled the forest floor. There was a big anthill ahead and moorland off to our right so I steered us left a little.

Jamie shuffled away from the anthill and shook his legs. 'You sure we're going the right way?'

We carried on and came to a clearing. There was a dead oak tree in the middle and primroses grew around its roots. A stream ran through the damp ground and he hobbled over to the tree, leaning against it.

'You all right?' I said.

'What, after being in a freezing river and dragged through a forest?'

'Should be coming to the camp soon.'

I didn't really know where we were but telling him that wouldn't help. Stopping for a minute or two would give me time to work out the layout. I opened my rucksack and drew out the bottle of water and offered it to him. He took a drink and passed it back. Up here it was warmer than down by the river, the air still. I drank the water in great gulps then put it down on the bag. 'Sorry about the river. And your gun.'

He picked up the water again and drank some more.

'If I'd have thought it was that bad I'd have gone another way.'

'I bet you wouldn't have made Laura wade through it.'

I snatched the bottle off him and put it into my bag 'We need to go.' With my rucksack fastened I led off, keeping ahead. We pushed our way between rhododendron and stunted pine trees.

It wasn't true about Laura. I'd have asked her to cross the river if we'd had to. And I'd tried to warn him about the deep water. Jamie was just pissed off about his gun.

The ground started to climb up some more. We made our way through birch that stood straight without branch or leaf.

Jamie stopped 'Wait, Trent, this doesn't feel right.'

'It's fine.'

'I think we've gone the wrong way.'

'We're fine.'

I continued, hoping we'd come upon the camp soon. The trees thinned out until we came to an open piece of ground covered in twisted heather. The rest of the forest lay before us and the sun hung low over the treetops in the distance. The land fell away down a yellow cliff and below was the river that snaked through the trees. From this high point it made it easier to work out the route.

We'd been heading off to the north, way off track.

'We need to head back a little,' I said.

Jamie sat on a log. 'Jesus. I knew this would happen. I knew we were going wrong. I just knew it.'

'We don't need to go too far.'

For several minutes we rested there, the woods and river below us. Then I led off again. We passed the birch, the rhododendron and the fallen tree, going to where the vegetation thinned to scrub, joining the moorland. Then I stopped.

He sighed. 'Well, where now?'

'I'm going to have a look around.'

I left him and walked through the scrub onto the moors. The sky was pale blue flecked with white clouds. Half a mile away there was further woodland: twisted ash trees with a massive redwood thrusting up behind them. This wasn't where the bikers had their camp but we were getting closer, we had to be. I guessed it was the other side of the big redwood.

He glared at me when I went back. 'Well?'

'This way.' I turned round and pointed to my left.

'You sure about this?'

'Completely.'

Maybe I wasn't quite that sure but I had a good idea where to go. I took us back through the trees, down towards the river then further off to the right, past marshland and a clearing with a two dead beech trees in the middle. We wandered through thick hazel and carried on up high ground.

Jamie stopped. 'Come on, I've about had it now.'

'It's up here.'

He slumped down on a log. 'No. no. That's me done. No more walking for me, Trent. You'll have to do it on your own.'

'You'll be fine after a rest.'

He shook his head and leant on his thighs, staring at the ground.

I took out the bread and cheese. It was damp and I set it out on the log. We ate it and drank the water, emptying the bottle.

'Feel any better?' I said.

Jamie picked on at crumbs on his legs. 'No. Not really. What now?'

'Don't wander off.' Taking the water bottle I left him with my rucksack, as he picked up another piece of cheese and chewed on it. He didn't look round as I went.

Going through the woods I counted my steps, carrying on in a straight line for eighty paces until the route was blocked by impenetrable hawthorn. There was a stream nearby so I leant down, filling the bottle from the shallow water that bubbled on its stony bed. To the right the trees thinned onto low undergrowth of gorse. This was where I went next, pacing it out until I came out onto the moors, lit bright by the late afternoon sun. The giant redwood was off to my left and in the opposite direction, several hundred metres off, was the bikers camp.

A track at the far right led to an archway made of motorcycle parts. A figure stood by it with a bike at his side. In the distance there was smoke from a fire and rock music played accompanied by singing and shouting. Caravans, ramshackle huts and bikes were visible, figures dancing beside them. Behind it all was the double-decker bus. Surrounding the whole area was a barbed wire fence, possibly with a ditch. Between them and me it was just open moors, nowhere to hide.

I'd have to sneak in after dark, once they were all asleep. Rushing the sentry didn't seem sensible so I'd have to go through the wire. If I wasn't spotted, it would just be a case of creeping back to the trees, back to Jamie and off. If I wasn't spotted. But seeing as I didn't know where the valves were or what other security measures they had, being spotted seemed quite likely. I'd have to run for it, across the open ground.

This was where Jamie was supposed to come in. Once I'd grabbed the valves he was meant to give covering fire, keeping the bikers at bay, winging a couple if he had to. Probably not a good idea, really.

Anyway, now I was on my own.

From the camp there was a cheer and something smashed. They needed time to party out, settle down for the evening, but that wasn't going to be for a while. In the meantime there was planning to be done. Somehow I had to cross the barbed wire. Nearby there were some branches from a dead oak and I grabbed two, the girth of my arm, a metre long. I left them on the edge of the moor by a tree stump.

Then I went back into the woods, through the gorse, by the hawthorn bushes and stream, swinging left and counting my steps. I carried on down the hill picking my way through the trees until Jamie's head showed above a log and I made towards him, shifting a heavy branch so it pointed the way I'd come.

He looked up, my blanket wrapped around him. 'That you, Trent?'

'I've found the camp.' Offering him the water I sat down. 'I'll head off later.'

He took a drink and laid the bottle on my rucksack. 'Aye? That mean we can we have a fire now?'

'Not so close to the camp. Don't want them to see the smoke.'

He hunched up. 'I bet you don't order Laura around like this.' He was needling again but there was no point taking the bait. He'd had a rough day but we were nearly there.

'Just think of the deal and what it'll mean. Think about what you can do with all that money.'

'If we ever get there.'

'We will. Get some rest. Once I've got the valves we're off.'

'What am I supposed to do until then?'

'Get some sleep. Wait for me.'

'Is that it?'

'Pretty much, yeah.'

'Pretty much.' He grunted, taking deep breaths, saying no more. I relaxed into the leaf litter as the sounds of the woods surrounded us: the rattle of branches and movement of animals.

It was calm, peaceful.

I lay there for some time, just Jamie and me in the woods. Unlike Setmarch with the plant and traffic. The drunken workers and Armstrong's thugs. This wasn't even like being on the road, always waiting for the next car to appear, wondering if it was scavengers, or people like Maxwell.

This was more like Shangri-La. Gary's place.

That bubble of calm, in its own valley north of here, away from the big towns.

My last visit had been five years ago, when Jamie and Lawson were cashing in their earnings at Gretna casino, the weekend after the job in Faeston when I'd needed to recuperate.

I'd arrived just before the party started, parking the Evora in the courtyard by the farm buildings. Gary greeted me like he always did, with a great bear hug, him dressed in a hand-knitted jumper, all colours. With that smell of fruit and homemade wine.

'Hello Gary,' I said.

He held up a hand. 'Listen.'

There was a gentle hiss from the breeze in the grass. Maybe some sounds from the forest that surrounded the pastures. Nothing distinct. 'I don't hear anything.'

'No?' He stared at me. 'Wow,' he said.

'What?'

'You've aged.'

I laughed. Gary could make anyone laugh.

'You've actually got older, Trent. Have times been that tough?' Before I answered he strolled off and I followed him into the building, as he tapped a tune on his teeth. We went into the main hall, a high ceilinged room, whitewashed and decorated with wall hangings, where several people sat on yin and yang cushions. They were dressed in homemade clothes, their hair unkempt. Each spoke to Gary, smiled.

'You want to stay?' said Gary.

'If that's all right.'

'Of course it is. Of course. Always.'

'Can I get washed somewhere?'

'You know the layout.' He pointed down a hallway. 'There's a room free there. Party soon after sunset.' Then he was off again, his footsteps echoing into the building.

By the time I'd washed and gone back through, the hall was busy. As well as the homemade wine there was a bong going around filled with their own weed they grew at the back. At the far end was a table laden with food. It was mainly apples and pickled things, the kind of stuff they grew. Most people were in the middle dancing as Gary and several others played simple instruments.

After a pull on the bong I poured myself a tall glass of fruit wine and settled in the corner. A slim woman with red hair sat beside me. She said she was called Ash and launched into this story about a dream she'd had, where she was in a great storm. She paused and took a smoke then rolled her green eyes up in her head, toppling over, sprawling across my legs and the cushions.

Now Gary was in the middle of the room. He'd abandoned his drums to dance with two women in kaftans. He laughed as they raised their hands and did this pushing motion.

I eased Ash away from me and she slid across the cushions onto her side. Her long red hair splayed out around her head, lips parted. She lay there with her mouth open and thick lashes flickering. I picked up my wine and went out of the building, to the Evora, its hard lines alien at Shangri-La. There was a cart at the far side and two donkeys stared out from their stalls. As music came from the main hall I opened the car and popped the engine cover. I examined the plug leads and distributor cap that I'd recently had grafted on after the electrics fried. Then I closed the engine cover and opened the rear hatch. When I tapped the jerry-can and LPG cylinders they each made a ding.

Gary came out of the building and strolled over. 'Getting some air?'

'Something like that.'

He leant against the car. 'What are you going to do?'

'Come back in, have a couple of drinks—'

'No, you know what I mean. Are you going to stay? For a while?'

I closed the hatch on the car and drummed my fingers on it. 'Probably not.'

We stood there as the sound of the party filled the courtyard. 'What can you hear now?'

'Voices. Music.'

He smiled then walked off. 'It's only just warming up.'

I followed him. He went back on the dance floor beside the two women in kaftans who wrapped their arms around him. He grinned and they smiled back, moving in time to the music.

Ash was where I'd left her, still sprawled but now with her thumb in her mouth, her other hand between her knees. I ran my fingers through her hair, touching her face. It was soft, smooth and I felt my own, dry and stubbled. She stirred, woke and looked up at me. For some time she just lay there, her soft eyes on me.

Then, smiling she sat up and without a word enveloped me in her arms. We kissed as the music played, her body warm against me.

Later we went off to her room and I spent the night with her, sleeping entwined after making love.

The next day I drove out.

I'd not seen Shangri-La since.

CHAPTER THIRTEEN

Camp

I awoke in the dark woods. It was silent apart from Jamie's snores. I lit my Zippo. He lay beside a log, wrapped tightly in his blanket, his mouth open. The branch I'd left as a marker was just by my foot and I followed it, going off between the trees, the shadows twisting around me.

I emerged from the woods onto the moors, lit black and white by a half moon, something I'd not seen in Setmarch. There was no sign of the branches beside the tree stump and I had to crawl around, feeling for them on the cool earth. It took some time to find them, but at last I put my hand on the rough bark, hauling them up. With one branch in each hand I crept out. The figure was in the archway up ahead, marching up and down, occasionally drinking from a bottle. I moved on, staying low as I crossed the moors.

Once I was past the archway I slunk over to the ditch and crept alongside it. Off in the distance were the caravans, huts and bikes, outlines in the moonlight. There was no music or voices so I kept going, stopping at a section where the barbed wire was flatter than elsewhere. I put the branches on the ground, going down into the ditch. The soil was soft and shifted under my feet. I bent down and put my finger in the liquid at the bottom. Lifting it up to my nose I sniffed. It was old engine oil that had mixed in with the soil. Elsewhere this would have been reused, filtered and mixed with new stuff to stretch it out. The bikers obviously got enough from Setmarch to throw it away.

Grabbing the branches I dragged them over to the ditch, setting one across the oil to stand on. It sank a couple of centimetres but held so I tried the other one. It twisted round but took my weight as it squelched into the mud. With my arms extended I picked my way across, stopping at the far side. There was only a thin strip of ground between the ditch and the wire. Leaning down I picked up one of the branches, pulling it out of the oil, lifting it up to lie on top of the barbed wire. The other branch had sunk in and I had to dig around in the slime to pull it out. It came free but I fell forward, throwing my hand out to the side of the ditch. I held myself up but my face was close to the slime as my arms strained to hold me. Heavy fumes wafted up as my feet slid. Using all the strength in my right arm I shifted my weight, pushing on the branch and digging it into the soil. With a twist I moved my hand, forcing myself up.

For a second I was upright but I overbalanced and fell back onto the barbed wire. It cut into my jacket, through into my back and shoulder with sharp stabs. Holding my mouth shut I lay there, my feet sinking into the mud and my body pinned where I was pierced.

Then I reached over and grabbed the branch that was

on the wire. Using it to push the barbs away from me I leant on it and pulled my feet up. With my hands in my sleeves I grabbed the wire and dragged myself out. The barbs cut through the jacket and into my hand, slicing into the skin. Turning round I used the stick to press the wire down but some still pricked into my legs and tugged as I moved through it.

I made it to the other side where I stood, cut and oily. My hands, legs and back stung but I was through. Setmarch was off in the distance, beyond the trees, factory-lights shining up through a blanket of smoke, an orange mushroom cloud. In the opposite direction were the vehicles, huts and caravans of the bikers and I lowered myself onto my haunches, creeping towards them.

As I got closer there were snores from the huts and I moved round the back of a caravan, past two bikes: a rusty 1100 and hand-painted 750. Someone grunted and said something so I stopped for a moment before carrying on to the double-decker. The back door was open. I crept in.

Inside it smelled of diesel and damp cardboard. There were boxes stacked up along the length of the bus. The cuts from the barbed itched on my arms and back. I ignored them and flicked my Zippo on, standing it by the boxes. Some had labels and others were plain. The first I opened held cans of beans and soup, right the way down to the bottom. I took them all out, lining them up on the floor, slow movements to avoid sound, before putting them back. Another was full of bottles of wine that chinked as I slid them out; the third held tools on top of shirts and packets of pencils.

There was a noise and I put my lighter off. A bearded

man moved around out in the moonlight, coughing and undoing his trousers. There was a hiss as he pissed, before he farted and coughed again. Once he'd finished he did up his clothes and staggered off. There was no more movement and I lit the lighter and opened more boxes. The next contained women's lingerie, shoes and scarves, bottles of beer and cider.

There was no pattern to how the boxes were arranged. The bikers would be awake by the time I'd gone through them all, or their guard would have noticed me. Even if the valves were in the camp they could have been hidden somewhere else, in a building or buried. Maybe they hadn't even got the valves. They could have dumped them in Setmarch. Or Dan faked the raid to sell the parts on. Sold them to Armstrong. This could all have been a set up.

If they weren't here we'd really have to do something else with the car. Dump it and take another. We had the deal to do and we needed to get out of town away from Maxwell, who might have found his BMW. Nixon could have contacted him, let him know about us in Setmarch. It wasn't like we'd just taken some of his dope, what we had was really rare.

My fingers were rattling away on the side of a box, drumming away. This wasn't helping. I needed to focus. If the valves were here I'd only find them by looking.

The next box contained pickles, jars of vegetables in vinegar and sauces. I shook it and there was a rattle of glass on glass right down to the bottom. I ignored the rest of the contents and went on to another. This case was better, full of smaller boxes holding batteries, light bulbs and switches, all from vehicles. Under these were minor components: wiper motors and lamp casings, but no valves. The next one held pistons, new and packaged, connecting rods and bearings.

But these were motorcycle spares, and there were no valves. I went through another case. There were more bike parts. A few for cars or lorries. Not what I needed. Then I pulled out a pack shoved down the side, covered in filthy fingerprints with letters and numbers on it: RX 350 and 24. The valves. The parts I'd hauled around in the car for so long. The fucking valves for the Lotus. I opened the box. All twenty-four were there. I gave out a sigh. Seemed I'd been holding my breath. Alongside the pack were two flares, large fireworks . They looked interesting so I picked them up as well, putting them under my other arm. I knocked the lighter off and crept outside.

There were snores and groan from the huts as I headed for the ditch, the air cool after being in the bus.

A woman appeared, smoking a roll-up. Her hair was red, shaved at the sides and she was heavily tattooed. She smiled when she saw me. 'You catchin' some air?'

'Yeah,' I said.

She laughed as I walked on. Maybe she'd thought I was one of the gang and I'd be fine. Maybe I'd walk straight out of the camp.

As I passed the caravan she shouted out. 'Whoa!'

Maybe not. I ran. Racing towards the ditch, the box of valves under one arm and the rockets under the other I stumbled across the rough ground.

'Hey you, you! Stop there!' She ran after me.

The valves jiggled around in the box as I kept going. The woman was a little way back but sticking with me. If she had a gun I was finished. I ducked down to make myself a smaller target, as if that would help.

This time there was no messing with the barbed wire. I charged through the bit I'd flattened down and chucked the sticks onto the oily mud. I was over in several strides and off onto the moors. There were shouts behind me and lights came on at the camp. The woman was over at the archway, straight past the guard, avoiding the ditch.

As I crossed the moorland the bike engines started. The woman was a shapeless form running towards me as I made for the woods. She was flat out but had further to go so I picked up the pace, the valves clattering in their box.

I charged into the trees, aiming the way I'd come, one hand out in front of me as the other held the fireworks and valves. My foot caught a log and I fell against a tree, holding onto it. Voices shouted over at the camp and I lowered myself onto the ground, sliding behind the tree's trunk.

Blood rushed around my head and I took deep breaths. The cuts on my back stung and itched.

Someone came crashing into the forest nearby, probably the woman. I put the valves and flares down, feeling around on the ground, grabbing hold of a branch. It was trapped under other undergrowth and wouldn't move. I felt for another one. There were sticks and rotting leaves. Nothing big. I leant back and groped around behind me. There was a short heavy branch and I picked it up.

Twigs snapped as she came closer. There was a chance she'd go past, not find me. But there was a risk I'd get caught, taken back to the camp. Lose the valves and face whatever punishment they fancied. At best I faced a beating, at worst something like the Glasgow gangs did, where they skinned their prisoners and hung them by the roadside. Must have taken hours to die that way.

The woman was right next to me, shifting around. A lighter lit up, sending uneven light around me, onto me.

I swung the branch up. It hit her full on the forehead with a crack. Before the lighter flew off there was a flash of red hair and tattoos. She dropped like a sack of coal.

Stamping her lighter out, I lit my own and checked her over. She lay with her mouth open, eyes shut, completely out cold. I felt at her neck. Maybe there was a pulse, maybe not. It was hard to say if she was breathing either. But I didn't have time to sort her out, not with the bikers coming.

Retrieving the valves and flares I left her and carried on into the woods.

The leaves were flattened down where Jamie had been, but there was no sign of him, just my rucksack leant against a log. Ramming my haul into the bag, I headed down towards the river, the lighter showing the shifting forest around me. My back and arms stung and my shirt was stuck to me with blood. The bikers shouted and revved their machines back at the edge of the wood but no one else had come into the forest, yet. I picked my way down through the trees, between the warped shadows. For some minutes I carried on.

At the river I extinguished the lighter and walked along the bank in the moonlight. This was where he'd come. He wouldn't cross on his own. The water rushed past, gurgled over the stones, a dark ribbon with a distorted moon twisted into it.

I made my way to where we'd had a fire and I found him huddled in my blanket next to the cold ashes. His face was grey in the moonlight. He glanced up, no smile or greeting. 'Christ, what a racket.'

'Why did you move?'

'Didn't seem safe. You get them?'

'Yeah.'

'Don't suppose you got any food, did you?'

Like I'd had time to pick up food. 'We need to go.'

'Now?'

'Yeah.' Behind us the river rushed by, as full as the day before. 'Maybe we'd best find somewhere else to cross.'

He snorted and muttered something.

'The bikers are coming we need to go.' He didn't move so I made my way to the riverbank, letting him follow. The weak light caught the water as it swirled past, the surface dark apart from the foam. Out of the shade of the trees the rocks showed as dim shadows. I headed upstream until I found a section with two small islands. Jamie joined me, the bikes roaring in the distance.

I pointed. 'This might do.' I wasn't keen on crossing in the dark but I didn't want to freak him out.

He stared at the river. It was hard to work out his expression in the faint light.

I stripped off my boots and socks, packed them in my rucksack and shouldered it before wading out into the water. The river was cold and sucked the heat from me. My feet slid across smooth boulders on the way to the first island, a hump of straggly grass and mud. Water roared between the two islands, fast but only a metre or so wide.

If I made a mess of this there was no chance of Jamie coming to the rescue. This was it. I stepped back ready to go then stopped. Maybe there was somewhere better to cross? But there wasn't time.

I went for it, jumped, thumped down on the thin soil of the second island, my feet still in the water, slipping on wet rocks, hands clawing, body tense. I started to slide back in and grabbed at the earth. Bit by bit I hauled myself up and lay on the rough ground. Then I stood and crossed the island before trudging through the shallows, not stopping. At the far bank I put my rucksack against a tree, the water churning past. Jamie was at the other side, almost invisible.

I waded back and shouted over to him, encouraging words. 'It's pretty easy.'

'Is it? Like it was last time you mean?' His voice mixed with the hiss of the river.

'I'll help.'

'You help? That's the last thing I need.'

'It'll be fine.'

'I'll find somewhere else. Don't you worry about me.' He was being stupid now. He had to cross. The bikers wouldn't laugh this off. I'd stolen from them. Killed one of their women.

'There's nowhere else. And the bikers are coming. Now.'

He took his socks off, stumbling through the shallows and across the rocks onto the first island. At the fast flowing water he stopped and hopped around. 'Come on, Trent, I can't cross that.'

I made my way back to him, reaching out a hand. 'I'll help.'

'Even you didn't find it easy, did you?'

'I'm here.'

He stepped back. 'No. No. I can't do this. You go on. I'll sort myself out.'

'Come on.'

He crossed his arms, gazed up the river and stood with his lips tight. This was like at Coldstream, where he'd yanked the handbrake on and refused to cross the bridge because of a crack in the road. We'd had to wait four hours, until a heavy-laden farmer's cart went over, before we could take the Evora over it.

'This is ridiculous,' I said. 'I'm off.' It was ridiculous and he was going to get us both caught.

'Oh, is it? Is that what it is?'

'Look, the fucking bikers are coming.'

There was the option to tell him about the woman I'd hit. How angry the bikers were going to be when they found her dead; what they'd do if they caught us. But there was no point pushing him too far because he'd get into a flap.

'You go then. Don't worry about me.'

I made as if to move off. 'Laura will be waiting for us.'

He snorted. 'Laura! I bet you'd carry her across this, eh?'

'You want me to carry you?'

'No. No.' He stared into the water.

'I'm going.'

I turned and crossed the island, sliding into the cold water and wading over to the far bank. Maybe he'd be there until daybreak or the day after. Forever.

Then he spread his arms out, stepped back and leapt, clearing the gap, clipping the edge of a stone with one foot and falling forward, his legs dangling into the torrent. He lay there and grunted, a squirming shadow in the grass.

I ran back to him, my legs slow through the water,

stumbling over the smooth stones onto the island, reaching over to him. I held him by one hand and leant back, hauled him out of the water, onto the sparse grass. He stumbled up and joined me, gasping and shaking his wet feet.

'You made it.'

'Yeah.' He took deep breaths. 'I didn't need your help. I was doing fine.'

We both carried on through the water to the riverbank.

I put my boots and socks back on. He only had socks and rolled them on little by little. Like there was no rush. Once he'd done both we headed up the hillside to a fallen tree.

'We should stop here,' I said, sitting on the log.

'I thought you said the bikers were coming?'

'They are. But they'd make plenty of noise crossing the river. Anyway, they'll probably keep to the roads and edge of the wood. We'll be safe here.'

'So you say.'

'We need to lay low.'

Jamie said nothing but lay at the other side of the log.

'You all right?'

'Fine.' His voice was flat.

'Get some rest.'

'I'll never sleep,' he said. 'Never.'

Within minutes he was snoring.

CHAPTER FOURTEEN

Pick Up

When I awoke Jamie was digging through my bag, the box of valves lying on a log. It was barely dawn, light fighting through the trees.

'What you up to?' I said.

'Looking for food.'

'There's none.'

He held up the bag of grass and a bundle of money, the last of our cash. 'So I see.'

'You been awake long?' I said.

'Long enough.'

He kicked some leaves and avoided eye contact. We both needed breakfast. There'd been food on the bikers' bus but that hadn't been my priority. There was no use even telling him about that. Not with the mood he was in.

After a drink of water we pushed up through the ferns to the top of the valley, towards the far side of the woods. Laura wouldn't hang around, not with the bikers wound up. They'd probably found the woman by now. Or at least noticed she was gone. It still didn't seem worth telling

Jamie about her.

For next hour we carried on up through the woods, between the leggy sycamores, light dappling the forest around us. The bikers were out there somewhere but we had the valves. All Dan had to do was fit them and we were off. That felt good. Being away from town had put it all in perspective. The place was such a mess.

'What are you grinning at?' said Jamie.

I hadn't even realised I was smiling. 'Mission accomplished. Once we're past the bikers –'

'Yeah, once we're past them, Trent, once we're back and the valves are fitted, then I'll be happy.'

I let this go. He was tired and hungry. We pushed on without talking, up the hill, where the woods thinned out. I picked up a stick, waving it at him. It was a metre long with the ends smoothed off. 'You want this?'

'You could have done this all on your own.' He took it and put his weight on it. 'I didn't do anything, really. Look at me.'

Although I wanted to say how much help he'd been, how it was because of him we'd got back, it really wasn't the case. Instead I said, 'Sorry about your gun.'

'Damn right you should be sorry. Losing that was a fucking tragedy.'

As we came to the edge of the trees. There was the sound of motorbike engines. Shouts. I waved Jamie over to an oak tree and we stood behind it as the bikers milled around. There were three bikes, a couple of racers and an old trail-bike.

'Shit,' he said.

'They can't see us here.'

'What about Laura?'

'She can look after herself.'

The bikes stopped, the trail-bike's rider getting off, examining marks on the ground. He said something to the others and they both pulled off in a roar of engines before he joined them, disappearing along the road.

Once the bikers had gone we shuffled onto the track. Jamie was in torn socks and my trousers and jacket were ripped, the rucksack stained with mud. The cuts on my hands, legs and back itched.

'Do you think Laura will come?' he said.

'I'm sure.'

We carried on to where we'd been dropped off but there was no car or sound of a car. Even though we were late I thought she'd have waited.

'There's no sign of her.' He stopped and put his weight on his stick.

The trees hissed in the breeze behind us and the bikers' machines droned off in the distance. Then there was a whirr from a starter and a dull engine note as Laura's Mondeo emerged from some ferns. It bounced its way across a rough track over to us. I knew she'd have waited.

'Well,' he said.

'Told you.'

She parked and stepped out, looking us up and down, all serious. 'Had to hide from our friends.'

'Good plan.'

'You're late.' She kicked the stones and dirt of the track with her toe. 'You get them? The parts?'

'Yeah.'

'Great,' she said, with a smile, but it wasn't much of a smile. Maybe us being late and the bikers showing up had unsettled her. I went over to her, ready to put my arm around her and thank her for coming back but she turned away, opening the boot so I could stash the rucksack there.

'We did all right,' Jamie said.

She looked at his feet. 'What happened to your boots?'

'There's a story.'

As I put the rucksack in he opened it, taking the box of valves out. He grasped the box and kissed it before replacing it and getting into the car.

'We need to be on our way,' said Laura.

'Now I'm happy,' he said. 'Soon have our wheels fixed up. Fixed up and gone, gone, gone.'

'Sure will,' I said.

Laura frowned before flashing a smile at me. But as she drove off the smile faded and she gazed out at the tyre-marked road, speeding us back to Setmarch.

CHAPTER FIFTEEN

Visitors

She dropped us on Front Street with a curt goodbye and we returned to the guest house, all cheered and ready to get the car fixed up. When Jamie opened the door to our room he shouted out. 'Fuck,' he said. 'Fucking hell.'

Our clothes were all over the place and the wardrobe hung open. The drawers lay on the floor, now empty, surrounded by pages ripped from Jamie's catalogue.

He went to the middle of the room. 'Christ, Trent.'

'Looks like they were in a hurry.' The lock on the door was intact with no sign of being forced. At least I'd taken our grass and money with us. And they didn't have Jamie's gun, though neither did we.

He started to pick up clothes and put them on the bed. Within the mess was his prized phone. The screen was smashed and case cracked. For some minutes he just stared at it, pressing the button to try and bring it to life but it was dead. I wanted to say to him that it would be okay that we'd replace it but we both knew that wasn't true. He took the phone and slid it into his bag, a slow movement. Then he dropped in the magazine's pages, one at a time. After that he was motionless.

'We need to go to the garage,' I said. 'We know what were they after.' God knows what they'd done to the Evora.

He came to life with that, digging around, getting his spare shoes and slipping them on. 'The payload? Jesus Trent, if that's gone...'

'Yeah.'

I kept hold of the rucksack and led Jamie off. At the bottom of the stairs we met Mrs Newry, standing in a cloud of imitation-tobacco smoke. She never left the house, always just hanging around, smoking, drinking, occasionally cleaning.

'Hey!' Jamie said. 'Someone's been in our room.'

She crossed her arms, sucked hard on the cigarette, her wrinkled face all screwed up, over-plucked eyebrows halfway up her forehead, like she didn't care. 'You sure?'

'Come on, you must have heard something.'

She adjusted her pinafore. 'Nah.' When I eyeballed her she looked away at the banister, licking a finger and rubbing some dust off it.

'Who was it?' I said.

'Don't know nothing.'

I stepped forward and she backed off, her eyes widening.

'I don't know.'

Slapping my hand on the wall I leant in close towards her. She didn't know I'd never hit her. 'Who?'

Several lads shouted outside as we faced each other in the hallway, in this cloud of smoke.

'Some man,' she said, her voice weak.

'Man?' I said.

'Some man.'

'You know.' I felt in my jacket pocket. When I drew out my papers and grass she flinched. 'What was he like?'

She cleared her throat. 'I'll get into trouble.'

Jamie glared at her. 'You're in trouble.'

She straightened her pinny. 'I don't know–'

I rolled a single-skin joint. 'Tell us.' Flicking my lighter I wafted it in front of her, making her nose twitch. 'Well?'

'Some man–'

'So you said.'

She sighed. 'Rough. One of the town fellas. Tracksuit and tattoos.'

'And?'

'Lots of tattoos. Pistol on his pants. Nasty.'

I lit my joint. 'Sikey.'

Jamie was hopping around as if he was going to hit her, so I steered him out. At the doorway I stopped and looked back. 'Don't let this happen again, you hear?'

She didn't reply, turning and disappearing into the back of the house. We went out and off to Dan's, neither of us saying much as we shoved past workers in the dusty air.

When we got to the garage the pair of them were busy with the Evora. Dan lay under the boot while the lad crawled around inside undoing the seats. Acetylene cutting gear stood off to the side.

I sidled up to the back of the car. 'Hello Dan.'

There was a thud from under the car then nothing. The lad ducked down inside, his backside a hump where the passenger seat should have been. Jamie limped round to the driver's door, opening it.

'Looks like you're busy,' he said.

Dan slid out avoiding me and going over to the bench. 'Checking it over.' The lad stepped out of the car and joined him. The both picked up tools randomly and shifted them around. There was a bottle of whisky on the bench and the lad took hold of it, unscrewing the top.

'Who set you up to this?' said Jamie.

Dan shrugged. 'Like I said, just checking it over…'

I grabbed hold of the whisky, screwing the top back on and sliding it into my pocket. 'I want this car ready to go.'

Dan mumbled something while the lad glared at me. Then I took off the rucksack, opening it and handing the box of valves to Dan. 'Here you go.' He just gazed down at them as if they were objects he'd never expected to see.

'I want them fitted.' I felt around in my jacket for the last of the money from Maxwell's suit. One note at a time I counted the money onto the valves. 'Fit the valves and you get this.' Then I put the money away again.

Dan reached out towards the box, touching it. 'But we can't.'

'Get it done and we'll pay you.'

'If you don't do it, we'll take it personally,' said Jamie. He gazed from one to the other, pointing at each. 'We know where to find you.'

I opened the box and laid the valves out on the bench, tapping each one in turn. 'I want it done for tomorrow morning.' Dan started to moan, about having another job to do but I held my hand up. 'Have the car ready for tomorrow and you get the money. And we're gone.'

Jamie prodded the lad on his overalls. 'We'll never be back.'

I stood by Jamie, close to Dan and the lad. I picked up a heavy spanner, 30 odd millimetre, and raised it up.

Him and the lad gave each other looks, movements of eyebrows and shrugs.

'Fine,' said Dan. 'We'll do it.'

Then they started to work. Without a word to each other they picked up tools and went over to the cylinder heads.

'We'll be here at ten, tomorrow,' I said.

Dan grabbed a cloth, wiping a camshaft as the lad inspected two valves. They stood by the bench and leant over the engine parts, passing things between each other, cleaning, loosening.

Me and Jamie headed out, onto the cobbled street, then down to the main road, joining the workers in AHI overalls that shuffled along the pavement for the ten o'clock shift. We didn't say anything but stopped as two men pulled up in a van, setting up a ladder.

'Do you think they'll do it?' said Jamie.

'They'll do it.'

'Not if someone leans hard on them.'

I slid out the bottle of whisky I'd taken, opening it, taking a swig. Dan had the tools and facilities to do the work, we didn't. There was a chance things wouldn't work out. But people like Dan weren't brave. And were greedy. He was scared of us and wanted the cash. We had to trust that.

Jamie twisted his stick on the ground, his feet moving. Now we were back in town he was starting to wind up. I smiled at him but my teeth were tightly clenched so it probably didn't look so good. After taking a swig I offered the whisky to him. The men with the ladder shouted to one another as they attached coloured flags to the Bank

He drank and handed the bottle back. 'I guess we

should tidy our room.'

I pointed off across town. 'I need to see someone.'

'Already? We've only just left her.'

'No, not Laura.' I drummed my fingers on the whisky bottle, trying to avoid scratching the cuts on my hand and back from the barbed wire. 'It's my brother, Rory. I need a word.' This wasn't something I'd thought through but now we were back there was no harm seeing him.

'Right.'

'It's something I have to do –'

'Right. Fine.' Then Jamie was off along the main road.

'You heading back?'

'What do you care?' Jamie disappeared past the bank and shops, amongst the workers.

For a couple of minutes I just stood there as workers passed by. As the two on the ladder adjusted the flags. I drank more whisky, tipping it down my neck in preparation.

When I got to the *Church of Reform, Abstinence and Piousness* there was a note on the door saying it was closed. That Rory was conducting a funeral at central cemetery at the other side of town. I set off for the cemetery but I detoured round the back of the old council offices, looking for the driver I'd given the message to. There was no sign of anyone there. No cars and no one waiting. I sat on the wall for a few minutes then carried on.

It was only a short walk, passing through the market place past men setting up flags on lampposts; lads kicking a ball outside the boarded up law-courts. I had no idea what I was going to say to Rory but I had to see him.

A rusted black car was parked just inside cemetery's gateway beyond the busted stone wall. The driver was in a

worn suit and chatted to one of the mourners. The rest of
them stood further along the path, between the cock-eyed
gravestones and in front of a stone cross. All were dressed
in black and in the centre of the group was Rory, mad
haired and eyes ablaze. His cloak shifted around as he
waved his arms, enjoying being eccentric, or unable to
help it.

Rory was the odd one out in the family, the quirky one.
He'd been quite typical as a kid but had taken ill the
winter of 2011. At first it seemed like normal measles. He
had a rash and felt sleepy but then it got worse; he
complained about a sore neck and started to act odd. At
last Dad took him to the hospital and they told us he had
an infected brain. The membrane or something. They put
him on a drip and gave him loads of medication but
there'd already been damage. Rory was in there for days,
not talking or moving. Within a week he was up and about
but he was never quite the same. After that he'd always
been a bit odd.

Now Rory waggled his fingers above the grave, his voice
clear in the still air. 'The power of resurrection. And all
that.'

A woman joined him and the man put his arm around
her when she cried. Rory stared down at the ground,
taking a deep breath. He looked at the people around the
grave. 'Don't linger. Not too long. You know?' Nobody
moved so he stared at each in turn until they trudged off
towards the car. The old man and woman approached
him and said something. Rory shook his head. He clasped
each by the shoulder, frowning, pointing towards the
gateway.

Everyone left apart from me and him. He stood there

by the stone cross and cracked headstone, gazing into the open grave then at me as I approached. He closed his eyes and muttered to himself.

'Hello Rory,' I said, soft, trying to be friendly.

'Lord. Give me strength!' Close up he showed his age, his faced deeply lined and hair thinning at the front.

'Been a while,' I said.

'And so. So! Out of the wilderness the beast returns...'

'Rory, I just—'

'And we shall know the beast! By what he says. And does. And doesn't!'

He was getting all worked up. 'I just want a chat. Catch up...'

He shook his head. 'Chat? What would *we*, us, chat about? Hmm?'

'Catch up on things. People.'

'Here's an idea. Let's not talk. You go. Just go!'

Behind us the funeral car moved off. Three mourners pushed it as several others sat inside. Everyone else walked. Rory pulled his cloak around himself even though the air was warm, as he leant against a gravestone.

I stood next to him. 'Just to let you know I'm only passing through. I won't be staying.'

'I see. Bye-bye. Nice journey.'

'I don't want to play games.'

Rory laughed. 'Games? Games you say? That's all you do. All you've ever done.'

'I wanted to talk before I left.'

'Talk?' Rory touched the gravestone. 'How many years is it, Trent?' He counted on his fingers for effect. 'Over twenty years. Getting on for thirty. All these years you've been away.' He rocked back and forwards on his feet. 'You go. Then reappear. Then go.' As he moved he kicked dirt into the grave, onto the coffin with its patched lid and name scrawled in chalk. We stood like that for a while.

'This isn't about me and you, Rory.'

Rory circled the grave. 'Oh. I see. Tell me, hmm, what is it about?'

'Like I said, I wondered how you were getting on. And how Dad is.' There was someone I'd not meant to mention.

'Dad? Did you say, Dad?'

'Just wondered how he was…'

He stopped and laughed. 'Oh. Oh, oh, oh!' He ran his hands through his beard. 'Very subtle.'

'Come on, Rory.'

'Guess what? He's not here. Not at all! Where, where, where? I haven't got him.' Rory cupped his hands around his mouth. 'Dad! Oh daddy! Dad dearest!'

'Come on.'

'Sweet daddy, hello?' He was really freaking out now.

'Rory, stop this.'

He lowered his hands and took deep breaths. Then he blew out a long sigh. 'Very well.'

'You know, don't you.'

'No, Trent. No. I don't know and the answer is no.' Rory raised his hands up in mimic of the stone cross he now stood under. It was some kind of act, like he was a parody of himself.

'You're as crazy as ever, Rory,' I said, throwing soil into the grave. Then I left, going back through the cemetery. Rory stayed under the stone cross, stationary, his arms outstretched, his head turned up towards the sky and his eyes closed.

I didn't feel ready to go back to the guesthouse so I walked across town just to look over the place. For the last time.

I drifted up the lane towards Tropicana Nightclub, the pavement all dog-shit and dried spew. I carried on into the East End Estate, now labelled *AHI Housing* past a grocers, also Armstrong Industries, the other shops boarded up. There were shabby semis, some devoid of windows or tiles. Then I found myself in front of one in particular, its lawn a rough pasture of dandelions and daisies.

Dad's house. Our old family home.

This was Rory's fault. Seeing him had triggered something and sent me up here.

The rendering was cracked and windows rotted. The rest of the row was boarded up or windowless, empty. Outside our place was a Ford Focus, Dad's old car, parked at the side, dust coated and flat-tyred. After all those years it was still there.

The sun was overhead but obscured by black clouds from the plant. There was no movement in the road or from the house, just blank windows looking down on me. I went along the drive, determined to make sure there was nobody there. My hands were doing that thing again, where they were all jumpy and fidgety.

The front door rattled in its frame when I tried it, the handle creaking but solid, locked. I knocked. There was no movement visible through the frosted glass and when I opened the letter box stale air drifted out, the smell of decay. Through it I could see the empty hallway with its carpet stained and trampled. When I looked in the front window I saw into the living room. There was a sideboard but no other furniture, just stacked boxes.

I went to the side of the house. The Focus was grey with dirt and the flat tyres hung off the rusted rims. Weeds grew out around it and the seats were blotched with mould. The house's back door was patched with rot, its paint peeling off. When I knocked a dog barked some way off. A car engine turned over in the next street but didn't catch and I knocked again before continuing round the back.

The garden was all dead grass and overgrown flowerbeds. I kicked at a dandelion looking up into the empty rooms. Those were the rooms I'd stood in all those years ago, me, Rory, Dad, and Harry. Where we'd chatted and played. Argued. Dad hanging round the house all day, giving orders, feeding us tinned food. Telling us we had to pull our weight now Mum was gone. Him drinking with Harry while Rory sat in his bedroom reading the bible and I went off to find my own space. When I came home late Dad was always there, in the living room with that table light on. Asking where I'd been what I was up to. Harry had been free to do what he liked and Rory hadn't done anything, especially after his illness. So I'd been the difficult one. The trouble maker. We'd had some rows in there. Some fights.

Of course that was nothing compared to later on, after Harry's accident. When Dad blamed me for what had happened.

Back on the pavement I scrutinised the house, every fissure in the rendering, splits in the window frames. After a few minutes I walked off towards town, my hands locked into fists. The plant was in the distance under its own cloud, flanked by slag heaps, as more smoke rolled up and curled out across the town.

CHAPTER SIXTEEN

Distracted

That evening we put everything together, preparing to leave. Jamie muttered on to himself as he packed up, his bust phone wrapped in spare clothes.

I'd been to the car park to see if the courier was around but there'd been no sign of him. I'd hung around for a while then given up.

We'd have to chance it and assume Sandhu was all right with the changed date.

I had my own stuff to think over, regrets at not finding out about Dad, or seeing more of Laura, but the deal was the big thing. That was what I kept reminding myself. Maybe afterwards there'd be an opportunity to come back to town, tie up some loose ends.

Maybe.

In the morning, with our gear packed up and set out in the room, we made our way to the garage. If Dan had done his work we'd pick the car up and be gone. He had the valves and the offer of money so it felt reasonable that he'd do it. A light drizzle fell on us, filthy rain sifted through the smoke.

When we got to Dan's there were no sounds from inside and no one in the lane. I tugged at the doors and they rattled but didn't open. Pulling again it was clear they were locked.

'Looks like they're not here yet,' said Jamie, taking the handle himself.

As he hauled at the door I went round the side of the garage, past the derelict cars, round to the back window. There were tools set out inside, the Evora with its engine cover open, the top-end still in bits.

Water dripped on me from the roof. Nothing seemed to have been done since the day before.

It was possible there was a part they needed to do the reassembly and they'd gone to get it. Or they hadn't got a particular tool and trying to borrow one from somewhere. There were reasonable reasons why they hadn't finished it. But we'd have to push them to sort ours out. They had to get a move on.

Then Jamie shouted out. 'Ah, man!' he said.

I joined him at the front door where he pointed to a piece of paper nailed on the panelling. It was a small notice, the ink streaked with rain. It said that the business had been closed pending an investigation. It had an official Armstrong Heavy Industries stamp. As I read it, a siren gave a short blast from the plant

'Jesus!' said Jamie. 'What the fuck is going on?'

There was no way I could soften this one for him. Things had screwed up. We went over to the wrecked cars, leaning against them in the drizzle.

'This better not stop us going!'

I said nothing. There was a steady drip, drip, drip of

water off the Citroen's bodywork. No valves, no car. We weren't going anywhere. We'd struggle to make the deal. Maxwell would have more time to track us down. The bikers might figure who raided their camp. Killed one of their women.

'We need to get out of here!' He was really getting wound up.

I tapped the roof of the Picasso behind us, with its mildewed seats and mouldy carpet, as water made rivulets in the dirt on the windscreen. 'At least they're not stripping it down. Trying to find the load.'

'Don't even talk about that!'

'Maybe they're ill? We could get another garage could have a look.'

'No.' Jamie closed his eyes. 'No way. This is so messed up!' He opened his eyes and pointed at me. 'You need to sort this.'

'Yeah, don't worry.'

'We've got a deal to make.'

'I know, don't worry.'

He grabbed my jacket, shaking me. 'Trent, we're supposed to be going!' As he shook me spittle sprayed in my face. He went on and on about how this was my fault. I pushed him off and stepped back. This was bad news but there was no need to get so overexcited.

'This isn't my doing, Jamie.'

'All your fault, all of it! If we'd got another car we could have been off…' Then he swung at me, a wide hook that I blocked, shoving him away. He staggered back and straightened himself up, his face flushed.

'Jamie, fucking calm down.'

'Hey, save it, you know?' Then he turned and stormed

off, down the lane in the drizzle. 'I'm going to get pissed.'

After taking a couple of strides after him I stopped. He needed time on his own. Doing the deal was important. Really important. And we didn't want to get caught by Maxwell. But for some reason being stuck here didn't feel that bad. I wasn't that bothered. It was like I'd lost my normal energy, become rooted in the place.

I went round to Dan's flat and knocked on the door. There was no answer so I tried again. Nothing. When I looked through the window there was no sign he was in. His overalls lay folded on a table and there was a spanner next to them. I stayed there for several minutes then tried the door again. Still no answer. After that I went to the garage's side window. The car was untouched from the day before. There was no sign Dan had been poking around in the chassis.

I grabbed a rock up from the ground ready to smash the lock on the door and break in. Cut the car open and take the Gehenna, our precious load.

But the car was quite safe locked up in the garage. Our guesthouse room was no safer. I dropped the rock.

After a moment just standing there I walked into town but in the opposite direction to Jamie, towards Belmont Street. I crossed Setmarch in the drizzle.

Beside the Belmont Hotel there were wooden benches, cracked and gapped, that faced the town park now turned into a tip. I sat down on one of them and turned the collar up on my jacket. Gulls flapped around the rubbish as kids picked at the edges. At the far side was Rory's church, half hidden by the piles of rotting vegetation.

Jamie would go off and have a drink somewhere. He'd mutter to himself then I'd catch him up. Now and then he needed his own space, time to reflect. Usually he'd do something with his gun, check it over, clean it. Or mess with his phone, read his magazine. But they weren't options now. He only played his guitar when he was in a good mood so that was out. He was all wound up with no way to let it go.

I'd work out a plan at some point, once it was clear what was going on at the garage. It was probably just some technicality, something to do with forms and bureaucracy. Dan would soon be back to work and sort the car out.

In the meantime, I needed to unwind. Get some perspective.

I left Belmont Street and bought a bottle of whisky walking around Setmarch in the rain, letting the sounds of the town roll over me — men who complained to one another on the way to work; women on the benches in the market place moaning about AHI and the state of the schools.

I stopped at The Globe and hung my coat on a chair to dry. When the clouds cleared outside I tried a few more pubs to see where Jamie was.

It was early evening when I found him in the Grey Bull. The air was damp but tawny sunlight filtered through the filthy windows. Old rave music played out of bashed speakers on the wall and several young men jostled around a table lined with pint glasses. At the far end of the room Jamie sat on a stool at the bar, a beer in his hand.

I leant against the bar near him. 'How's things?'

He stared into his glass. His face red and eyes watery. 'Oh, it's you.'

'Sorry about earlier.'

'Yeah?'

'You pissed yet?'

He took a drink then belched. 'Aye, well, I'm getting there, bit by bit...'

'Can I join you?'

The lads at the far end laughed as they put empty pint glasses on their heads.

I pulled a stool up and sat down. 'I'll sort it out.'

'You'll sort it out. How many times have I heard that?'

I waved to the barman ordering a whisky. While he was over I asked him where we could go to later, somewhere for entertainment. Somewhere with women. He gave me an address up on the Veston Estate, once one of the best parts of town.

The music stopped and the lads cheered. There was a crash as a glass smashed followed by a groan. The barman swore at the lads and they laughed.

The whisky arrived and I took a sip. It was rough, cheap AHI junk. 'Come on, Jamie. Let's go back.'

Jamie didn't move, the slight wobble of his head showing how drunk he was.

I downed my drink. 'Jamie?'

'What?'

'Come on. Please.'

He finished his drink, standing by me as I led him out. One of the lads balanced on a stool and waved his arm as the barman argued with another about the broken glass

Outside it was cooler, the shouting from inside muted. The pavements were packed with people. Men, women and children who stood around, expectant, many still in overalls.

'Don't think I'm happy about all this, Trent.'

'I know.' I took the bottle out and drank from it, passing it over to Jamie. Drumming came from behind us. The sun had set and there was only faint light from pubs and houses. 'We need some fun.'

Jamie drank the whisky as we shoved through the people. 'What about us getting away from this place?'

'I have a plan.'

'A plan? You?' He swigged more booze.

There was a flash of light as we turned and faced up the road, where a group of men came around the corner, black robed and barefoot. They carried burning torches and led a cart with women on it, also in robes and with painted faces. The men drank from bottles and blew out the liquid, paraffin type stuff, lighting it, sending flames into the air. The women on the cart twirled torches and danced, their movements slow and their eyes closed. They were followed by the drummers who beat in time to the men's footsteps.

'Come on, Trent, what's this plan?'

Although I didn't actually have a plan, now wasn't the time to say so, not when he was full of beer. Not after everything going wrong with the car. I still thought it might just sort itself out.

'I'll tell you later,' I said.

Across the road, caught in the light of the procession were two figures, one in a tracksuit. It was Sikey with a woman. She was pinned against a building as he pushed his elbow against her throat, ripping her dress open with his free hand. She struggled and squirmed as he laughed and ran his fingers across her bare flesh.

'No, no, you tell me now,' said Jamie.

Without replying I headed over towards Sikey, away

from the procession. I fought my way through the crowds, against the tide of partiers smelling of booze and sweat.

Jamie caught up and grabbed my sleeve, just as the woman ran towards us, her clothes ripped and eyes wide, staring.

'Wait,' I said but she stumbled past, off into the crowd, swallowed up by all the people. Sikey had disappeared as well, vanishing into the festivities.

Jamie leant against his stick. 'What was that about?'

The procession carried on, the floats passing by with drumming and dancing, lit by the occasional swirl of fire. For a few minutes they slid by.

'Come on,' I said, taking Jamie down a side road, away from the noise, past bigger and bigger houses, really old, soot-coated like everywhere else, their long gardens of dried earth and dead plants. We went up a hill where the houses were detached.

'Where we going Trent?'

'Just wait.'

The house I'd been told of was set back from the road, a big stone place with bay windows. There were lights on all over but the curtains were pulled. Men came out, smiling and talking to one another. Music played, like there was a party but more civilised.

Jamie slowed 'Trent, what's this to do with the plan?'

'Jamie, it'll be good.'

He started hopping around. 'Ah man, I don't know about this.'

I led him on towards the door and he followed, as old music came out, vintage rock from the nineties. This was what we needed. A break. We'd sort out a plan when we knew what was really happening. I pulled the door open leading into a hallway lit by lights with fancy lampshades. There were exotic plants in chipped pots and the music warbled from speakers at the far end. Three women were wedged onto a settee at the side and another sat behind a table with lace covering. Jamie hung around in the doorway then came in.

The woman at the table smiled and waved. 'Come in, come in!' She looked us up and down. 'You boys after a good evening?'

'How you fixed?' I said, dropping some of our remaining money in front of her.

She pointed over to the women on the settee. They smiled, grins that appeared quickly and went away just as fast. They were in their twenties, wearing white dresses. There was a thin blonde, another curvier blonde and a brunet.

Going over I sat between curvy blonde and the brunet, their bodies warm, smelling of perfume; men. They laughed and put their hands on my shoulders but Jamie didn't join us.

'You sitting down, Jamie?' I said.

'I'm okay here. Don't worry about me.'

'Yeah, come on Jamie, join the fun,' said the brunet. She smiled at him and this time it had more to it, like she almost meant it. 'I'm Ruby, you know, like the stone?' Then she went over to him, taking his hand. He was immobile for a moment then let himself be led across the room and up the stairs. He glanced back and nodded to me.

The two blondes were pushed tight against me.

'Who'd you prefer out of us?' said the thin one.

I looked from one to the other, at their made-up faces,

long hair and painted nails. 'Who's the oldest?'

She grinned at me. 'We're both twenty-one, can't you tell?'

'Who's the craziest?'

'Oh, that's Candy.' She pointed at the curvy blonde. 'She's up for anything.'

Candy laughed as I stood. She took my hand. Her grip was firm, like someone used to manual work. Her eyelashes flicked across bloodshot eyes as she led me upstairs.

We went to a room at the far end of the landing, shutting and locking the door. It was lit by bedside and table lights. There was a dark carpet, thick rugs and flock wallpaper, prints of old paintings on the wall, *The Birth of Venus* and *The Creation of Adam*.

'So, you're Candy.'

She started to undo her dress. 'That's me. Sweet as.' She stripped to her underwear. Her skin was orange tanned and she had dimples on her thighs. She wasn't thin but she looked good. Her cleavage rose and fell as she breathed.

I undid the buttons on my shirt, sliding it off and lying back on the bed. 'Let's see how crazy you are.'

She laughed, slipping off her underwear and gliding over to me.

CHAPTER SEVENTEEN

Football

In the morning I took a walk to the garage, to see if Dan was back at work. There was a chance we'd got worried about something unimportant. Unrelated to us. I'd told Jamie I'd see him later at the football ground. I'd whispered to him when he was still half asleep, getting a grunt, leaving before he fully woke and started asking hard questions. I thought I'd sniff around on my own, without him getting all emotional on me. If Dan was back at work we'd not need a new plan. It would just be a hiccup and we'd be on our way again.

The garage was still locked up with the notice on the door. No sign of anything going on inside. The Evora was unmoved from the day before. The sun popped the tin roof but there was no other sound. When I tried Dan's flat he didn't answer. I hammered on the door for the best part of a minute, the echo of my fist thudding though the building. When I stopped there was silence, not even a creak or rattle. Through the window I saw the old pair of overalls and spanner on the table. Either he was away or avoiding me. Whatever he was up to, the car wasn't getting fixed.

I carried on across town thinking through a plan, something to tell Jamie. All over there were bright banners and coloured flags, but still men went to work in their grey overalls. With their dead faces.

Any plan had to make the deal the priority. To do it we needed some transport. That could be the Evora or another car. Maybe some other vehicle would do, or be better. There'd be no need to hide the payload in its chassis, not if it was just a straight run. Although the Lotus was a fabulous car, it was becoming difficult fix it. Despite having the valves we were stuck.

So that was it, find a car, take the payload out of the Evora and make the deal.

But if we left the Evora, that would be the last I'd see of it. It was a unique car, a classic. It had memories, family connections. There was something else as well, something that bothered me about this, like I was giving up.

I stopped at the post office, now another AHI place, semi-derelict. There was a door to the side for deliveries and another that said Public Phones, wires hanging down. Further on I saw the council offices, windowless. I went round the back to the car park looking for the driver I'd given the message to. There was no one there. Rather than carry on I waited, as the smoke rolled over the houses, hiding the sun. Sounds clattering in from the plant.

Ideas went back and forward in my head — leave the Lotus, fix it up.

About half an hour later a courier arrived. It wasn't the fella I'd spoken to. He parked and gave me an eyeballing, staying in his car. Some time afterwards a Vauxhall came in, its discs grinding. This was my man. He passed something to the first driver who headed off. Then I went over to his car, tapping the window. Although reluctant to open it far, he slid it down enough to talk.

'You pass my message on?' I said.

'Message?'

'To Sandhu. In the city.'

He nodded then smiled. 'Aye, and got a reply. Think you owe me.'

'What did he say?'

The driver made a hand-sign, rubbing thumb and index fingers together. I rolled out a couple of notes and held them, retracting when he reached for them.

'What did he say?'

'Agreed the date. At the quayside, three pm, look for the Gold Jag.'

I paid the driver and left the car park. At least that was one thing sorted out.

I carried on across town, by the ruined swimming pool, the old police station, its windows bust, just down from the Masonic Lodge, all spic and span.

By chance I passed Laura's house. Without thinking about it I was in Hope Street. Talking through a plan with her was an option. I went to knock on the door but stopped with my hand raised, letting it fall at my side. There was a shout at the end of the road as a man dropped something, smashing it. Apart from that there was just the usual drone from the factory. A lorry's engine way off.

Laura wasn't the one to talk to. She'd have her own perspective, skewed in favour of the town. I knew what she'd say: stay around, take your time. Then we'd catch up about the old days, get all cosy. What I needed was space to think. So I didn't bother calling on her. Instead I scribbled a note and shoved it through her letterbox, suggesting we meet up later on. By then I'd have some idea what I was up to and be in the mood for socialising.

I continued to the football ground, the place I'd come to with Dad and Rory to see Setmarch Rovers play, years and years ago. It was amazing it was still here. And there were players practising, a ropy bunch in the town strip belting the ball around. Like the rest of town, the stands and their kit were plastered with AHI.

I sat alone in the oldest section, amongst cigarette stubs and the smell of stale beer, as the players practised. Some bulged out of their strips, bellies sagging over their shorts, while others vanished beneath folds of material. At least they'd kept the team colours: green hoops on white.

I'd come to quite a few games here with Dad when I was a kid. He'd always got tanked up beforehand and swore like crazy all the way through. That was before football got wrapped up in the chaos that hit everything else. Despite all his faults, Armstrong had got the team going again.

For some time I watched the players kick the ball back and forward, thud after thud. I slid out some of our grass and rolled a joint, slipping it unlit into my jacket.

Then a figure came in from the far side. It was Jamie, head down, weighing heavily on his walking stick, the one we'd got from the woods. I'd not worked out a plan yet. Maybe the trip to the brothel had calmed him down a little, softened him up. Coming closer he didn't look too cheery.

'How you doing?' I said.

Without a word he held out an envelope to me. It had *Trent and Partner* written on it and it had already been opened. He thrust it to me and sat down as I read it, him watching me. It was from Armstrong. He wanted to meet up, have a parley. Chat about our predicament and a solution. We had to meet him in his club later on, evening time.

'Where did this come from?' I said.

'Waiting downstairs for us.'

'Doesn't sound great.'

He snatched the letter back and gripped it in one hand. 'Cheer me up. Tell me about your plan.'

Rather than stall him I launched in with some ideas. 'Well, we can either patch up the Evora and use that or pick up another car...'

'Is that it? Is that your plan?'

I took the joint out and rolled it around in my fingers. Now seemed a sensible time to light up. Chill Jamie out. The team volleyed the ball between one another, calling out, dropping it frequently and swearing.

He shook his head. 'You've got no idea, have you?'

It was true, it didn't really sound like a plan, as such. More an outline. A few thoughts. 'I just need to think some more.'

'Come on, last night you said you'd sort it—'

'I will. I thought your time with Ruby would have cooled you down—'

'Don't!' Jamie laughed, jigging around. 'This is just typical, typical of you. Ah, man, you knew I wanted to go to the coast.'

'We can go afterwards.'

'That won't happen, will it? Anyway, we're past that. You're risking the deal.'

'Sandhu's fine. I've heard back from him. It's all set—'

'But we can't get there! We haven't got a car, Trent. We could have got one days ago.' He leant in towards me. 'Listen, Trent, is this about her?'

'You saw the garage,' I said, standing and lighting the joint. 'It's not about anyone.'

It wasn't about her, or me or Jamie. If it was about anyone, it was Armstrong. He was the one who'd stopped us. We had to sort him out and then we'd be able to go. That was why Dan had been stripping the car and they'd trashed our room. Armstrong just wanted a payoff and then we'd be able to fix the Lotus, leave.

The team formed into a line and took turns shooting at the keeper in goal. One sent it flying off over the net and the others groaned and called for him to fetch it.

Jamie grabbed the rail, pulling himself up alongside me. 'I said we should never have come here.'

'Jamie, I've got an idea...'

Without a warning he swung a punch at me but I shifted out of the way so that it just clipped my shoulder. He went for me again. 'I ought to sort you out, Trent.'

I stepped backwards, out of the stand and onto the edge of the pitch, him following me all the way, still gripping that letter. 'Jamie, just cool it.' The team waited for the ball to return and looked over at us.

'You piece of shit. All that about having a plan.'

I grabbed him as he swung again, flicking him backwards onto the dried soil but he held onto me, pulling me with him. As we both fell the joint flew out of my mouth and he ranted on and on. 'It was all worked out.

Off to the coast, then the deal but you had to maroon us here. This shit hole....'

I moved round to sit on his chest. Pinning him down. 'I never mean for us to stay so long.'

'Here with Sikey and Armstrong, and her. She just *happened* to be here –'

'Jamie...'

'All this supposed help she's given us –'

Then I was grabbed from behind, dragged backwards off him as someone pulled me. Stepping to the side I faced my attacker, ready to strike back.

It was Laura. 'What the hell are you both doing?' she said.

Jamie sprawled out on the ground as I brushed dead grass off myself. He struggled to push himself up. The team stared at us from the pitch as Jamie dusted himself down. 'What are you boys looking at?' he shouted. The keeper kicked the ball to the players and they passed it between themselves, dull thuds back and forth.

Laura helped Jamie straightened his clothes. 'This is ridiculous. What are you fighting about?'

'Haven't you heard? We're stuck,' said Jamie, jabbing his finger at the letter. 'AHI has shut down our mechanic.'

I picked up the joint, relit it and smoked while Jamie rambled on about what had happened, how it was my fault. He jabbed me on the shoulder but Laura stood between us, stopping him getting any closer; getting his hands on me. Then he shoved the letter at her. The three of us stood there as the team kicked the ball, stopped the ball, passed the ball. Sometimes they glanced over, but most of the time they worked together. Like everyone did in this town.

She scanned through it, giving it back to him. 'So what are you going to do?'

'Go with it,' I said.

'What?' said Jamie, getting agitated again.

'I think we should accept the invitation. Visit Mr Armstrong.'

'Is that it?'

'We work together, Laura knows this town. And we negotiate with Armstrong, giving him something so we can go off, make our deal.'

One of the players kicked the ball way up in the air and another ran beneath it calling out, claiming it as his. Laura had perked up at the mention of the deal, or something. It was time to let her in on it, get her to help.

'And if he won't play, Trent? What then?' said Jamie

'We find another car.' I looked over at Laura.

'My car?' She turned away from us, as if the football practice was more interesting than what we were talking about. The ball slammed down onto the forehead of the expectant player, bouncing off across the field and sending him backwards. The rest of the team laughed as he fell to the ground, his hand on his head.

'I'm not sure...' She took the spliff off me. 'Buy me lunch, talk it through and I'll consider it.'

'All right,' I said. 'Let's go and make a plan.'

Although Jamie gave me a dirty look he followed when I walked off, Laura at his side. We made our way across the pitch, watching the footballers as they carried away their injured player.

CHAPTER EIGHTEEN

The Club

After a lunch at the pie shop we spent the afternoon at Laura's, planning. She was disappointed in the lunch and Jamie wasn't keen to work as a three, but after a glass of cider they cheered up and we agreed to form a partnership. For Jamie and me, getting the Evora fixed and doing the deal was the main thing. Laura was to get a small cut of our payment, though Jamie wasn't too happy about this, eventually settling on ten per cent, adding an extra five per cent if our car was unfixable and we had to use hers. Laura asked me what we were trading and I was vague, talking about technical papers, rare documents, avoiding talk of military secrets. Weapons. Jamie narrowed his eyes at this but didn't ask. She seemed satisfied. The point was, Armstrong didn't know what we had either. He didn't have a clue what we were transporting. We'd string him along a little, give him some cash then get out of town. He'd never know it was a big deal. That people like Maxwell were so keen to have it.

We decided to meet Armstrong as requested, agreeing

that we weren't going to take any weapons, which was just as well as we didn't have a gun anymore. We'd stick together, not letting him drag us off into another room. The club was a public place so there was limit to what he could do.

I said I'd lead the discussion but we all were going to chip in. Armstrong was after something so we had to negotiate, make sure he didn't take too much. But we did want to have an agreement. I'd seem keen while Jamie and Laura were to appear less so, to balance it up. Our final gambit would be to storm out, pretend to leave, hang around by the pie shop for ten minutes then go back and force a better deal.

With it all settled we had another drink before heading to the club.

When we arrived the place was rammed. Despite only being early evening there were loads of people there, all semi-smart, men in dress shirts and the women in skirts. Most of them were in their thirties and forties but there were a few younger ones, though even they dressed older. They milled around the building, a low ceilinged place that had been a budget supermarket when I was a kid, now chopped up by walls. The windows were boarded up but the strip lighting remained, quite a few of them lit up. It was bright, too bright, possibly a showcase for the electricity Armstrong's plant was kicking out. Or maybe they just liked it bright.

We passed through the hall, past tables with pints of beer lined up, by the queues at the bar where men struggled with trays filled with overflowing glasses. The club smelled of beer, chips and imitation-tobacco.

At the far side of the room was a darts' board and a

man stepped forward, flexing his arm, a dart in his hand.

'Game on!' a voice announced on a PA system, another of Armstrong's gimmicks.

The conversations carried on but most of the people looked over towards the board.

'Over there, Trent, there he is.' Laura pointed to a table set away from the others, at the far side of the room. Armstrong was at one side, dressed in polo-shirt and pressed jeans. Sikey and some other thug sat at the other side, both in sportswear. Though Sikey's outfit was immaculate, the lad beside him had holes in the jacket showing a dirty T-shirt.

'Eighty-five!' the voice announced. There were boos from the audience.

A man nearby shouted 'Get off, you're shit!'

Carrying on across the room I went right up to Armstrong. Jamie and Laura were either side of me, just as we'd agreed. Armstrong stared at the darts-board and player as if we weren't there. There was a bottle of whisky in front of him with empty glasses. Since there were no free seats at the table, we didn't sit.

'You wanted a word,' I said.

Armstrong carried on watching the game. Sikey smiled, shifting his baseball cap and playing with his gold chain. His companion stared at us.

'Thirty-nine!' the voice announced. There were some shouts and several people swore.

Armstrong still didn't look away from the darts board. 'You like darts, Trent?'

'Not much,' I said. Seemed he knew who I was.

'It takes a lot of skill, getting the tip in exactly in the right place.' He looked at me for the first time. 'You've got to be good with numbers as well.'

He wasn't that scary, old Armstrong. Just an overblown business man.

Sikey pointed at us. 'Hey, let's fucking kick them around and throw them out.' His friend grinned.

Armstrong shook his head. 'We don't want to spoil the game.'

'Yeah,' said Jamie. 'Do what your owner tells you, Sikey.'

Laura laughed and Sikey drank his lager, staring at Laura's crotch as he sipped, then muttering something to the fella at his side. The pair laughed, coarse crude laughter.

'Word is you're settling into the town nicely, Trent,' said Armstrong.

'That so?'

'One hundred and one!' the voice announced. There was applause and a few cheers and Armstrong clapped his hands, slow claps.

Sikey flicked out a fifty note, folding it. A waitress tottered past, some young woman, and he grabbed the hem of her skirt, stopping her. 'We need more drinks,' he said.

She stared at him as he took hold of her blouse. He pulled at the material so she had to bend down towards him.

'Get us a bottle of whisky. Another couple of beers.'

The girl nodded and he shoved the note into her cleavage, leaving his hand there, only letting go of her blouse after several seconds. As she turned to go he slapped her on the backside, laughing. She disappeared off to get the drinks.

'She's all right,' he said. 'I'd do her.'

The fella snorted.

Jamie shook his head. 'Jesus, you're some gentleman.'

Sikey ignored him and smiled at me. 'Heard you were up at the tart house. Have a good shag with the prossies?' He pointed at Laura. 'She's not up to it, eh?'

I didn't bother to reply. Laura fidgeted a bit beside me, straightening her hair out as Jamie jiggled his stick around. We were right in enemy territory here but at least it was public.

Armstrong took a drink and stared at the darts board. 'I guess you're trapped here at the moment, Trent. I guess you can't get that car of yours fixed up.'

'Something like that.'

'I guess you need my help now.' He smiled and took another sip of his drink, gazing around the room then over at me, the smile disappearing. 'Without me you can't go anywhere.'

There was some whisky in the bottom of Armstrong's bottle and I poured it out into a glass. 'Why would you care?'

'Forty-five!' the PA announced. There were groans.

'Good question,' said Armstrong. 'Here's another question: why are you here, Trent? Why Setmarch of all places?'

Jamie came round and leant against the table. 'We're just on our way somewhere, you know?'

Sikey frowned. 'Who the fuck asked you?'

Jamie and Sikey eyeballed each other. Neither looked away and it seemed like they'd stay like that all evening. The other fella tried it on me but couldn't hold it.

The girl came back with a tray of drinks and squeezed

past us, breaking Sikey and Jamie's stare-off. As she bent to arrange the glasses and bottle Sikey put his hand on hers, a light motion but he leant forward, right up to her face. 'What's your name, pet?'

She carried on with the other hand. 'Julianne.'

'You're a good looker.'

'Thanks.'

He put his other hand on her thigh. 'Aye, real good looker.'

She finished off but couldn't move off as he held her, his hand sliding up into her skirt and feeling around. 'Hang around at the end,' he said. Then he removed both hands and sat back, smiling to his friend. Possibly he did it to impress us, show how much power he had. Or maybe it was just what he did.

'You're a sleaze,' said Laura.

'One hundred and eighty!' the voice announced. There was loud applause, cheers and shouts. Some people stood up.

Armstrong looked into his glass then up at me. His brow was furrowed but he smiled. 'Look, let's not waste time. I know what goes on. I have my eyes and ears. Maybe you are just passing through but you've stood on a few toes. Put things out of kilter. You need to pay your dues.'

'We just want our parts, then we'll go,' I said.

'This isn't one of those free-for-all places, you know. Everyone contributes in this town. Everyone. You've outstayed your welcome and you need to cough up. We want what you're carrying.'

'Maybe we don't want to give you it.'

Armstrong grinned. 'Maybe I should get Dan to rip

that car of yours apart.'

There were cheers as a player got a bullseye.

'Come on, I don't want to get all heavy handed,' said Armstrong, 'but you owe the town. Hand over your load and you're free to go. Take you car and drive off. I'll even throw in some cash. Just for goodwill.'

'What load?' I said. He could have been guessing, taking a leap in the dark. There was no point making it too easy. Guessing we were couriering something wasn't unreasonable. It was what we did. The problem was that we didn't have drugs or ammo on this run. It wasn't a bag of gems that we could share out.

Jamie leant towards me. 'Don't give him a thing, Trent.'

He was playing his part but maybe too hard. I wanted to string Armstrong along, make a deal and get the car fixed, not just piss him off.

'What are you after?' I said.

'Without knowing what you've got, it's hard to say,' said Armstrong. 'What is your load?'

'The usual.'

Armstrong played with his glass. 'Rumour has it you got something special. Something really big.'

This was unexpected. It could have been a guess but I had a bad feeling

Laura prodded me. 'No more than ten per cent, Trent.' She was following the plan but the game had changed.

Armstrong locked his eyes on me. 'I want the documents, all those charts and details, or you don't go. Simple as that.' From the way he looked it was clear he knew what we had. And he knew I knew. My left hand had started drumming on my leg and I forced it to stop, inspecting my fingernails for a second, not wanting to look over at Armstrong or his idiot sidekicks. We had nothing to play now. He knew what we had and that it was in the car. I was ready to turn and run out of the club but even that didn't feel safe.

'If you don't hand it over, Trent, you don't go.'

Right as planned Jamie pulled at my sleeve. 'Let's leave it.' He delivered the lines so well that it was a shame they were of no use. Armstrong had changed the rules. If he knew about Gehenna we really were in trouble and bluffing wouldn't help.

'Yes, let's go, Trent,' said Laura, chipping in. They were both going on as if nothing had changed.

'"Yes, let's go, Trenty,"' mimicked Sikey. The fella next to him laughed.

Armstrong shrugged. 'Big mistake. Big mistake.'

'Come on, we don't need this.' Jamie turned and walked off, his head in the air, all too phoney.

There was nothing else to be said so I followed him, Laura at my side. I half expected them to come after us, grab us. They'd slice the car up, have Gehenna and they'd stick us on their lorry. Parade us around town.

But Armstrong returned to watching the game, as if that was all he'd been doing all night. Sikey and his companion had their eyes on us but didn't move.

'Ninety-four!' the voice announced. There was weak applause.

We left, pushing our way between tables.

'Ah, man, what people,' said Jamie.

'We're blown,' I said.

'I though it went well. We'll go back, negotiate some deal.'

'He knew what we had.'

'He was guessing, Trent. How could he —'

'He knew.'

Laura said nothing but she had a serious look on her face and she was playing with her hair like crazy. We came to the door, going out into the passageway. It stank of stale piss and bleach. Women queued for the toilet and men came out of the gents, barging their way back into the main room.

Jamie was getting agitated again. 'How could he know? Christ, I don't even know what we're carrying.'

A cheer came from the hall. 'I'm not sure,' I said. Maybe it was Nixon. Or Dan could have spotted something. Whoever it was, we needed to get the documents out of the car.

The passageway was busy and we pushed past the club members.

Silhouetted in the frosted glass of the main door were the outlines of fire jugglers, stilt-walkers and drummers outside. The door handle was stiff, having once been an automatic door, so I had to shove on it a couple of times before it burst open, sending us out into the street, amongst the noise of music and shouting, dark compared to the glare of the club. The drums echoed off the buildings and there was the smell of fireworks, sweat and beer. Giant papier-mâché heads bobbed past and Roman candles flared above us.

We'd have to go straight to the garage and take the documents out. Then work out what we were going to do. If we could stall him and get the valves that would do it. Or just blast off in Laura's car. We'd got complacent, lazy. Now it was time to go.

We pushed through the people, across the road and

onto the other side, jostled and bumped all the way. We stopped outside the pie shop as the procession passed by. There was just the two of us, me and Laura. 'Where's Jamie?' I said.

She looked around. 'He was with us.'

The crowd passed but Jamie didn't appear. 'Where the hell is Jamie?'

'I don't know. He was just here.'

The carnival went by but there was no sign of him. I led Laura to alleyway and we slid into it.

'Trent, what's going on?' she said.

'They've got him. They've got Jamie.'

We stayed there in the shadows. Ten minutes or more passed but he didn't appear.

They'd taken Jamie.

CHAPTER NINETEEN

Vanished

'Maybe he wandered off,' said Laura. 'He might have got caught up in the crowds.'

It didn't seem likely but we had to rule it out before we got into a panic.

I let Laura guide me through the Setmarch Carnival as it meandered through the streets and people cheered, drank and drummed. We followed the procession, with the drinkers, dancers, drummers and women with rattles. Men with no shirts or shoes.

We moved towards a float, a cart covered in fake skulls and bones and black material. The drumming was everywhere.

Laura took my arm. 'If he's not here there's a chance that he went back.'

'He wouldn't go without me.'

There were all these faces, sweaty skin and glazed eyes. One cart came level with us. It was rammed with women whose painted bodies writhed to the music as they shook maracas. There was the smell of burning and beer.

Flaming torches waved around us and one dancer put her arm around me, her skin warm, sweaty. I pushed her off.

Laura led us away from the floats. From the noise and movement. 'He probably lost us in the crowds and he's gone back, I'd say.'

'Back?' Armstrong had taken him, I was sure of that. Now we really were in trouble.

'He'll be at your guesthouse I'd bet.'

I closed my eyes against the movement, my hands on my ears to keep out the sounds, the endless thud, thud, thud. The crowds passed by, pushing and jostling. Jamie might have gone back, that was true. Opening my eyes I shoved my way through the bodies, fighting my way towards the guesthouse. Laura trailed alongside me, holding onto my jacket, dragged through the drummers and acrobats, along the pavements sticky with beer and vomit.

At Valley View I strode up to our room, two steps at a time, the drums hammering through the building and torchlight mottling the windows. There was a chance she was right and he'd be there sitting on the bed.

The room was empty. I opened the wardrobe, our bags still stashed there.

'Christ, he's not going to be in there.'

'I know.'

She laughed, like this was all some big joke. 'He isn't that small.'

I grabbed her and held her arms tightly. My teeth were clenched. 'I was looking to see if his clothes were gone.'

'Okay. Sorry.' Her eyes were wide.

I let go of her and went to the window. Floats rolled past outside forcing their way through the people. It wasn't her fault that he'd gone missing but she didn't seem to see what a big deal it was. This wasn't some accident. It had been a trap.

She sat on the bed. 'What do you think happened to him?'

'Armstrong's got him.'

'Well, let's go back, talk to him—'

'No, that's what he wants. We've been set up.' I stayed at the window as drummers and performers passed by outside, the sound getting louder accompanied by my fingers beating out their own tune on the woodwork.

'What should we do now?' she said.

'Maybe it's best you go back to yours. In case he turns up there. Looking for us.' And I needed some space and time to think. If he was free there was a chance he'd go there but it was more likely he'd come here.

If he was free.

'Well, I'll be off then,' she said.

'All right.'

The bed creaked as she stood up. 'I hope he turns up. I'm sure he'll be fine.' This was when I should have turned, said goodbye, thanks for your help but I didn't. The door closed with me still by the window as the dancers, drinkers and drummers rumbled past.

Armstrong was tactical and played games. He'd played us and we'd lost. For this round.

For minutes I stood at the window as people and vehicles filed past. We'd been set up but why go to all the bother? Why not just burst in here and take us.

They didn't know Jamie had lost his gun. Sikey had had his pistol whipped off him and he'd seen Jamie with the rifle. They'd know we'd be less likely to go into the club with a gun and now they had him.

I moved from the window, grabbing up my bag, emptying clothes out and throwing some other bits and pieces in: tools and the two flares from the bikers' camp. Armstrong had Jamie and there was nothing stopping them taking the stash as well. The only bargaining power I had was in the Evora. With a bag full of gear I went out.

By the time I got to Dan's, the procession was across at the far end of town, a remote throb under the smoke-filled sky. The lane was empty as I took a long screwdriver out, ramming it into the padlock, shoving hard and twisting.

There was a crack. Pushing again the lock came loose. Drumming drifted in out from the distance as I opened the door. Dan didn't appear and there was no one around.

The garage smelled of oil and stale petrol. The light switch gave a pop before the lights flickered on. The Evora was parked as before, skewed with the passenger side near the wall. The cylinder heads lay on the bench with the old valves next to them. There was no sign of the box of replacements, the ones that had taken all that effort to recover. It was tempting to throw the car together, chuck the old valves back in and get it running. Blast out of the town.

But those kinds of repairs would take time. Expertise. And Jamie was still here. Stuck somewhere in the Armstrong empire. At Kelso he'd waited for me. He could have taken off in the Evora but he'd hung around. He'd done that at Callander as well.

Shutting the door I jacked the car up, lying under it. I shifted a section in the floor-pan trim and felt around in the side of the chassis, for the panel that was built in. Once I'd found the bolts I grabbed Dan's spanners, undoing them. With all three removed, an aluminium rectangle dropped out to reveal the container. Normally there'd be loads of packages in here, lots of packs of compressed grass or resin, precious metals. Ammo. Our usual trades. This time it was just a metal tube, thirty centimetres long, dark green and marked with stencilled writing that said HMS Gehenna. I put it into the bag with the two flares. Then I slid the of chassis panel into place, bolting it up again before popping the floorpan back.

Outside the lane smelled of smoke. The sound of drums faded in and out as I shut the garage and put the padlock back. As I headed up the hill shouts and laughter came from the town.

CHAPTER TWENTY

Festival

I didn't sleep well. I'd gone to bed late, after walking up to Dad's to hide the stash and rockets. With the door wedged by Jamie's bed I fidgeted all night, eventually getting a couple of hours sleep just before dawn. I hoped Jamie would show up but there was no sign of him.

When I awoke I went downstairs and there was a note waiting for me from Armstrong. Mrs Newry held it out to me between her thumb and forefinger, watching me as she smoked. It was roughly written with *TRent* on the outside. Inside it said: *GoT him. Cough UP.* I went upstairs with it. In the bedroom I barred the door with a chair and turned the note over, as if something else would jump out of it.

Nothing did.

I lay there for a while as the sounds of the town filled the room.

Then there was a knock at the door.

I moved to the side of it, ready for it to burst open. 'Who is it?' I said.

'It's Laura. I just want to chat.'

I let her in and we had an awkward moment where we both stood either sides of my bed. Then she sat on it and I sat on Jamie's.

We talked about the weather, how busy the town was with the carnival. Small stuff. Then she suggested that we should go look for Jamie. She'd taken the next couple of days off, while the festivities were on, letting one of the barmen run the pub. She seemed to think the festival was a good place to look. She gave me a description of the site and what went on there. The words rolled over me as I sat there, numb.

But I had no better suggestion so I agreed to go.

With that as our plan we grabbed a tent from Laura's place and carried it down to the showground so we could merge into the crowds. This had been the site of Wild West Land, the town's fairground. The main feature had been the roller-coaster and that still rattled around in the middle, now surrounded by marquees and what was left of the original metal fence, patched up in places. All of the other rides seemed to have disappeared: the stampede, chair-o-planes and cable car; the runaway train I'd gone on three times in one afternoon with Dad. Behind it all was the disused railway and station.

We pitched amongst all the other tents as smog drifted across the field, whiffs of shit from the toilet stalls at the far side. Despite being the middle of the day there were lights on all over the festival.

Laura tightened the guy ropes. She'd changed into a short dress and light jacket, her hair tied up. The dress fitted her waist, showed some cleavage. It followed her body and was tight in all the right places.

It had only occurred to me as we'd set out the bedding

that we'd both be sleeping next to each other in that small space. Me and her in that little tent.

Still, that wasn't important, finding Jamie was.

'Why here?' I said.

'Here?'

'Why do you think they have Jamie here?'

She gave a guy rope one last pull. 'AHI don't run a prison. They parade people on the lorry or run them out of town. So they've got nowhere to hold him. Here they have all kinds of caravans and things.'

'Yeah?' I wasn't quite convinced but we were here now.

With the tent fastened we made our way across the field, our way lit by hazy sunlight. Around us there were muted voices, laughter. People sat out and drank. They smoked and danced. There were a few bonfires. As we carried on along the track we passed a couple on the ground, naked, having sex.

The main entrance was up ahead and to the left of it was a plinth with Rory on it, shouting and gesticulating. He was flanked by eleven figures in robes. Though I'd not expected him it wasn't a massive surprise to find him here.

'Oh, Rory,' I said.

'Is that your brother?' She'd met him in the old days. Only a couple of times but he'd made quite an impression.

'That's him all right.'

Rory's voice came to us over the sound of the generator and music. He ranted, moved around and pointed, he reached up to the heavens, rolling his eyes up in his head.

We joined the entrance queue, shuffling forward slowly. Two of Armstrong's thugs stood on the gate, fat, in tracksuits, bald and flat nosed. They looked everyone up and down and took money before they let them proceed. They grabbed a man in an old waterproof coat and pulled him out of the crowd, pushing him to one side. When he protested the biggest thug hit him in the belly before slapping him across the head.

As the queue crept forward Rory pointed and shouted. 'You people of Setmarch. Lost souls! Why fall prey? Why give in to the power of drink and crude pleasures?'

'Piss off,' shouted a man near the front and there was laughter.

Rory raised his hands up and closed his eyes. 'You may argue, fight with what is good. But deep down, way, way deep down! You know it. You know what is right!'

We moved forward and I lowered my head as Rory shouted, jumped and gnashed his teeth. He stopped and pointed at me. 'And here. Here he is. The real viper! The real snake in the nest! Snake in a dirty, filthy vest!'

This was just what I didn't want, him spotting me, making a fuss, attracting attention.

Rory formed a fist and beat the air. 'Here he skulks and sulks. The *ultimate* sinner. Cooked dinner.'

Some people in the queue turned to one-another, whispering. The men on the gate glanced over.

'Oh, but watch, be wise to how he tries to hide. Hide his sin! In the sin-bin.'

Reaching into my pocket I took out my bottle of whisky. There was a mouthful left and I opened it, knocking it back.

Rory jumped on the spot. 'See the sinner drink. Sup the evil liquor!'

I put the top back on the bottle and threw it. It flew through the air catching the light before it hit him in the chest with a thud. He exclaimed and stumbled backwards on the plinth, falling onto one of the disciples, his hands flailing.

There was a cheer.

The crowd moved forwards and the men on the gate laughed. Rory lay in a heap and his helpers milled around.

We paid and slid by Armstrong's men, going into the festival.

Once inside we passed the stalls where drinks, drugs and potions were sold. Signs proclaimed their benefits and gave a price while distorted music blared out of speakers. The roller-coaster clattered past overhead and women screamed on the big dip. Up ahead were several marquees flanked by stages. On one stage were four women in their underwear, Candy and Ruby and two others. They paraded up and down as men stood staring and pointing at them. Beside them was a man in a boxing ring who pranced around as a bloodied lad was helped onto a stool.

Laura stopped at a stall selling crystals. 'It's all grown so much bigger over the last few years.'

The beaten lad was being sponged down, diluted blood running down his face and onto his shirt. 'Real quality stuff,' I said.

'So where are we going to look for Jamie?'

'I don't know. I've never been here before. It was your idea to come.'

She rotated the crystal in her hand, so the light caught it. 'I've never done this kind of thing. Sneaky stuff. Like you do.'

'Sneaky stuff?'

'You know what I mean.'

I did know what she meant. She wasn't used to the dangerous things Jamie and me did all the time. Working without a plan. Second guessing. I looked around at the stalls and stands. All the people milling around. If he was here he'd be hidden round the back, out of the way. 'We just need to get the feel of the place.'

'Think they'll be waiting for us?'

'I'd expect so.'

Laura put a crystal down. There was a cheer as Ruby took of her bra, squeezing her tits together. Men waved money in the air, rough looking fellas. Ruby smiled but it faded as she looked at the men. Their hungry faces.

She pointed towards one of the marquees. 'Fancy a drink, just while we're looking around?'

'All right.'

Having a few drinks would help blank out all the crap from the festival. Let us fit in as well. I'd expected more security. Maybe that meant they didn't have Jamie here. It was hard to say. Chances were they'd be waiting for me to contact them, turn up with Gehenna. Not go sniffing around.

She led off to one side, past the boxing ring, round the back of a stall where a tall man was next to a short woman and the sign said *Freak Show*. The woman grinned at us but the man's face was lowered.

The beer tent was long and thin with a bar that ran the length of it. Bottles and barrels were stacked up behind it. It stank of stale booze and sweat. At the far end was a small stage where a man was lit by electric lights. He wore a trilby and bright waistcoat, holding a microphone that wasn't connected to anything so he had to shout his lines. 'My wife,' he said, 'my wife.'

'He's a local comedian, apparently,' said Laura.

The comedian paced up and down the stage. 'She's so fucking fat.'

'Want a drink?' I said.

'I definitely need a drink.'

At the bar I ordered a gin and a large whisky. We drank as the comedian told his jokes. A few people laughed while others talked.

'So what do you think, Trent?'

The comedian shifted the hat on his head. 'Two nuns in a bath.'

'Not my kind of thing,' I said.

'I meant about Jamie.'

'I'm not sure.' There was something about it that didn't feel right, Armstrong sticking him here. For some reason Laura thought it was a likely bet and she knew the town better than me. How AHI did things.

The comedian prattled on and we drank. Laura looked good in her outfit. She wore clothes that suited her, worked well with her body shape. And in this town she could still get decent kit. Places like Setmarch drew in quality merchandise. Where there was money, trade followed. Rough as it was, the town had some advantages.

I knocked back my whisky. We needed to find Jamie. 'Let's go look around.'

Laura finished her gin and joined me.

As we left the comedian hit his punch line. 'Wears the soap,' he said. 'Wears the soap.'

It was an old one but some people laughed.

We headed towards the bigger marquee, passing the talking-dog show, fish-boy and the jars of pickled stillborn-babies. We avoided the three men fighting over a bottle of beer and a couple fondling against the mutton-pie stall.

We came to the marquee. Loud guitars and drums came from it and a heavy power cable snaked into the tent. 'Doesn't spare the juice, does he?' I said.

'This is the big event. When the town can let it all go.'

'When doesn't the town let go?'

Setmarch was a bubble of pubs, fuel, food and drink. Awash with them. Away from here there wasn't all this stuff. All the junk Armstrong had given them.

'What's at the other side of the marquee?' I said.

Laura shrugged so I led her on.

We found fuel containers and piles of wood. There were animal's cages, all empty. Tarpaulins pilled up and containers of booze. There didn't seem to be anywhere to stick Jamie. No caravans or smaller tents within the perimeter.

A couple of Armstrong's men were over at the far side, one I recognised from the club with Sikey, but they were chatting and didn't see us.

'There's not much here,' said Laura.

Then Armstrong's men glanced over, noticing us. Without a word to Laura I grabbed her and pushed her against the marquee's side. I kissed her and wrapped my arms around her, holding her tight. She made a noise then embraced me, joining in with the ruse. Her lips were warm and soft and she tasted of gin. Her breasts pushed against me through her dress and I could feel her thighs against mine.

I could have stopped sooner but it felt good so I carried on.

When we slid apart she was soft eyed and I felt unsteady. The men were still at the far side but talking again, which was just as well as we didn't move.

'Sorry,' I said.

'Sorry?'

'That was to fool the men. So they didn't see us.'

'I see.'

'Sorry.'

'So you said.' She turned and walked away, back towards the main festival. I caught her up, took her hand and stopped her. She was taking it all personally while Jamie was in Armstrong's hands. 'Look, we're here to look for Jamie. It's not about anything else. Don't get all huffy.'

'I see.' She looked at me but her eyes wandered off, like she was bored.

'We need to find him.'

'Stop bossing me around, Trent.'

'I'm not bossing you around.'

'You've got no idea.'

She was the one with no idea but there was no point telling her. 'All right, where do you want to go?'

'I need to eat.' She led me to a stall that had a pig roasting. She ordered a pork sandwich and ate it as I stood beside her. It took ages for her to eat it, as she picked on with the crackling. At last she finished and handed the plate back.

'Now what?'

She shrugged. 'You decide.'

She really was being difficult. 'Let's go in here.' I pulled open the flap on the side of the marquee. Warm air and music poured out. Even if I had unsettled her with the kissing thing, we were here to find Jamie. That was the purpose of this.

We went in behind a group of women who staggered

around with bottles in their hands. The band was at the far end, the lead singer singing about working in the colliery. This group had microphones that worked and some kind of sound system. It was distorted but loud.

I needed Laura to help with the search so I had to chivvy her along. Without asking I went to the bar and got her a gin, another whisky for me. When I handed it to her she took it but said nothing. I downed my whisky, pushing the glass into my jacket pocket, taking out some of my precious grass which I rolled into a small spliff. This was bound to help her mood. I lit the joint and passed it to her.

She smoked and swayed to the music saying nothing to me.

If Jamie was here they'd have him within the perimeter, where they could keep an eye on him. He had to be nearby.

Some fella in a bike jacket was wandering around, tapping people and saying something as he slid between them. He came up to us. 'You want to get out of it, eh?' he said.

'No thanks,' I said.

'What you got?' said Laura.

He opened his coat. There were pockets sewn up and down the inside and he lifted a small paper bag out of one. Opening it he held it under her nose. She nodded and handed him some money then he was off.

'What's that?' I said.

She thrust the bag at me. There was grey powder in it. It smelled of bleach and sugar. 'Moon Dust.'

'Moon Dust?'

She gave me the joint back and I smoked as she licked her finger and dabbed the powder. She slid it into her mouth, washing it down with the gin, taking a deep breath and closing her eyes. Maybe this was just the thing to cheer her up. I'd give it a few minutes then we'd go look around. We watched the band, drank our drinks and I finished the joint. Then I went to the bar and got us another whisky and gin. When I handed Laura hers, she lent over to me. She said something about being glad I was back in the town but I couldn't hear the rest for the music. She offered me the Moon Dust and I tipped some in my drink. More went in that I'd planned but there was plenty left.

'It's song,' she said, or something.

I drank the whisky and took down all the Moon Dust. It tasted of sherbet and salt. Laura took a dab before she slid into my jacket.

Then she grabbed my hand and led me out.

After the marquee the air was fresh, cooler. The roller coaster rattled and people laughed but the music was muted.

'What now?' she said.

'Keep looking round.'

We passed drunks, shows and fights. We didn't bother with more drinks so I dabbed the powder. It tasted all right, really.

My next thought was to find Armstrong's people. Maybe they had something set up on another part of the site, like a control centre.

When two track-suited men went into the comedian's tent I tapped Laura's arm and pointed at them. She followed me as I went after them. I offered her more Moon Dust but she refused it. I had a little more.

As we went into the marquee there was a power-kick

and the lights brightened.

The comedian was still on. He had a guitar and sang a song about his wife's hatred of anal sex. Armstrong's men were across the far side, watching the show. To fit in we bought a gin and large whisky, as drunken men and women jabbered on, a lot of them yawning. When I handed Laura her drink, the light caught the liquid, dancing around the glass. We drank and I added some Moon Dust to my whisky.

The comedian had picked up his show. '*She won't take it up the arse,*' he sang. It was a very funny line and I laughed, big roars of laughter so I had to lean forward to brace myself, hurting my face and lungs with the effort. Laura held onto me and said something but I couldn't make it out.

The comedian's song ended and I stopped laughing. 'That was funny.' It was the most I'd laughed in ages, certainly since coming to the town. I'd almost forgotten what fun was.

Laura took the bag of powder. 'Give me some of that.' She picked a few fingerfuls of it.

Armstrong's men just stood there. They weren't doing anything.

'Should we go look somewhere else?' I said.

We floated out past the stalls and came to the hall of mirrors. The sign was cleverly made so it appeared to float in the air. 'Let's look in here,' I said.

'Really?'

'Yeah, yeah.'

'Trent, do you think that Moon Dust is —?'

'I'm fine. Only messing.' I ran my fingers across the material of the tent, how it rippled in the light. They'd really put some effort into this.

Before searching around for Jamie we tried out the mirrors. The first one made us several metres tall and we moved our arms, stretching up to the ceiling. In second we were tiny with giant foreheads and we could change the shape by moving up and down. Laura laughed so hard she cried. I laughed too.

'We look completely crazy,' she said.

'Yeah.'

'We look just so bizarre.'

'Yeah.'

'We look like freaks from a freak show.'

Something about that didn't seem so funny and I moved onto the next mirror. The room spun for a second, probably due to the light distortions, and I had to hold onto the tent. The third mirror made us wider, like we were really fat. Laura laughed and turned sideways. 'Looks like you're pregnant,' I said.

'I don't think —'

'Like you, but if you were having a baby.'

'Oh, Trent, don't—'

'Nine months gone. Ready to have a kid.'

She started to cry so we went out. Women were often sensitive about their weight. I'd pushed it with that comment.

She held her hands to her face as I reached into the bag and took out a pinch of Moon Dust, eating it. She cried and her body shook so I put my arm around her. 'It's just the Moon Dust,' I said. When the festival spun I closed my eyes. We stayed like that until she didn't cry anymore. Then she ran her fingers through her hair, wiping her eyes.

'Should we go and look somewhere else?' I said.

'Please.'

At the entrance for the roller coaster I stopped. It rose up before us on old wooden boards. 'Here's an idea. We'll see the whole place.'

She looked up at the ride. 'Do you think it's safe?'

'It's fine.'

'I don't know if I like things like that.'

The wooden structure towered about us with its metal rails that shifted in a slight side to side sway. The car rattled down and to the start point, just in front of us.

I stepped forward. 'It's fine.'

We took our seats, waiting as it filled up. The car was hand painted, patched with riveted plates here and there.

'Didn't we go on this in the old days?' I said. 'Just before your twenty-first?'

'Don't think so. I can't remember.'

'I'm sure we did. Unless I was with Elise Tucknall…' I massaged my forehead and pulled at the skin on my cheeks. It had all gone numb. The car drifted like a boat in the water.

She said something but the attendant had pulled a lever so we had started to move. Her words were lost in the clatter as it set off along the rails.

'What?' I said.

'What took you so long?'

The car started on its ascent to the first dip. It clanked and juddered as it was pulled up, so that it pointed towards the sky, filled with dark smoke. My skin moved back and forward on my body as if waves ran through me, as the roller coaster climbed. Then we levelled out at the top. Setmarch was laid out in the valley around us.

Laura said something but the car accelerated down the other side, dropping fast, clattering down the track. She screamed and I gave out a low moan, as she held onto me, closing her eyes. We ran over two more dips then slowed and jolted to a stop.

The attendant let us out and I fell forward, staggering onto the path. Laura joined me as I got out the bag of Moon Dust, dabbing more, as the festival shifted around me. 'Jamie would have *loved* that,' I said.

Jamie, yes.

We had to find Jamie.

'We need to look for Jamie,' I said.

'Not with you in that state.'

I stumbled around and pointed at her. 'We need to!'

This was important, the reason we were here. We'd got side-tracked and now it was time to find him, rescue him, get the hell out of here.

'You're far too trashed to do anything, Trent.'

'No, I'm all right, really.' I was wobbly but fine. I'd been much worse. Much, much worse, many times. And always got the job done. Always.'

'Can we go back now? We can look tomorrow.'

'We need to look. For him.'

'Trent, you're too messed up at the moment.'

'I'm okay. Fine.' I slipped and fell, lying face down on the ground. Maybe Laura had a point, possibly the Moon Dust had done something to me.

She helped me onto a bench. 'I really think we need to rest. Let's go back to the tent. We can break and come out again later this evening.'

She eased me up and we set off. The festival wobbled in front of me as I took giant steps, determined not to trip over my feet. The ground was so uneven and the Moon Dust didn't help. I walked ahead of Laura balancing myself.

Then there was a noise behind me. The noise came again and I turned back. Laura screamed and waved her arms around as several men held her. Two shadows moved around me so I swung a punch but missed, stumbling forward. Straightening up I punched again but my hands were pulled aside and I was kicked in the gut, hit in the head and everything spun around me. There was soil in my face and something appeared over my head, something rough that smelled of oil and damp.

It was dark. Very dark.

CHAPTER TWENTY-ONE

Caged

I woke in a cage, one of the ones round the back, something they'd kept animals in. It had metal bars and there was straw on the floor. My lips were dry, cracked and it felt like there was a tight band round my head.

Laura lay asleep at the other side, lit pink by the sunrise that filtered through the smoke that hung above the festival. The cage was surrounded by empty barrels and chopped wood stacked against another cage, smaller than the one we were in. The roller coaster had stopped and its lights were off but there was still music and shouts from the marquees. I ran my fingers over the rough floor, lifting them up and sniffing them. They smelled of dried piss and something rotten.

People milled around outside, shaven headed lads in tracksuits. Beyond the fence, across the show-field the bikers had parked their bus and their women danced semi-naked around a fire, the smoke hanging over their tents and bikes on the trailer. I watched for a moment to see if the woman I'd hit was there but they were too far off. Not that it mattered anymore. We other things to worry about.

Laura woke and sat up, her eyes bloodshot. 'Where the hell are we?' She shuffled over to me and touched the bottom of the cage. 'Christ Trent. What kind of animals do you think they have in here?'

'Us at the moment.'

She slumped back against the bars and leant her head forward. 'I can't believe they've got us in here.'

'Looks like you were right about one thing. They certainly have places to lock people up at the festival.'

She grunted.

A figure appeared outside, walking around. It was Sikey, his baseball cap tilted back, a smile on his lips. He circled us, slow steps around the cage, stopping behind Laura and pushing his fingers through the bars, prodding her. She gave out a squeal and he laughed. 'Rats in a trap,' he said. 'Rats in a fucking trap.'

I slid up to the bars. 'Where's Jamie?'

He didn't even acknowledge what I'd said, instead prodding Laura again so she moved away from the bars. 'Bit fucking fat, I reckon,' he said.

'Come on, Sikey,' she said, 'what's going on?'

'Oh, you know what's going on.' He grinned at her, before turning and swaggering off into the showground.

Then it was just Laura and me again.

'What now?' she said.

I grabbed hold of the bars, pulling at them. The steel didn't flex or rattle. The door's hinges were welded in place and the lock had no opening on the inside. Even the boarding was rot free and without gaps. There was no way out without tools or a key so I sat down next to her. 'We wait.'

'There must be a way out.'

My head ached, as if someone was standing on it. 'I need to rest.'

'Great.'

I leant against the bars and closed my eyes, letting the sounds of the festival roll over me as I took deep breaths. The drone of the generator was like a car engine, like being back on the open road, driving the Evora.

I passed the dried moorland that went on for miles and miles. Came to Glasgow with its barricades and bodies strung up on scaffold. On to that abandoned village in the forest, its trees bare of leaves. Bodies piled in a pit. The other one with the pile of bones in a church. Human bones. Skirting Carlisle, seeing the warning signs for the west coast where the leaks were. Whole towns, livestock left where they fell.

The road rolled by under the snout of the car.

Mile after mile.

Suddenly I was back in the cage, as my head jerked back and my arms yanked against the bars. Something thick and rough was pulled around my neck and both arms. As I kicked and strained forward, coarse material dug into my skin.

'What the hell is going on?' said Laura. She came over to me and tugged at whatever was round me. 'Leave him alone! You're strangling him!'

Harsh laughter came from behind me. Then there was a jangling sound and two lads came into the cage both wearing scruffy tracksuits, their beer bellies bulging out of the jackets. One was the fella from outside the pub, holding a shotgun again, a replacement for the one I'd taken off him. The second man was Sikey's sidekick from the club. He had a rubber cosh. They waved the weapons at Laura and backed her away from me and against the side of the cage. She kicked out and they laughed, the one with the gun swinging it until she was against the bars. They leapt forward, grabbed her and she cried out.

'Get her fucking hands, Gaz!' shouted the one with the gun.

'I'm getting them!' said Gaz, grappling with her.

I strained against the ropes but couldn't move as Laura screamed, the lads dropping her down, pinning her to the floor, as she scuffled and shouted. This went on for some time.

Then they stood up. She lay with her hands tied behind her back, mouth gagged and dress rolled up on her thighs.

The lads laughed again and a deep chuckle came from behind me, the ropes on my neck and arms jiggling, sliding up and down.

'Leave her,' I said, my voice thin. Then the rope tightened around my throat and I gasped for air.

Sikey strode into the cage, standing over Laura. His black tracksuit was immaculate and his trainers wiped clean. 'Like a fucking Christmas Turkey,' he said to Gaz. He came up close up to me, until his nose was only millimetres away. He smelled of soap and bleach. 'Hey. Might slice you up. Feed you to my dog.'

The lads laughed again and he moved over to Laura. 'Get her feet,' he said.

Gaz and the other lad obeyed. They dropped down and grabbed a leg each. They leant on her and held her still as she tried to kick. They eased her legs apart.

Sikey reached down and ran his hands across her body.

He worked his way over her shoulders and breasts, down her torso and crotch, worming their way down her thighs. 'As I thought, a bit flabby,' he said.

She moved around, grunted. When I tried to speak only a gurgle came out and the gruff voice came from behind me.

Sikey took a folding knife out of his trousers, flicking it open and holding it up, moving the blade around. He knelt and touched it against Laura's chest, circling her breasts and running it over her dress as she squirmed and twisted. It looked like he was going to cut her up so I shouted, made some sound but the rope was pulled tight again.

Then he sliced the blade up the dress and slit it open. The material flapped aside and she lay there in her underwear.

'Hey,' he said. 'This is better.'

The lads snorted.

Sikey turned to Gaz. 'Does she look temptin' to you?'

Gaz and the other man mumbled.

'You know my saying, it's more fun when they're not willing.' He hooked the blade inside her bra, turning it and pulling hard. The material snapped and he yanked it off.

She struggled in her bindings and against the lads, flicking her head up towards Sikey, fighting against him. But he leant on her, forced her back.

Then he hunkered down until he sat between her legs, running the knife across her skin before he put it aside and grasped her breasts, holding them tight and jiggling them around. He started singing: 'Jelly on a plate, jelly on a plate, wibble-fucking-wobble, wibble...'

They all roared with laugher at this.

He started with the blade again; ran it across her belly to her knickers. He cut the material.

The ropes on my arms were still tight but the one on neck had slackened so I leant forward, turning my head to one side, needing to get free, to do something. 'You wait!' I said, my voice rasping.

Sikey looked round and frowned. 'Shut him up, Robson!'

This time the ropes jerked really hard around me, forcing me against the bars. I was trapped as Sikey ripped Laura's knickers off her. She grunted and shifted around but the lads held her firm.

Now she lay naked before him. He shuffled around between her legs so that he sat between her splayed thighs, as she twisted and wriggled. 'What now? What d'you think Gaz?'

'Fuck her,' said Gaz.

The other lads laughed. Laura moaned and I pulled at the ropes on my neck and arms.

Sikey sat up and moved so that his knees were under her backside, her naked crotch against him.

She shrunk back.

'Don't know,' he said. With her pinned down he took hold of the top of his trousers, eased them down a few centimetres.

I tensed up my right arm, using all my strength, dragging at the rope around it.

For a moment he didn't move then he sat up, pulling up his tracksuit bottoms. 'Not here, with you all fuckers watchin!'

'Go on,' said Gaz.

'Later. Later. Then it's free-for-all.'

The lads laughed. Sikey stood and adjusted his pants. He came over to me and swung his hand, slapping me hard across the face, pulling at the rope on my neck. 'And another for luck.' He slapped me again, harder, then he shook his head, pointing at me. 'Need to quiz this one. Take him to mine. Work him over.'

'Now?' said Gaz.

'Soon enough.'

'And her?'

'You'll get your turns.' He strode out of the cage, the lads following him. They locked the door and the ropes slid off my neck and arms.

I slumped forward and put a hand to my throat as Laura lay there with her eyes closed.

We sat like that for some time until I shuffled over to her, slipping off the gag and picking at the rope on her hands. 'Are you all right?' I said.

'No. Not really.'

'Don't worry, I'll get us out of here.'

She nodded, pulling the rope off her and curling up, her ripped dress wrapped around her. Both of us just lay like that for some time, as the sounds of the festival carried on around us.

It wasn't long before the lads in tracksuits came back.

Robson had a bunch of keys and carried the rope he'd held me with. He unlocked and opened the door as the other two stood to one side, one holding the shotgun and Gaz gripping his rubber cosh.

I stayed beside Laura. She had her torn dress pulled around her body with her legs and arms crossed in front of her.

'Come on,' said Robson, jangling the keys.

The other man jabbed his gun at me. 'Watch him, Robson.'

'All right, Doddsy.'

Doddsy waddled round to the side, prodding me with the shotgun, telling me to get up, so I did, helping Laura to her feet. Her head was slumped forward and her arms wrapped around her.

'Come on,' said Robson. 'Out.'

Laura followed me down the wooden steps to the ground. Doddsy joined Robson and Gaz so that the three of them were lined up, staring at us, at her. She crossed her arms tighter in front of herself and hunched up. As I led her the lads backed off, less sure of themselves without Sikey.

'This way,' said Robson going towards the barrels and woodpile in the direction of the main marquee. The others moved to the side, watching us.

This was our chance to get away, escape before Sikey got hold of us. I limped forward, my face twisted up.

'Come on,' said Gaz.

Bending I touched my leg. 'Sore ankle.'

'Don't try anything.'

With a groan I stumbled, falling forward and grasping my ankle as the lads laughed at me. That was what they were good at, laughing at people, humiliating.

Then I swung round and kicked Gaz in the leg. He staggered to the woodpile, dropping his cosh and I hit him in the belly, the saggy flesh yielding under my blow and folding him up. As he slumped against the logs Robson faced me, sliding a key between his fingers, between the tattooed *I love AHI*. In his other hand was the rope. As he swung out I sidestepped, kicking him between the legs, causing him to moan. Then I punched him between the eyes, just where his eyebrows joined, a quick clout that cracked against the bone. He staggered and wobbled back and I gave him an uppercut to his chin, flicking his head back. He collapsed onto the ground.

Doddsy stared at Robson collapsed there, Gaz off at the side. His gun hung loose in his hand. When he raised it up I grabbed it, hauling it from him.

'You can go. I won't stop you,' he said.

I moved towards him. 'I know.'

He backed off. 'I've got nothing against you.'

'Yeah? What about Laura?'

'Laura?'

I pointed to her. 'You seemed happy to let Sikey mistreat her.'

'That wasn't my idea!'

I swung my arm, slapping him across the face, like Sikey had done to me, causing his head to twist round. A spot of blood burst from is lip. He staggered off to one of the barrels and climbed up it, trying to scramble onto the other cage. I reached up, seizing his tracksuit bottoms.

He shook his leg. 'Get off. Get off!'

I pulled at the synthetic material, off balancing him, hauling again so that he wobbled on the worn wood then fell backwards. He landed splayed out on the ground and I cocked the gun, pulling both triggers. Nothing happened so I spun it round, swung it, hitting him in the ribs with its stock. He cried as I swung again, this time clipping the end of his nose, busting it and spraying blood into his eyes and mouth.

'That is for what you did to Laura.'

He lay and sobbed, a hand to his face. Like a great big baby.

Laura came over to me. 'Come on Trent. Leave them.'

I stepped back.

Doddsy lay there and cried. Robson was out cold. Gaz still leant against the woodpile, holding his belly, groaning and rocking. He seemed brighter than the other two, less stupid, at least. I approached him. 'I have some questions,' I said.

His face was twisted into a sneer, defiant. 'You can fuck off.'

I hit him in the leg. 'Let's try again. Tell me about Jamie.'

He screwed his face up and touched his thigh. 'Dunno.'

Raising the gun I hit him in the groin and he bent forward, giving out a silent cry.

'Now,' I said, 'let's try again.' Once more I lifted the shotgun. 'Where's Jamie?'

'I don't know!'

I smashed it into his left hand.

Laura grabbed the stock. 'Please, Trent.'

Shaking it free I lifted it high, this time aiming it at his head.

'He's at the plant!' said Gaz.

'Where exactly?'

'I don't know!'

'Where?'

'I don't know!'

Laura grabbed for the gun but I avoided her, hitting him across the arm. 'Think!'

'I don't –'

'Wrong answer.' I swung hard and hit him across the

head with a dull crack.

He collapsed down, his eyes half open and his mouth slack. His arms lay off to his side at odd angles as if half way through some dance.

'Jesus, Trent.' Laura bent and touched his neck. She held it for a moment. 'He's not dead.'

I dropped the shotgun and took her arm. She squirmed out of my grip but joined me as I marched off, away from the lads and the cage.

She held her dress around her. 'I thought you'd killed him.'

'So what if I had?'

We climbed over the fence around the carnival, off into the camping field.

CHAPTER TWENTY-TWO

The Pit

After stashing the tent back at her house Laura wanted to take a walk. I joined her, guessing she'd need company after what had happened to her. I wanted to think out my next move. How I'd find Jamie at the plant. She led me up to Setmarch Mine, not saying much on the way.

It was deserted, closed for the festival with no lorries in the parking area. Warm sun filtered through the haze down onto us, warming the coal-speckled ground. One of Armstrong's men stood over at the pit-head. He watched us but didn't come over.

'Why are we here?' I said.

'I just wanted to get out of town.' She led me to a rock at the end of the lorry park, well away from the guard. She took out a pack of cards and sat down. Above us smoke flowed along the sky like a filthy river, drifting and breaking up and dropping a mist of ash. Seemed the plant didn't shut for anything.

'You all right?'

'Not really.' She shuffled the cards and cut them, as I

kicked pieces of coal across the ground. The festival was visible at the far side of town, the marquee and roller coaster hazy outlines, beyond the plant with its smoking chimney and a pile of cars in the scrap yards down below us.

'Sikey's a head-case,' she said.

'Yeah.'

She stared up at me, eyes red-rimmed, like they'd been since we came back. 'Emily Snowball,' she said, picking out a card at random and putting it back. 'She was the first.'

'What?'

'Sikey's first victim. Her and her brother.' She cut the cards again. 'Leo Snowball was trying to set up a union and Sikey shot him. Not bad enough to kill him but to put him in hospital. Then he went for Emily. Assaulted her. She was only a kid.'

Laura shuffled cards faster, sloppily. She frowned as she did it and after every couple of cards flicked her hair behind her ears. For some time she did this.

'The thing is, we got away,' I said.

'Yes, this time.'

'But he's still got Jamie.'

She slid the cards back into the packet then popped them out again.

A burst of steam came from the plant and there was a distant rattling sound. 'That's where he is,' I said, pointing at the factory. 'People like Gaz don't have the imagination to make things up. We need to go and have a look around. Try to find him.'

'Not now. Not festival time.'

'All the more reason to head over to the plant. It'll be

quiet…'

'Not now.' She put a card down, the King of Hearts. 'Stuff happens at the end of it. Security is tighter.'

I picked up a stone and threw it across the barren land, towards the winding gear and dark buildings beyond. The guard shuffled around, now accompanied by another man. 'We could just nip down there.'

'Trent, can't you trust me on this?'

From the distance came a crack of fireworks and faint drumming. She put the pack of cards down and looked over at me. 'Did you really want to kill him?'

'Gaz?'

She nodded.

'At the time. Maybe.'

'But you wouldn't normally…'

I shook my head. There was no normally. There were situations and things that happened, some of them good and some not so good. But there was no point trying to explain all this.

The road beyond the parking area had several people on it, a steady trickle heading into town. I pointed over towards the plant. 'Look. Jamie's there now — '

'For Christ's sake, Trent.' She threw the cards down. 'Okay, let's go.' She stood with her hands on her hips and glared at me.

'Right.'

'But don't say I didn't warn you, okay?'

'I won't.'

'Don't complain when it all gets screwed up just because you wouldn't listen.'

'I won't.' I headed off across the filthy ground with her behind me. At far end there were shouts and voices as more figures appeared along the track. Bangs, cries and drums bounced off the wall.

'See?' she said. 'I told you this would happen.'

'It's only a few drunks.'

She laughed. 'Oh, that's all right then, isn't it?'

The people came up the road, a couple at the front spitting out paraffin, igniting it and sending clouds of flame above them. Others banged drums as a group of lads lit and threw fireworks. There were carts behind them, chinking and rattling, laden with beer bottles sitting in trays of water. Everyone held at least one bottle. As they pulled level, a man painted black and dressed in mucky loincloth came over, handing Laura and me a bottle each. The glass was cool, damp and I opened it on the wall, drinking from it. The beer was strong, thick and yeasty.

Laura opened hers on a rock and dipped her finger into it. 'Festival beer. Careful, it's very strong.'

The procession carried on past, dozens of town folk all drinking and laughing. Some drummed on tins and boxes and empty bottles. I sipped the beer as they thumped past. 'How many are there?'

'Christ, Trent, it's most of the town. The plant is on full security to stop them getting in and causing bother.'

More people passed and bottles smashed accompanied by cheers. A man in rags lobbed a firework at us, which I dodged, letting it land in the mud to explode in a shower of dirt. The thrower laughed and carried on. 'When does this end?'

'When they run out of beer.'

'All right. Let's wait it out.'

She smiled, climbing up onto the wall, sitting on it. 'Now that sounds like a good idea.'

As the people passed on the track staggering, singing and drumming I joined her, drinking the beer. Once it was empty I lobbed the bottle in the air and it spun towards the procession, twirling through the air. There was a crash and cheer as the people filtered past.

CHAPTER TWENTY-THREE

Works

The festival ended that night in a final carnival. It sounded like war had broken out so I sat in my room, as the drunks shouted and smashed bottles outside. Laura had invited me round but I declined, trying to keep our partnership professional, business-like. She'd agreed to pick me up in the morning, part way through the early shift, so we could look around the plant.

Sure enough she turned up just after breakfast in her Mondeo. We crossed town as AHI men swept and cleaned. Empty bottles and drunks were collected and taken away.

We drove beyond the plant and back in from the riverside, through the South Estate, around the broken glass, burnt out furniture and smouldering bonfires. The works was up ahead, spewing black smoke that mixed with the steam from a vent and hung across the houses, a stinking mist. We drove on past the tree stumps, chewed up grass and the pavements strewn with used condoms and dog turds. At a side road she dodged the charred remains of three tyres.

Two shaven-headed lads leant against a fence with a Bull Terrier on a rope. They were early-teens, a rough looking pair.

'Looks like this hasn't improved,' I said.

'Of all of Setmarch's shitty estates, this is the shittiest.' She turned the engine off. 'He might not be in the plant –'

'We've got to try it. Gaz wasn't bright enough to make it up.' She nodded at this, even if she wasn't convinced. It was possible that Gaz had lied to save his neck but it was all we had to go on.

When I got out of the car, the lads came over, dragging the dog, their hands in their pockets.

Laura slid a couple of padlocks through the hasp and staples she had on the car's doors and joined me as I shouldered the bag and faced the lads. One held onto the dog while the fatter one stood behind him.

The one with the dog tapped the car with a filthy hand. 'Not a good place to park, this.'

'You reckon?' I said.

'Not safe, like.'

The fatter lad nodded.

I took a joint out, slid it into my mouth and lit it with my Zippo as the dog raised its leg and pissed on the Mondeo's tyre. 'There some way we can make it safer?'

The lad with the dog stared at the joint and smiled, his teeth grey and chipped. 'Maybes.'

I offered the joint to him. He reached out, grabbed it and drew hard on it, closing his eyes.

'There's more of that,' I said. 'If you keep an eye out.' It was worth giving away our stash to keep the car safe.

The lad blew smoke out of his nose and smiled as the

dog growled.

His fatter companion came round so he could inhale the smoke. He raised his nose up and made sniffling noises. 'Don't hog it, you fucker.'

We left the lads smoking and walked down the track towards the plant, its soot-covered chimneys standing over the pipes, gantries and buildings, framed by the tangle of wires that ran off across the town. There were rumbles and hisses and creaks as heaps of slag were fed by a conveyor ejecting waste.

We carried on past stunted elders, along the mud decorated with bottle tops and dog turds — different shades of brown in heaps and swirls. Ahead was the chain link fence that surrounded the plant. On the far side, the ground was sprinkled with coal dust leading to the grey buildings. A sign on the fence said *Armstrong Heavy Industries. Keep Out.*

A hundred metres away a man in a boiler suit patrolled along the inside of the fence, leading an Alsatian on a chain. We waited behind an elder as he came level, the dog snuffling and pawing at the ground. The man muttered something and continued on.

Once he'd gone I opened my bag, taking out a pair of wire cutters, cutting a section of fence and peeling it apart.

'This is it,' Laura said. 'We're at the furthest point from the gate. But once we're in, we're on Armstrong's turf.'

I put the cutters away and opened the hole some more, sliding the bag onto the blackened soil. 'Some turf.' I crawled through, standing on the crushed coal and mud, an explorer on an alien world. Laura glanced up and down the track before sliding through next to me.

I closed the fence and led her across the filthy ground. We passed ancient shipping containers, the names of long gone firms on their sides, some in foreign languages, strange lettering. We carried on towards a doorway. It was locked from the inside but was easily levered open. Checking there was no one around we entered the plant.

The furnaces creaked and hissed and there was a flash from up ahead. The air was hot and smelled of tar, coal and ash.

'This is mad, Trent. Really daft. Where are we going to start?'

'Maybe he's in some side room.' There was a rattle as coal passed on a conveyor overhead. Several men in overalls came towards us so I ducked behind a large piece of equipment, pulling Laura with me.

Once the men had gone we slid out and carried on through the plant. There was a rumble as another load of coal thundered overhead, off towards the far end. Up ahead workmen shovelled up pieces that had fallen from the conveyor. The pipes hissed and gurgled and dust hung in the air.

The place was massive with machinery in the central section and corridors off to the sides; dirt everywhere.

Laura kept glancing around. 'If Armstrong's people get us, we're screwed. You know that?'

'Yeah.' I wasn't sure if that was meant to be a joke after what Sikey threatened to do to her but she wasn't smiling so I kept a serious face.

A machine chewed up coal above us and dust sprinkled down. A group of men came out of a doorway nearby, all in overalls, typical AHI workers.

That was what we needed to be, typical workers. No

one else came out and I crept over to the door. It said *Shower Room*. It wasn't marked male or female. There were no women factory-workers in Armstrong's backward new world.

Laura grabbed my arm. 'Trent, where are you going?'

'Trust me.' I gave her a smile but she just messed with her hair and sighed.

The corridor led to a long room with rows of pegs carrying overalls and hard hats on one side, lockers opposite and an entrance to communal showers at the far end. It smelled of sweat and soap. There were no men in the room but someone whistled in the shower. I set my bag down and picked up a pair of overalls and held them against me. They were too short and I put them back, grabbing another pair and reading the label. They were medium and I pulled them on. There was a badge attached with the AHI logo and a name.

Laura got close, her voice low. 'Are you completely mad?'

I thrust some overalls at her. 'Kit yourself out.'

She frowned then pulled them on over her clothes. Doing mine up I handed her a hard hat and grabbed one myself.

Wet footsteps padded out of the shower and a man came into the changing room, drying his hair with a towel. Laura pushed her hair into the hat and turned around to do up the overalls. The man slid the towel around his waist and cleaned his ear with a finger. 'How do,' he said.

'All right,' I said, as if I was a fellow worker.

He whistled, put his foot on a bench and picked at his toes. Another man came out and joined him, chatting about the AHI football team. Grabbing my bag we headed out of the room, back out to the machines and conveyor belts.

Laura read her name badge, tugging at the overalls. 'Well, this is very chic, I must say.'

'Yeah, well it'll do the job.'

We carried on through the plant, looking just like the other AHI staff. Now we were spies. Whether that made things worse, it was hard to say.

CHAPTER TWENTY-FOUR

Containers

We wandered around for another couple of hours, up and down the factory, into side rooms, the canteens and storerooms. Everywhere apart from Armstrong's office that sat in the centre, the middle of his web. We stopped at what was labelled *Condensing Section*, where liquids gurgled past in the pipes above us. Coal dust hung in the warm air as I drummed my fingers on a stanchion.

There'd been no sign of Jamie.

Laura took her hard-hat off, adjusted her hair, sliding it on again. 'So are you satisfied?'

'Not really.'

'You did your best.'

We headed outside through the door we'd entered. A black cloud spewed from the chimneys above us. The guard wasn't around.

'We can look again tomorrow,' she said. 'Or try somewhere else.'

'Yeah.'

'There's only so much you can do.'

The guard appeared over at the far side. 'Did I tell you about the time at Kelso?'

'Trent, you've not really told me anything.'

We passed the scrap heaps and piled up metal. 'He put himself on the line. It could have gone wrong but he waited for me. That meant a lot. Still does.'

She gave me some look but it was hard to make out what it meant. Possibly she was impressed.

We carried on towards the fence, over crushed coal and pools of slick, past the row of old shipping containers. Slicing through the middle of them were tyre tracks, trampled in places, but really wide tyres, like from a fancy car. Not the kind of thing that would drive round a factory site.

'Look at these,' I said.

'They're just tyre tracks, from a lorry or — '

'No, no.' I knelt down, touching the fine crisscross pattern, feeling the imprint, imaging the tread. Then I followed them as they snaked off between the rusted containers. Most were open, filled with worn parts for recycling: shock absorbers, brake shoes and batteries.

Laura followed me as I traced the tracks to one container.

'They wouldn't put him in there.'

'Wouldn't they?'

'Trent, even Armstrong –'

'Let's just have a look.'

She leant against it, cupping her ear.

'Can you hear anything?' I said.

'Shh!'

There were sounds of lorry engines and hisses from inside the plant. The smoke curled off into the distance, rolling off above the cables and pipes.

Laura closed one eye, looking at me with the other one. 'I heard something.'

I joined her and put my ear to the metal. There was no sound from inside, just the lorries and the factory echoing through the container, bouncing around the empty shell.

Laura got close to me. 'Hear it?'

'No.'

'Well, I heard something.' She tugged at the chain padlocked round the handle. 'Are you going to do something?'

Even if there was a chance he was in there it was worth exploring. I opened my bag and took out the wire cutters. There was a rusty link and I put the clippers on it, applying force. The chain bent but didn't snap. I tried again and leant down on it, twisting as the clippers bit together. The link broke, pinging onto the ground and I clattered the rest of the chain through the handle.

The door resisted when I pulled but moved when I hung my weight off it, creaking open. The container smelled of damp and mould as the sounds from the plant reverberated through the metal.

I flicked on my Zippo and stepped in. There was a pool of water in the doorway and screwed up paper on the floor. Boxes and parts of machinery were piled up alongside water pipes.

I checked back outside and saw that the guard was across at the far side, well away from our hole in the fence. I shut the door, sealing us into that dark place of muffled sounds. The lighter's flame flickered and shadows moved around us as we picked our way to the back of the container. In the corner were several sheets of cardboard and on them a roll of carpet.

Beside that was Jamie. He was gagged with his bandana, his hands and feet tied. His eyes were dark in his bruised face as he stared up at Laura and me. I put the lighter on a pile of rusty metal. Then I knelt down and took the gag out of his mouth. He gasped and licked his lips.

'Are you okay?' said Laura.

He sighed as I undid his hands and feet. Then he pointed over at the roll of carpet with a swollen hand. 'She's in there.'

'She –?'

'Look.'

Laura grabbed the edge of the carpet and I helped push it across the cardboard. It unrolled and a naked leg, smooth and white flopped out. As it unfurled some more we found a young woman. It was the waitress from the club. She was naked with a trail of blood from her mouth. Her eyes were open, one bloodshot. Bruises covered her body, especially on her thighs. I touched her neck and the skin was cold. She smelled of damp carpet, stale sweat and fake-cigarette smoke.

'Oh, god,' said Laura. 'Oh, God.'

'We need to get out of here,' I said.

This was Sikey's work. He'd kill us if he caught us here. After shouldering my bag I helped Jamie up. Laura was immobile, staring at the body.

'Laura. We need to go.'

She pointed at the waitress's body. 'We can't just leave her like this.'

'We need to get out. Nothing we can do.'

'But just lying here, like this.'

I went to the door holding Jamie up, the lighter in my other hand. 'Laura you need to help.' But she'd frozen. Maybe it was the first dead body she'd seen. Or the first murdered one. She was certainly taking it badly. 'Laura, we really need to get out of here.'

From outside there were clangs from the plant and the thud-thud of a machine. Stashing my lighter I opened the door, checking it was clear, leading Jamie out, his body limp. 'Laura?'

She was still inside, knelt down by the body, looking up at me, her eyes filled with tears.

'Come on.'

She came over and hooked Jamie's other arm over her shoulder then we started off across the rough ground, him slumped between us, her breathing heavily. His arm kept slipping off me as I aimed us at the gap in the fence.

'How are you, Jamie?' I said.

'Dunno.' His eyes were shut and his head lolled around.

The guard was ahead of us, near where we'd come through. 'We've got company.'

Laura slowed. 'Christ, this is just what we need.' Her voice wavered and her head was down.

I pointed at the nearest section of fence with my free hand. 'This bit's closer. I'll cut a new hole.'

'We'll be miles from the car, Trent, we'll not make it.'

'We'll be fine.'

She adjusted Jamie's arm on her and we staggered over to the fence, over crushed coal and mud and pools of slick. She slowed as we continued then stopped, her eyes closed. 'He's heavy.'

'Yeah.'

'Can't we rest, just for a minute? I'm all in.'

'Jamie?'

'Hmm?' he said.

'Can you walk?'

'No…Not really.'

I led off again, Laura faltering alongside. We carried on towards the section ahead of us. The guard had found the cut piece, prodding it with his foot. His Alsatian sniffed around at his side.

Laura took in great breaths as I wrapped my arm around Jamie to keep him up. It was hard to say if she was struggling with Jamie's weight or thinking about the dead waitress.

We came to the fence and she leant against it with him propped up. I worked on cutting a new hole, the cutter unwieldy in my hand as I snapped the links, rushing, not focussing, glancing across at the far side where the guard kicked the hole in the fence.

'He could easy see us, you know?' she said. 'What would we do then?'

'Just let me cut.' I clipped the wire, my hands dusty with coal, the fence resisting the tool. There was no use getting into a discussion with her on this.

'We're out in the open, just standing here….'

'I know.' At last the links were all cut. I slid the clippers into my jacket, lifting the chain-link and rolling it up. At the far side, the guard stared at the ground near the other hole. 'You go first,' I said.

'All he has to do is look round and he'll see us…'

'Laura!'

She looked at me. 'Sorry?'

'Go on.'

She opened her mouth as if ready to say something else

and I was tempted to grab her, throw her through, but then she ducked into the gap, turning and squatting as I shoved Jamie to her, pushing him through feet first.

His legs folded up and I twisted him round. 'Come on, Jamie.' He moved his feet but still wouldn't go. Another man had joined the guard and they talked to each other. Then a siren sounded, a low wail in the distance. 'Come on, Jamie!'

He groaned, moving round as I climbed over him, reaching back and dragging him.

The guards marched over towards us, pointing.

Laura hauled on Jamie as well and we slid him right the way through. 'We're not going to make this.'

I lifted him up between us, determined not to snap at her, not to tell her to shut the fuck up. 'Let's go.' We staggered off up the track with one of his arms each.

The guards sprinted over and the dog barked, running alongside.

Laura swayed as we struggled along the track. 'Oh, Trent, I just can't do this.'

'You can.' We ran along the mud and shit towards the car.

The guards had turned round in the plant and now dashed back towards the other hole in the fence, their Alsatian alongside us. They were going to cut us off.

Laura slowed and shifted Jamie's arm on her. 'We're not going to make it.'

I ran faster as Jamie bounced around between us, pulling Laura along. We passed the spot where we'd first gone in as the guards approached it. 'Not far.'

'Oh, Trent...

Jamie jiggled all over the place. Up ahead was the car

with one of the lads leaning against it. There was a bark behind us as the guard released the dog, sending it after us.

Laura dropped to a walk and Jamie's arm slid off her shoulder.

The lad straightened up as we approached, his companion coming round from the far side of the car with the Bull Terrier on its rope. He smiled, staring past us, undoing the knot that held the dog. It leapt forward, towards us.

Laura stopped altogether. 'Oh, no...'

The guard dog and Bull Terrier closed in on us from opposite sides. I pulled the wire clippers from my jacket. It was something but not enough to fight off two dogs. The Bull Terrier was close, its teeth bared and its ears flat against its head. Laura gripped Jamie tight as I raised the tool.

But the Bull Terrier ran past and carried on along the track towards the Alsatian. It leapt at it and there were yelps, growls and barks as the two dogs jumped and bit and twisted.

There was a howl and the Alsatian ran towards the plant as the Bull Terrier strolled back to its owner with blood on its muzzle and hair in its mouth. Passing Laura and me it seemed to glance up.

We hauled Jamie up and lurched on to the Mondeo, leaning against the bonnet. Someone had scratched ARSE along the doors. The two lads moved away, one smiling and patting his dog. 'Well done Hitler,' he said.

'Nice work,' I said to the lads.

The thinner one tickled the dog behind its ears. 'Looks like you owe us.'

'Looks that way.'

Laura opened the back door and we laid Jamie across the seats. I felt inside my overalls and into my jacket then pulled out my stash, taking some grass and offering it to the lad.

He looked at it and bared his teeth. 'We saved your fuckin' skin back there.'

I took out more, handed it to him, leaving me only enough for a couple of joints. The lad gestured to his friend before they both swaggered off.

'Hoy,' said Laura. She pointed at the writing on the car. 'Did you do this?'

The lads carried on, laughing.

I got in as Laura slid onto the driver's seat, starting the engine. We slid our hard-hats off and dropped them in my footwell. She accelerated past the lads, away from the works and through the estate.

Jamie lay in the back of the car, groaning, holding onto his stomach with his swollen hand, rolling his eyes up in his head.

CHAPTER TWENTY-FIVE

Armstrong's House

We took Jamie back to Laura's, deciding that the guesthouse wasn't safe. Parking in the back lane we manhandled him into her house, up to the spare room. His face was bruised on the side and his lip bust, his hand all curled up.

We cleaned him and put him in some men's clothes Laura had lying around. I didn't ask where they'd come from and she didn't say. After that I sat with him as he lay flat out in the bed, a blanket wrapped around him, his eyes closed. I was there for some time.

Late afternoon Laura came up. 'How is he?'

'The same. Weak.'

She nodded, then leant forward and touched his hand. Held it for a second. 'At least he's warm.'

'Yeah. Thanks for helping. At the plant.'

'No problem. We made a good team.' She smiled. 'You know, you don't have to watch him all the time.'

'It's fine.'

'Can I join you?'

'All right.'

She pulled up a chair and we sat in silence for a minute. A cart squeaked past outside and a door slammed.

'That waitress,' she said.

'I know.'

'They killed her.'

'Yeah.'

'Why would they do that?'

I shrugged.

'I can't believe they'd do that.'

'I know.'

Laura shuffled in her seat. She looked around the room and moved the chair. Fidgeted. 'I've got a few things to sort downstairs.' She patted Jamie's arm. Touched me on the shoulder, kept her hand there for a few seconds. Then she went out and shut the door.

Once her footsteps had gone down the stairs I leant over to Jamie. 'Jamie.'

'Eh?'

'Who did this?'

He sighed and rolled around, his eyes closed.

'Who was it?'

'What?'

He shifted his hands to his face, rubbing his cheeks, coughing. 'Sikey.' Then he lifted up a little and half-opened an eye. 'Trent?'

'Yeah?'

'I need a drink.'

I stood up. 'I'll get you one.'

He nodded and closed his eyes again, lying flat on his back. There was an empty glass on the beside table so I took it and went to the bathroom. I ran the tap, let the water flow, holding my hand under it and feeling the coolness. I filled the glass and took it back, lifting his head up, supporting him as he drank.

'It's going to be all right, Jamie.'

After he'd had the water he lay back and was soon asleep. With him dozing I left the room, going down stairs. Laura was in the front room, reading a historical book. She held it in front of her but didn't seem to focus on it.

'He's much better,' I said.

'Good.'

'Had a drink and gone back to sleep.' I sat down, ready for a rest after our last few days.

'So what now?'

'Now?' I'd been so wrapped up in getting him out I hadn't thought about anything else. But I had to keep Armstrong and his people off our back. There was nothing stopping them dropping in here. 'Where's Armstrong's place?'

'His place?'

'His house. Where he lives.'

'Why do you need to know that?'

'I need to make a deal with him.'

'Really?'

'Really.'

'Is that a good idea?' She put the book down, came over and sat beside me on the settee. Her eyes were bloodshot and she blinked a lot.

'We have to do something. It was Sikey driving things at the festival. Armstrong just wants to trade. He's more greedy than crazy. Just tell me where he lives. I'll be careful.'

Laura sat close and took my hand. 'Promise?'

'I promise.'

'Bellendale Road, a big place. It was a hotel once. Opposite the old tax office.'

'Thanks.' I slid out of her grip. 'Can you keep an eye on Jamie?'

She kissed me, just a peck on the cheek, and I took this as a yes.

So I made my way to Armstrong's, walking up the back roads in case Sikey and his friends were around. Bellendale Road was in the west end. It was tree lined with clean pavements. Driveways disappeared into huge gardens, the houses set too far back to be seen. His place was easy enough to find, with his name slapped on a sign at the gate. A long gravel drive led up past shrubs and flowerbeds to the detached stone building, double fronted with fake castellations and leaded windows. There was a garage at the side and the driveway carried on round the back. The gravel crunched as I walked up.

The front door was a heavy oak thing with metal studs and a knocker shaped like a gargoyle. As I hammered on it I thought about my options. But it was hard to guess what it was going to be like in there. I'd have to be flexible. Be prepared to bail out if things got tough. The door creaked opened a minute later, a woman standing there. She was in her early thirties, heavily made-up wearing a black dress and black stockings.

'Yes? Can I help?' Her voice was slow, with some foreign accent.

'I'm here for Armstrong.'

'He's busy.'

'It's Trent. I've got a deal for him.'

She nodded and shut the door on me. I kicked gravel

around as I waited, a crow flapping down and watching me from a bush.

Soon the door opened again and the woman waved me into a panelled hallway, high-ceilinged with doors off at the side. I could hear piano music coming from one of the rooms.

'Mister Armstrong will see you,' she said.

Stairs went up to the right to a landing lit by a tall window, some big ornament beside it. She led me along to the back of the house, past the PVC tables, garish plastic vases with polystyrene flowers and cast plastic statues on stands. The house smelled of polish, fried food and imitation-tobacco. The woman strode on ahead, her backside wiggling in the short dress and her heels silent on the carpet. She stopped at the room that the music came from. As she opened the door it could be heard more clearly, less impressive without the door muffling it. She stood at the side, indicating for me to go in.

The room was large with French windows at the far end looking out to a paved patio and a garden of lawn, low hedges and neat flower beds. There was a croquet lawn that led into an area of ornamental shrubs in the distance. Armstrong sat at the far corner of the room, surrounded by PVC chairs and occasional tables, all nasty bright colours. He was in a yellow polo shirt and pressed trousers, waving his hand as if conducting the music. At the nearest wall a woman sat at a piano. She was in her thirties like the other one but wearing only her underwear. She stopped and checked the music every few notes, her forehead creased.

Armstrong motioned to a chair beside him and I went across and sat on it. The plastic was smooth and slippery, not at all comfortable. The woman played and Armstrong watched, now moving his head to the music, but not necessarily following the rhythm. It was some classical piece, slow and intricate. She stopped, stood up and Armstrong applauded. I clapped twice as she took a bow, her tits drooping forward.

'Should I go now?' she said, her accent foreign too.

Armstrong ignored her and turned to me as she sat back down. 'What do you think of that, Trent?' Talking to me like I was an old mate.

I shrugged.

He leant back and interlocked his fingers. 'I love this kind of music. Amazing. You want a drink?'

I shook my head.

He turned to the woman. 'Get me a vodka, Freda. And not the cheap stuff, you hear?'

She nodded, tiptoeing out.

'So, how are things? How's your friend?' He smiled, all friendly, too friendly.

'Fuck you.'

'It's nothing personal. Things can get out of hand, you know? But points have to be made. Lines drawn under actions.'

'And what about Laura?'

'Sikey and me have had a few words. He's a good worker but, you know how it is. People go too far. All of us....' He waved his hand, made some sound in the back of his throat.

It was tempting to go over to his chair, slap him around a little, like he'd had done to Jamie and Laura. To the waitress.

'Look around you, what do you see here?'

The room was filled with plastic things: seats, tables, vases and lamps, all bright colours. 'Loads of junk.'

'Products, Trent, products. All from my plant. All from my works. All this choice, like people used to have. Have you any idea how rare plastic is these days, have you?'

'No.'

'It's really scarce, I'll tell you that. Like hens' teeth. We make it and fuel and chemicals as well, all from one simple ingredient.'

'Do I have to hear this?'

He snorted. 'It's from coal, Trent, coal.' Going over to a display case he slid something out, taking it to me. 'Look at this, will you?'

It was a piece of coal, sliced open and there was an imprint of a leaf in it.

'You know how old that is?' He handed it to me. This really was some kind of show.

'No.'

'It hundreds of millions years old. What do you think of that?'

'Amazing.' I wanted to take the coal and shove it down his throat. Instead I put it on the table. 'Look, Armstrong, this is all fascinating but I want to talk business.'

'Don't be so hasty, Trent.'

The door opened and Freda came back in carrying a drink. She offered it to Armstrong and he took it without speaking and drank. 'Is this the good stuff?'

'From big bottle?'

He thrust the glass back at her. 'For fuck's sake. The little bottle is the good stuff.' She took the glass and minced out. Armstrong stared at her backside as she left. 'Can't get the staff. Still, she's good at other stuff.' He grinned at me.

'I've come here to make a deal.'

'See, Trent, I'm thinking big picture. Strategically.'

I sat back in the seat and rocked on it, the plastic legs creaking. Twisting round I could see out onto his garden. Beyond the flower beds at the back of the house there was a kind of greenhouse built on, the wood neatly painted, glass intact. What they used to call an orangery. The glass panes reflected the afternoon light.

Armstrong was still droning on. People like him always had to make speeches, like everything was a sales pitch. 'I started small Trent, like you, doing minor deals in Setmarch, some illegal stuff, but I've moved on. I've got plans for this town, ideas to take AHI and Setmarch forward–'

'Look –'

'I can trade with some of the players in the city, for glass and beer and such like, complementary goods, but I need stability. We've done up houses for workers, got half the town electrified and I'm looking at getting the phones going —'

'Save this for your board meeting.'

'I just wanted to give you some context... I do good stuff for this town.'

'And plenty bad.'

Armstrong frowned. 'You can't make a fried egg without breaking the shell!'

The door opened and Freda came back in with his drink. He grabbed it, tasted it and waved her away. 'Proper vodka. All the way from Russia.' He took a good mouthful. 'What was I saying?'

'You were talking about eggs.'

'You really don't get it Trent, do you—?'

'What's the deal, Armstrong?'

He drank and stared at me. 'All right. All right. First of all, I need to know more about what you're carrying. Do you know what it is?'

'Seems you know enough already.' There was no way I was telling him more about Gehenna.

'I get to hear stuff, Trent. I keep my ears open. But let's be straight, man-to-man. Give me the details.'

I drummed my fingers on the side of the chair, a hard rattling sound. He must have spoken to Nixon. That was the only way he'd know what we had. 'I've not really looked at it. Just looks like a pile of papers.'

'Come on, Trent.'

'You seem to be the expert on everything...' There was no harm seeing what he really did know.

'Knowledge, that's what it is. Knowledge on how to find something. Something amazing. Something that will change all the rules. An old world weapon, that's what it is, Trent. There, I've said it, you hear?' He was getting all worked up now. But it sounded like he had a pretty good idea what Gehenna was all about.

'So, say I trade, what would I get?'

He laughed. 'To live without fear.'

'I've emptied the car, hidden the documents. Got Jamie back. You haven't got that much to trade with.'

Armstrong flushed, jabbing his finger at me. 'I've got your valves and I've closed your mechanic's place. And this is my town.' He formed a fist and started banging it on the table. 'This is my fucking town and no one does anything without my say!' He thumped it down especially hard with the last word, spilling his drink onto his pants.

He stood up swearing and shouting for his helpers. When one came in he swore at her and got her to fetch a cloth.

'So that's it?' I said.

'What's what?' He pulled his vodka-infused trousers off his skin.

'No money?' No sweeteners?'

He shook his head. 'That was good vodka. What a waste. What a shame…' The woman came in and dabbed at his crotch as he stood there holding the empty glass.

I stood up, facing him. 'Forget it, Armstrong.'

Armstrong held his hand up. 'Don't get all screwed up. What do you want?'

'I want the valves back so I can get my car fixed. I want fuel. And safe passage out.'

'Right.'

'And I want a couple of thousand. Scottish notes.'

'No chance. No chance.'

We stood in the room eyeballing each other as sounds came from the rest of the house. People working in the kitchen, someone moving around upstairs, coughing. The woman wiping his crotch.

'One thousand, just for goodwill. Take it or leave it.'

'All right,' I said.

'Heron's bridge. Thursday. Seven pm. No later and no messing around, you hear?'

I went for the door, keeping eye contact with him. 'See you Thursday.' I went into the hallway with its plastic vases and polystyrene flowers. Cast plastic statues on stands. Waiting there was the other woman, just standing there. She followed me as I left, slamming the front door behind me.

CHAPTER TWENTY-SIX

Laura's

By the time I returned to Laura's it was early evening. She was cooking something so I let her know I was there before going to check on Jamie. He was splayed out in the bed, snoring, his damaged hand held on the covers.

'Soon be sorted out and ready to go,' I said, sitting next to him, letting him sleep.

After some time I left him and I went down. There were a couple of plates of set out on the table with a glass of cider for each of us.

'I've cooked pasta,' she said, a light in her eyes, a look she'd not had for a little while. Hopefully she'd got over the shock of seeing the dead waitress. As I sat down she grabbed hold of a pan from the kitchen, filled with spaghetti and sauce, dishing it out for both of us.

I tucked in, rolling it onto my fork and sliding it in. It tasted great, really good.

Laura picked at hers. 'Jamie can stay as long as you want, you know. He seems fine in the spare room. He's quite settled.'

'Yeah, thanks.'

'And obviously you can stay. I know you'll want to keep an eye on him. There's plenty of room here…'

'Thanks.' I licked my lips, drank more cider and swallowed. 'Great food.'

For a minute we ate in silence, me swirling up the pasta with the sauce and Laura sliding it onto her fork, eating slowly, watching me. The only decent food I'd had since arriving had been at Laura's. I was so hungry, it was like I was making up for the years of meagre rations on the road.

'How did it go?' she said.

'He's offered another deal.'

'Really?'

'It's not a good one. A little cash. Reopen the garage. Give us our valves back.'

'And he wants your whole load?'

'Yeah, but he's not getting it all.'

She nodded and ate some more, chewing slowly then washing it down with a mouthful of cider. 'And then what happens? After you've dealt with Armstrong.'

'Go to the city, do the rest of the deal.'

'And then you're off?'

'We'll settle with you first.'

We ate without speaking, just the sound of our cutlery; distant noises from the plant. She shifted round until we were face to face across the table, her eyes soft. She was thinking about something but her face was hard to read. Leaning forward her dress showed a little cleavage. She'd put on makeup for the evening as well but I'd been too busy eating to notice.

'I appreciate you putting us up,' I said, giving her a big

smile, to show I really meant it.

'No problem.' She pushed her spaghetti around. 'Listen, Trent–'

'Yeah?'

'It's, well... I don't know.'

I pointed at the food left on her plate. Loads of spaghetti. 'You not want that?'

'No, no, you go on and help yourself.'

I took her plate and slid the spaghetti onto mine, shoving it around with my fork, eating it then drinking the last of my cider. It had been a really good meal. 'I never realised you were such a good cook.'

'No?'

'Yeah, I'm impressed.'

'Thanks.' She messed with her fork, taking deep breaths.

'That's some house Armstrong's got.' Him and his type always had nice places. It was one of their weaknesses. Maybe all the thugs in town got smart houses given to them. 'Does Sikey live up at that end of town as well?'

'Sikey? No, he's up on the Spenwood estate. A nineties place. Detached.'

I finished my food, standing up. 'I'll wash these.'

'Oh, you don't need to –'

'My pleasure.'

In the kitchen I piled the plates up in the sink and ran the tap to fill the bowl, tipping in warm water from the kettle on the stove. Back in the dining room Laura sat at table drinking the last of her cider.

It was odd staying here, me and her eating and drinking together, almost like going back to the old days. With what had happened I'd slipped into it, like putting on a pair of old pants or something.

The bowl filled and I turned the tap off, running water being one of the treats of Setmarch. Bad as the place was, there were conveniences. That was what Armstrong relied on, bribing his workers with home comforts. Home comforts that we'd soon have to do without, once we fixed the car and left. Got on the road again. After the deal Setmarch would just be another place we'd stopped off at. Another on the list.

But it meant more than that. With all the memories. On the road I'd not thought about the past. About Rory and Harry. Laura.

She was entwined in things that had happened to me in the town. Those last few years before I left.

She'd been with me at Harry's burial.

We'd been going out for a couple of years by then and she'd offered to come to funeral without being asked.

Up at the cemetery chapel she'd stood by me, both of us dressed in black, Dad over at the other side with Rory, well away from me. As the vicar said his piece Laura took my hand, not something I normally liked but seeming right on this occasion. When I glanced at her she smiled, just a little, her eyes soft. That seemed to say more than all the religious stuff.

Despite being June it was cold at the graveside. A wind came up the valley and blew at our funeral clothes. Once the coffin had been lowered in Dad and Rory lined up, Laura and me pushed to the side.

Afterwards I walked back with her and for some reason she cried. Even though she'd not really known Harry she stopped and sobbed by the graves.

'Are you all right?' I said.

'Yes. I'm okay.'

'I didn't think you knew him well.'

She shook her head. 'I didn't. It was for the whole thing. You know.'

I didn't know but I held her close and we walked back together, separate from the rest of the family. Later on we'd had our own wake at the pub, drinking until the early hours.

Now here I was in her house. Back with her, kind of. I started on the washing up, stacking the crockery on the draining board as I went along.

As I cleaned the chopping board Laura came up behind me, her breath on my neck.

'Thanks for doing this,' she said.

'No problem.'

'I don't recall you doing a lot of washing up in the old days.' Her warm body was close to me as she leant forward.

'People change.'

'In some ways...' She slid her arms around me, held me as I wiped the soap off a knife. We stood like that for a minute, me immobile. Then she turned me round and as I faced her she kissed me, a warm kiss, my hand still holding the knife.

We slid apart and she smiled at me. 'Want to go upstairs?'

I put the knife down and she led me off.

In the bedroom she pushed me against the wall, holding my hands as she kissed me before undoing my shirt, throwing it onto the floor. Then she knelt and undid my trousers sliding them and my underwear down. With me naked she wrapped her arms around me, pulling me close, nibbling at my ear as I unfastened her dress, took off her bra.

We dropped into the bed and I slid the rest of her underwear off, looking down at her naked body.

Then we made love, our fingers digging into each other's flesh, moving slowly as we always had.

Afterwards, as I lay next to her in the bed she put her arm across me and turned towards me with her thigh on my leg.

'I love you, Trent,' she whispered.

I said nothing, lying there in the dark.

CHAPTER TWENTY-SEVEN

Back to Business

I was up first in the morning, going into the bathroom where the sun shone in under the dark clouds. I turned the shower on and stepped into it, the water running over my head and down my back. How I'd wished for something like this when I was on the road. But everything came with its price, its complication. I lifted my face up and let the warm stream run into my eyes and my mouth, resting my hands against the wall I slumped forward, as the water gurgled into the plughole.

The bathroom door opened. Laura came in and stood by the shower, an outline through the shower curtain. 'How you doing, mister?' She slid her dressing gown off and stood there naked. 'I'm sure there's room for two.'

It was so tempting, her standing there and me here. But it would only make this more difficult, harder to unravel once I had to leave.

'I'm finished,' I said, stepping out, my shoulders slumped as I avoided looking at her.

She leant over, kissing me and putting her arms around

me. 'That was quite an evening we had together, don't you think?'

'Yeah.' I kept my arms loose by my side as she enveloped me, her warm body pushed against me, those breasts and smooth thighs. It took so much effort not to drag her back to bed, make love all morning. 'I'm wet,' I said, reaching over to a towel and wrapping it round my waist before I left the bathroom, leaving her there.

I stood at the bedroom window, staring out and pulling on my clothes. A black cat tiptoed along Laura's wall, picking its way along the rough surface.

When Laura came back through I was dressed. She kept the towel round her and stood next to me. 'Look, Trent, is there something we need to –'

'I've got a lot to sort out.' I didn't turn to face her. Looking into her eyes made it much harder.

'I can help you–'

'No. No thanks. Time's been getting away.'

Her tone changed, hardened. 'I suppose it has. You don't want to waste time, do you?'

I turned to her, with her hair all wet and eyelashes damp. 'Last night was, you know–'

'Oh, I know, me. I know *exactly* what last night was.'

She didn't but she thought she did.

'No time to waste with talk, Trent.' She sat on the bed and folded her leg up, drying her foot with the end of the towel. 'You better get going then. Before time *completely* runs away from you.'

For a moment neither of us moved then I went to the door. She stayed on the end of the bed, her lips tight and one hand now running through her hair. 'See you later,' I said.

She gave a snort and shook her head, not looking at me as I left.

On the way out I grabbed her spare key and a bag from the hall.

As I walked across town I tried to concentrate on what had to be done before we left. Upsetting Laura hadn't been my intention but last night had taken us too far. Into a place that we shouldn't have gone to.

Now I had to get back on track. First I needed to sort the car out.

When I arrived at Dan's the garage's doors were open and Dan was leaning against the frame, smoking. He jabbed his cigarette at me. 'We nearly got closed down cos of you.'

The lad glared at me, his lips curled. The Evora was still parked in there, its seats out, the carpet lifted and wire hanging out of the dashboard. Seemed they'd done some poking around but Gehenna was out of it. Hidden. Dan shook his head. 'And we got broken in to. Someone messed with your car.' If he guessed it was me he didn't let on.

'Have you got the valves?'

'You kidding? They got taken when we were shut down.'

'Armstrong is going to give them back.'

They both laughed.

'I want you to put it back together.'

Dan grunted so I pulled out the shrinking bundle of cash, peeling off a couple of notes. I gave them to him and he snatched them away.

'We'll tidy it up,' he said. 'Don't hold your breath for those valves.'

I left the garage as they flipped the carpet into the car, put the seats back, starting to bolt them in.

Next I had the load to pick up.

I walked across town to the East End Estate, past the shops and the house with the flags. When I came to our old house I stopped on the pavement. A dog barked then something smashed and a man laughed. There was no other sound after that.

I went down the drive, past the Focus and the split back door. The gate in the side fence was shut and I opened it, carrying on into the back garden.

The stones were as I'd left them and I lifted them, feeling around. The soil was dry and I dug into it with my fingers, pulling out the Gehenna's tube and the two rockets. I blew the soil off them before putting them into the bag and going back through the gate.

Instead of leaving I went to the back door, trying to open it. It resisted a couple of shoves so I stepped back, kicking it. On the second kick it split and with the third it burst open, thudding against the kitchen units. Stale air drifted out, the smell of decay and damp carpets.

There was a hammering noise several houses away but no other sounds.

The lino stuck to my feet as I went in. There were boxes stacked up, bags with kitchen utensils in them. The worktops were stained and cupboard doors hung off. The tap dripped a steady beat into the sink.

I went into the hall where more boxes sat on the flowered carpet, the whole place smelling of mildew. In the living room there was a sideboard, stained, gouged and three-legged. There was no other furniture so I went back into the hallway and up the stairs where the wall was marked by outlines from photos. The landing carpet still wore the imprint of two bookcases and there were more ghosts of pictures on the wall. A hiss came from the bathroom at the far end as a tap dribbled brown water into the bath. I turned it off and it gave a hollow gurgle. The shower-head hung broken on its hose, the curtain speckled with mould.

The back bedroom's window looked out onto the garden, a mess of long grass, brown shrubs and weeds. I stood there for a while before turning to face the room. There was a bed and some outlines on the carpet, more imprints of the past.

In the front bedroom there was only a bedside table and marks from a bed patterning the carpet. I crouched down to bed height, staring out of the window at the roofs of houses. Smoke swirled up from the valley and mixed with clouds.

Me, Dad, Rory and Harry had lived here for years, the hard years after Mum died. When Rory had his brain virus and Harry had his final accident.

I set the bag down, opening it. This seemed a good time to have a good look at Gehenna's documents. See what all the fuss was about. I slid it out. The tube was dark, heavy in my hands, flecked with bits of dirt. Apart from one quick glance I'd not had chance to examine it properly. I wiped it clean, opening it, taking out the contents and laying them out on the floor. There were maps and charts, lists of codes and schematics. The first time I'd looked at them it hadn't seemed that special, loads of documents, technical stuff, plans of some kind of ship and sea charts. It was only the Top Secret and Ministry of Defence stamps that gave it an edge.

Others seem to see the significance. When I'd told Sandhu that I had plans for Gehenna he'd got really wound up. Maxwell had kept them well secured. And Armstrong was keen to get hold of them.

So now I took a good look at them. There were six sheets. The one with the Top Secret stamps was cross-sectional plan. But it was clear that it wasn't a ship. It was a submarine. At the bottom it said HMS Gehenna and was dated 2026. By this date I'd left town and stopped following the news. If it was anything like the subs that had been around when I was a kid it had to be loaded with weapons, possibly nuclear. That was what it was about. That was why they were all after it. Weapons. I skimmed through the other sheets. There were two charts showing sea and land, all different shades of green and blue lots of little lines. Odd names and tiny numbers. This had to be where it had last been seen. Or still was. The other documents just had codes on them. I didn't really follow them. But that didn't matter. If this thing was still out there, loaded with weapons, the last person I wanted getting it was Armstrong. Or Maxwell. We'd done the world a favour stealing it from him.

I slid the sheets away and sealed the tube.

I left the house and pushed the back door shut, slipping the tube into my bag.

Back at Laura's I made as little noise as possible when I went in, creeping into the kitchen. I pulled the plinth off the bottom of the sink unit, feeling around. There were a few crumbs of food there, some cobwebs. Opening the bag I took out the metal tube and slid it in before putting the rockets in and pushing the plinth back.

As I stood up Laura appeared in the doorway. 'Christ,

Trent, what are you doing? I thought you were a burglar.'

'Just got back. Sorry.'

She held onto the door frame and looked me up and down, weighing me up. Then she turned and went through into the front room, still distant, upset.

I went and sat with Jamie for the rest of the evening.

Things were moving on. With the payload stashed I was one step closer to making the deal. Once the Lotus was fixed we'd be ready to go.

CHAPTER TWENTY-EIGHT

Harry

The next day I went to Dan's garage first thing. He was there with the lad, pottering around, smoking and drinking. The Lotus was now parked outside, a dilapidated Peugeot 208 having replaced it in the garage. The Evora's cylinder heads lay on the workbench behind it.

'Any sign of the valves?' I said.

'Told you,' said Dan. 'No chance.'

The lad muttered something and they both carried on with their work, bending over the Peugeot's front end.

I inspected the Evora. At least the dashboard was back on and the seats in place. Dan had shut the engine cover and locked it all up. Although it was tempting to argue with Dan, give him a hard time, it wasn't him stalling. It didn't look like Armstrong was going to cough up the parts. I left the garage and made for Bellendale Road. I'd confront Armstrong, make him hand them over. Then I'd take them to Dan, get them fitted straightaway.

At Armstrong's house I hammered on the heavy front door, letting the sound echo through the hallway. After knocking three times the door creaked opened and the same woman greeted me as last time.

'I need to see Armstrong,' I said.

'Mister Armstrong is busy,' she said. 'Are you Trent?'

'Yeah, I'm Trent.'

'There is a message.' She took a breath, thinking it through. 'Parts when trade.'

'What?'

'That's the message. Goodbye.' Then she slammed the door.

Parts when trade. What was that about? I'd get the valves when we traded? That wasn't what we'd agreed. I banged on the door again, not stopping until it reopened.

'Yes?' she said, like she'd never seen me before. This time I didn't ask, pushing past her, making my way in. I burst into the living room but found it empty.

The woman followed me, blocking the doorway.

'Where is he?' I said.

'At work of course. At the factory.'

'Of course.'

I walked out, along the panelled hallway, past the PVC tables, plastic vases and cast plastic statues. The door slammed behind me.

Going to the plant was an option, but it all seemed fruitless. He wasn't going to cough up the valves without Gehenna. At best he'd give some big speech and more false promises. At worst, well, this was his town so there were lots of things he could do.

That was it. That was the Lotus ruined. Without the valves it couldn't be fixed and Armstrong wouldn't hand them over without a trade. And there no way he was getting Gehenna. Especially now I knew what it really was.

I wandered across town, thinking about making a mock up of the Gehenna plans. But the valves had to be fitted once we got them and he'd soon spot fake documents. Or I could give them to him and steal them back. But there was the whole town to hide them in.

So the trip to the bikers' camp had all been a waste of time. Armstrong had beaten us. On this, at least.

I walked up West Road, past the golf course and closed garden centre, still weighing up the options. I carried on to the cemetery. The stone gatehouse was still there, as was the chapel and caretaker's house, though all dilapidated. The cemetery was set higher up the valley than the rest of the town. Below me smoke came from the plant, clouds of black intermingled with white steam that ran in grey shadows across the rooftops and scorched moors. The breeze shook dead branches in the trees as I wandered up through the dry grass amongst stones that were laid flat, past a soot-stained angel and stone teddy bear.

I came to the section on the slope that adjoined the moors. Just off the path were two graves. Harry and Mum's. I'd put off coming here since I'd arrived in town. The wind rattled the boughs against one another as I stared at the weeds around the gravestones. I undid my jacket and knelt down, pulling up weeds and tearing out the grass. Once I'd cleared part of the plot the red gravel showed through. I tugged and dragged at the remaining vegetation, my hands and knees stained green.

I took a rag out of my pocket and spat on it, scrubbing the gravestones, one at a time, Mum's first. The wording appeared out of the filth, her name and age, the date: 14th October 2014. She was only thirty-eight, younger than me now. Then there was Harry's. Twenty-five, that's all he had been. Died 25th June 2024, in that sunny summer all those years ago.

Such a hot summer.

Old-timers had talked about it being as hot as one from the seventies, not knowing that the weather was all going to pot. That there'd be hot summers, followed by no summers, droughts, freezing winters, warm winters. Storms. That the old weather patterns had gone, forever.

It had been the hot weather that killed Harry.

Not directly, but the dry conditions had made us ride faster than normal, pushing the bikes to their limits on the sticky tarmac.

I scrubbed at his headstone, cleaning the filth off it.

That evening, Harry's last evening, we'd really been blasting.

Halfway through the run we'd had a few drinks in The Angel at Laybridge, before riding back to Setmarch, past the castle and under the dual carriageway's bridge. I was on my little Suzuki, him on his newest machine, one of the two Triumphs he owned, his Speed Triple. He was way out in front, the note of his bike's three cylinder engine rising and falling, up and down the rev-range as he eased the power on and off, the bike cranked-over on the bends, flying ahead on the straights. He shot ahead as I trailed some way off, fighting to keep up.

Then he disappeared. He should have been visible on the final straight but there was no sign of him. Passing the bend at the cricket ground I saw the hole in the fence. The smashed wooden rails. Dropping down through the gears I pulled my bike over, flicking the stand down. For a few seconds I didn't move, as traffic droned in the distance and a blackbird sang in a cherry tree at the roadside. Black tyre marks wove across the road, thick black line that twisted and swerved then swung onto the verge; through the fence and across a field, its crop lying dead in the heat.

I removed my helmet and walked over the parched soil, by the snapped posts and rails. I followed the furrow made by his bike, not looking ahead as if that would change what was there, as if not seeing would make it all fine.

There was the Triumph, trapped in the dry-earthed channel it had cut. A spacecraft crash-landed. Meteor fallen to earth. Harry was still on the saddle. I ran over, ready for him to slide off, say, 'Shit, that was a tough one,' or something.

But he didn't move. He was slumped there, his hands still at the controls, the oil light glowing, red. Like the blood that ran down his leathers, onto the dark lump of the engine, hissing where it dripped. It streamed from his neck. Where a shard of wood was wedged.

I turned the bike's ignition off and walked away, slow footsteps across the lifeless field. I sat on the verge by the tyre tracks. I was still there half an hour later when a car finally stopped, the woman driver asking what had happened.

I'd just pointed towards Harry on his bike.

Harry who was now buried in this cemetery.

The wind dropped and the branches stilled in the trees. The sun shone down through the smog but there was a coldness in the air. When the breeze picked up I exhaled.

'So Harry,' I said.

If he'd been alive I would have explained that now was the time to leave the Lotus. His Lotus, the car he'd given me. That it had been a good car and lasted me for over two decades but now it had come to done its last run, Setmarch being its final resting place. I'd have told him it wasn't from lack of trying but the odds were stacked against me.

But he wasn't alive so I left the cemetery saying none of it.

There were things to be done, preparations to be made before we left Setmarch.

CHAPTER TWENTY-NINE

House Call

When I got back to Laura's I packed my and Jamie's bags ready to go. I was supposed to meet Armstrong later but it was the real deal tomorrow, with Sandhu. That was what mattered, what had always mattered. Armstrong was never going to give up the valves so we'd have to go in Laura's car. I'd thought through ways to make it work. We'd make the trade then pick up a second car, bring Laura's Mondeo back and give her a cut of the money. Where we met up could be sorted out later — maybe outside town. But we'd have to abandon the Lotus. Leave Harry's car.

Armstrong had caused all this. He needed to be brought down a few pegs, given something to think about. Him and Sikey needed a kick up the arse.

Laura came home from work, tidying the kitchen as soon as she was in, scrubbing the stove.

'How was your day?' I said, friendly.

She had her head in the oven. 'Fine.'

'Busy in the pub?'

'Trent, what are you after?'

'After?'

She sighed, sitting back on her heels. 'I'm not stupid.'

'No,' I said, 'no, you're not. I need to borrow your car. To meet Armstrong, tonight.'

'Fine.' She returned to the oven.

'And tomorrow. To do the deal in the city.'

'That still going ahead?'

'Yeah.'

She might have made a grunting noise after that, or it could have been the sound of her cleaning. It was hard to say.

When I went out into the back lane, clouds were building up above the smoke from the plant, rising above the town in great dark swirls, the sun dipping below them.

Instead of driving towards Heron's Bridge I turned off onto Quay Lane, skirting the scrap yard with ancient cars piled up, picked bare of all decent parts. I passed the ruined garden centre where skeletal greenhouses stood surrounded by shards of glass, beyond the AHI fertiliser depot and the terraced houses where the tannery workers once lived. I drove on to the riverbank.

The river ran sluggishly between worn stones, thick with turds and food waste, reflecting the orange clouds as the sun burnt down into the horizon. I parked the car on the sandy bank, walking down to the trees at the water's edge. I leant against the trunk of a dead oak, its bark peeling.

Across at the other side was a silver Rolls-Royce. Armstrong walked around it while his driver inspected the bodywork. An orange Nissan 350Z drove down and pulled up beside it, the headlamps turning off. Sikey joined

Armstrong, speaking to him. They were all there with their fancy cars, waiting for me. Waiting to do the deal.

Maybe this was a good time to get even.

I slid back behind the tree and over to the Mondeo, driving off to the Spenwood estate. The houses had neat gardens and some driveways even had cars, though they had odd-coloured panels. Side windows replaced with board. I carried on past the lawns, statues and begonias, pulling the car in opposite a detached house with black fence and black gravel. The dark blinds were drawn and the gravel wore the imprints of wide-section tyres.

Laura said Sikey lived up here. This had to be his house.

No one came, asked me what I was doing there, why I was hanging around. There was nobody in the darkening road, in the gardens or at the windows. I approached the house, along the gravel of the drive, past a rhododendron with no leaves and a defoliated buddleia.

The gate and fence to the back garden were painted black and there was a sign with a picture of a Rottweiler and BEWARE written in red letters. Noises came from the other side: sniffs, growls and shuffles, and there was the smell of shit. I tried the handle but the gate was locked.

Jumping in with a vicious dog was a stupid idea. But without smashing a window or the front door there was no other way in. I examined next-door's fence, looking for a way through. There was nothing obvious. Then a cat came past, some mangy thing with fur missing. It wasn't bothered about me being there and walked on by. I grabbed the creature and it clawed and bit as I pinned it down on the gravel. It got a couple of good nips on my hand but I grasped the back of its neck, taking it to the fence and flinging it over.

Yowls and barks came from the garden and I pushed off from a dead shrub and scrabbled up, pulling myself onto the fence then over.

I landed on flagstones littered with dog turds. The back garden was paved with black stones and in the centre stood a statue of Apollo surrounded by smaller mythical characters. There was a shed and kennel at the end but no grass, plants or flowers. The Rottweiler was the same as the one I'd seen Sikey with in town. It was at the far side, barking at the cat on the shed's roof.

As the cat hissed from its safe position the dog shifted its blunt head, opening its mouth to show loads of teeth, jagged and drool coated. Before it noticed me I went over to an ornament, grabbing the nearest statue. It was a model of Pan holding his pipes, just over a metre tall, solid plastic, marbled grey and brown. It was heavy when I swung it, as I let the momentum pull me round.

The dog spotted me and bounded over on its heavy legs, slobber dribbling from its mouth. A low growl came from it then a sharp bark as it curled its lips back, baring the teeth. But I was already swinging Pan in a low arc, bringing the base of the statue round with a thud into the dog's flank. The dog yelped then growled, now focussed on the moving statue. I swung again and hit it harder, this time in the ribcage. It staggered to one side as Pan completed another circuit now moving fast. The statue's base hit the dog across the front of its skull, sending it off to one side.

As the animal eased itself up I raised Pan before I smashed it down into the dog's head. There was a crunch. The Rottweiler collapsed down onto its fore legs, its tongue lolling out and dark eyes on me, a low whine coming from it. I held the statue above it then rammed down one more time, the dog's head distorting and blood spurting out. It laid still, head sideways, hind legs askew and fore legs splayed as if about to perform some trick.

I stood there for a moment, in the fading light as the blood ran out of its head across the dark flagstones, a stream of red.

Killing it hadn't been part of the plan. Still if it was Sikey's dog that was fair enough.

I swung Pan at the French windows and smashed the door. The glass shattered and I reached through, turning the lock and opening it. Pan had lost one arm and a horn.

The glass grated on the black painted floorboards as I crunched through the living room. There was a leather settee, table, metal lamps, an old TV set and shelves, all black. Above the fireplace there was a framed photo, a rare thing now. It was of a car. Sikey's car that I'd seen earlier. Ancient porn magazines lay on the seat and tables, some open and other closed and dog-eared. There were also DVDs, lined up, all porn ones, presumably why he had the telly. I placed Pan by the TV and picked a magazine up and flicked through it. There were pictures of women with other women or pissing onto men. I threw the magazine aside and walked through into the hall, past a fish tank with black fish. There were shoes piled up at the bottom of the stairs, some men's trainers, black, but also women's heels, small and large.

I walked along into the kitchen. There were dirty plates, opened tins and bottles of beer. There was a knife block and I grabbed the biggest knife.

The door to the front room was locked and I pushed at

it before giving up and going upstairs, the bare stairs creaking.

The bathroom had black towels, tiles and a dark bathroom suit. Even with the light on it was gloomy. It smelled of stale soap, piss and blocked drains. There was a pile of dildos and vibrators in a box and leather straps on the bath taps.

The back bedroom was filled with plywood boxes. Opening one I found women's jackets and coats. Another had blouses and skirts and trousers. A third was part-filled with stockings, knickers and bras. All the boxes had women's clothes in them.

His bedroom had a double bed with metal rails. There was a wardrobe of shirts and tracksuits, all black. There were several free weights on the floor next to a chest expander. The bed had two sets of handcuffs on it, belts tied to the headboard and stirrups with leather straps on the other end. A drawer was open with a tub of AHI petroleum jelly in it and on the floor was an old camera as well as plastic fruit, vegetables and vacuum cleaner attachments. The wall above the bed was marked and scraped and the sheets ruffled and stained.

I left the room and returned downstairs, trying the door into the front room again. It had to be locked for a reason. I stepped back and kicked it. It cracked but held so I kicked again, bursting it open.

The blinds were closed and the room was hot, smelling of oranges and something rotten. I felt for the light switch and flicked it on. The walls were hung with photographs. The pictures were of women, all naked. Some were bent over and others were chained up. Many were strapped to the bed and had the items from upstairs inserted in them.

A few were in the bath tied to the taps and covered in soap. Sikey was in most of the pictures but some had Gaz and Doddsy as well, other track-suited lads on top of the women, under the women — having sex with the women. They smiled but the women closed their eyes or turned their heads away.

I paced around the room twice, my footsteps loud on the bare boards, looking at the photographs of Sikey and his idiot friends. The women.

I raised the knife and slashed at the pictures and flung them off the wall, stamping on them. I swirled, cut and smashed every one.

In the back room, I tore at the furniture, cutting the curtains and shredding the magazines. I put the knife in my belt and grabbed Pan, swinging it into a lamp which flew across the room, breaking against the wall. I kicked over a table, stamping on a leg then jabbing Pan at a shelf, snapping it in two and letting some ancient porn films fall on the floor. Next was the TV. When the statue hit it the screen cracked then split, pieces rattling around my feet. I made my way out into the hall to the fish tank, smashing Pan into it. The glass cracked but held. I swung again, Pan losing another arm, but the tank split, water pouring out. The fish flapped on the floor and gasped, squirmed and died with me standing over them.

Stepping over the small black bodies I went round the rest of the house, kicking out balustrades, breaking ornaments, walking across the beds and chairs with my shoes covered in dog shit. I unhinged doors, broke drawers and smashed dildos and plastic fruit. I used the knife to slash pictures, rip curtains, tear clothes and shred bedding.

I trashed Sikey's house.

When I'd finished I set Pan in the hallway with his smashed arms, split head and bloodstained base. The knife was jammed into the statue's neck.

I left through the front door, out into the fading light, the air heavy. Once in the Mondeo I revved it hard and pulled off fast, away from Sikey's house.

CHAPTER THIRTY

Masonic Lodge

I drove across town past Armstrong's club. The lights were out so I parked outside. The clouds were really starting to build up, great creamy cumulous that mixed with the smoke to hang low over Setmarch.

I waited around for a while. No one came or left. When I went to the front door there was a notice up saying it was closed for a lodge meeting. One of Armstrong's stipulations, no doubt. There were no security staff,

I hadn't planned to go here but this was too good an opportunity to miss.

Taking a screwdriver out of my jacket I went round to the fire exit, feeling around the edge of the door, pushing the tool into a gap. I fed the blade in and levered it as I pulled the handle.

The door eased open. There was a growl of thunder some way off as I opened it all the way, stepping inside.

The club smelled of stale beer and smoke. The door creaked shut behind me and I stood there on the carpet sticky with spilt booze. I took out my Zippo and flicked it into life. It was the same hallway we'd been in the other night, when Jamie was kidnapped. Without all the drunks it looked much bigger. I walked along to the door at the far end.

Thunder grumbled through the building as I went through into the main bar, my Zippo sending shadows round the room, across the flowered wallpaper and chairs set around tables; the bar and darts-board.

I approached the bar, opening the hatch and sliding through. There were bottles of spirits lined up on the wall, all with Armstrong Heavy Industries on the labels. I put a glass to the whisky optic, filling it up and drinking. The whisky burnt and tasted of chemicals so I spat it out. Behind the other AHI spirits there was a bottle of Glenfiddich so I filled a glass, taking a drink, savouring the smoothness. The lighter flickered and I raised the drink above my head, my shadow wobbling across the bar. There was a crack of thunder.

I took out the screwdriver and messed with the till, picking at the locked drawer. With a ching it popped open revealing two bundles of notes and small trays with coins. I scooped the notes up and slid them into my jacket along with the screwdriver. Then I finished the drink, taking the bottle of AHI whisky off the optic. I headed across the room, holding the bottle upside down and letting it pour out onto the floor. At the door I tipped out the remaining whisky and threw the bottle down.

There was a menu on a table nearby and I picked it up and played the lighter under it, turning it in my hand and dropping it onto the floor. It flickered and flared up, the carpet burning with a blue flame as I flicked the Zippo off. I propped the door open with a chair but the fire raced over towards me, licking up the side of my leg and catching my trousers, making me stamp around. I ran along the hallway lit by my burning trousers. At the exit I shoved the handle, spilling into the street.

It was raining, heavy drops that bounced off the car park and I slapped at my trousers, holding the material out to catch water as it ran from a bust gutter. The flames died down, sending smoke up around me and I got back into the Mondeo. The rain drummed off the car's roof as smoke rolled out of the building.

I drove into the storm and left the burning club.

The Masonic Lodge was at the other side of town, but only a short drive. I parked in a side road near to it, just down from the abandoned high school. The rain rattled on the windscreen and poured down the road, streaming into the gutters.

I opened the door and stepped out into the deluge, walking with my jacket over my head, the screwdriver in my hand.

The lodge was set on its own piece of land, behind the derelict chapel and across from the old police station. Its stained glass windows were intact, the stone plinths soot free. A light lit the symbol of compass and the square set up above the doorway. The door was open and two men stood just inside talking to each other, shaking their heads, pulling their tracksuit jackets around themselves. There was a road that ran down to the back of the building.

Rain poured off the lodge's roof, down the gutters to form rivulets around my feet as I walked to the back door. In the car park two other men in tracksuits stood by the cars, probably most of the vehicles in town. The men huddled under an umbrella. Armstrong's Rolls-Royce was parked beside a Mercedes C class with no grill.

So he was here, presumably having given up on dealing with me.

The back door was wooden, painted battleship grey. The paint had peeled and the hinges were rusted. Above and to the side of it a pipe poked out of the wall, black smoke belching out, accompanied by a growl from an engine. I took the screwdriver and slid it along the edge of the door and levered it near the lock. It resisted even when I pulled hard and I had to put my weight on it. Then there was a crack and the blade bust out of the handle. I threw it on the ground, picking up a stone, shifting it from one hand to the other before dropping it. There was no way I'd break in that way, not without making loads of noise. The rain ran down me, into my clothes. Time for the direct approach.

I walked round to the front. One of the men looked up when I approached. Neither were fellas I'd seen before.

'Hello,' I said, all friendly, just another lodge member.

The other man straightened up. 'You're late.' He looked me up and down, especially at my burnt trousers. The two of them were track-suited, heavy built, smelling of beer.

'Got stuck in the rain.'

The first man stood in front of me. 'We don't know you.' He was the wise guy, the one to watch. I flicked out my hand and hit him in the face, a thud that made him stagger back. Not giving him time to fight back I stepped forward and hit him again, this time under the chin, on the saggy skin, stubbled and spot-flecked. He made a gurgling sound then slumped down.

The second man stared at me and as I raised my fist he put his hands to his face so I punched him in the gut, folding him, extracting a sigh. Then I elbowed him on the head and he collapsed down, seemingly out cold.

I was about to check him over when the arms of the first man appeared around my chest, pulling me backwards. I staggered off balance across the foyer grabbing at the forearms that encircled me, trying to pull them off. He dropped himself down, taking me with him and we lay on the floor writhing. Even though this was a real pain I had to admire his style.

As he tightened his grip I grasped one of his fingers and bent it back, making him cry out and loosen off. Then I shot an elbow back, winding him. With his grip loosened I struggled up, punching down at him, hitting him hard on the jaw. He attempted to rise so I hit once more, then again until he was still.

They both lay there, slack mouthed and stinking of sweat. My hands hurt from hitting them and I flexed my fingers. Not a tidy way to gain entrance, but I was in.

The curtains at the front windows had tasselled tie-backs and I pulled them off, putting two in my pocket and going back to the men with the others. Once I'd manoeuvred their hands behind their backs I tied them up, leaving them there in the open, not wanting to drag their dead weight around. It was risky but quicker.

I continued further into the lodge, along the passageway. There were two doorways, one beside me and one at the far end and it was this one I went to, along the thick carpet. The corridor was lined with photos of lodge members in ceremonial clothes, some other ones of men in uniforms, wearing their medals. Setmarch seemed to be the only place where people still took photos. The door was a panelled one labelled *Temple*. Muffled voices came from the other side and I pushed my ear against it. One man recited verse and others joined in on some parts. Taking the tie-backs from my pocket I tied the handles together.

Then I returned to the second door, opening it to the smell of oil and drone of an engine.

I flicked the lights on and went down to the generator. There were wires and switches on a panel and the exhaust disappeared through the wall above the back door. I unbolted the door and grabbing hold of a wire flicked the biggest switch. The generator slowed and stopped. The lights flickered, dimmed and went out. With a yank I pulled the wire out of its connectors, hauling on it again until pinged out of the generator. The room was dark, silent. There were shouts from upstairs.

I slid out of the door into the car park. The men still stood at the far end smoking and talking to each other. The rain had slackened to a light drizzle. On my way back to the car I threw the wire over a wall.

As I got into the Mondeo figures appeared outside the lodge, some with robes on, others in suits. They stumbled around, pointing and waving their arms.

I started the car, accelerating hard and driving off.

CHAPTER THIRTY-ONE

Leave Town

So it was the day of the deal. I'd been up for some time, washing, getting dressed, thinking about things. The plan was still to make the trade then pick up a second car, bring Laura's Mondeo back and give her a cut of the money. After that Jamie and me would be off in our new car, away from Setmarch.

Something wasn't quite right but I couldn't put my finger on it. I'd been so wrapped up in preparing to go, and giving Armstrong and Sikey a bloodied nose, that some of the other details weren't in place.

When I met Laura on the landing I was still working this out. After some awkward pleasantries, vague answers as to what had happened the night before, I thanked her for the loan of her car seeing as it was critical.

'What happens after the deal, Trent?'

'We return your car. Some money…'

'And that's it?'

There was a cough from the spare room as Jamie cleared his throat.

'I guess,' I said.

Laura was up really close, her eyebrows tight down over her eyes, her finger spinning in her hair. 'I want to come with you.'

I didn't reply. This needed some thought.

She pushed past me, going into the bathroom. A few seconds later the shower started running so I went into the spare room. Jamie was sprawled out just like the day before. I said his name twice and he didn't respond, just changing his breathing a little. Even when I opened the curtains there was no reaction. Faint light shone onto his pale face, patched with bruises.

I went downstairs and pulled off the plinth from the sink unit, taking out the Gehenna and flares, loading them into my bag and setting them by the back door. Then I had a glass of water and chunk of bread, chewing slowly, looking out into the yard.

Laura coming with us made sense. Jamie wasn't well so he could rest in the back of the car while she read the map, drove her own car back, helped out, no more than that.

When I went back upstairs she was dressed, waiting outside the spare room. 'Well?' she said.

'I just want to check with Jamie. Make sure he's all right with it.'

She sighed and I led her into the spare room. 'Jamie,' I said. He didn't respond. 'Jamie, it's time to do the deal.' Even when I shook his arm he didn't wake. Sweat ran down his forehead and there was a slight wheeze at the end of every breath.

Laura came up close to me. 'He's not well enough to travel, Trent. He needs to rest after something like that.

263

He got kicked around and was dumped in a wet container. It takes time...'

'We haven't got time.'

'Maybe you should rearrange.'

'We've got to go. We need to deal.'

Laura put her hand on my arm. 'I know this means a lot to you, but taking him along, well, it wouldn't help.'

'Just give me a moment. With Jamie.'

She stayed there for a minute then walked out of the room, leaving me next to him in the bed.

I grasped his good hand between my own. 'Jamie. Can you hear me? Jamie, we need to make the deal.' He lay there and panted. His injured hand was red, the skin tight. The eyelashes on one eye flickered but otherwise there was no movement on his face.

'Sorry, Jamie,' I let go of him, going out.

Laura was on the landing. 'So, what happens?'

The bathroom window was red with the sunrise.

Leaving Jamie here wasn't great, especially after what I'd done the night before, but we had to meet Sandhu. We had to trade today. 'We leave Jamie. You and me go.' I said. 'But I'd prefer to drive.'

'Okay.'

We went out into the yard, me carrying the payload and rockets in the bag. There was a red glow on the horizon as black smoke hung across the town. I put the bag into the boot and we got in the car. I sat in the driver's seat, Laura next to me.

'He wasn't up to the journey,' she said.

'I know.'

'You really care about him, don't you?'

She was starting to needle me. I slid the key into the

ignition, started and pulled off into the sunrise. 'Let's get going.'

We drove down to the end of the lane, onto Hope Street. A car was parked in the middle of the road, an orange 350Z, the paintwork gleaming. Sikey's car. He was beside it, stretching and looking at the houses, reading from a piece of paper. As I pulled out he glared at me, getting into the Nissan.

I revved the Mondeo and accelerated hard onto the main road.

Laura grasped the grab handle. 'What's going on?'

'We need to get moving.'

Sikey's car came up behind us, the lights on as we raced into town. The roads were empty and we flew though the marketplace, up Moor Road, by the billboard that said AHI ACADEMY: A FUTURE FOR YOUR CHILDREN.

Laura glanced back. 'Trent!'

I swerved onto a side road. 'Is Mill Road still open?'

'What's this about?'

The Mondeo slew around as I pushed it into another bend. 'Is it?' The Nissan was up close, the lights hidden by the Mondeo's rear hatch.

'Yes, it's open but—'

'Fine.' I took the Mondeo over a junction and past the old council offices, swinging hard left onto Quay Lane, past the scrap yard and straight on. The car pitched and tossed on its decades-old suspension, handling well but no match for a sports machine like Sikey's.

'Hell, Trent, you're going to kill us!'

The 350Z was close, its snout just behind the Mondeo. I accelerated and turned off to the right, just before the overgrown garden centre. The Mondeo's tyres howled as we slid around the corner and the front end lost grip, under-steering so that I that had to throttle back. The car gripped again, tucked in and turned as I put the power back on.

Laura banged her shoulder on the window. 'Trent! For Christ's sake!'

'Sorry.'

The road narrowed and I took us over a rise, braking with increasing pressure over the brow, scrubbing off much of the speed. We dropped down to a ford, the car in second but I slipped it into first as we entered the water. It sloshed around as we drove through, gurgling past the sills as we came out onto the other side, steam rising up from the exhaust. There was a hiccup but the car kept running and I drove on in first gear keeping the revs up.

Sikey's car appeared over the dip, the engine snarling as he flew into the ford. The water sprayed up over the bonnet, round the windscreen and the car pinked, gave off steam and stalled. Water swilled around the Nissan in great waves as Sikey tried the starter. It turned over but didn't fire.

'What on earth's going on?' said Laura.

As we crested the rise Sikey was still in his car, the window open and his arm out. As he raised his gun we drove off, onto the East Road.

CHAPTER THIRTY-TWO

The City

We drove out of town as the sun rose up, burning down on us, unimpeded by cloud. We made our way down the valley, past the old paper factory and the abandoned industrial estate. After crossing the river by the East Bridge, we came to the junction for the dual carriageway but instead of joining the by-pass I swung left onto the old road, the one to Laybridge. 'Let's stay on the back roads for now.' I didn't explain that this was for the sake of memories, that I wanted to relive some stuff from the past. Laura didn't ask, maybe she knew or maybe she didn't care, either way she never said anything.

'So what was that with Sikey?' she said.

'He's crazy.'

'Thought he'd be sweeter after you cut him and Armstrong in on the deal.'

We passed the field Harry had crashed in. The fence had gone, the cherry tree just a stump. The ground was filled with sickly potato plants. There was no sign anything significant had ever happened there. Though I felt like stopping, I carried on. There was no importance to that field other than in my head.

'You did do the deal, didn't you?' she said.

We went by the old cricket ground, now overgrown, the clubhouse stripped of its boarding to leave bare foundations.

'Trent?'

'Yeah.'

'So it went okay?'

'Fine.' There was no use telling her what had really happened. None of it would matter once the real deal was done. Even though Jamie wasn't here we could still pick up a replacement car, slide him into it later and head off. With the money from Sandhu we could do what we liked. As the day went on I'd iron out the other details.

We passed the castle ruins and went under the dual carriageway's bridge with no sign of any other vehicles on the road. I eased the car round the roundabout, joining the main road, its surface pitted and broken.

'Rules of the road now,' I said.

'Oh? What rules are they?'

'There are no rules.'

'Oh, of course, those rules.'

We passed a lorry tipped on its side, its panels and mechanics stripped, then swerved round a burnt out car, some hatchback, probably the work of the bikers or other neo-reivers.

We drove on towards the city for the next half hour, dodging derelict vehicles and litter on the road, a couple of carts pulled by sickly animals. Laura chatted on about how it had been along here at one time, when there was lots of traffic and people travelled all over the place. As we passed the tattered airport sign she talked about some holiday she'd had as a kid, to a Caribbean island with warm seas and white beaches, like the stories I told Jamie.

Up ahead was a bridge. On it were motorbikes, maybe a dozen, beside them their double decker bus. Just what we didn't need. They were parked so they faced up the road, towards us, like crows on a fence. In the centre of them sat the tall biker with plaits, astride his tourer. We drove on towards the bridge as they gazed at us. Their eyes tracked the car, stared at me, then Laura.

'You never know, maybe they are just curious,' she said.

'That's not what you said when you drove us to the woods.'

'This is the open road. It's different.'

But not that different. And she didn't know about what had gone on in the woods, when I'd killed one of their women. There was a chance they hadn't seen me or wouldn't recognise me, but it wasn't one worth risking. I put my foot down and let the car pick up speed. There was a chorus of starter motors and the roar of engines. Some bikes revved-up with a shrill bark.

'Christ,' said Laura.

The first of the bikes appeared alongside us as we passed the end of the roman wall. It was a hand-painted cruiser, its saddle held together with tape. The gruff drone from its water-cooled four changed tone as the rider took it up and down the gears. I swung onto the A1, the Mondeo lurching as we navigated the roundabout onto the slip road, its surface cracked and strewn with broken glass and rusty metal. We joined the main carriageway and I swerved round the debris. So did the bikers. We passed over the section of the bridge that was intact, by piles of scrapped vehicles, mountains of rusting steel. Up ahead smoke sat above the city. There was a side road to the brewery, where steam rose up from chimneys as carts lined up amongst men with guns.

'What are you going to do?' said Laura.

There was a junction up ahead, the turning for the old Shopping Mall and I knocked the car down a gear. The engine pitch rose as the rev counter's needle swung round the dial. Two racers joined the cruiser, their four-valve heads clattering amongst the primary-drive whine and cacophonous exhausts.

I gripped the steering wheel and jerked it, taking us down the slip road. The bikes swerved to the side as we accelerated hard and flew straight onto the roundabout. With its tyres squealing the Mondeo slid sideways. Laura clung on as I steered round and straightened up, taking us into the complex.

'Trent!'

'Hang on.' I kept the power on and drove towards the building, swinging into a car park entrance way. The car bounced onto the ramp, going round and round and up. At the third level I pulled past burnt out vehicles and smashed shopping trolleys. We flew to the far end. There was a stripped Toyota Avensis, the rear hatch and prime parts gone; a Transit van similarly picked clean. I squeezed the car in between the two, turning the engine off.

Before the bikers found us I was out, ripping the bumper off the Avensis and laying it across the front of our car, popping open the Mondeo's bonnet and dumping in a few busted engine parts that lay around. As long as they didn't look too close we were just like any other stripped vehicle.

The growl of the engines echoed through the car park. I lay across the Mondeo's front seats, drumming my fingers on the steering wheel. Laura slid into the back, staring up at the roof lining, her playing cards gripped in her hands.

'Are we going to be late for the deal?' she said.

'Not much we can do.' We weren't late but there was no saying how long we'd have to hang around, if we got away with it. At least we were half hidden.

'Are you sure they will wait?'

'I'd think so.'

'It's a shame Jamie couldn't make it.' The car steamed up and she wound down the back window letting the stale air out and the sound of the bikes in.

'Yeah.'

'So what happens after the deal? Now he's not with us?'

'Pretty much the same as before. Grab a car. Go back. Pick him up.'

'Drop me off?'

There was a low rumble from the bikes as they rode around, the engine notes rising and falling.

Even though the plan was to leave, get out of Setmarch straight away, Jamie needed to recover. That would mean hanging around in Setmarch, chancing that Armstrong didn't stick us on his punishment lorry. Sikey and him'd be really pissed off with what I'd done. If I'd known how poorly Jamie was I'd not have caused all that chaos.

Laura held up a playing card, an ace of spades. 'I know you've been up to stuff, Trent.'

'Stuff?'

'All this skulking round, meeting Armstrong. That thing

with Sikey. I know you're up to something.'

In the past there'd been no plan, nothing complicated to work out. Me and Jamie had gone to one town, traded, picked up stuff, moved on. Stopping in Setmarch had screwed all that up.

'I've gone along with it, but I'm part of it now. I'd like to know where it's all going, that's all.'

There was a bark from outside, a loud howl from a four-into-one and a whistle of gears. I lay down on the seats, peering through the steering wheel. A Kawasaki appeared between the Transit and Avensis, a decrepit late model, hunching down on its forks, the seat gone and engine casings scraped. The rider wore an open faced helmet and tattered leathers, standing on his foot-pegs to look around. The cam-chain growled like an angry terrier as the bike settled to uneven idle, stopping between the van and Toyota to show a rear wheel of furred alloy and gap-toothed sprocket. Laura sat up a little, staring at me, some look that meant something. The bike rolled backwards propelled by its owner's booted feet. He turned towards the Mondeo and he seemed ready to step off the bike.

Then he banged on the Transit's flank before winding on the bike's throttle, swinging a wide arc and short-shifting back through the car park, the engine a choir of exhaust, worn chains and under-shimmed valves.

'That was close,' she said. The Kawasaki's exhaust yowled off into the car park, joining the other distant growls.

'Too close.'

'So, what's the plan, Trent? After the deal?'

I messed with the ignition key, turned it on, lighting up

the dashboard with a small click from a relay. The bikes were like the hum of bees round a beehive; wasps around a jam jar.

'You working the roads again,' she said. 'Trading in the borders?'

'Not if I can help it.'

'So when Jamie's better, you and him will be off again? Just the two of you in some old car?' Laura ran her fingers through her hair, narrowing her dark eyes.

'Something like that.'

'Where will you go?'

'I don't know. Somewhere else. Somewhere quieter.' It sounded like the bikers had given up on us.

With a shrug she wound the window further down. 'Maybe, you know, I could join you? After the deal. The three of us.'

The only sound was a dull drone from the bikes, now fainter.

'I wonder if Jamie will be okay?' I said, opening the car door.

'He just needs to rest.'

'I meant being left in the house. With Sikey around.'

'Sikey wouldn't go that far.'

'He did with the waitress.' I stepped out into the car park. The bike engines were fainter. I walked round the wires and upholstery stripped from the Toyota then threw the busted bumper off the Mondeo and cleared all the duff parts out of the engine compartment, shutting the bonnet.

Laura stood beside me. 'So what do you think?'

'Think?'

'About me coming with you?' She gave me a smile and

leant against the Toyota.

These were the details I'd not sorted. What happened about Laura. About Laura and me. I couldn't imagine her spending time on the road. Then again, with the money from the deal I wouldn't need to trade anymore. It'd mean the end of couriering. Finding somewhere to settle down. 'You've got a lot tied up in Setmarch. With the pub and your house.'

'The house is rented. I can sell the pub. AHI would snap that place up.' The smile was still there but she ran her fingers through her hair, twisted a few strands around.

'And that's it? You'd sell up and leave?'

She looked away from me, across the car park. 'I never meant to stay in Setmarch. Not forever. But it's hard to leave a place. When you've got stuff. I suppose I needed something to happen. Something to shake things up...' She faced at me, wide-eyed with a slight frown, like she was waiting for me to give the right answer.

'I need to check on the bikers.' I turned away from her and walked over to the parapet. The road below was clear apart from several bikes that accelerated back along the A1, where the road snaked along the river's edge towards the west end of the city and factory stacks poured black smoke.

So Laura wanted to join Jamie and me. Would that work? Despite all those years in Setmarch she seemed to have stayed out of Armstrong's pocket. Not been corrupted. And we'd worked well together in town. Made a good team. Once the deal was done we wouldn't be on the road anymore. With the money we could do whatever we liked.

I went back to her. 'They've gone. We can go.'

'So what do you think? About me joining you?'

'It's a possibility.'

She rested back against the Avensis, with its dashboard hanging off, seats ripped and wires hanging out, running her hand over the twisted door frame. As I opened the Mondeo's door she leant over to me, pulling me close to her, kissing me. I held onto her, gripping her tight.

We stood like this as the bikes' rumble faded into the distance

CHAPTER THIRTY-THREE

Meet Up

We drove past the Angel of the North, its wings sprayed with graffiti and peppered with shotgun marks. We carried on into the city through the south side between rows of dilapidated houses. I told Laura where we were meeting Sandhu, down by the quayside. Normally Jamie did the navigating but today it was her job.

She examined my map, an old battered thing, one of many we'd kept in the Evora's glove compartment. 'Okay, turn down here.'

We carried on down towards the river, passing an upturned car, bricks in the road and smashed bottles. Three lads sat on a wall and one threw a stone which bounced off the roof. As we carried on round a bend we came upon a long queue outside a shop with wire meshed windows. People with bags lined up on the pavement, silent as they walked forward. Two men with batons stood at the doorway.

I drove on down the hill.

'It's just round here, I think,' she said.

I slowed the car and pulled up on the side of the road, winding down my window and turning the engine off. There were sounds of singing, shouting and glass breaking.

'It's at the end of that road there,' she said. 'By the river. Maybe we should walk?'

I laughed. 'Are you serious? There'd be no car to come back to.' Starting the engine, I slid it into gear, driving down the hill.

At the bottom, the road swung round towards several bars and cafes, derelict and windowless. Beyond a smashed fence the river flowed past, brown and sluggish and we pulled up by the pavement facing a Jaguar S-type, its gold paintwork gleaming despite the smoke veiling the sun. I got out of the car and Laura joined me.

'Sandhu's car?' she said.

'That'll be the one.'

Gulls flew overhead, their calls echoing off the buildings.

Two men stepped out of the car, one old, thin, dark-haired and dark-skinned, Sandhu. The other was in his twenties with a similar complexion but shaven–headed. They both wore sportswear and had gold chains around their necks.

The rear doors of the car opened and another man stepped out: heavy-built, middle aged and white. He wore a dark suit, white shirt and bootlace tie, his thinning hair combed over his head. It was Maxwell.

'Fuck,' I said.

'What?' said Laura.

'The payload. It was his.'

Maxwell grinned, a wide smile across his heavy-jowled

face. His eyes sparkled, those cruel eyes. There was a roar from an engine and a BMW appeared from the side road, a silver 5-series. The car stopped and blocked the road behind us.

Maxwell stepped away from the Jag. 'Hey, Trent!' he shouted. 'You fucking owe me.'

The gulls cried overhead and there was thud from somewhere across the city, possibly an explosion.

'Yeah?' I said.

'Come on, you know what you owe. Don't fuck me about, Trent.'

'I'm here to deal.'

'Ha! You've got nothing to deal with!'

I pointed at Sandhu. 'I'll deal with him.'

Maxwell laughed. 'We've already spoken, me and Bal. He knows the fucking score!'

'It's a deal or nothing.'

Maxwell clapped his hands, high up like a flamenco dancer. The door of the BMW opened and Nixon stepped out, sliding a pump-action shotgun from the back seat. He walked round and joined Maxwell leaving another man in the BMW. 'Hello, Trent,' he said, like we were old friends.

We really should have left him in that upturned car.

Maxwell smiled. 'You're screwed, Trent. You'll have to hand the whole lot over. No funny business, you hear?'

I went to the back of the car and Laura followed me.

'Just give it to him, eh? We can't take on all of them,' she said.

'You think he'll let us go?' Opening the hatch I undid bag, taking a rocket and the payload out.

Laura grabbed my arm. 'Trent, come on, let's just give them the load.'

I shook her off and walked around to the side of the car, unscrewing the metal container and holding the flare under my arm.

'Hah,' said Maxwell. 'We going to have a firework show?' But he looked at the open Gehenna tube. That got his attention.

I took out my Zippo and flicked it into life. It blew out so I relit it. 'Either we do a deal or I blow everything.'

'Don't be a twat! You're outnumbered!'

I played with the lighter above the documents.

Maxwell shuffled around. 'Trent, listen, don't be hasty! You got any idea what that stuff is? What it means? Burning it won't save you.'

'That so?' I said.

'That's a real game changer. Whoever gets his hands on that will really wipe the floor.'

'But it'll burn a well as any other paper.'

'Don't be daft, Trent, that's worth more than you'd guess.'

The lighter was still lit, held above the tube. If Gehenna meant that much, could make such a difference, he wouldn't risk it getting damaged.

Sandhu's man and Nixon moved forward, hesitant steps as they looked at one another and back to Maxwell. Nixon raised the shotgun, pointing it towards me but he didn't shoot.

Then I shifted the lighter to the rocket. It was time for me to do something while they dithered. The fuse caught and hissed as it burned. The men stayed where they were as Laura grabbed for the flare.

'Stop him for fuck's sake!' said Maxwell.

Nixon raised the shotgun so I ducked behind Laura's

car, pulling her down. When I flicked my head up he fired, spraying pellets across the roof of the Mondeo. As Laura tugged at my sleeve I shifted the lit rocket to my other hand and bowled it under her car, sidelong across the road. Watching through the Mondeo's windows I saw it spin over towards Maxwell who jumped out of the way, letting it go under the Jaguar. He backed away from Sandhu's car pointing at it. 'Fucking stamp it out!' he said.

Nixon fired again, smashing the passenger window of the Mondeo as Sandhu shouted something to the younger man, going behind his Jaguar. Laura crouched next to me with her hands over her ears.

The rocket burst into life and shot up into the wheel-arch of the S-type, a stream of flame firing out of it. Nixon had gone round to the other side of the BMW with Maxwell while Sandhu peered underneath his car, grabbing at the rocket but keeping his hands away from the flames.

I opened the Mondeo and got in, dumping Gehenna on the back seat. I started the engine and shouted for Laura to join me. She jumped in as I revved the car, slamming it into first and pulling off towards the BMW.

I accelerated hard, the Mondeo mounting the pavement, clipping the rear of the BMW, shifting it forward. With my foot hard down we flew up the road, the wheels clawing for grip and engine screaming as I held it in second.

There was a bang behind us, followed by cracks and pops then a louder explosion.

Without slowing we carried on up the hill, past the upturned car, bricks in the road and smashed bottles. Lads pelted the car with pebbles as we roared past the shop with its queue; the men with batons.

'We need to hide out,' I said.

'Christ, Trent, that was crazy.'

'You got the map?'

'I thought this was just a deal? What's going on?'

'You got the map?'

'It's here somewhere.' She fumbled around, picking up the map from the footwell, shifting it. 'I don't know… we could try here.' She pointed off to the left.

I swung the car up a side road, past boarded houses, rubble and a pack of dogs tearing something apart. We turned down another road and came to waste ground with a smashed play area. I drove onto the grass and crept the car forward, down towards a clump of undergrowth, parking behind it.

Laura put her hand to her forehead, closing her eyes. There was glass all around her from the bust window. 'I can't believe you did that.'

'They wouldn't have let us go.'

'But you blew his car. Jesus. You might have killed someone.'

'Or we might have been killed.'

We sat in silence. There were shouts and distant crashes from outside. Smoke rolled over from the far side of the city but above us the sky was blue, the sun burning down on the straggly bushes and play area with its empty frames and cracked concrete.

'What now?' she said.

'Lie low and wait.'

'Can't we just go?'

'We'd struggle to outrun the BM.'

I messed with the CD player, tugging at the disc

jammed into it. She ran her finger across the jagged glass of the passenger window. Tuning the radio I picked up nothing but static and background noise before finding a station playing old dance music then one where someone screamed, the scream going on and on. I turned the radio off and stepped out of the car, taking Gehenna and going over to a wall, sitting on it. The river shimmered beyond the rows of houses and thin white smoke rose up from where Sandhu's car had been. Maxwell might still be there or he could have left straightaway. He was hard to predict. There was a loud crack from several streets away and laughter.

Laura came and sat beside me. 'Is that the deal screwed?'

'Seems so.'

'Is that it?'

A car revved up not far away, a powerful six-cylinder machine, like a BMW. Grabbing Laura's hand I pulled her over to a house. The door was boarded up so I kicked at it as the sound came closer. On the second kick the door burst open letting out musty air. We dashed in, slamming it behind us.

The engine's growl came and went as it drove around the nearby streets. I peered through a gap in the door frame but there was no sign of the BM.

'My car's out there,' she whispered, her face lit by light through a poorly boarded window.

Raising my hand I put a finger on her lip. Her eyes widened and she frowned but she didn't say anymore. There were no more car sounds, just occasional laughter; things breaking. The dust made me want to sneeze but I held it in.

After a couple of minutes I eased the door open. There was no sign of Maxwell's car. We went out, both of us coughing.

'Can we go now?' she said.

'Yeah.' After putting payload in the boot we left, past boarded houses, rubble and the pack of dogs, now dozing in the sun.

We drove out of the city in the damaged Mondeo. Back to Setmarch.

CHAPTER THIRTY-FOUR

Candy

I sat at the bar in the Turk's Head, topping up my empty glass and slugging the whisky down. There was only a little left in the bottle and I poured it out, drinking it, slamming the glass on the bar.

The barman came over. 'You wanting some more?'

I shook my head and stood up, wobbling. After getting back I'd done little else but drink, sitting here all evening, blowing some of the money from Armstrong's club. There didn't seem much else worth doing, seeing as Gehenna wasn't traded, Jamie was still resting and Laura wasn't saying much. I'd expected her place to be trashed after what I'd done to Armstrong's club and the Masons. Even they seemed to have lost interest.

The barman frowned. 'Hey, you okay?'

'Fine.' I stumbled across the room, my footsteps slow, unsteady as I went out onto the pavement. It was dark outside, faint light coming from buildings. A gap appeared in the smoke and stars shone through, specks of brightness in the black.

A woman came up and stood in the pub's doorway, side lit. 'You enjoying the view?' She had blonde hair, a handbag on her shoulder and wore a short skirt. She was familiar, smelling of soap and vodka.

'I know you,' I said. Her skin was orange tanned, a good bit of cleavage on show. 'Candy?'

She raised a finely-plucked eyebrow. 'How sweet, you remember.' She adjusted the front of her dress, pressing her tits together. 'Want some company, big guy?' She prodded my shoulder. 'Just for fun, you know?' She flicked her hair back and offered her arm to me. 'I've got an idea where there's a party.'

I took her arm and let her lead me on, since I had nothing else to do.

We headed across town, past the gangs of drunken men and the women who sang ancient pop songs. She told me about how great the party was going to be and how much I'd enjoy it. She pulled a bottle of AHI vodka out of her handbag and we both drank from it, as we carried on down Quay Lane, by the bare outline of the garden centre's greenhouses. We passed AHI Fertilisers where a cracked spotlight caught the dust-filled air and lit the carcasses of dismantled cars in the scrapyard across the road. We carried on until we came to a row of terraced houses by the old tanning works. Several were boarded up but light came from the windows of one where loud music thudded through the stonework.

'Here we are, party man.'

I let her direct me in.

We pushed through a hall of people drinking and smoking, into a room lit by candles on the fireplace and windowsills. An old record player rattled out music, wires running out of it to two car batteries. The song was fast, discordant with incomprehensible lyrics. Three women danced in the middle of the room with one man. Two of the women had their arms around him while the other danced in front of him. Couples sat on the floor on beanbags, some drinking, others smoking and one pair making love. The room smelled of fake tobacco, whisky and sweat.

Candy tilted her head and smiled at me. 'Like the look of it, lover boy?'

It reminded me of somewhere, somewhere almost forgotten. Somewhere safe. She got up close to me, grabbed my hand and put it onto her leg, her bare thigh, the skin warm, smooth and soft.

We drank from her bottle. 'You want to take a look around?' she said, dragging me by the arm. We shoved our way out into the hall and up the stairs with its ripped carpet and loose banister. Two women waited to get into the bathroom, both in short black dresses and with dyed blonde hair. A man lay asleep on the floor, his shirt undone. The music thudded up through the building.

Candy opened a door into a small room. It was a bedroom with an iron bed, a table and a wardrobe. A candle burned on the windowsill and she picked up another lying beside it, lighting it from the first. They cast sallow light on the unmade bed, used condoms and a pair of knickers on the floor. Several more packs of AHI condoms lay on the table next to an old engine part used as an ashtray, filled with stub ends. Pushing the door closed she shoved me against the wall, kissing me hard on the lips as I slid my hands up her skirt, feeling her underwear and the soft flesh underneath.

She stepped back from me, dumping her handbag on the bed. She pulled her top off and undid her skirt, standing there in her underwear, the skin on her legs rippling as she sidled over to the bed and lay on it. 'Want to join me?'

I took my jacket off and threw it onto the floor, slipping of my boots, dropping my trousers and falling next to her. She rolled me over and sat on me, pinning me to the bed as she undid my shirt. With her head leant forward she kissed my chest and worked her way down my body.

I closed my eyes and sighed as she ran her mouth over me and caressed me. She rolled down my underwear then stopped. I opened my eyes and her face was up close.

'I need the toilet,' she said.

'You're kidding?'

Grabbing her clothes she shrugged and went out, slamming the door behind her, rattling it in the frame. I lay on the bed as sounds from downstairs came up to me. The music was slower, quieter, some ballad that I didn't know. There were shouts from several people and the music sped up, turning into a familiar old grunge song.

I sat up, reaching over to grab Candy's bag to have another swig of her booze. The bag had gone, as had my clothes. I slid off the bed and looked under it to see if they'd rolled underneath but there was no sign of them, just my boots and the detritus from earlier visitors. When I tried the door it was locked. There were voices outside - a couple of women arguing and a drunken man but no one who sounded like Candy.

She'd taken my clothes and locked me in.

I tapped on the door, then banged louder but there was no answer. The door was hinged to open inwards so when

I yanked on the handle it came off. Ramming it would have jammed it harder into its frame so I didn't even bother.

I went to the window. It was an old double glazed thing, the seals blow so it was filled with condensation. When I grabbed the handle it didn't move, either locked or seized. Outside I could see the low roof of the kitchen, pitched towards the yard, the cracked tiles letting light up from the room below.

The music stopped and there were raised voices. Heavy footsteps came up the stairs and I heard Candy outside. She was talking to two men, one who I recognised as Sikey. She'd got Sikey with her. The voices came closer and Sikey laughed, a low gruff sound, no doubt pleased to have me trapped.

I had to get out, fast.

Pulling the sheet off the bed I wrapped it around me like a toga, slipping my boots on. Then I picked up the ashtray, tipping the stubs out. It was a piston from a lorry engine, blackened and scorched beyond use, the rings melted into place. Putting it on the windowsill I slid the table over to the door, putting the candles on it then hauling the bed up against it, wedged tight. As the key rattled in the lock I grabbed the ashtray and swung it against the bottom windowpane. It cracked but held. Swinging harder the glass smashed into large chunks, two dropping out. I hit again, now catching the second pane, shattering it onto the roof outside.

There was a thud as they charged the door. I leant backwards and kicked the remaining glass out, clearing as much as I could while the table and bed shifted from the door's movement, the candles sending rippling light round the room. Hanging onto the window frame I swung through, keeping my back raised from the shards that pointed up towards me while avoiding one that hung down.

When the door flew open the table fell across the room and the candles died. I planted my feet on the roof, slipping on the busted slates, still holding onto the window. With a flick I let go, flying out, the sheet tagging on a splinter and coming off me. As I clattered towards the edge I grabbed for the sheet and caught hold, twisting round when it jerked tight. I was splayed out across the tiles, my feet in free space and arms at full stretch. A head appeared through the window, Robson's blank face gazing out.

'He's here,' he said, turning back.

Then there was a ripping sound and I flew off the roof, still holding the torn sheet, smacking into a woodpile and rolling onto the ground. Sikey growled something out of the window as I stood and pulled the sheet around me.

'Trent!' he shouted.

I stumbled out of the yard as two shots roared from the window, one zinging off the ground. Sikey shouted my name again as I joined the alley at the back of the houses. I ran into town wrapped in the sheet.

CHAPTER THIRTY-FIVE

Gaz

When I got to Laura's she only let me in after a few minutes of hammering at the door. I tried to explain what had happened but she said nothing, giving me a good looking over, prodding the sheet. She turned and went upstairs when I got to the part of the story about meeting Candy.

I lay on the settee with the sheet as my bedding, soon settling into deep sleep.

A loud bang woke me up. It seemed only like minutes later. Early light shone in through the blinds so some hours had passed. There was more noise from outside, a crash and a thud then a crack. I rolled off the sofa. Then there was a smash and a crackle. I peered through the blind at the smoke that spilled over the wall.

I went upstairs and craned my head through the bathroom window. Flames came from Laura's Mondeo out in the lane, feeding a cloud of black smoke that rolled across the houses.

There was a thump and the gate to the back yard burst

open. Gaz slunk in, sidling along the wall, a sawn-off shotgun in one hand and a can of fuel in the other. He put the can down and made for the back door, pulling up the collar on his tracksuit.

I went downstairs and into the kitchen, crawling along the floor. The backdoor rattled as he pulled at the handle. I crouched down and flicked a knob on the cooker, lit the gas under the kettle that was on the ring. Then I opened a cupboard to slide out the biggest frying pan before I reached into the knife drawer and took out a carving knife.

The kettle hissed as it warmed up and there was a crack as Gaz levered something into the door frame. I put the pan and knife on the worktop and moved up to the door. The key was in the lock and his outline was clear through the glass. I opened the kettle's lid. There wasn't much water in there and it was already bubbling at the edge. Gaz bashed against the glass panel in the door. I unlocked it and stepped back.

When the door burst open he flew in and I picked up the pan and swung it, hitting him on the forehead so he staggered around, one hand to his head and the other on the gun. I grabbed the kettle and threw the contents at him so that the hot water hit him in the face, making him cry out.

I picked up the knife. 'Drop the gun.'

He staggered and shouted but held onto it, a dark-metalled sawn-off, not the piece of junk Doddsy used.

'Drop it.'

He turned towards me, only one eye open, waving the shotgun around and pointing it at my feet.

'Drop it, Gaz.'

He swung the gun up and fired, an explosion that blew

a hole in a cabinet and filled the kitchen with shrapnel and smoke.

I thrust the knife at him just as he stepped forward. It was to prod him, warn him that he had to drop the gun. The blade caught him just below his ribcage but he stumbled towards me and it sank further in. He gasped and straightened up, grabbing for the knife, dropping the gun as his hands spasmed, his neck arching. He opened and closed his mouth but made no noise, pointing at the knife's handle and staggering towards me. I backed off as he groped for me, his eyes wide and a guttural sound coming from his throat. I pushed him away and he slumped against the worktop then fell forward, collapsing onto the floor, groaning as the knife was forced deeper into him, the blade angled upwards. He moved his arms and legs as if to crawl, twisting on the ground, grabbing at the knife and writhing, his eyes bulging. He lifted his right arm up towards the shotgun. Then he slumped forward and didn't move.

I stayed where I was for some time, the kitchen now quiet. Then I leant over to the body, touching the warm skin on the back of his neck, a crimson pool forming around him.

Laura appeared in the doorway in her dressing gown. She stared down at Gaz, opening her mouth but no words coming out.

'He wouldn't drop it,' I said.

'Trent, what the hell have you done now?'

'He wouldn't drop the gun.'

He lay sprawled on the floor, blood all around him. 'Oh my god, what have you done?'

I shut and locked the back door before going to Laura,

stepping over Gaz's body. Gaz's dead body.

'If he'd put the gun down it would have been fine,' I said. 'He trashed your car. Tried to break in.'

'Christ, Trent, is he, you know?'

'Yeah.'

I'd expected something back from Armstrong's mob after what I'd done. This looked like Sikey's work, sending one of his thugs out. But it was odd only sending one, Gaz on his own.

Maybe he'd sent more.

I grabbed up the shotgun, pushing past Laura.

I went to the front room's window. Robson and Doddsy were at the front door, messing with a can of petrol. I slunk out into the hallway, to the door. They muttered outside as the fuel sloshed around.

I shoved the gun through the letterbox. 'Get the fuck away from here!'

There was scuffling and agitated voices, movement visible through the small glass panel. Then I pulled the trigger and the gun fired its last cartridge, a great roar that shook the weapon in my hand and thundered through the hallway.

When I opened the door I saw the pair of them running off. Neither had been hit, which was a shame.

When I went back through to the kitchen Laura was in the same spot, staring at the body. There were probably words to say, things that would have made her feel better, though it was hard to be upset about Gaz.

So I just stood there with her, next to Gaz as he bled on the floor.

And there was a lot of blood in that body. 'We need to get rid of him,' I said.

Laura faced away from me, unable to look at him. 'You do, Trent. You need to get rid of him. You can handle this.'

He lay sprawled, his podgy face slack, wet lips open, this red pond spreading out, filling the floor. 'I need your help. To move him.' Times like this I didn't feel anything, like it was something distant from me. Stuff had to be done and I just got on with it.

'I can't.' She closed her eyes. 'You're asking too much of me, Trent.'

I went over to her and put my arm around her, as she took deep breaths. 'It'll take two of us to get him out.'

She opened her eyes and gazed down at the body splayed out on floor. 'You killed him,' she said. 'You killed him in my house!'

'He's just dead.'

She looked away, out of the window, her eyelids red. Turning to me as if to speak she spun around and walked out of the room.

I knelt by Gaz. His skin was warm, dry. There was a smell of blood and something sweet. I reached into a drawer and pulled out a towel then I grabbed the knife and eased it free of him. It was in deep and had to be wiggled out. I dropped it into the sink then shoved the towel into the wound, holding it there with the top of his elasticated pants. There was blood everywhere so rinsed my hands and the knife. A thud came from the black lane as something blew on the Mondeo. It shook the windows and there were clangs as parts rained down on the yard.

The towel in Gaz's wound seemed to stem the bleeding so I knelt and felt through his pockets. There were some coins, a pack of AHI gum and four shotgun cartridges. I took the ammo and unwrapped a stick of gum, flicking it into my mouth, taking away the taste of booze from the night before.

Laura came in wearing dirty jeans and a jumper. 'Here you are, use this.' She handed me a sheet and dropped another on the floor.

I chewed. 'What for?'

'Are you eating something?'

I pointed at Gaz. 'It's his gum.'

She groaned. 'Wrap him in the sheets,' she said, standing over me, her hands to her eyes.

I fed the material round his back, wrapping it around him, doing the same with the other sheet. He was covered apart from the top of his head.

'All done.' I said.

'Christ, do you have to chew that gum?'

I took it out of my mouth and held it. Searching around for somewhere to put it I pulled the sheet off Gaz's head and shoved the gum up his left nostril.

'Jesus Christ, Trent, you really are…' She unlocked and opened the door, stepping out into the yard. I joined her. The sun was rising into the smoke across the town. The Mondeo added its own plume that rose and fed into the dark blanket. Twisted and burnt components from the car lay on the ground. She went to the gate, looking out at it as it burned, already blackened. 'Jesus Christ…' She crossed her arms in front of herself, hunched up, smaller than usual. I enveloped her, holding her for a minute, as her breathing slowed and she made a sound from the back of her throat.

'Are you crying?' I said.

'No.'

'It's all right if you are –'

She pushed me off, walking away. I followed her into the kitchen but left her to wander off into the house, get her thoughts together.

I had Gaz to deal with. First I grabbed his feet and turned him round. Then I dragged him outside, laying him against the wall in the yard.

There was a shed at the far side and I opened it. Inside was a bucket, an old broom and rusted tins of paint or something. I went back to Gaz and hauled him over to the shed with my hands under his armpits, walking in backwards. His heels slid over the scorched parts from Laura's car. Once he was all the way in I stepped over him to get out, shutting the shed door. I went back into the house.

That was enough for now. There were more important things to sort out.

CHAPTER THIRTY-SIX
Patch Up

I changed into fresh clothes and knocked on Laura's bedroom door. When I went in she was sitting on the bed, dressed but not doing anything. Just staring out of the window.

'Are you in work this morning?' I said.

'Yeah. Yeah.'

'Do you want to meet up?'

She looked at me for the first time. 'What did you do with him?'

'He's in the shed.'

'Christ…'

'It'll do for now.'

She sighed, her face expressionless. 'What happens now?'

Armstrong and Sikey were stepping up the fight. We needed to leave Setmarch. But with the Mondeo gone we had no car, no way to get away. Because the deal hadn't gone through there wasn't enough money for a new car so there was only one option. Fix up the Evora. It wasn't ideal but it was all we had. 'I'll talk to you later. At the Feathers.'

When she didn't reply I went downstairs, grabbing a bag, slipping a few bits and pieces in before going out.

The air was heavy with smoke and I pushed through AHI workers as I made for Dan's.

When I got to the garage him and the lad were outside, smoking imitation-tobacco. The Lotus was still at the side, parked by the wrecks.

'I need my car fixed,' I said.

Dan jerked his thumb back to an Astra in the garage with the back end jacked up. 'Got a snapped spring to sort out.'

'I need it tomorrow.'

'We've got other stuff to do. Anyway, tomorrow's Sunday.'

'I need it all put back like it was.'

Dan shrugged. 'Can't do it.'

I dropped the bag and grabbed Dan by his overalls, pulling him up close. There was no time to reason with him, chat him up. A more direct approach was needed. 'I need the car.' The lad looked over. Dan's lips tightened on his cigarette as I shook him. 'Tomorrow.'

'Armstrong said we can't. He took the valves.'

'Carrot or stick?'

'What?'

I let go of him, opening the bag and taking out the shotgun, the sawn-off barrels stained with blood. I held it under Dan's chin. 'This is the stick.'

Dan swallowed hard and looked down at the gun as the barrels pushed into his skin. The lad made some noise and stepped forward. They knew that the gun could blow his head off, send his brains into the air in a pink spray. That's what I saw looking into their eyes.

I felt in my pocket and brought out some cash, a few notes from the money I'd stolen from Armstrong's club. 'And this is the carrot.' I shoved the cash into his overall pocket, the rough material of it greasy.

'Well?' I said.

His eyes bulged. 'It's not that simple –'

'I think it is.'

'Armstrong will –'

'Forget Armstrong. He doesn't need to know about this.' I pushed the gun harder under his chin. The lad stepped back and closed his eyes, putting his hands to his ears.

Dan's chin shook, the cigarette wobbling in his lips. He smelled of tobacco and sweat. 'The old valves are shot.'

'They'll do. There's more money. Or…' I cocked both barrels and placed my finger on the triggers. This was the moment. If he didn't do it after this, he never would.

'Okay. Okay!'

I let go of him and he straightened his overalls. He took his cigarette out of his mouth, staring at the gun then he rubbed his chin, the cigarette shaking in his hand.

I lowered the gun, taking a breath. 'See you tomorrow.'

Dan frowned but glanced at the lad before sliding the cash out of his pocket. As they both examined the money I backed off into the lane. Once out of sight of I opened up the unloaded shotgun, sliding a couple of cartridges into the empty breech and dropping it into my bag.

The Feathers would only just be opening up but I was ready for a drink.

I had to push through a crowd in Back Lane, people standing around, talking, shaking their heads. The pavement was strewn with burnt wood and shattered glass.

Laura was there amongst everyone, facing the pub. What was left of the pub.

The doors lay on their sides, charred chunks, a glass pane showing part of *The Feathers* etched into it. The filthy sign still hung on the wall, now black and misshapen. The windows were gone, their frameless spaces open into the blackened interior.

Laura shook her head. 'I can't believe it. I can't believe what they've done. This was all I had. This was my work.'

'I'm sorry,' I said.

Her footsteps were slow as she made her way to the doorway, kicking at the debris and stepping over the smashed doors before carrying on inside. I followed her, crunching glass and charred wood under my boots.

She stood beneath the ruptured ceiling and near the bar, now black and split. Ash lay around her on the floor that was littered with fragments of tables and chairs.

'It looks worse than it is,' I said.

She kicked a table, causing it to collapse in a pile of charcoal. 'Christ, do you have to be so damned sensible about it all?'

'Sorry.'

'This is your fault!'

'Not directly—'

'Can't you take some responsibility?' She picked up a charred table leg and jabbed me with it. 'All your fucking fault, Trent! You and your fucking plans.' She kept prodding me harder and harder but I didn't move or resist. It wasn't exactly my fault but she had a point. She carried on then smacked me with it before dropping it onto the ground, into the ashes.

'Sorry.'

'And stop saying that! It just a word, it doesn't make it any better!'

'I know.' I headed over to the bar, round to where the optics had been. Most of the bottles had cracked, empty of their contents, but I found one intact. Wiping the soot off I saw that it was cognac. I took it and went back over to her, kicking up grey dust that floated in the still air, a stinking cloud.

Laura had lost her business and it was my fault.

Like what nearly happened last time.

I unscrewed the cognac and took a swig, coughing. It wasn't real brandy, more likely Armstrong's stuff. As I drank it Laura walked around the gutted bar.

This time her business was finished. That's what they'd threatened to do last time, all those years ago when I'd had to leave town.

I'd not wanted to leave but I'd had no choice.

It had started to go wrong when I helped Harry with his dodgy deals, shipping dope and pills into town through a few couriers. After his death I took over the whole lot.

When the stuff arrived I met them down at the old supermarket, now demolished for AHI's plant, and picked it up, paying in cash.

Then I stashed it in Laura's flat, at the bottom of the drawer I kept my clothes in. Someone must have informed on me because one night the flat was raided.

It was one o'clock in the morning and Laura had just come up from the bar, tired and ready to rest. I was tinkering on with some parts from my car. As I was cleaning up there was a knock at the door and Laura went to get it. From the living room I heard her turn the key, but then the door burst open with shouts and lots of thumping around. Several armed men charged into the flat, the private-security thugs that had taken over after all the police cutbacks. One twisted Laura's arm up her back and another groped his hands across her body. As I ran over to her a third one cracked me over the head.

When I came round I was tied up and lying on the floor. Two of them stood over me, one really old guy and another middle-aged. There was no sign of Laura. 'What's going on?' I said.

The younger one held up a bag of pills, much more than I'd had in the drawer. 'We found these.' His partner laughed.

'So?'

He kicked me in the ribs, a hard jab from someone who'd done this kind of thing before. Enjoyed it. 'There's other stuff. We're taking it and you're going away.'

'It's for personal use.'

'We've found guns as well. You're in big trouble.'

The older fella held up a plastic bag with a revolver and two semi-automatics in it.

'I don't do guns,' I said.

He grinned. 'Seems you do.'

They'd set me up. Whoever informed them was probably a competing dealer, wanting me out of the way.

The younger one leant down towards me. 'You and the woman, you're going away for a long, long time.'

'She's nothing to do with this.'

They both laughed.

'She'll go away and lose all this.' He waved his hand around the room. 'But….There could be a way to sort this problem.'

He went on to say that if I left town within the next forty-eight hours they'd leave Laura out of it. As long as I didn't come back to town again, ever.

So I'd gone. I'd left the town. And her.

But this time it was going be different. I'd be here for her.

'Now you'll have to come with me,' I said. 'I've still got something to trade.'

'This was my place. I've lost everything—'

'It'll work out.'

Laura said nothing at this but her face softened a little. I passed the bottle to her but she pushed it back, heading outside, stopping at the split door frame.

As I joined her she took the cognac and drank hard, wiping her mouth on her sleeve. She picked up a piece of glass with part of the pub's name on it, twisting it round so the light caught the sharp edges. Then she threw it into the burnt-out shell and turned away.

We both walked back to her house in silence, her leading.

Armstrong and his people really were playing it harder now and we needed to get out. But before we left we had to find somewhere safe to stay. And make him back off.

Once we were at her place she settled in the front room with a glass of gin. I said I was going out for a while, to sort things. That I wouldn't be long.

She made some sound and looked at me for the first time, her eyes red rimmed.

'It's all going to be fine. Don't worry,' I said.

'Don't worry. Really?'

'We'll work it out.'

She threw her glass at me and it bounced off the wall.

I thought about talking through plans with her, try and cheer her up. Instead I let her be. It seemed sensible to give her time on her own.

Anyway, I had more to do.

I took the bag with the shotgun and the set of AHI overalls I went up to East End Estate, towards Dad's but not stopping at his place, instead walking up and down the road. Most of the houses in the street were empty, abandoned, decaying. Dad's house was too obvious a place to go but one of the others would do fine. Armstrong wouldn't guess we'd picked somewhere close by, with any luck.

Choosing one house at random I kicked in the door and went in. There'd been a water leak and the carpets were white with fungi, rotting. The place smelled like a fish shop, from the days when there were fish shops. When I tried the taps in the kitchen they were dead, to prevent further leaks presumably, which was going to make things tricky. The next one had had a fire but there were some tins of food left in the kitchen cupboards, which I slid into my bag.

The third house was the best of the lot. The taps worked and there were some old beds. Many of the front windows were boarded up but that didn't matter, in fact it was an advantage. Emptying my bag in the kitchen I went back to Dad's place. The house still had that smell of damp and neglect. I went round the rooms, tipping out every box, going through it all, seeing what was useful. Most of it was junk. Old books, smashed lamps, maps, some screwdrivers, a crowbar, and cracked photo-frames. The whole lot clattered on the floor as I turned the place over.

In the kitchen drawers and cupboards there was the usual stuff. Cutlery, pans and cracked crockery. There was also an empty soup tin on the windowsill that rattled. I tipped it out, going through foreign coins, bottle tops, rusty keys for mortise locks, Yales or windows. There was a Ford one as well, for the Dad's Focus by the looks. Shoving them back in the tin I slid them into my bag and went out. Kicking a fence panel out of each of the back gardens I was able to ferry stuff along without being seen on the road.

Once that was all done it was time to have a chat. I slid on the AHI overalls and hid the shotgun then set off for the plant.

I was ready to talk to Armstrong.

CHAPTER THIRTY-SEVEN

Offer to Armstrong

I joined the afternoon shift, dressed like everyone else. There was a chance someone had noticed the overalls were missing but my guess was stuff went astray all the time in somewhere this size. That was what I hoped.

I went into the factory alongside all the other workers. The fires in the furnaces lit the plant orange, smoke rising up around me. In the toilets I slid the gun out of my overalls and into the bag. It was loaded with two cartridges, just in case Armstrong had some of his thugs with him.

I wasn't sure what mood he'd be in after me trashing the club and Masonic Lodge; Sikey's house. But Laura's car and The Feathers were now wrecked and he didn't know what I'd done to Gaz so maybe we were even.

I carried on through the factory, the place stinking of coal and chemicals, until I came to the steps for the office. The door was glass paned with MANAGER DO NOT ENTER written on a brass plaque. I strode straight in. It was a large room with a desk, several chairs, wall charts and four filing cabinets. Armstrong was at the desk, papers spread out in front of him and a pen in his hand. Windows looked out on the factory.

He sat back in his chair. 'Well, well, well,' he said, looking behind me, as if expecting more people. As if Gaz or Sikey would be herding me in.

I grabbed a chair and pulled it over. 'I want to deal.'

He slid the pen into its holder, shuffled some of the papers and opened a drawer, dropping them in. 'Do you, now, Trent. That sounds familiar.'

'It's time to talk.'

Sitting upright he leant on his elbows, adjusting his shirt-collar, his lips tight. 'What happened to you the other day? Wasn't that the time to deal?'

I shrugged. 'I didn't like the set up.'

'Is that so?'

'We need to make a new deal.'

'I sent Gaz with a message for you,' he said.

'Yeah?'

'Don't suppose you've seen him have you?'

I shook my head. 'Not that I can remember.'

'Gaz's just a foot soldier, a doer. He knows the line. He doesn't get carried away. Now if you're planning on getting even with what happened to your friend...? Well, remember Gaz has folks, people who care.'

'I'm sure deep down he is a lovely man.'

Armstrong pointed at me. 'You know, things can get out of hand, Trent, things can go so you don't know where the line is and when you've crossed it! You don't want to get run out of town again, leant on and scared off –'

'You want to deal or not?'

He coughed and reached over to a drawer in his desk. I

slid the shotgun out of the bag and aimed it at him and he moved his hand back, staring at the gun. 'What makes me trust you this time?' he said.

'Maybe now's a better time.'

'You caused some chaos the other night, mind. Maybe I don't want to deal with you anymore.'

'Business is business. I still have the documents.'

'Perhaps I'm not interested?'

'Yes you are.'

He eyeballed me for a good minute. 'Say I *did* want to deal, what would I get?'

'Same as before.'

'Really? How do I know it's worth what you say?'

'You know it is.'

Putting his hands flat on his desk he licked his lips. 'Just to show I'm reasonable, a thousand, take it or leave it.'

As he leant in towards me I drummed my fingers on his desk. 'As long as you back off. No more visits.'

'Sounds reasonable.'

'And I want the valves back. The new ones.' If I had those we could be off.

Armstrong smiled, a nasty grin. 'Oh, don't want you running off. You try and leave town and I'll have my patrol pull you in.'

I glared at him but the grin remained. He wasn't that stupid.

'Do we have a deal?' he said.

'All right.'

For a moment neither of us said anything or moved. Then Armstrong thrust a hand out to me. I didn't respond until he waggled it and I reached out, shaking it, his grip tight. Then he leant back, flicking his feet up onto the desk, so I could see the soles of his shoes, plastic things. Around us the plant rattled and rumbled. 'So this deal, how would it happen?'

'We meet up somewhere I like.' I picked up one of Armstrong's pieces of paper and started to doodle a map. 'How about—'

Armstrong shook his head. 'Oh no, we meet here.' He jabbed his finger on the desk. 'At the plant. Somewhere secure.'

I shifted the gun from one hand to the other, giving the impression I wasn't sure about this, that it didn't suit me, which it did. I didn't have the details but somehow I was going to disrupt Armstrong's little empire.

'All right. Couple of days time?'

'Monday. In the morning, here…at ten.'

I got up, sliding the gun into my bag.

Armstrong stayed behind the desk, his hands flat on it, surrounded by his cabinets and charts. I left the office, going off through the factory and away from him.

CHAPTER THIRTY-EIGHT

Evora's Back

Laura spent the rest of the evening packing up. She stayed in her bedroom and only came out to collect a few bits and pieces. I told her about the new deal with Armstrong. How it would keep him off our back. She muttered something about it being too little, too late and went back to her room.

When night fell I sat in the back room with the shotgun, just in case. No one came but I stayed awake the whole time.

At first light Laura was up, clattering around before coming down sometime later. When I went through into the kitchen she was there, sorting through more stuff, still in her dressing gown.

'I'm sorry about this,' I said.

'Hmmm.'

'I didn't mean it to go like this.'

She turned to me, holding a spatula. 'Just leave it, Trent.'

So I left her to her packing and went to Dan's garage.

The Evora was already parked outside, looking surprisingly good in the morning sun. Dan and the lad were beside it, each with a mug of tea and an AHI caramel wafer. They drank and ate, staring across the lane at the waste ground with the weeds and rubble. They didn't look at me.

I walked around the car. 'All fixed?' I said. The car's engine cover was shut and the paintwork wiped clear of fingerprints.

Dan grunted.

I tapped the Lotus's flank. 'How's it running?'

He chewed on his wafer, his lips smacking, mumbling something that was lost with all the food.

'It's got the original valves back in?'

He thrust his wafer at the car. 'This took us all of yesterday. Into the evening.'

'It's running like it was before?'

When he shrugged I got into the car. The key was in the ignition so I started it up. It ticked over with an uneven beat and when revved up it misfired and hiccupped. The revs dropped and it stalled so I started it again.

Dan tapped on the window, his mouth full of biscuit. 'You owe us. For labour. And some parts.'

I revved the engine, slipping it into gear, pulling forward a little, just to try it.

'We've spent time on this!'

I knocked the Evora it into neutral, blipping the accelerator to keep it running. I felt around in my pocket, taking out the rest of the cash I'd stolen from Armstrong's club. Then I rolled it up into a bundle, opened the window and held it out. 'Don't spend it all at once.'

He grabbed it without a word, counting it as I put the

car first and pulled off.

The Lotus hesitated and hunted as it eased down the lane. In the mirror I saw the lad join Dan, his mug of tea and a caramel wafer still in his hand. They both stared down at the cash as I left in the car.

It ran like a bucket of nails across town, but it did run.

I parked it behind the burnt-out Mondeo and flipped both of the seats forward before I went into Laura's house.

She was in the kitchen just standing there, one arm crossed around her waist. She'd changed into jeans and a checked shirt, her hair tied up.

'You ready to move out?' I said.

'Suppose so.'

'There are a couple of things we have to do first.'

'Oh?'

'We need to get rid of Gaz's body.'

She groaned and closed her eyes, putting her hand to her forehead. Although we could have left Gaz's body in the shed there was no need for Armstrong to find him. That would really push up the stakes.

'I can't, Trent,' she said.

'We have to.'

'This is too much.'

'It's just got to be done.'

I led her to the shed opening the door and going in. She stood in the yard, gazing off at the sky and the wall. At everything apart from what was inside.

'This won't take long.' I bent over his body, now smelling of shit and decay, sliding my arms under his shoulders. 'Can you grab him?'

She stooped and took hold of his wrapped feet. 'You owe me for this, Trent, big time.'

I stood up and so did she, raising the body, cold and heavy. He'd stiffened at an odd angle, half-curled up. We walked out towards the car but going through the gate the sheet slid off an arm. It was rigid at his side, crooked at the elbow, the fingers discoloured.

'Christ, Trent, it's his arm!'

'Just look at me.'

'I thought you were going to wrap him up properly, you know?'

'Look at me.'

She looked at me as we continued on to the Evora. I popped the door open with one hand before crouching down and creeping into the back of the car, pulling the body into the tiny rear seats. She let go of his feet and they stuck out of the door, his body impossible to move.

'Laura, please.'

Twisting her head away she grabbed his trainers, lifting as I dragged him in, a gaseous fart rasping out of him. I had to haul him right to the far end and wedge him in diagonally, his head against the car's roof. Then I squeezed out, flipping my seat down. He stank and I waved my hand in front of my nose.

'This is just a big joke to you,' she said.

'No, it's not... '

'Something to laugh about. A good story.'

'You feel better once this is done.'

She sat in the passenger seat but kept the door open, her hand over her mouth. Then she jerked forward, leaning out and retching into the lane. I patted her back as her body convulsed.

'You all right?' I said.

She heaved once more but nothing came from her.

Wiping her mouth with a hanky she straightened up in her seat.

I slid a pack of gum out of my pocket but put it away again. 'You ready to go?'

She nodded, her eyes closed. A dog barked in the next street and someone slammed a door. Laura's eyes tightened at the sounds. The car smelled of vomit. Gaz's rotten body.

I started the engine and she curled up on the seat, pulling her knees up to her as we drove off. She wound her window down as we drove across town.

We went to West Bridge, not far from the old mill feed. It was a narrow bridge that ran over Mill Burn and led to a disused quarry. Even when I'd lived in Setmarch it hadn't been much.

Laura stared ahead, shaking her head as I parked the car halfway across the bridge.

'You going to help?' I said.

She said nothing so I stepped out, going over to the edge of the bridge. The road was split and potholed and stones had dropped from the top of the parapet. Below the fast water foamed and gurgled past, turds and toilet paper appearing in the flow.

There was no one around. No vehicles or people.

I went back to the car and opened my door, folding the seat forward and tugging the sheet off Gaz.

The body lay in the foetal position and I took hold of the trousers, dragging him over the doorsill. He was heavier than ever and as I pulled, his arm caught on the rear seatbelt and his tracksuit bottoms slid down to show blood stained boxer shorts, paunch and pubic hair. The towel I'd stuck in his wound fell out as I jiggled the body onto its side and over the sill. With a last tug his head thudded out onto the road.

Laura made some sound, as she sat twisted away from me in the passenger seat.

I adjusted my grip, scraping him along the road to the edge of the bridge. This section had lost several stones so it was lower than the rest but there was still half a metre to clear. I dropped down and wrapped my arms around him, lifting him, using my hands to support me against the wall. He really was heavy. His arms jutted forward and he smelled of blood, rot and damp hair. The tracksuit bottoms rolled down below his backside so that I was pressed against his filthy underwear. He was now fully upright, like a curled-up and stiffened drunk leant against the bust wall.

I braced myself read for the last push. Back at the car Laura gazed out of the windscreen in the opposite direction, towards town.

I slid Gaz's pants up and hauled him some more, so his upper body protruded over the side of the bridge, pivoted on his crotch. Bit by bit I shoved him further across the parapet, his tracksuit's material tugging on the rough surface. When his weight shifted sufficiently his feet rose up and I had to grab his ankles, holding the cold skin as the body balanced on the edge. He lay across the smashed wall, awkward. I let go and stepped back so that his legs swung up and he flipped over.

When I looked over Gaz's hand waved from the water. He was jammed on some rocks and the water dammed up behind him so that he swayed in the current. I grabbed a stone and chucked it at him but it bounced off his head. The next two plopped into the burn. Then the built up water started to drag him along and his body glided down towards the river, away from town.

I returned to the car and sat next to Laura. 'All done,' I said.

We drove back to Laura's in silence.

After I'd parked in the lane we put all our stuff from the house in the yard, ready to load the car.

Then we helped Jamie down the stairs. He barely supported his own weight to begin with, Laura grunting as we held him up, but by the time we were in the dining room he'd straightened up. He walked with just a hand on each of our shoulders.

We slid him into the back of the Evora, where Gaz's body had just been. His lips had pinked up and he sat upright as Laura packed the bags around him. The holdall with the payload and one last rocket went in the passenger footwell, between Laura's feet.

'You all locked up?' I said.

Laura pulled some face, her mouth all screwed up but she didn't say anything.

We drove off, past her burnt-out Mondeo, away from her house, the Evora's engine backfiring.

We headed across town, past Dad's house with the old Focus. We carried on to the empty houses I'd selected, parking on the drive beside the side door.

Laura stared out. 'It doesn't look much of a place.'

Three lads pushed a wheelbarrow along the road behind us, piled high with old bits of machinery.

'We'll be safer here.' I got out and Laura joined me. 'Ready?' I said

'I suppose.'

We eased Jamie out, helping him into the house and up

the stairs, to the back bedroom, laying him out on an old bed.

Once he was settled I took a panel out of the back garden's fence and drove the car onto the lawn, out of the way.

Then we cleared the rest of the bags. Laura took hers into the front bedroom while I dumped most of my stuff with Jamie in the back room. As Laura unpacked I took one bag down into the living room. I walked up and down the worn carpet listening for loose floorboards. There was one that creaked and rattled so I rolled the carpet back, feeling around. It levered out easy enough and I slid the bag into the void under it. The bag with Gehenna and the rocket.

Once the plank was back in place I lowered the carpet.

CHAPTER THIRTY-NINE

New House

For the of rest the evening Laura tidied the new house, getting me to shift and carry. AHI ran town gas through the old natural-gas pipes and I bypassed the meter and bodged the connection so we could cook. We'd brought candles so the lack of electricity didn't matter. By the time we went to bed the place was functional. I slept on the floor in Jamie's room and Laura had the front bedroom alone. As Jamie snored I heard the town around us: drunks that passed by and sounds from the factory, things I'd probably never hear again. Being several houses down from my old home was odd as well, unsettling. There was no sign Dad had been there for some time but it wasn't like he'd moved. Or died. More like he'd vanished. Rory had to know where he was. He was hiding something.

I woke up first and walked into town, dropping a note off at Rory's church, to get him out of the way. Give me a chance to sniff around his stuff. Crowds were already building up for Maxwell's weekly parade — the lorry with his victims strapped to the back. As the kids lined the pavements I pushed my way through and returned to the East End Estate.

Laura was preparing food when I got back so I examined the stuff from Dad's to see if there was anything useful. She'd brightened up since we'd set up in the house, throwing herself into organising and getting things working.

She held a rusty can of beans on the worktop. 'Why don't we leave today?'

'Before the deal?'

She pushed the can opener onto the tin and turned it. It slipped off and she tried again. 'Trent, you can make the deal somewhere else.'

'Yeah.' I was busy looking for the keys I'd found in Dad's and brought round. She did have a point. There was a chance Armstrong wouldn't pay up and leaving town would be the sensible thing to do. Even though we'd struggle to outrun one of his patrols. But meeting with Armstrong was about more than a trade. I wanted to give him a bloodied nose. Really screw up him and his empire.

She opened the can and tipped the beans into a pan. 'Well, we're ready to go. Jamie's okay to move.'

'You sure you didn't see any keys? They were in an open tin.'

'No, I don't think so.' She put the pan on the cooker, tuning on the gas ring. 'Anyway, let's load the car tonight, eh?'

'I've got stuff to do tonight.'

'Stuff. You and your stuff. What have you got to do?'

'I need those keys.'

'I'm sure you care more about your stuff than you do about me.'

I stopped ferreting around, straightening up and looking at her. This was one of those questions of hers, the ones with no right answer. The sound of two dogs barking came from outside, one deeper than the other. A man shouted and they were silent. I opened a cupboard and distractedly lifted out tins and jars.

Laura returned to the beans, stirring them fast then slow. Then she pointed to an old soup tin on the windowsill. 'That's full of bits and pieces. It was on the cooker so I shifted it.'

I reached over and tipped it on the worktop, raking through the foreign coins and bottle tops, flicking through the rusty keys and key fobs. Amongst them was a plastic-handled Ford one, the key to Dad's Focus. I took it and went outside.

The Evora had old sheets and blankets on it, a lumpen shape that couldn't be seen from the road. Slipping round it and through the side fence I made my way to Dad's via the back gardens. The house's back door was open so I went in. Cupboards were open and the stuff I'd left behind strewn across the floor, kicked about and trampled. It looked like Armstrong had sent some of his people round.

I went back out to the Focus. If it was fixable then we'd have more options. Being here intact was a miracle but Setmarch had some odd rules. Maybe cars parked on drives weren't allowed to be salvaged.

The key slid into the door lock and turned with a rasp. There was no sound from the central locking, which wasn't a surprise. The handle was stiff and the door didn't move at first so I pulled hard, creaking it open, as it sagged on its hinges. It smelled of damp and mould. The seats were stained, the plastic cracked and upholstery ripped. Cosmetic stuff. I went round to the front and opened the bonnet release with a clunk. The catch was seized and the bonnet had to be forced open, its hinges groaning. There were rotting leaves round the edges of the engine bay. The inner wings and bulkhead were dotted with rust, the brake servo and inlet manifold coated with a pale beard of corrosion. The air filter hung at the back, its plastic split and the exhaust lay at the front with the plug leads dangling into space. There was no cylinder head, alternator, radiator, battery or starter. Piston-less con-rods sat two-up-two-down in rusted bores with the cam and fan belts flopped at the side, both cracked and stained. The car had already been stripped. I lowered the bonnet on the dismantled engine, shoving it shut before slamming the car door and going through the gardens and into our kitchen.

'Right, are you ready to eat?' said Laura.

I sat down to a plate of beans in front of me, shovelling them in and staring out of the window at the Evora. It was that or nothing now.

Laura sat with me and ate. 'You think things are going to work out?'

'Yeah. It'll be fine.'

After eating I took food up to Jamie, sunlight filtering into the bedroom through the smoky clouds and cracked window, patched with board. He was on the bed adjusting the strings on his guitar, sitting up. This was the best he'd been for ages.

'How you doing?' I said.

He put the guitar down and shrugged. 'Not so bad.'

I gave him the plate of beans and he scooped up a

forkful using his good hand, munching away at them.

'Laura's tidying up,' I said.

'So what's the plan?'

'We'll be off in a couple of days.'

'Hey, how did the deal go?' He licked the sauce off his lips and shuffled up another load of food. There were sounds of Laura putting things away downstairs, the normal noises from a house.

'There were problems –'

'Problems?'

'Don't worry.'

He dropped his fork down onto the plate. 'Tell me it went through, please.'

I walked around the room, stopping at the window. The Evora took up most of the garden, like a corpse in its shroud of blankets. I turned back to Jamie, his face red. This could have been handled better. Jamie was always more cheery after food, drink, a few compliments. 'You're looking a lot fitter.'

'Trent, don't start all this. What's going on?'

'There's a new deal. In two days.'

'Hey, come on –'

'It'll be fine.' I pointed out of the window. 'Got the Evora back –'

'What happened to the first deal? You said Sandhu was a big cheese…'

'This one will be fine.'

Jamie slapped his bad hand on the bed. Then he grasped it in his other hand, his face twisted up, shaking his head. 'Tell me!' He was really getting wound up.

'Jamie, you're going to –'

'Trent!'

'Maxwell was at the deal...'

Jamie closed his eyes. 'I don't believe this. All that work you did setting up with Sandhu.' He opened his eyes and pointed at me. 'I told you Kelso would catch up with us.'

'Nixon was there too. We should have left him in the wrecked BM.'

This shut him up. I sat on the bed near him. There was still bruising on his face and his swollen hand was red and shiny.

'So?' he said, calmed down. 'What about the new deal then?'

'It's with Armstrong.'

He laughed. 'You're kidding.'

'I know how it sounds –'

'Like he's someone we can trust.'

I faced the window my back towards the door. The sun fought through the smog, back-lighting the clouds a sickly yellow. Outside the valley it would be a sunny day. 'Jamie, look...'

He picked on at his food again, his fork scraping on the plate as he chewed noisily. At least he was eating. Sometimes when he was annoyed he refused food.

'I'm going to give him a surprise.'

He ate some more but didn't look up.

'We'll get the money but maybe he'll never get the payload. I'm going to screw up AHI.'

'That sounds more like it, Trent.'

There was a clink, the sound of glass on glass. Laura stood in the doorway holding a bottle of whisky and two glasses. 'I thought you might fancy a drink, with us going.'

'Ah, that's a great idea.' Jamie shifted his plate aside.

She brought the glasses over, putting them and the

bottle on the bedside table. If she'd heard any of that she didn't let on.

I stood up. 'I was just telling Jamie –'

'Were you?' She moved towards the door, not looking at me. 'I'll go and tidy up.' She disappeared out.

Jamie opened the bottle and poured two glasses of whisky. She'd heard all right. Now I'd have to chat her up as well, convince her it would all be fine.

'Hey, Trent,' said Jamie.

'Yeah?'

'Goodbye Setmarch!' He raised his glass and drank.

CHAPTER FORTY

Bike

I helped Laura tidy up after the meal and she gave no hint of being suspicious about what I was up to. She was in reasonable spirits, excited about us going.

When I told her I had stuff to sort out she said nothing, fixing herself a glass of gin.

After grabbing the shotgun and crowbar I drove the Evora across town, creeping up to the tip in first gear, parking at the far end, hidden from Rory's church by a pile of cabbages. As the afternoon sun filtered through the smog Rory eventually appeared, walking off, heading on the wild goose chase I'd sent him on - the note inviting him to a bible reading at the Masonic Lodge. He'd be disappointed when he got there, but never mind.

Once he was long gone I took up the crowbar and walked over to the building.

The notice that said JESUS WANTS YOU NOW, NOT LATER! had been defaced, with *Fuck Jesus* scrawled across it. The door was locked so I positioned the crowbar next to the handle, pushing. There was a crack but the door stood firm. With another shove it opened and I was into the church.

I went straight through the vestibule into the main building. There was a door by the pulpit and I went through. It led into a hallway, lit by a narrow window opposite that faced the tip. At the far end there was another door. It was unlocked and I opened it. The room was dark so I pulled the curtains, light catching the dust that floated on the warm air. There was a bible and empty glass on the bedside cabinet. A creased up paperback lay on the bed, some historical story, its spine broken. Two candles on the drawers were melted stubs.

I put the crowbar on top of the set of drawers before examining them. The first held socks, underwear, shirts and trousers, the next dog collars and a spare cloak. The last one was trousers. All Rory's clothes. There was nothing else in there or down the sides.

There was a bowl in the bedside cabinet which held small change, cufflinks and some buttons. There were a few novels and religious books in the cabinet but otherwise it was empty. I knelt and lifted the mattress, poking around in the worn material. The fabric was stained and musty but there were no cuts or openings for secreting anything. There was no other furniture in the room, no hatches in the wall or cupboards. I picked around the room some more but there was nothing interesting. Nothing.

I'd broken in for no reason. What had I expected? A diary or something at least. Or some of Dad's stuff.

I drummed my fingers on the top of the drawers, a steady beat, then banged my hand on the crowbar in annoyance. There was a rattle, a faint tinkle so I did it again.

On the underside of the drawers' frame there was something heavy and sharp taped up. It was a bunch of keys. I tugged then out, holding them up to the fading light. The key ring's chrome was worn and there was a leather fob, the writing scuffed off. There were three keys, two small metal ones, sharp with plastic grips and one longer and thicker. The two were off one of Harry's bikes and the other was his garage's key. Harry's bunker, where he kept all his stuff. His precious things. Maybe everything was still there. Still intact.

I put it all back in place and pocketed the keys. With the crowbar under my arm I walked back through the church, stopping at the picture of Rory on the cross. His eyes were raised up and he wore a crown of thorns. Saint Rory. I slashed out with the crowbar, ripping the picture before I left.

Back in the Evora I rolled the keys around in my hand.

Then I set off. The drive to the top of the East End Estate was only a short one but it took much longer than it should have. The car misfired and I crunched gears, something I never normally did.

Instead of turning off to our old house I carried on past the shops to where the houses gave way to overgrown playing fields. I continued along a gravel lane to where the hill steepened, eventually forming the bank of the town's reservoir.

There was the bunker up ahead.

I parked the Evora's on the gravel track and approached the bunker's rusted and flaked steel doors. It had been an air-raid shelter or something in the last century then Harry had bought it and converted it into a garage, a place secure enough to store all his valuables once things got shaky.

I'd kept it out of my head, not even thought about it, because Harry's bunker was all about him. Him and everything that happened to him.

It was amazing that it was still there, intact and locked up. There was a chance there was nothing in it, that Dad or Rory had cleared it out and got rid of everything. But it was Harry's stuff and neither of them had been good at accepting what happened to him, moving on. They'd kept me away from here in my last days in Setmarch, a defiler of Harry's shrine.

I lifted the lock's cover, taking the key and putting it in. It was stiff but turned with a click. I grabbed the handle, pulling it. The door was heavy but it did move, creaking as it opened up for the first time in decades. I walked backwards and let the stale air out, my eyes on the ground, not daring to look in, in case it was empty. Just a dirty shell.

At last I allowed myself to see the inside of the bunker.

Harry's Triumph stood in the middle of the space, a chunk of black metal and alloy. Still here, after all those years. The tank was dusty and I wiped it, the green paint unblemished underneath. The tyres sat cobwebbed and half-inflated on wooden blocks that kept them off the floor. I ran my fingers across the saddle, along the side panel and down the engine's fins to the alternator cover, across every centimetre of the bike, Harry's Scrambler.

The sun cut through the clouds as I walked around the bike, the stark light extenuating the width and length of it. This was his fun bike, the one he'd taken out for more relaxed runs, while he burnt tarmac on his Speed Triple. The Speed Triple he'd died on. It was part of him, his history.

Behind it were boxes on the shelves, all with labels in his writing. Most of the shelves had Scrambler pencilled on them but one said Speed Triple and another Evora 3.5. These two were empty.

I looked the bike over, marvelled that it was still here. For decades it had been secured in the bunker. Forgotten and ignored. But this was more than a oddity. It was an opportunity, a way to escape the town.

I selected plugs and an oil filter from the Scrambler's shelves before going to the tool rack. Nails were hammered into wooden board with sizes in millimetres written below them. Most were bare, with faded shadows where the spanners had hung.

I left the parts on the workbench and took a cloth from the shelf, cleaning the bike, exposing the painted metal. For some time I tidied it.

Then I slid the small key into the ignition and turned it. The oil and neutral lights didn't illuminate. It was hardly surprising that the battery was dead after all the years.

I took the key and left, shutting the door on Harry's bike. With the Evora beating an uneven tune I drove away from the bunker, off to Dan's garage. Now that I had a way out of town the Evora was disposable.

I went to Dan's but he'd shut up for the afternoon. The lock was still bust from the last time I'd broken in so I popped it open and collected what I needed, piling it on his bench. There were jump leads, a roll of wire, another screwdriver and a switch, stuff for sorting out the bike, and spicing up the car. Some kind of plan was forming for dealing with Armstrong.

A noise came from outside and Dan came in wearing a

vest and long trousers. No overalls. 'What's going on?' he said.

'I need a few tools.'

'Tools?'

'I'll just borrow them.'

He scratched his chest through his vest, examining his fingernails afterwards. 'What d'you want them for?' He picked up the jump leads. 'Is this for the car?'

'I've got a bike to sort out.'

'A bike?'

'You don't need to know.' I organised the tools on the bench and he picked up the switch and wire that was lying there.

'What's this for?'

'Like I said, you don't need to know.'

He put the switch and wire down, opening his mouth as if to speak. Then he turned and walked off. With his hand raised he left the garage. 'Take what you want.'

I collected up the tools and went back to the Lotus. From the distance a low throb came from the plant as I loaded the car with the gear. I pulled off in the Evora and passed Dan standing by the wrecked cars, his shoulders slumped, shaking his head as he watched me go.

Back at the bunker I set everything on the bench and started work on the bike.

First I gave it a fuel flush then removed, cleaned and refitted the plugs. Finally I reversed the Lotus, connecting its battery to the Scrambler's with the jump leads.

The Triumph's neutral and oil lights illuminated with a soft glow. I turned it over on the starter for ages with nothing happening. I gave it a break then tried again. And again. It took four more shots before it fired then died with a sharp bark and pop. After three further attempts it burst into life, hesitating, backfiring as it revved up. As I disconnected the jump leads a haze of smoke rose up off the exhaust and casings. The bunker smelled of burning oil and petrol fumes, echoing with the growl of the engine.

I knelt and put my hand on the clutch cover, feeling the warm metal and the movement of crank, primary drive and gears within. As the engine settled into a steady idle I loosened the brake callipers, adjusted the chain and pumped up the tyres. Once it was warmed I turned it off, changing the oil and filter. Giving everything a final check.

Then I restarted it and slid onto the saddle. Sat where he'd sat. It bounced on its shocks as I clunked it into first gear and rode into the lane. I smiled to myself as it cruised in second, as I steered from side to side, easing the brakes on and off. On the main road I took it up to four thousand revs, letting the two-into-two bellow as I gunned it through East End Estate.

After the ride out I parked the bike where I'd found it and stashed the shotgun, cartridges and crowbar with it. The rest I put in the car. I locked up the bunker as the sun dipped under the clouds in the west.

The Evora took several attempts to fire up and the tachometer jiggled around as the revs rose and fell.

Then I drove back to the house. To Laura and Jamie.

CHAPTER FORTY-ONE

Preparations

When I got in Laura was drunk, ranting on about the town and how we should leave straight away, trade somewhere else. She walked around the house with a glass of gin in her hand.

I didn't comment, going off to grab the bag from under the living room floor then setting to work in the kitchen. I was starting to firm up what I had planned for Armstrong.

'Christ, what have you been up to?' she said.

I laid out the wire I'd brought from Dan's and grabbed a kitchen knife. Behind me on the worktop was some of the junk I'd brought over earlier from Dad's place, road maps and travel guides. 'Sorting stuff out.' I scraped insulation off the wire with the knife.

She continued to pace, pointing at the wire, the switch and the pliers. 'And what's all this for?'

'You worried about something?'

'Yes, Trent, I'm worried that you are stalling and we won't be able to leave. Why can't we just go now?'

'Not yet.'

She topped up her glass and drank some more. 'What are you planning?'

'You know, the deal tomorrow, then go.'

She pointed at the wire with her glass. 'What are you keeping from me? I know you're up to something. I'm not completely stupid, believe it or not. And what was that you said to Jamie?'

'Never mind what I said to Jamie.' I cut through some of the strands of wire.

She sat opposite me. 'Just tell me, Trent.' She smiled. 'Please?'

I stopped and stared at her, as she drank and watched me twist the wires. I wasn't even telling myself about the plan, just letting it fall into place round some rough ideas. Stuff I had. The wires and car. The rocket. 'If I let you in on it...' I shook my head. Once she knew, that was it. There was no way to unlearn something. The Gehenna stuff was valuable and dangerous. That meant I couldn't give it to Armstrong. In fact I wanted to take stuff from him. This town had steamrollered me once before but it wouldn't this time. 'You don't want to know.'

She picked up the wire I'd striped, moving it around. 'This doesn't look good to me, all these wires...'

I took the wire off her. 'As I said, you don't want to know.'

'Listen, Trent, I'm no fan of Armstrong, you know that.'

I flicked the switch on and off, attaching it to the coiled wire. It was the only sound in the kitchen. Maybe it was time to tell her everything. Trust her. Even though she was a little drunk. 'Do you know why I left Setmarch —?'

'Trent, come on —'

'Just listen. I was told to leave. Forced out. I'd done some dodgy things but they came down hard on me. It was leave town or I'd suffer. And you.'

'Me?'

'They said they'd do stuff to you if I stayed.'

'Right.' She took a drink and picked up the wire. 'So where does this all fit?'

I held the wire and switch up to her. 'See, this wire gets connected to this switch.'

'And where is all this going?'

I looked out of the window towards the Evora in the back garden, a darkening shadow. Then I scraped some more insulation off with the knife.

'Hang on.' She went to the window, staring at the car. 'It's going into the car? The car you are doing the deal in and that we are leaving in afterwards?' She drank more then topped her glass up again.

I inspected the wire, straightening the strands, twisting some of them together, smoothing them.

'Trent, I know you're pissed off with Armstrong, but there's no point trying to get even. You just need to deal and leave.' She came back and sat opposite me again tapping the wire. 'You're going to do something to the car, aren't you?'

'Well, you wanted to know –'

'This isn't the answer.'

I straightened out the final piece of wire, put the knife down on the edge of the table and arranged all the pieces. She picked up the switch and flicked it on and off. There was only the click, click of the switch as she messed with it.

I took it off her, grabbed the bag and books and

roadmaps off the worktop before I went to the door. 'Don't worry.'

'*Don't worry*,' she said. Her voice flat. '"*Don't worry*," says Trent. That *is* a time to worry.'

As I went out she sat at the table with the pieces of shredded wire and her glass of gin.

I opened the Evora's hatch and placed the switch and wire next to the rocket. Then I set out the maps and books beside Gehenna's stuff. A rumble came from the plant in the distance.

Laura was visible in the kitchen, as she lit a couple of candles. She ran her hands through her hair, drinking from her glass. She didn't like what I was doing but hadn't tried to stop me. I'd chat her up, make her feel it was all right. If she took it well I'd even show her the payload, let her in on Gehenna. She'd stuck with me through all this, and like she'd said earlier, we did make a good team.

Tapping the metal case of Gehenna I closed the boot.

When I went back in she was facing me, her arms crossed in front of her, as she swayed.

'Look, Laura, it's all going to be fine.' I dumped the car keys on the table and approached her. 'Let's talk about it.'

'I see, all fine. That's what you say. But I know what you're up to. You're going to blow the car, aren't you?' She unfolded her arms. Showing the knife she was holding. 'I can't let you do this.' She stepped forward, an unsteady step, the knife held out.

I glanced over at the gin bottle. There was only a quarter left. She really had been knocking it back. Holding my hands out I eased towards her. 'You've had a few drinks...'

She thrust at me. 'Oh, that's it, I'm drunk.' She was

drunk. Completely pissed.

'Just put the knife down –'

'I can't let you blow everything.'

'Laura, there's more to this –'

'Don't!' She moved towards me, the knife aimed at my chest. 'This isn't the way. It isn't.'

I backed off and bumped into the table.

'We can leave, Trent...do a deal someplace else... maybe you could sort out Armstrong. Some other way...' She had the knife held out. Her face was flushed. 'Just forget about the plant, huh? And everything. Don't ruin things, the town, just to get even. Just forget it...'

'Fine.'

'Fine?'

I smiled. 'All right.' I held my arms out. There was no point arguing with her, not when she'd made her mind up. And she was drunk. Words wouldn't fix things.

'What does that mean, Trent? What?'

'I'll go to the car and take it all out.'

She held up the knife, looking at it all cross-eyed. 'You mean this? For real?'

'We'll load up and head out.'

The knife wobbled in her hand, her eyebrows raised. Her body straightened up as she lowered it a little. 'Is this a trick? Trent?'

'I was being crazy.' I reached over to the car keys. 'All right?'

She waved the weapon. 'No messing. This is serious. I don't want you tricking me!'

Then she slashed out, caught me across the hand, made me bleed. Before she did anymore I grabbed her by the wrist, twisting her hand hard, pulling at her skin and forcing the ligaments to their limits. She cried out but held onto the knife, tightening her fist on it.

'Drop it!' I said.

'Christ, Trent!'

I twisted some more, making her shoulder slump. 'Drop it!'

She dropped it. I pulled her arm round, shoving it up her back. I leant her forward and pushed her arm further upwards, my body tight against hers. Her breathing was fast and uneven, rasping out of her.

'Trent, you're breaking my arm!'

'And what were you doing?'

'I didn't mean to hurt you, but you can't blow it, you just can't!'

'You've said your piece.'

'Trent, I would never have hurt you, really!'

I eased off the pressure, grabbing her other arm, shifting my leg under her and pushing her forward. She shouted as she fell onto the ground and I knelt on her back, pinning one arm with my knee.

This wasn't how the day should have gone but she'd crossed the line. Using a knife was a serious stunt.

'Let go of me! Now, Trent!' She growled in the back of her throat.

Grabbing her shoulder, I turned her over onto her back and she looked up at me but her eyes rolled around in her head. Then I lifted her up and half carried her along the passageway, leant backwards so that she had to walk to stop herself falling.

Opening the front room door, I shoved her in, so she staggered over then fell onto the floor. She sprawled there, almost pushing herself up. As she was about to say something she leant forward and threw-up a great pile of sick, before lying down beside it.

Taking deep breaths she muttered to herself, trying to get up then slumping back down.

Back in the kitchen I filled a glass of water, letting it run clear. Maybe she had a point about going too far, getting carried away. That we should just leave and forget about it.

But she'd not lived outside the town, experienced life without AHI. There was no way Armstrong was going to rebuild the old world. Not that it was worth rebuilding. He was just another gangland boss but with better marketing.

And there was the personal side of it. How the town had treated me, and her. Driving me out all those years ago.

That had burned in me and now was the time to balance things up.

I took the water through to her. If I could sober her up a bit we could talk about the plan properly.

When I went into the room she was asleep, arms splayed. I went upstairs to collect a pillow and sheet. Jamie was on the landing.

'What the hell's going on?' he said.

'Just having a chat.' I collected the bedding and returned to her, turning her sideways as she slept off the gin. After touching my hand on her cheek I left her resting, going out the Evora.

Working on it by the house didn't seem sensible, attracting unwanted attention, so I drove across town to the bunker. By the time I got there it was dark. I turned the Evora's tick-over up and opened up the steel door. The engine rattled away as it ran, providing light that caught the Scrambler's exhaust through the dust.

Before I set to work there was the payload to sort out. I took the Gehenna container and emptied it out, stacking the plans in the bunker. Then I replaced them with the old roadmaps from Dad's, opening each one out and rolling them to make them look similar before sealing the container again. Armstrong wasn't going to get the real thing. By time he figured it out it would be too late.

In the reflected light of the Evora's headlight I jacked the car up, undoing the panel in the chassis, popping in the junk-filled Gehenna container and bolting it up tight so it would take a while to get out.

Next I slid further under the car, wedging the rocket between the bodywork and petrol tank, near the fuel-line, gaffer-taping it in position and tying the scraped wire near the rocket's fuse. I shuffled on my back across gravel and earth, leading the wire under the car, taping it to the chassis. With the wire gripped between my fingers I fed it along the wiring loom, balancing it under the gearbox linkage.

Inside the car, I undid the centre console and gearshift cover, pulling the wire through and fitting the switch, linking it to the cigarette lighter and twisting all the wires in place.

I flicked the switch and crawled back under the Lotus, feeling the wires where they were stripped. They were soon hot and I jumped back in the car, knocking the switch off.

Once the wires had cooled I wrapped them round the rocket's fuse before lowering the car off the jack.

With everything in place I drove it back to the house, ready to deal with Armstrong.

CHAPTER FORTY-TWO

To the plant

That night I dreamt of Shangri-La, of fields and woods; dancers wearing kaftans. Clean air and animal sounds.

I woke in Setmarch, smoke rolling out across the sky and clattering coming from the factory. After picking on at some food I left the house at eight. Jamie was just waking and Laura still asleep. It was too early for the deal so I drove round and round the town, back and forward on the main roads, having a final run out in the Lotus. Taking the Scrambler out would have been fun, but today wasn't really about fun.

The approach to the plant was flanked by slag heaps and shrouded by a dark cloud. In the gloom I parked by the gate, stepping out. It was quarter to ten. There was still time to jump back in the car, drive away. Pick up Laura and Jamie, get out of town. The place smelled of coal, oil and soot as a man in overalls came over to me, some balding AHI employee. He looked me up and down. 'You Trent?'

'Yeah.'

He came over. 'I've got to check you over,' he said. 'No search, no entry.'

I opened my jacket and pulled out my pockets showing the lighter, skins and grass. The tiny amount I had left.

He pointed at the Evora. 'Didn't know you'd have a car. Need to check it as well.'

I took the skins and grass, starting to make a joint, a one-skinner. Something for me to do while he messed with the car, stop me fidgeting and making him suspicious.

He shifted the driver's seat forward, leaning into the back then feeling under the seats and through the door bins. Then he went round to the passenger side, opening the glove compartment and lifting out old fuses, the small spanner and maps. As he shifted the gear-stick, he flicked the switch I'd fitted. 'What's this?'

I held the half-made joint to one side. 'Rear heated window,' saying it all casual, as if it was obvious.

He flicked the switch off and on again. 'There's a switch for that already.'

'Bust.' I leant in and flicked the switch off. 'Don't want to run the battery down.'

He opened the boot, examined the floor, sides and fuel containers, then popped the engine cover, lifting it and peering around the engine. He cried out when he put his hand down the side of the cylinders. 'Bloody hot.' Then he went under the bonnet poking around as I lit the joint and smoked. He came over to me. 'No smoking in the plant.'

I nodded.

'I need to look under the car.'

This was the problem time. If he spotted something I'd either have to give some story or deal with him. Neither was great.

He lay beside the front of the car. It was too low to the ground for him to slide right the way under but he squeezed his head under the sill, prodding. I drew on the joint and blew out a thin stream of smoke. Next he went to the back of the Evora, struggling to shove himself under the bumper. There were tapping sounds as he shifted around, exploring probing. I inhaled on the joint, kept the smoke in. The man moved, shuffled and slid back out, coming over to me. My chest expanded as I held the smoke, waited for his verdict.

'It's in a bit of a state.'

I blew out the smoke, a great cloud that engulfed him, making him cough.

'It's an old car.' I slid into the Evora, pulling the door shut.

He tapped the windscreen. 'There's no smoking in there.'

I opened the window and threw the spliff at his feet, letting him stamp it out as I revved the car and drove forward, through the gate.

The plant's smoke rose up above me like some dark angel. Clanks and hisses came from the machinery as I approached the factory building, aiming for the giant doorway underneath the thick cables and letters A, H and I, where a lorry roared off with refined fuel. I had to be near the juice if the plan was going to work.

Sikey appeared out of the building, playing with the zip on his tracksuit as he swaggered over. I pulled forward towards the factory entrance but he stood in front of the car shaking his head. His cap was tilted to one side and he came up the side of the car, kicking the bodywork. 'Get out,' he said.

I ignored him and steered round him into the entrance, past the piles of coal dust and pulling up in front of one of the tanks with CTL PETROLEUM on it. I parked but let the engine run and kept it at two thousand revs, as it hunted and hiccupped.

Sikey came over and kicked the car again, waving to some men in a nearby office. I turned the ignition off and there was a backfire.

He pointed at the car. 'You weren't meant to bring a car. Where's the fucking stuff?'

'Where's the money?'

'Stuff first, money later. It can't stay here. Reverse it.' He walked over to the office, talking to a man in there. The man picked up a phone, dialled and spoke into it.

I felt around with the bolt down into the floor. The Lotus had to be locked in gear for this to work. But the bolt wouldn't line up and Sikey was about to return. He'd want to drive the car out.

I found the slot, screwed the bolt in, covered it with the carpet and hauled the handbrake on as hard as it went.

Sikey came over, poking his head in the open window, up close to me, his breath sickly sweet, his eyes opaque, unfocussed. 'I said move the car.'

I stepped out as the worker came and stood by Sikey. Two other hard-hatted men joined him, blocking my way. Then the first fella slid into the Evora and started it. It stalled and he restarted it, revving it up, pulling on the gearstick. It lurched forward. Sikey banged the car's roof, his other hand on his pistol. 'Move it.'

There was a clunk and the car lurched forward again, stalling. The man got out of the car. 'It's jammed in first.'

'Sometimes does that,' I said.

Sikey glanced over at me. 'Where is it? The stuff.'

'Safe. In the car. When's Armstrong getting here?' I didn't want him missing the show.

Sikey clicked his fingers at the men, making them cluster around him. 'Right, slice it.'

'Where?' said one.

'Start at the front and work back. Fucking chop it up.'

I didn't want the car cut up, not with the explosive in it. 'All right,' I said, tapping the Lotus at the bottom of the driver's door. 'It's here. Under a panel. Now give me the cash. And I want to see Armstrong.'

Sikey waved his hand and the men set to work. One jacked the car up, another sliding under, pulling the bodywork off, fishing around for the blanking plate. Once he'd found it he called to the third man for a spanner. They were efficient. Too efficient. This wasn't good. I should have stalled them some more.

The factory rumbled around us. Men came and went further on in the works, the odd one coming through and dropping off dockets in the office.

There was obviously no cash. Armstrong wasn't going to show up. So now was as good a time as any to flick the switch, set it off and run.

I stepped towards the car but Sikey pulled his Glock out, shoving it into my chest. 'Where you off to?'

I tried to read him. 'You wouldn't fire that next to this fuel.'

'Your guts'll damp it down.'

Several men came out from the office as the panel under the car opened up, a slice of aluminium dropping out followed by the metal tube. A man held up the container. Sikey waved the others over with his gun. 'Hold him.'

Two men grabbed me but I elbowed one, slipping free, diving into the Lotus. Even Sikey wouldn't risk firing towards the fuel tanks. As I reached out for the switch another man dragged me out of the car into the open. I punched him in the face and he bounced off the flank of the Evora, but his partner swung his hard-hat and clipped me on the head, a hard blow that sent me spinning off to the ground. They fell upon me and pinned my arms as the factory lurched around me.

Sikey put his arm round my neck, his tattooed muscles taught on my windpipe as they dragged me backwards. Then they hauled me up against the wall, forcing my arm against a rusted pipe. Sikey leant against me and the men disappeared. His mouth was next to my ear and he muttered, 'Gotcha.' Then he laughed.

The men reappeared and he let go of me as they pushed my arms against the pipes, binding me tight before they secured my feet. Workers coming and going in the factory glanced over then moved on.

They stepped back. I was immobile, arms raised at my side and feet together. Crucified on the factory's pipework.

Sikey came up and punched me in the stomach, knocking the air out of me. He grasped my hair and raised my head up, his face up close. 'This is for Gaz,' he said. He hit me again hard. There were several more punches before he lost interest; went over and grabbed the Gehenna container.

I dangled there, stuck, trapped.

For some time I hung on those hot pipes as my lips dried and cracked. Sikey strutted around, swinging the fake Gehenna with one hand, the other on his pistol in his trousers. He talked to himself and jerked his jaw out.

It seemed it couldn't get any worse then a car pulled up outside, a silver BMW. A BMW five-series like Maxwell used. The same one I'd seen at the quayside with a smashed rear bumper.

Maxwell slid out of it with Nixon. They both strolled over into the factory, joining Sikey.

The three of them stood before me.

There were thuds and rumbles from the plant as I squirmed in the rope, pulling at it. 'My three favourite scumbags,' I said, my voice thin.

Maxwell smiled. 'How you fucking doing, Trent?'

Sikey passed the Gehenna's metal tube to Maxwell who opened it up, smiling. After flicking through the papers he resealed it.

'Do you know what this is, Trent?'

'I know enough.'

'I don't think you do. If you had any idea you wouldn't have messed with it.' He pointed at me. 'This is the big deal. Powerful stuff. It's a floating powder keg, out there somewhere.' He jabbed the container at the river, towards the sea. 'It's a powder keg waiting to be lit, waiting for someone like me.'

'It's just a load of old paper.'

He got up close. 'You just don't get it, Trent. The old world stuff is all out there. Waiting to be picked up. Used.' He waved Nixon over. 'Enough chat.'

With a nod from Maxwell, Nixon raised his hand and slapped me across the face, flicking my head against the pipe. He slapped again, sending my head the other way. I hung forward on the ropes.

'Hurt?' said Nixon.

Maxwell and Sikey laughed as blood ran into my mouth. Nixon slapped me again, forcing the air out of me. Alternating hands he hit me repeatedly across the face, hard blows that made me see flashes and hear thunder. He carried on until I slumped on my bindings.

As Nixon went to hit me again Maxwell stopped him. 'Not too fast. Slow finale for him. We want him to feel it all.'

Sikey grabbed my head and tilted it up, so I was forced to look at him. 'Don't worry. We'll be back for you.' He took his knife out and held it to my face. 'Going to slit you open like a pig at the slaughter house.'

Maxwell took his arm. 'Let's talk business.' He led Sikey and Nixon over to the BMW.

I hung on my ropes as they disappeared into the car. By squirming around I took weight from wrists and arched my back to give some space between the hot pipes and my skin.

As I shifted around a figure came from behind the Evora, over towards me. Maybe this was some other punishment from Sikey. A secret beating when Maxwell wasn't looking. The fella was stooped, with grey hair, dressed in AHI overalls — not like Sikey's track-suited pals. He stopped by the pipes and glanced around before continuing on. There were two men in the office but they were well into some gossip, waving their arms and laughing. The fella slid up behind me, grabbing the ropes on me. Untying them. 'This is for what you did.'

I eased free. 'What I did?'

'My bag,' said the man. 'Sikey tried to take my bag.'

I hadn't even recognised him. It was the fella Jamie and

me had helped days ago. Flexing my wrist I straightened up but maintained my position by the pipes. Maxwell, Nixon and Sikey were still in the BMW, smoke rolling out of the open doors. 'Thanks.'

He turned to go back into the factory.

'Wait,' I said. I had to warn him. 'Get away from here. From the plant.'

The man frowned.

'Just go. Now.'

He stared at me, nodded and slunk off past the Lotus.

I moved away from the wall, extending my arms, staggering over towards the car. The smell of fuel and coal dust clogged my chest and my face was numb from the slapping.

As I touched the burns on my back Maxwell burst out of the BMW. 'Trent!' he shouted.

I slid into the Evora, reaching the centre console, flicking the switch and rolling back out.

As Nixon and Sikey sprinted towards me I stumbled off into the factory.

There were conveyor belts, piles of coal and rows of pipes that disappeared off. Men with shovels worked amongst the dark machinery. There were crashes and thuds and hisses as coal passed into a machine and powder came out the other side. Furnaces and pipes stood to my right but daylight came from my left so I headed towards it.

The men were still after me as I continued under the conveyor clanking and rattling, pieces of coal falling in black hail. The noise and smells added to tightness I felt in my head, the pain from the burns on my back, all slowing me, making me want to stop, rest.

But the fuse was lit and burning.

Coal sat in great heaps in the delivery area. A lorry unloaded up ahead, an old Foden with its back tilted up as it added to the pile. Nearby, men shovelled the coal onto the conveyor. I staggered past them towards the lorry as it lowered its tipper. The ground was all loose chunks that slid under my feet. The lorry's back thudded into place and I reached up and grasped it, hauling myself to perch on the edge.

There was a bang from way off in the factory, no more than a muted explosion. The Lotus had blown but the plant was still intact.

A hand tugged at my trousers and I kicked backwards, hitting Nixon in the face. The Foden clunked into gear and juddered forward with me holding on and him grabbing at me. As the lorry picked up speed it pulled me free but Nixon raised his shotgun. He grinned as he aimed it. I held the top of the tipper and heaved myself up but he had me.

Then there was an explosion, a great roar. Nixon dropped his gun as he was engulfed by the blast which flung me into the back of the lorry, the interior littered with coal shards.

CHAPTER FORTY-THREE

Meet Up

The sound thundered around and through me and I held my eyes shut, rolling around in the back of the lorry. The Foden rocked and shook but carried on as I covered my ears, staying like that until the sound faded and the heat had gone. Then I peered out of the tipper. The lorry made its way along the track away from the works and towards the gate. The exit from the factory building was a dark orifice and Nixon lay sprawled beside it, something imbedded in his head. Several workers ran along a track at the far end where the Evora had been, now obscured below a yellow fireball that rolled out above the factory which had split down the middle, an opened sardine tin. Smoke belched out from every side of it.

Growls and thumps came from inside the plant and there was another explosion, the roof shaking. The top of the building lifted as flames licked out and smoke rose up. There was a smell of burnt oil, burning coal, hot metal and something cooking. The lorry stopped at the gate and I clambered up and out of the tipper, jumping off and going round to the front, still unsteady. The driver gazed out at the fire, shaking his head. When I tapped on the cab he looked down at me, opening the door. I grabbed him, hauling him with what little strength I had so that he fell out, sprawling on the ground. Then I climbed into the seat and shut the door. He ran off, away from me and plant, past the guard who ignored him. There was another explosion and more flames came from the buildings. In the distance a figure staggered from the side where Maxwell's BMW had been, a shambling form with burning clothes and scorched skin.

I examined the lorry's controls, pressing the clutch, moving the gear lever and shoving it into first, all the same as on the ones I drove years ago. It jerked forward as I revved the engine, ground the gears, pushed it from first into second, steering towards the figure. I slowed and wound the window down. 'Maxwell,' I shouted. 'Maxwell.'

The figure turned towards me, a roasted man in tattered clothes.

'Maxwell?'

He staggered around and made some sound. What hair he'd had was burned off and his skin peeled. Even though it was Maxwell, ruthless bastard that he was, it was hard not to pity him.

Then he felt inside his shredded suit, reaching into a holster that hung on his chest, grasping a pistol, waving it towards me. Same old Maxwell.

I revved up and steered round him, turning sharp right and swinging round, the tyres scrubbing as I held it on full lock to take it in a wide circle. I let it turn and straighten up so that Maxwell was now in front of me, still gesturing with the revolver. I kept my foot on the accelerator and there was a shout and a thump but the Foden barely moved on its suspension. In the mirror I saw a crushed body on the ground. A suit with limbs at odd angles.

As I approached the exit I kept the power on and the lorry picked up speed. The man on duty stared at the plant, at me, pointing and shouting something but I kept the Foden aimed ahead. The lorry hit the gate and jerked as it smashed through, carrying on to the road. Another explosion ripped through the works.

A bottle of fizzy drink rolled around in the cab, AHI lemonade, and I reached down, picking it up and opening it. I put it to my dried lips and drank, the warm liquid the best thing I'd ever tasted.

Now I had a visit to pay. Finishing the drink I headed out of the town centre, up towards Bellendale Road.

When I came to Armstrong's house I swung hard into the gateway, knocking one of the posts off, accelerating the lorry along the driveway. Pushing it through the gears it rattled over the gravel, round the side then round in an arc. I held on tight as the Foden bounced over the grass and flower beds, previously trimmed and tidy, piling through the wooden structure of the orangery at the back. It lurched and bucked as it smashed through the glass and framework that shattered and splintered around the cab, obscuring the view with a wave of wreckage. The lorry emerged through a border of begonias and pitched across the lawn. I dropped it a gear, keeping my foot rammed down on the accelerator. It charged across the grass, through a low hedge and rose bed, the tyres churning the croquet lawn as I steered it back in a tight circle towards the house. At the back of the garage I straightened up, tightening the seat belt as the lorry revved out, entering the wooden structure with a thunderous smash, half-mounting the car parked in there, juddering forward until it jerked and stalled, now halfway into the garage.

The fuel pump whirred and coolant gurgled. The belt was locked around me and lights glowed on the dashboard. There was a crack across the windscreen and the passenger mirror had gone. Most of the garage had collapsed around the lorry, the roof fallen to show blue sky. I turned the ignition off, undoing the belt and opening the door. It was stiff and I had to kick it with my foot. As it creaked open I slid out and down into the ruined garage that groaned around me. The lorry was surrounded by smashed wood and glass. Buried under the front bumper was Armstrong's Rolls-Royce, its boot forced forward onto the rear seats. The bonnet was rammed partway through a steel door.

I clattered through the debris onto the lawn. There were deep tracks where the lorry had swerved across in a wide arc. At the far side of the house was wreckage from the orangery that spread out in the lorry's wake.

The French doors into Armstrong's drawing room burst open and he flew out in smart-shirt and pressed trousers, holding a revolver, waving it around. 'What the fuck is going on!' He saw me and levelled the gun at me. 'What the hell are you doing here?'

There was a crack from the pistol and I turned, going back towards garage.

'Look at my fucking garden!'

I got to the back of the lorry and leant against it. When I looked out and there was another shot.

'Look at my garden! And my car, my fucking Roller!'

I carried on round the lorry, wading through the debris until reaching the far side of the cab. I eased myself up, opening the door and sliding in, turning the ignition on. With the lorry running I could drive over him, finish him off like Maxwell.

'Don't think I can't fucking see you!' said Armstrong.

I tried to start the lorry. The engine turned but didn't catch. He fired twice. One shot ricocheted off the tipper and the other was wide. I tried to start the lorry again. The starter motor whirred but the engine didn't ignite.

Armstrong was at the back of the garage, looking all smart in the mirror. His fist was balled up and in his other hand was the pistol pointed at me. There was a crack as a bullet whizzed off the lorry's door. With a thud another jammed in the cab. I opened the window, leaning out.

'You ever thought you might need glasses?'

'You fucker.' When he aimed and fired, the gun clicked and he frowned, trying again. It gave another click.

I opened the cab door, jumping down and picking up a piece of wood, swinging it. It wasn't heavy enough so I dropped it, picking up another, heavier one.

Armstrong pocketed the gun and shuffled backwards as I came towards him. 'Now, Trent.'

I walked on, forcing him across the lawn, making him backtrack towards the house. 'Quite a deal you set up.'

'Deal?'

'At your works.'

He looked behind him and carried on away from me, towards the French doors.

'Or should I say ex-works.'

'Ex-works?'

'Seems you've had a little accident there. Didn't you

hear it?'

Armstrong's brow furrowed. 'That was my works?'

'Seems something went wrong there.'

He backed himself into the drawing room. 'Look,' he said. 'You've messed up my house and trashed my car, my beautiful Rolls-Royce!' He took a breath. 'You didn't need to do all that, Trent.'

I moved to the centre of the room. 'And there's your plant. That's pretty well done for.'

'Christ, I was on your side, Trent.'

'Oh yeah…' I swung the piece of wood. 'You were with me all the way.'

'You've got it all wrong.'

'How silly of me.' I jabbed him, causing him to stagger back.

He raised his fist, like an aged prizefighter in smart-casuals. 'You idiot!'

'Temper.' I lifted the piece of wood above my head ready to swing it.

'Who do you think kept Sikey off you?'

'Save it, Armstrong.'

He shook his hands. 'And Laura. I let you have her. We could have stopped all that ages ago.'

I swung and smashed a table sending orange plastic flying. 'What about Jamie?'

'Things happen, Trent, things happen…'

'Is that so?'

'It's not too late. We can deal and work together.'

'Why would I deal now?'

'I run this town. And I know what you're dealing with, what you had hidden in that car of yours. What it could lead to. Do you realise the importance of it, Trent? Do you?'

I swung hard at him, forcing him to jump out of the way. He'd had his time to talk, now he had to face reality. 'Time's up.'

'Wait! Wait! I have something that might help.'

'Too late, Armstrong.'

'No, serious, something important. Something – someone you're bothered about.'

I laughed. 'Nice try. Game's over for you.'

Raising his hands he waved them. 'Really, Trent? Really?' He smiled, a crooked smile. 'What about your family. Your dad.'

'You're just stalling.'

'No I'm not, not at all.'

I lowered the piece of wood and paced around the room, going to the window. Outside the lawn was all chewed up and the lorry's tipper showed out of the back of the garage. This was a ploy, the one thing he thought would catch me out. And he was right. He was playing me. I turned and faced him. 'You're just stalling.'

'Your dad.' He moved away from the piano and came over to me, the most genuine I'd seen him. 'He's here.' He strode over to the door and when I didn't react he carried on into the hall.

I followed still holding the piece of wood but it was now limp in my hand. He really knew how to work people, I had to give him that. I'd see what his game was, then leave. His empire was finished without the plant. He led me past the plastic chairs, plastic vases with plastic flowers and plastic statues on plastic stands. A woman in a short dress watched us from the far end. She didn't move or say anything.

We carried on upstairs, stopping on the landing next to a plastic model of Michelangelo's David. He pointed at a door. The house smelled of roast meat and polish.

'Listen, Trent. You know, me and your family go back some years.'

'First I've heard.'

'I know your...' Armstrong cleared his throat. 'I knew your family.' He stared down at the carpet then took the door handle. 'Come on then.'

I waved the piece of wood at him. 'You first.' There was still a chance this was a trap. That there'd be a couple of Sikey's mates in the room.

Taking the handle he turned it, pushing the door open and going in. 'You've got a visitor,' he said.

I took a deep breath and stepped in.

CHAPTER FORTY-FOUR

Armstrong

The curtains were closed and the room warm. There were clothes on the floor, a bedside table with books and a glass of water. Under a chair with was a pair of shoes, worn and scuffed. A figure lay in the bed wrapped in the bedding.

'Matt?' said Armstrong.

The blankets shifted. There was a cough.

'Matt, you've got a visitor.'

The figure groaned and turned round in the bed, his bald head shifting. It really was Dad.

Armstrong leant over to me. 'You want me to leave?'

I dropped the piece of wood on the floor. I didn't know what I wanted. Armstrong sloped out and closed the door behind him. Dad snorted but didn't speak.

I approached the bed, got close. 'It's me, Trent.'

His face was old, wrinkled, peppered with grey stubble but there were still the hard cheekbones. He opened his eyes. They were blue, cold as they'd always been. 'Who?'

'Me, Trent.'

He shook his head. 'No.'

'I've come to see you.'

'No, no.' He looked past me at the door then sat up, rubbing his head. He smacked his lips and made some sound in the back of his throat then lay back. 'Christ.'

I undid my jacket and leant against the chair. Here he was, still alive and living in Armstrong's house.

'Where's Armstrong?' he said.

'He's busy.' I went over and tugged at a curtain, letting sunlight in.

'What are you after?'

'Just to talk…'

Dad laughed. 'Talk?'

I undid the catch and opened the window, fresher air drifted in. The lawn was a badly ploughed field. I'd given up on seeing Dad — not thought about what I wanted to say to him.

He laughed again, a hoarse crackle. 'I told him not to let people in.' He twisted in the bed so that his back was to me. 'I told him to keep people away.' Then he turned over again, pushing himself up and reaching over to grab the glass of water. As he drank his throat pulsed, then he held the glass so as to stare into it. 'But I knew you'd come. Come back to gloat. To win the final round.'

'I don't know what you mean.'

He shook his head and stared at the ceiling, gripping the glass. 'You know. You fucking know.' After glancing over at the set of drawers he closed his eyes. 'I want you to leave.'

'Dad, look, what's up–?'

'Don't call me that.'

I touched my face, still numb from all the slaps. My

back and legs hurt as well. Footsteps sounded outside on the patio. 'Is this about what happened with Harry? Or me leaving?'

'Don't!' He leant forward and pointed at me. 'Don't you start.'

I went over to the set of drawers. There was an old photograph in a cracked frame. It was of Harry, Rory and Dad showing them sitting together, arms around one-another all smiling. Just the three of them

'I want you to go.'

I drummed my fingers on the picture. 'Why are you here?'

'I need to rest. I'm not well.'

I turned to him. 'You're ill?'

'Questions, questions!' With a shrivelled hand he pointed at the door. 'Get out. You're a nasty piece of work. Nasty.' He lay there twisting in the bed, his face all screwed up. Bitter and angry.

This was how he'd been in the old days, just before I'd left town. After Harry's accident he'd been angry all the time. Angry with me. It came out one evening, the time he got drunk and ranted on.

'Why Harry?' he said. 'Why him? Why not you?'

He stood in the living room and pointed the bottle of whisky at me. Gave me a look of hate.

'It was an accident, Dad,' I said.

'I know you, Trent. What you're like. Always want to get one up on people. Always jealous of Harry. You forced him into a race. Forced him to crash. Your mother had a soft spot for you. Now she's gone...'

'Harry was the one—'

'Don't! Don't you dare speak ill of him! He was my

flesh and blood. Mine!'

'Same as Rory and me.'

He laughed at that. Laughed and then told me to get out the house. That had been the last time we'd spoken.

Now here he was in Armstrong's house with those same angry eyes.

'You don't get it,' he said.

'There's nothing to get.'

'You're not my son. You're nothing to me. Never were.'

He'd spent his whole life trying to disown me. Shove me out of the family. I thought he'd have mellowed, put it all in context. Seems not.

Dad snorted. 'Piss off downstairs. Chat to Armstrong. You and him have a lot in common. A hell of a lot.' He laughed at this. A laugh that turned into a cough.

I felt around in my pocket, dug around until I found the Scrambler's keys, bringing them out and holding them in front of Dad's face. 'Know what these are? Loving son Rory wasn't too careful with his stuff. Harry's stuff.'

'You piece of shit. You have no right to have his things. No right! You know, if I was fitter I'd sort you out.'

I sat on the edge of the bed and got close to Dad's face. 'But you're not fit. You're far from it.' There were noises from outside, muttering and clicking so I went over to the window. Armstrong was on the lawn feeding bullets into his gun, saying stuff to himself. He fidgeted, struggling to slot them in. I moved away from the window and across the room, opening the door.

'Listen, Trent, don't you get it?'

'Goodbye Dad,' I said. He started to talk but I left slamming the door, knowing I'd never see him again.

Out on the landing I went to the window, opening the

catch, easing it up. It squeaked and Armstrong looked up, pointing the revolver. I ducked back in as there was a loud crack and the bullet bounced off the stonework.

'Trent!'

I leant against the wall beside the window, next to the statue of David. When I moved towards the window there was a pop and the whistle of a ricochet.

'Trent, those were warnings, right? We need to deal. Things have changed.'

'What do you want?'

'I want to deal. Get the documents. Gehenna.'

I crept over to the statue, grabbing it and pulling it. It was solid plastic, heavy. I eased it towards the window, standing it at the side of the frame. 'I know your deals.'

'You want to live, I want to live. What's the problem with that? We can make a deal, I'll give you something, you hand me the papers for the ship....'

I dropped down to the bottom of the window frame so I could see out. Armstrong was just below. He pointed the gun, waving it around and I pulled one curtain so it obscured the window.

'A curtain won't stop a bullet, Trent.' He fired again and the bullet zinged off the masonry.

'You can't hit me if you can't see me.'

'Trent, Trent, it's not about hitting. These are just warning shots. We can have a win/win situation here.'

'Yeah?' I manoeuvred the statue up to the window, just behind the curtain.

'It was me watching over you in this town, me, Trent.'

'Yeah?'

'Me who kept Sikey off you. And away from that tart. Come down and we'll talk.'

'No way.'

'You can't get out of here. I have a handful of ammo.' Armstrong fired twice more, bullets ricocheting off the wall. 'Just warning shots.'

When I flicked the curtain aside I saw him below, holding his hand up. It was full of bullets.

'Give me Gehenna and you're free.'

'How do you know I still have it?' I put my arms around David hidden by the curtain.

'Me and your dad, you know. We had history. I was your guardian angel.'

Grabbing David I pulled him closer to the window. 'Sounds ropy to me.'

'No, Trent, listen, we can still have an understanding. Man to man. Despite what you've done I'm ready to move forward. Despite you fucking up my business and car and house! Despite that…'

'I need more before I can trust you.'

'Christ, come on. I'll even put the gun down.'

I flicked the curtain out of the way. Armstrong was directly below and held the gun down as he reloaded it. With David's midriff on the sill I stepped back, lifting the base, pushing the statue through the window.

It thundered out and there was a heavy thud, a scream.

CHAPTER FORTY-FIVE

Rory's chat

When I went down to Armstrong I found him pinioned by the statue. The plastic arm was jammed in his side and the gun lay on the ground, surrounded by bullets. He groaned, his eyes rolled up in his head as blood pooled around him.

'Still want to deal?' I said.

He gasped for air. 'This wasn't meant to happen.'

'It's how it is.'

'Help me,' he said.

I knelt and picked the gun up, loading it up with the five rounds lying next to it, levelling it at him.

'I wanted to make a deal. Make things good.'

I waved the gun at him. 'Deal time is over.'

He gasped and tried to move. 'Trent, there's something I've got to tell you. It's important. About your Dad. See, he's not—'

'Leave it, Armstrong. Talking time is over.'

'I know…he's not…I know. It's true…'

I passed the gun from my right to my left hand and let it

swing with its weight. I glanced up at the bedroom window, where Dad was, then down at Armstrong lying trapped in an expanding pool of blood. He now seemed small, fragile. Even in his final minutes he was trying to make a deal, negotiate. 'Goodbye Armstrong.'

'Wait…Trent, your Dad…your Dad. He's really here… here.'

With one last look at him I slid the gun away, heading across the lawn and towards the lorry. In the garage I picked my way through the wreckage, climbing onto the Rolls-Royce's boot. There was a chunk of wood wedged into the lorry's front. I hauled it out and popped the Foden's engine cover. There were long splinters stuck in the drive belt and radiator. I pulled them free and a trickle of water ran down. A wire was off the injector-pump solenoid so I put it back on.

I climbed into the cab and turned it over. It fired up but ran unevenly. I blipped the accelerator, reversing over the wreckage of the garage. The structure shifted around me as the wheels bounced over the debris, dragging the Rolls-Royce a little way before it clanged free. The lorry's cab slid from under the roof, sending it falling onto the floor. The Foden backed across the lawn.

Armstrong still lay under the plastic David, his arms motionless and head back. At the doorway to the lounge several staff stood and gazed out. There was no sign of Dad.

I revved the lorry, pulling off and driving across his lawn. Going down the driveway I joined the Bellendale Road.

Further into town steam rose up from the radiator and curled around the lorry in a creamy cloud. There were lights on all over the dashboard and I pulled in, turning the ignition off. The engine ticked and hissed. There was no traffic on the road, no lorries that roared down to the plant. The air was clear, smoke-free, with clouds drifting over the town. No thuds or rumbles came from the works. Even the pit on the hillside seemed still.

I got out of the cab, inspecting the revolver and carrying on into Setmarch.

Sun shone on me from a blue sky as I passed the old fire station and continued down by along Belmont Street, past the tip. To the *Church of Reform, Abstinence and Piousness*.

The church was empty. No sign of Rory or indication of where he'd gone. But I knew where he'd be. I walked across town but this time south, up the valley side. People lined the pavement: old men, women and children who stood in the sunshine and stared at the clear sky. The first time they'd seen it for years.

At the top of the hill I stopped and faced back. The air was clear and the blackened buildings heated up under the unhindered sunshine. Where the plant had been there was a space, a charred gap. Small fires still burned, tiny wisps of smoke. Chunks of the factory were strewn around the area.

I carried on towards an old oak tree, the tree — where we'd gone to play as kids, me Harry and Rory. It had fewer leaves and more dead branches but otherwise it was the same, with its long bough pointing off into the shire and roots that snaked into the ground. Roots that Rory sat on.

I joined him at the foot of the tree.

'Bang, bang boom!' He licked his lips, then pointed up at my face, where I'd been hit. 'Ouch.'

This was my chance to quiz him. Work out what had been going on and what his part was in it. 'Rory, what was the deal? You, Armstrong, Dad.'

'Deal? Deal?'

'Why was Dad there? At Armstrong's house?'

Rory started to hum a hymn.

'Rory, why was he there?'

'He was. His choice. They were both at the Lodge. Masons. Went back some years. Not my thing. Hmm?'

I leant against the tree, beside Rory. A stab of pain came from my back where it had burnt on the pipes. My cheeks stung as well. 'Come on.'

'Nothing to do with me. Nothing. Zilch.'

'Really?'

'Really, really.'

Maybe that was it. They had gone to the same Masonic Lodge and they knew each other. Setmarch was a small town. Armstrong had wanted to tell me something as he died but he was so wrapped up in lies and plots it hadn't seemed worth listening. People like him didn't know what the truth was.

I picked at the bark on the trunk, sunlight dappling it through the few leaves of the tree. 'That it? What about you and Armstrong?'

'Nothing. He didn't believe. I did. I do.'

'What about the others? Laura, Dan...'

'Don't know. Nothing.'

I turned to him, staring into his bloodshot eyes. He stared back, his gaze steady. We stayed like that for some time, looking at each other, into each other. I could tell he'd not lied to me.

I looked away, across at the town with a great hole

where the works had been. All the damage I'd caused. Without Armstrong and the plant AHI was finished. It had been a blight on the town. 'This town was a bad place, Rory.'

'And now it's better? Huh?'

'There's no Armstrong to oppress the ordinary people —'

'No work, no money, no food, no fuel…'

'Rory, listen—'

'Gone, gone, gone, gone.'

I knelt and grabbed him, shaking him, getting him to look at me. 'Rory, I didn't mean for it to go this way. The town and what happened. I never planned this—'

'So. It was you? You did it?'

'I didn't intend this. To do so much damage —'

'You never do. Never do. It just happens. You destroy.'

I'd got rid of Armstrong but now Setmarch was dead, like so many of the ghost towns I'd seen in the borders. Had I gone too far, wrecking the place just to satisfy some grudge? I'd not thought what it would mean when I was doing it.

'Yeah, I destroy.'

'And my room. Was that you that came in? Took Harry's keys?'

'Yeah, I found them.'

'Harry left them to me. Left them to look after. Now you have them. Fine. Fine.'

He adjusted his cassock, standing up. Then he put his hands together and prayed. Although I didn't join him, I didn't interrupt, letting him mutter his words in the still air. When he'd finished he stretched up, head facing into the branches, arms wide. After a minute or so he relaxed.

'I have work to do, Trent. People to help; hope to offer.' He held his hand out. 'Might as well be civilised. I hope you are going now. Off into the wilds. Away.'

'Yes. I will be.' I took his hand and shook it.

With that he turned and went off towards town, arms still moving as he pointed and made fists. He disappeared down the hill.

For a few minutes I stayed there, leaning against the trunk. That was Rory gone. Now it was time for me to pack up and leave.

I walked off, towards Setmarch, away from the tree.

CHAPTER FORTY-SIX

Joust

The crowds stood out in the street staring up at the blue sky. They watched and waited, lost. Amongst them were Robson and Doddsy, stationary on the pavement beside traffic-free roads, aimless men with no purpose. I headed through the market place, down the hill, past the grounds of the old Job Centre. On East Lonnen, the billboard said AHI: WORK HARD, LIVE WELL. I carried on by the Catholic Church and the lifeless orchard, turning right at the derelict playground, up into the East End Estate, going all the way to the top.

There were no kids playing football in the nearby fields. No one around.

At the bunker I slid the key into the lock and it eased open, letting out the smell of oil and petrol. I left the revolver and picked up the sawn-off shotgun, sliding it down the back of my jacket. The Gehenna paperwork went down the front. I popped the four cartridges into my pocket before starting the Scrambler and riding off into the afternoon sun, leaving the bunker open.

Now it was time to pick up Jamie and Laura. Talk about leaving. Three on the bike would be tricky. But we could probably grab a car.

Then we'd be gone, on the road. It was a fresh start; a new beginning.

I turned into the road where our house was.

There was Sikey's car, parked sideways, the door open and engine running. He was out of the car and kicked at the front door of Dad's house, shouting and punching at the wood, very much alive. His cap was gone, his tracksuit melted with some sections hardened. His reddened hands were clutched in fists. There was no sign of his pistol.

He carried on yelling and hammering then turned, staring at me. For a moment neither of us moved.

He ran over to his car, jumping in and shifting it across the curb so it faced me. It shot backwards, going right to the end of the road, giving him a long run up.

So this was it, a final joust, him and me.

I reached back and slid the shotgun out of my jacket, breaking it and slotting two cartridges in. With a click I closed the gun and laid it across the handlebars.

The Nissan's engine was a distant growl as I revved the bike, a snarl from the two-into-two. We faced each other but didn't move. Then the Nissan's lights came on. The revs picked up and the car shot forward. It accelerated towards me.

I thudded the Triumph into gear and moved off, raised the gun, holding it forward, making clutch-less change ups and aiming for Sikey.

I pulled the trigger. There was a blast and the gun jumped up, pelting pellets onto the Nissan's windscreen. The car veered off, hitting the curb and carrying on into a wall.

I pulled up, the bike idling as I flicked down the side stand, stepping off and walking over to the Nissan. Steam rose from the buckled front end, some other liquid forming a filthy pool where it had impacted the wall. There was a jagged hole in the edge of the windscreen and pellet marks across the roof.

The inside was full of steam or smoke. The passenger door burst open and Sikey staggered out. He had blood on his face and shirt. 'You'll pay for this.'

I levelled the gun, firing. He ducked as the blast took off part of the roof. Reaching into my jacket I took out two more cartridges, breaking the gun and loading it. I leant down, my head under the car. His trainered feet shuffled around at the far side of the car, beyond the exhaust, beside the rear tyre. As he made towards the back of the car I fired, the noise shaking the Nissan and jerking the gun in my hand. There was a cry and I went round to the other side.

He lay on the floor with his leg in his hands, his eyes shut. 'Nice shooting,' he rasped. Where his right foot had been there was a red mass of flesh, shredded trainer and tracksuit-bottom, blood pooling on the ground. He rocked around.

I aimed the gun at him, then lowered it. The injury would finish him without medical treatment and I wasn't going to shoot him, lying there. Not even him. As he bled on the ground I stood over him, the gun slack in my hand.

Laura came over and joined me, standing at my side.

'Christ,' she said.

She was freshened up from the night before but red eyed, like she'd not slept well. She was in light top and jeans, wearing a blue necklace. The one I'd bought her for her twenty-first all those years ago. 'How are you?' I said.

'Hung-over.' She put a hand to my face, the marks from the slapping earlier. 'What happened to you?'

'A disagreement with some of the locals.' I nodded towards Sikey who lay back beside the car, shifting his injured leg.

'What are you going to do with him?' she said.

'I don't know. His car might be useful though.'

If we could patch the radiator, tidy it up a little it would make a good replacement for the Lotus. There'd be enough room for the three of us and our kit. We'd dump Sikey somewhere and go.

Then there was a sound, a crack followed by another and my left leg gave way. I fell sideways and braced myself against the car, pain shooting though my thigh. A whole had been punched in my trousers, a dark red circle growing around it.

Sikey held a twin barrelled piston, a tiny low-calibre thing and he laughed, waving it at me. 'Gotcha,' he said.

I raised the shotgun and fired, his body bursting, jerking and falling back, scattered with holes. Blood seeped down the black of his tracksuit and tattoo.

Then I turned to Laura, also leant against the car.

'That's him sorted out,' I said.

She stared at me, eyes wide, mouth opening but making no sound.

'Laura?'

Her right hand was on her chest, just below her ribcage, where her top was stained red, soaked with blood. Slumping onto me I caught her, holding her as she gasped something, words I couldn't work out.

'Oh, shit, Laura,' I said. Her hand gripped mine, a tight grip as she took shorter and shorter breaths. 'We'll get you sorted, don't worry.'

She put her weight on me, her legs not giving much support, and I held her up, trying to walk her towards the house where I could put something on the wound, stop the bleeding. Her breath came out in pants, shallow. I put her arm over my shoulder and pulled, dragged and slid her towards the door. When her grip slackened I took hold of her arm and hauled her up but her body was getting heavier, only held up by me. Before we reached the door she'd stopped walking and hung off me.

'Come on Laura,' I said.

She slumped onto the ground, arms splayed and I knelt by her, listening at her chest, taking a pulse. There was nothing so I tilted her head, giving her a breath, starting compressions, my hands covered in blood, her blood. I continued with the compressions and breaths, keeping her going until we could take her to Setmarch General, where we'd get her patched up and let her rest, then leave in a couple of days. A slight delay and we'd be off.

Jamie appeared.

'Can you help?' I said. He knew first aid. Medical bits and bobs.

He didn't move as I worked on Laura.

'Come on,' I said.

He put his hand on my shoulder. 'Trent,' he said. 'Stop.'

I ignored him and carried on, one compression after another, after another. On and on.

'Trent, it's no good.'

Shaking him off I tilted her head a little further back,

opening up her airway, making sure there was no obstruction.

Jamie came round and grasped my hands. 'Trent. It's no good. You can't help her anymore.'

As I tried to move him off I looked down at her, at her closed eyes, head to the side. The great pool of blood over her and under her.

Then I bent forward and held her, staying like that for some time.

CHAPTER FORTY-SEVEN
The Tree

I buried her myself that evening, in the rain that came just after seven. I took Sikey's car and drove her body up to the tree.

Me, Harry and Rory had always said we wanted to be buried up there so it seemed the best place for her. Jamie came along but I dug the hole on my own, refusing help from him, my injured leg strapped up. The soil was hard but softened as the rain fell, churning up as I dug.

Once it was deep enough I lowered her in, wrapped up in old sheets. Then I put the soil onto her, spadeful after spadeful as the water ran down me and into the hole.

At dawn the rain stopped and Jamie joined me to say a few words, religious stuff he knew and an old poem from a book in the house. The sun rose up on the town, clear of smoke and pollution, no longer under Armstrong's control. As first light hit her grave I walked away from the tree.

I drove Sikey's car back and parked it on the pavement. Jamie wanted us to put Sikey into the Nissan so the two of us hauled his body off the road and slid him onto the front seats. He sprawled against the dashboard his clothes sticky with blood.

There was nothing left to do so we prepared to leave.

With a tea towel wrapped around my leg, I tied my kit tightly onto the Scrambler, Jamie joining me wearing his guitar on his back and carrying a small bag. 'You want to take anything else?' I said.

'This is all I have.'

I strapped his bag on, easing myself onto the bike, starting up. The big-twin engine settled into a lumpy tick-over. 'This your bike?' said Jamie.

'It was Harry's.'

Jamie got into position and shifted around. 'Who's Harry?'

'He was my brother.' With a burst of revs I pulled off, accelerating along the road, past Sikey's car with his body in it.

We met no other traffic in town or on our way up the hill towards the moors, the exhaust note echoing off the soot stained buildings. We passed the battered sign that said, *You are leaving Setmarch, home of Armstrong Heavy Industries.*

The bikers' bus was parked up across the road at the top of the hill, several bikes set in front of it. I slowed, dropping into first gear and stopping. The Scrambler ticked over a steady beat as we sat twenty metres from them.

Jamie leant forward. 'Just blast through them.'

I turned the engine off and warm air rose up off the bike, the engine pinging to itself. 'I don't think so.'

The big guy with the tourer came over, the others

staying on their bikes. His boots click-clacked and his plaits shifted on his head as he walked. 'You two bats out of hell?'

'Something like that,' I said. Faces stared out of the bus. There was no sign of the woman I'd hit in the woods. Maybe she was resting, recovering; dead.

The biker looked at my leg then back towards Setmarch. 'Been some kind of rumpus going on, eh?'

I shrugged.

'Looks like a big bean-fight.' He leaned against the headlamp of the Scrambler and slid his fingers along the paintwork. 'Still, this is some bike you got, a real smart piece.' He turned to the other bikers. 'Isn't it a real nice bike?'

They shouted their agreement back, laughing, all apart from one, a shaven-headed man with a jacket adorned with chains.

The big fella went on.' We could do with a nice bike like this. Would fit in. Always on the lookout for machines. Like this one.'

Jamie leant forward. 'We're not interested in selling.'

'Maybe we don't want to trade. As such.' He strolled around the bike. 'Real nice.'

'We need to be on our way,' I said.

'How about you step off?'

'I don't think so.'

'You just get off. Walk away. We say no more about it.'

'Let's get out of here, Trent,' said Jamie.

I reached into my jacket, took out my Zippo and popped open the petrol cap, fingering the lighter as if to light it. Warm fumes rose up out the filler. 'If I don't have it, no one does.' I wasn't in the mood for messing around anymore.

The biker looked us up and down, stepping away from the bike. 'That's crazy.'

'Wouldn't be the worst thing I've done.'

'I don't think you'd go that far. You're not that crazy.'

As I messed with the lighter, ready to flick it, send myself up in flames on Harry's bike, finish off what I started in Setmarch, another biker came over, the one covered in chains. His shaven head was marked with tattoos, patterns and shapes: dark flames, a crucifix and stars. He stared at me as he walked over.

'Let them pass,' he said.

No one spoke.

Then the big fella laughed. He glanced over at the town, at the wrecked plant, then back at me, at my leg with the bloodied towel on it. He patted the other biker on the back and they both strode off.

Once they were astride their bikes I stashed my lighter, closing the petrol cap and starting the Triumph, putting it into gear with a clunk. None of the bikers spoke or moved. The only sound was our machine's engine. I pulled off and accelerated along the road, past the double-decker and away from Setmarch.

CHAPTER FORTY-EIGHT

Coast

We rode across the moors for the rest of the day, carrying on north and east until the air cooled and the land dropped away as we came to the coast. The sea was ahead of us beyond the sand dunes, deep blue with white waves that dotted the surface. It faded off into the distance and joined the darkening sky. I pulled the bike up and switched the engine off. The air smelled of salt and seaweed.

Jamie took a deep breath. 'It's so beautiful.'

The breeze blew the sea air onto my face. 'Yeah.' We sat there for several minutes until I took us down a lane through the dunes. The waves crashed on the sand and rasped back.

We slid off the bike and limped onto the beach. 'Look at us, eh?' said Jamie.

'Yeah, look at us.'

We leant against a washed-up tree trunk, smooth and carved by sand and sea, as the waves roared and hissed. Jamie lay across his bag and closed his eyes.

I went to the bike and took my gear off it, setting it out

before gathering driftwood and piling it up. We had a fire as the stars came out above us, the moon mirrored at sea.

'What's the plan now?' said Jamie.

'Not sure.' I reached into my bag and took out a tin of beans, opening it and emptying it into the pan, the one Laura had used the other day. As it heated up on the edge of the fire I stirred it round and round and round, ensuring the beans didn't burn.

After we'd eaten I limped down to the sea and rinsed the tea-towel in the water. The waves sloshed around my feet, sucking them into the sand as I tied the towel back onto my leg. Taking a handful of cool water I washed my face, taking the grime off me. The sea went off forever, into the distance, cold and deep. I walked into it, deeper and deeper. After taking several more steps I turned and waded back.

When I returned to the fire Jamie had taken his kit out of his bag. On top of clothes and bedding was his bust phone and guitar. He picked the phone up, running his hands across the broken glass.

'There were videos stored in this. Made by some family. Of days out. Picnics.' He put the phone down, grabbed his guitar and strummed some notes. Stopping after a few chords.

'You going to play?' I said.

He stared down at his right hand and shook his head. We both gazed into the fire, how the wood burned yellow and orange.

'I'd love a joint,' he said.

I felt in my jacket pocket, dug around, finding a tiny bag of dope, making a spliff, lighting it from a twig. The logs had burned down to a red pile. 'We need more wood'

He took a smoke then made to throw his guitar onto the fire. 'No use to me.'

'Don't Jamie.'

Putting the guitar down he flexed his swollen fingers. 'Can't play the guitar. Or shoot. What use am I? Everyone needs a trick.'

'No they don't.'

We sat and smoked together beside the fire.

Once we'd finished the joint he got up. 'I'll fetch more wood.'

As he shuffled off I slid out the Gehenna documents, ready to ball them up, throw them on the fire. But they'd cost so much, the lives of so many people. I pushed them back into my bag, under the sawn-off shotgun and spare clothes.

Jamie came back with several logs. They steamed and smoked before yellow flames licked up their sides. They burned as we sat there, neither of us moving until they were just embers that glowed.

We both rolled out our sleeping bags at opposite sides of the fire. 'You crashing out?' I said.

'Not yet.' He threw sand onto the fire and let it crackle. 'Did I ever tell you about the bus? What happened to me as a kid?'

'Bits.'

Then he went on to tell me the whole story. About him as a teenager on that bus. How his parents had died. What the reivers had done to some of the survivors.

Once he'd finished telling me all about it he slumped back into his bedding.

The remnants of the fire crackled and popped as the sea shushed down the beach. There were things that could have been said about the story. And about Kelso and Setmarch but it was hard to work out where to start.

'Feel better?' I said.

'Some.'

Neither of us spoke for a while, as the waves rolled up and the embers burnt.

Then I took my boots off and slid into my bag. I pulled it up around me and lay back, facing up to the stars, gazing into infinity. I should have ached all over but I didn't feel anything. I was numb.

The sounds of the sea filled my dreams, as I floated alone on the water, drifting, lost.

When I woke up Jamie was already awake. The sky was light blue flecked with clouds and the sun lay low on the horizon. The tide had gone out leaving the sand smooth in its passing, the waves hissing in the distance.

'You sleep okay?' I said.

'Not really. You had nightmares. You woke me.'

'Sorry.' I stood, stretching, pulling my boots on.

'Listen Trent, about Laura–'

'There's nothing to say.'

'I just wanted to–'

'Please.' I raised my hand.

There really was nothing to say. Not yet, maybe not ever.

He packed up his stuff, sliding it into the bag. 'Where we headed now?' he said.

'Oh, somewhere else.'

'I think I'd guessed that.'

I had an idea of where to go but didn't want to say it. Think it, even. We ate our beans without talking then packed and rode inland, north, west across the moors, still and hot. We travelled on until we were in woodland of oak, sycamore and chestnut. Timber was stacked by the roadside and the air was fresh, cool in the shade. The exhaust of the bike barked through the undergrowth. We rode past the trees, bushes and wildflowers, up the hill by prayer flags and bunting. There was a field cleared in the woods where sheep grazed. The tinkle of wind chimes drifted in.

'What is this place?' said Jamie.

'Shangri-La.' I dropped the revs and headed for the only building, a low farm house, steering into the cobbled courtyard and parking.

Gary came out, his close-shaved head and heavy arms fighting their way into a purple jumper. He smiled at us. 'Out of the wild the wanderers come.'

'This is Jamie,' I said.

Gary gave Jamie a hand as he hauled himself off the back of the bike. Then he hugged him, holding him for several seconds. Jamie patted Gary on the back.

As I stepped off the bike Gary embraced me, his clothes smelling of lavender and cider. For a second I relaxed in his grip. Then he released me and circled the Scrambler, as it pinged and ticked. 'Different wheels?'

'It's a long story,' I said.

With a laugh he ambled off, tapping a tune on his teeth. Everything seemed to make him laugh.

Jamie shouldered his rucksack and guitar. 'Is he okay?'

I swung my stuff over my shoulder, a haze of petrol and oil fumes rising off the Triumph. 'He's fine.'

We followed Gary, going into the main hall where he sat in a corner on cushions patterned with yin and yang. There was no one else there and he indicated for us to sit next to him. I put my gear down and joined him, adjusting the rag on my leg.

'Oh, poor you,' said Gary.

I straightened my leg out. 'It's fine.'

Jamie stood for a moment then joined us, helped to sit by Gary as he held his right hand to his side. Gary inspected us, tilted his head with narrowed eyes, a frown creeping across his brow. He reached over and touched my face then took my hand, holding it, keeping his eyes on me. We sat like that for a while. After he'd released me he knotted his fingers together and exhaled, eyes shut.

'All gone,' he said.

'What is?'

Gary smiled at me, but not one of his big grins, something more thoughtful. 'It's windfall time, time to pick and ponder.'

'Can we crash here a while?'

'Of course, of course.'

'We don't want to impose.'

'All welcome at Shangri-La.' With a squeeze of my good leg he smiled. 'You're always welcome. You and your friends.' He looked from me to Jamie. 'Maybe you'd like to freshen up?'

'Thanks.'

Then he got up, talking as he went. 'You know where everything is, Trent.' His footsteps echoed in the building as he disappeared.

'How you feeling?' I said.

'Okay,' said Jamie. 'Is he always like that −?'

'He's a good fella.' I offered him my hand as he leant over and tried to push himself up. We limped across the hall and to the bedrooms.

Later that evening there was music and drinks, the usual thing for Shangri-La. Jamie sat with me at the edge as the others sang or danced. There was no sign of the woman I'd met last time I was there, Ash. When I mentioned her to Gary he seemed to have no memory of her.

After a few glasses of fruit wine Jamie got up, leaning on his stick.

'What you up to?' I said.

'I fancy a dance.' He went over into the middle of the room where a young man and woman linked him in their arms. Jamie grinned as he danced with them.

I watched them and drank some more, eventually making my way to my room, leaving the music and laughter behind.

CHAPTER FORTY-NINE
Shangri La

In the morning I woke before daybreak, sliding out of bed and grabbing my gear. The shotgun and Gehenna material were under my clothes and I wrapped them up, stashing them in my bag. In the faint light I made my way along the corridor, looking into the room opposite.

Jamie lay asleep, his guitar on the floor and a smile on his face. I considered going in, waking him, saying goodbye. Telling how good it had been working with him. How sorry I was it had all gone wrong in Setmarch. Instead I let the door close and carried on out of the building.

The sun was just coming up as I went outside, a fiery ball on the horizon. I crossed the courtyard and opened the door to the outbuilding, the creaking hinges joining the early calls of birds that came from the woods. The chain on the Scrambler rattled as I wheeled it out, the black bars and engine casings soaking up the early light.

There was no need to leave Shangri-La, it was a place everyone was welcome. But I needed time on my own, time to think through what happened in Setmarch. Seeing Dad. Destroying the plant. Burying Laura.

There was a sharp stab in my leg as I shifted around and took weight off it, my fingers drumming on the bike's fuel tank.

Then I took my gear and strapped it on. With everything in place I swung my bad leg over, flicking the stand up and aiming the Triumph down the road. I left it in neutral and nudged it down the track, the brakes hissing as it coasted past the prayer flags and bunting. Approaching the woods I turned on the ignition, clutching it into second and letting it bump start. It fired with a bark and accelerated off, the exhaust note bouncing off the trees.

At the road I stopped and slipped into neutral. The bike settled into a lumpy idle from the twin pipes. Shangri-La showed up through the trees behind me and ahead were the moors. To the left was south and to the right was north. I put the Scrambler into gear, feathering the throttle, riding slowly one way, then the other, doing a figure of eight in the road, the sun casting a long shadow of me and the bike. I could have done that all day, forever but I straightened the bike and rode off, the exhaust murmuring as I short-shifted up into top.

I rode off alone, north towards the border.

ACKNOWLEDGEMENTS

Writing can be a lonely hobby so it's good to have some people behind you.

I would like to thank George Green and Lee Horsley at Lancaster University for all the brilliant suggestions. Also Brian Baker, Andrew Pepper and Jo Baker for further guidance.

Thanks to Tom Grover and Colin Buchanan for reading early drafts and Troy Melhuish and Phil Hilbourne for the later ones.

To Tom and Janet Storrie for believing in me when no one else did.

Of course I couldn't have done it without Tara, Ethan and Lucy being so patient when I was too busy to play.

And especially to Debs Austin for all her moral and emotional support.